Christopher Bolsover was born in Derbyshire, England. He joined the Derbyshire Constabulary at sixteen, then the Royal Military Police, serving in Germany and Northern Ireland, the latter as an investigator with the Special Investigation Branch during the major troubles there. He immigrated to Australia in 1974 and was a private detective before starting his business career which took him to the heights of Corporate America with multi-billion-dollar companies.

After being shot in the back three times in a house invasion in South Africa, a wake-up call, he started writing the novels he had always wanted to, calling upon his abundance of experiences.

Christopher has lived on five continents, visited nearly every country in the world and currently resides in the UK with his wife and two children. He also has four grown-up children and five grandchildren who reside in Australia.

To my wife, Monica, for her inspiration and dedicated support without which I would never have completed this novel.

Christopher Bolsover

## THE HELLFIRE CLUB

*Chas*

*to my amazing wonderful brother!*

*Love You.*

*Chris B*

**AUSTIN MACAULEY PUBLISHERS™**
LONDON * CAMBRIDGE * NEW YORK * SHARJAH

Copyright © Christopher Bolsover (2021)

The right of Christopher Bolsover to be identified as author of this work has been asserted by the author in accordance with section 77 and 78 of the Copyright, Designs and Patents Act 1988.

All rights reserved. No part of this publication may be reproduced, stored in a retrieval system, or transmitted in any form or by any means, electronic, mechanical, photocopying, recording, or otherwise, without the prior permission of the publishers.

Any person who commits any unauthorised act in relation to this publication may be liable to criminal prosecution and civil claims for damages.

This is a work of fiction. Names, characters, businesses, places, events, locales, and incidents are either the products of the author's imagination or used in a fictitious manner. Any resemblance to actual persons, living or dead, or actual events is purely coincidental.

A CIP catalogue record for this title is available from the British Library.

ISBN 9781528917698 (Paperback)
ISBN 9781528936064 (ePub e-book)

www.austinmacauley.com

First Published (2021)
Austin Macauley Publishers Ltd
25 Canada Square
Canary Wharf
London
E14 5LQ

# Prologue

The payphone rang in the little, red phone box. It rang five times. He picked up the phone and wiped the handset with his hanky before placing it to his ear. He was a large man in a grey American style trench coat and a trilby hat sitting skew on his head.

"Is it done?"

"This package will cause you no more problems, boss."

"Disposed of how?"

"Eeeish boss, I do not reveal that to anyone, just be sure it is out of the way for good. Your friends can rest easy."

"This is very important to my people? Can you assure me no comebacks?"

"Yes, boss."

"Good. I will wire the balance."

"Yes, boss. Thanks, boss."

The caller rang off. The man in the trench coat wiped the phone again with his hanky before replacing the handset and limped away in the rain, thinking that maybe he should have asked for proof of death.

# Chapter One
## McAllistar's Cottage

The walk from the bus stop in town was slow and painful. The weight of his army kit bag, backpack and small attaché case was weighing him down against the power of the gale-force wind and driving rain which was bitter cold piercing into every part of his body. Pushing him back, resisting his every move. He strove with determination to make slow headway up the winding hill to his final destination. There was no pathway, just grass verges. Both sides for miles were just green fields protected by dry stone walls. He thought how good it was, despite the weather, to be back in the English countryside, back where he used to belong. Free on the outside.

It was very dark now and the road was deserted, there were no street lights in the countryside. Every now and then he would stop, take a breather and listen to the howling wind welcoming him home. He thought he could hear words and laughter, hysterical almost screaming. It was only the ghosts in his mind playing tricks, coming back to him in a blast of torment, speeding by like the wind, untouchable and then whirling into the night. It was exhilarating, exciting and scary.

Cars would come along but always going the opposite direction, they would slow down, put their high beams on and after examining him briefly, sped away. It was as if they knew who he was, where he had come from and wanted no part of him. Even if one had been going his way, there had been no chance of them stopping for him, too late, too dark and too daunting a sight. He thought to himself, *better if I am not picked up anyway*.

He was a tall man, six feet four inches, with short salt and pepper hair underneath his beanie, the old black overcoat made him look far bigger than his muscular frame really was. His load of what was left of his worldly possessions adding to the size of the dark figure marching along, walking the lonely country road late at night.

"Just around the next corner," he told himself. He knew every inch of this road; he had dreamt about running away to this place since his problems started. This place represented his happiest and best childhood memories of summer holidays with his adopted family. It was during this last year that the dream had kept him sane. One of only two dreams he had left. The rest were nightmares filled with revenge and hate. He got his second wind and as he came around the last sweeping right-hand bend, he saw the driveway. The old dry stone walls separated the cottage from the barren fields surrounding it. They came right up to the big stone gate posts in the driveway, the iron gates were no longer there. The pebbled driveway was overgrown with weeds and wildflowers. He made it to the gateway and gently put down his load. He pulled out a pack of cigarettes and after huddling behind one of the large gate posts managed to light up after five attempts. He wanted to savour this moment. He took a long drag and looked up to the stone cottage at the top of the drive.

The cottage was in total darkness, the dark clouds seemed to spin over the chimney top. The full moon shone from behind, hitting the roof and adding some light to the general feeling of gloom. It was cold and unwelcoming, but this was his new home for now, his escape from his nightmares.

Or would it be?

Cigarette still in hand, he started trembling and had an uncontrollable urge to cry. He hadn't cried since he was nine years old, outside this very cottage, when he was being taken back home when his holiday had ended. This time, it was the build-up of the daily fear and suffering of the last year and the knowledge of what he had yet to face. Still, he thought there was no better place on earth for him right now.

He could barely read the new polished silver nameplate on the other gate post. He didn't need to, he knew.

It said, 'McAllistar's Cottage'

# Chapter Two
## Liberty Bell

Liberty had a very toned, young, petite and sexy body. Long legs decorated in black stockings, black pant shorts that could be mistaken for the smallest mini skirt ever, white blouse with a black jacket. Her short dark hair hung in curls around her baby smiling face. The cleavage was obvious but not too daring. The shoes with high heels complemented the package. Walking through the untidy, busy press office, everyone noticed her, including women.

Most took more than a passing interest. She knew the impact she had and always used it for her advantage. She knew too well how to play the 'corporate game'. When necessary, she wielded her physical charm like an axe, but she had other more powerful weapons in her locker. She banged against the editor's door rather than knock and without waiting for an answer, she walked straight in.

Gavin Hastings looked up in surprise, relief or shock. She wasn't quite sure. He was a battler, a war-torn vet of Fleet Street. A man who started journalism with great ideals and honesty, who thirty years later, found himself a master of the gutter press, the Tabloid guru. The only things that mattered were circulation, which fed advertising revenues and the power to influence a nation. He never remembered selling out his ideals and principles. It was just time and circumstances that slowly eroded the way he worked, what he believed in. The reality of his chosen career and the price of success had brought changes, some good and some bad. In the end, if nothing else, he was flexible and rolled with the punches. He now was who he was, a successful editor of a major national tabloid newspaper in the United Kingdom.

Sitting opposite to him was Sir Richard Carlton, the chairman of the *Daily Cryer*, called in for his weekly 'chat' and, as always, to pass on some of his comments (judgments), on the latest editorials, layout and leading stories. The tension was always high during these sessions. Gavin always had to listen and placate Sir Richard no matter what inane dribble he would come up with. Mostly from investors and rich friends at one of his clubs or dinner parties, whom Gavin suspected would not wipe their asses on *the Daily Cryer*. In his opinion, they wouldn't be seen dead with it but probably sneaked off secretly to their bathrooms to admire the 'tits' and 'bums' he lavished throughout the pages.

Sir Richard was a dapper sixty years old, with an immaculate blue pinstripe suit, silk yellow tie and yellow handkerchief carefully positioned in his coat top pocket.

Gavin saw him as a bit of a playboy, public schoolboy rogue, silver spoon right in his gob from birth and always a bit aggressive after four or five glasses of red wine at lunch.

He always felt a little shabby beside him. Gavin was often unshaven due to the late hours, which he kept both at work and on the town after, tie loose around his neck and suit that always looked like it needed cleaning and pressing. It was after lunch, so Gavin was holding his tongue, no use arguing with the booze, he knew from experience.

*Argue with a fool and no one knows the difference.*

Liberty's dramatic entrance was welcomed by Gavin even after his initial annoyance by her barging in. Sir Richard's attention would now be towards the sexy American and hopefully would close today's unwelcome information session.

"Sorry, guys, didn't mean to interrupt…I was told it was urgent," she said emphasising her New York Brooklyn accent.

"Liberty! Come and join us, we were just talking about you," Sir Richard spouted in a friendly gregarious tone.

"You were? I trust it's all good!" laughing, flirting.

"Always! Sit down. You have caused quite a stir young lady since you hit this town."

Sir Richard offered still in a friendly tone.

She realised she needed to work him, so she sat directly opposite to him and crossed her legs. He could hardly keep his eyes off her thighs.

"Liberty," Gavin tried to get back control, "Sir Richard has a complaint from the PM's communication department, Chief McClements, about the article we are about to print on Fish."

"Fish?" Sir Richard queried.

"The minister for trade, Sir Richard, Bill Stephens, we call him Fish," Gavin explained.

"Fish? I guess it's his mouth. Am I right?" Sir Richard seemed pleased with himself.

"Got it in one, Sir Richard."

"What's the problem with the article?" Liberty asked faking concern.

"They believe, in their opinion," Sir Richard took the lead, "that you have grossly misrepresented the interview, not so much in content but context and tone. They believe that it paints the wrong picture of a serious public servant and hardworking politician, bound for high office. No doubt, though, it would be good for us to have him onside so to speak."

"Gives the wrong impression," Gavin cut in to explain clearly.

"Well Sir Richard, opinions to me are like ass holes and everyone has one!" Liberty fired back.

Sir Richard sat a little stunned. He wasn't quite used to anyone addressing him in this manner. There was a silence and then Liberty took the lead.

"I have the tape of the interview; you can listen to it. The guy is a dick in my opinion and the public deserve to know about it. It is all in his own words, in the words of a self-serving big head."

"You taped it?" Gavin shouted a little louder than he planned. "Our deal with his people was no taping!"

Liberty stared in his eyes for a few moments, holding his gaze but letting go before he gave up and lost face.

"Good job. I got the tape then if it becomes an issue, she said. Besides he doesn't know I taped him; he was too busy trying to look up my skirt."

Gavin just shook his head. He wanted to laugh out loud and look serious at the same time.

Sir Richard coughed and immediately looked away. A moment of uncomfortable silence ensued, so he filled the space.

"Oh well, the editorial is Gavin's area," Sir Richard, unused to aggressive females started to run for cover, "I'm just passing on the information. I like that…opinions are like ass holes…I'm off then. Cocktails at Barney's at seven tonight, Gavin if you want to pop in and bring young Liberty here along, might liven things up there for us."

With that, he departed rather quickly. *Probably dying for a pee.* Gavin thought. *Saved by a weakening bladder!*

Addressing Liberty, he said, "Just what I need. Another few hours of advice on how to run my paper. I wouldn't mind if they had a fucking clue what the average person in this country thinks." Gavin got it off his chest. He continued, "If we printed what they wanted, we would have a circulation of zero, even so, they would never read it, the paper isn't long enough for their image and no one sees them secretly reading it in the toilet."

"Come on, Gavin, we both know you tell the people what to think, read your own editorials. You mould them like putty. You appeal to their basic instincts, you build up hopes, heroes and good news and then knock them all down."

Gavin raises his hands as if in surrender, "Stop! I don't need another lecture today of all days. Who told you I wanted to see you urgently, didn't Joan tell you the chairman was in with me?"

"Sure, she did. I figured you needed rescuing and you did."

"You've got balls, I give you that," Gavin snorted a laugh. She was hard to handle and something about her made you want to strangle and love her at the same time. He tried to pretend to be mad, but she always saw right through the pretence. When he was really mad, the end result was the same, he ended up admiring her and laughing with her. He had lost the power base and she treated him just as an equal, well, he hoped at least an equal.

"For a lady," she said in a fake English accent.

"For a lady, right. Now, let's get some work done before cocktails at Barney's."

"So, first things first. You have been with us for a month that is five weeks. We have had five complaints, let me see. That makes it one complaint per major interview which is one a week. Pretty straight batting average, I say. Remind me why we hired you?"

"Easy. One, you took me on because I am the fucking best thing you have seen for a long time. Two, all those interviews, I did have got life and spice in them exactly what you do here but with a bit more curry than you Brits can take! And three, what the hell does a batting average mean?"

"Oh, that's a cricket terminology. Have you got a three?" Gavin said almost laughing.

Most men like him liked spunk and this girl had it coming out of her ears.

"Well, number three, I'm twenty-six and I can count on my left hand, how many blow jobs I've had to give to get here. That's not bad eh?"

They looked at each other and both broke out laughing.

They both lit up cigarettes from their respective packets. Gavin leaned back on his chair, blew little smoke circles in the air without saying anything. He was thinking something through. Liberty had enough sense to let him go through this thinking process without interrupting. Finally, Gavin made up his mind, sat forward and leaned across his desk.

"I have a very interesting assignment for you. In fact, I think it's possibly a lead article for quite a few issues. It means a fully paid trip around the English countryside for as long as it takes. It is a difficult one, maybe some danger, how would I describe it?"

"Interesting," Liberty finished his thought. "And I'm interested already."

She was wary that she wasn't being fobbed off to some second-rate assignment. Had her aggressive interviews made it for her or had she gone too far? Was this a nice English way of putting her to one side, promoted to the House of Lords, out to pasture. She thought about it for a split second and then decided.

*No. This is not a nice industry, a chicken shit cheap paper and not nice management. They would put me on the next plane to the big apple if they didn't want me.*

Gavin leaned forward as if sharing a secret, "What's involved here no one is certain. I can give you our file and background information. This will be the biggest job of your career, maybe even mine. It involves we believe some pretty nasty people, dirty politicians, corrupt officials, perverts and local villains, gangsters that you 'yanks' call them. So, that opens up all the usual possibilities of drug cartels, prostitution, porn, extortion, sex trafficking, murder, all types of criminal activities, which suggest possibilities of corruption of police, government officials that without whom these crimes can't flourish and swamp our streets. Now there is a chance, this could all open up the biggest can of worms ever because of one guy and we need to be there and get this story first! Any questions?"

Liberty was chewing gum now and listening intently. "Yeah, what's cricket?"

Ignoring her Gavin continued, "By the way, we will need to let Fish off the hook this time, pardon the pun, you can get him later and if this article comes out okay, he will be easy bait the next time. You said it, build them up and knock them down. This is a huge assignment, a very interesting story and the complex guy involved, so let's not get into the balls talk again. Okay?"

"You're the boss. What's his name?"

"McAllistar."

# Chapter Three
## The Blue Haven

The old 'Dirty Cow' was now called 'The Blue Haven', a three-floor adult entertainment facility, bar and restaurant. The owners were Nick and Jimmy Harker, local criminals involved in all types of organised crime. The brothers were responsible for a good deal of the misery that flooded the streets of the United Kingdom.

It was very busy on a Tuesday night. In the heart of Soho, London, it was ideally located for the entertainment it offered. The first floor was for dancing. The disco music of the early seventies had been replaced by heavy house music. The people jerking around like rag dolls on bungee ropes. The second floor was what they called an entertainment area for the dancing ladies and as a more intimate seated area for personal lap dancing, the top floor was a fine dining restaurant. In between the second and top floor was a mezzanine floor which held a small VIP area and the owner's office.

The only difference from the girls dancing being the closer interaction with the girls that lap dancing provided given that touching their bodies was not allowed.

On the surface, the club offered a chance to enjoy adult entertainment in a protected clean environment. There were seven security guards on the entertainment floors to keep good order, with more on call. For the club's protection and business interests, there were at least fifteen people at any given time mingling in the crowd known as 'watchers', who integrated with the crowd, their job was to ensure no one brought in drugs to sell, no street prostitutes on the game there, no rogue undercover cops and most importantly to spot safe targets for the poison The Blue Haven offered on the first floor. The toilets only had hot water taps, which were set to steaming hot the instant you opened them. This ensured the drug users bought the expensive bottled water at the bar rather than quenching their thirst drugs gave them in the bathrooms. The drugs reduced the alcohol consumption and The Blue Haven was about profit whether you drank heavily or just took their drugs and water.

The Blue Haven club was classy and very clean apart from the smoking. The main reason it was full of punters was due to the sixty beautiful girls from sixteen to twenty-five, who plied their particular form of entertainment or as they called it dancing.

The Blue Haven had a varied clientele, plenty of lonely businessmen from all over the world, groups of men out on the town for whatever they had to celebrate, usually forthcoming nuptials, girl's night outs, a few single women either with the men or enjoying the dancers. Some just wanted a pretty girl to talk with and maybe flatter them somewhat, others to drink and watch the dancing, some creepy ones wanted more and would proposition the ladies whenever an opportunity arose.

Either way, it was a big money-spinner. Entrance fees, high costs of drinks, customers getting milked by the dancers when they come off stage. Talking them into buying them expensive champagne or cheaper bottles at inflated prices. Each lady had an evening sales target for the number of bottles they needed to sell. The place was protected by police contacts but still could come under another police scrutiny without warning at any time. Staff and the girls were well trained in what to say and how to say it to keep on the right side of the law. The owners of The Blue Haven owned three other establishments of a similar trade in other major cities across the country, they got their share of all the action that went on in the clubs one way or another.

The Blue Haven was very busy. There was very little spare space to sit. The back lap dance rooms were full. People stood around on the second level staring at the dancers doing their turns on the three small stages positioned around the room. Every two hours all the dancing entertainers would be introduced and paraded across the centre stage to whet appetites and promote the quantity and variety of girls on offer and lap dances.

Nick and Jimmy could see everything going on from their office on the mezzanine floor, overlooking the second-floor entertainment and lap dancing.

Their window was see-through one way and from there they could view all the action, looking down even the private lap dancing areas could be watched from this position. Even though they were curtained off sections with no ceilings and dominated one-third of the floor space, they positioned discreetly along the rear wall far away from all entrances. This gave a feeling of privacy for the clients and was the hardest area to access should there be a raid. By the time anyone got there if anything was not kosher, it would have stopped.

The ten video screens and recorders in the basement, officially for security surveillance doubled as peeping toms. They ensured there was no privacy, that every customer's indiscretions were recorded for posterity and use if it benefited the owners. The private areas were no exception and not even the toilets escaped surveillance.

Nick was forty-five years old, he looked and was extremely fit. He had a crew cut of brown hair and a diamond stud in his left ear. He weighed twelve stone and stood six feet tall. He had the markings of a boxer. His broken nose, bunched up cauliflower ears, a variety of small scars on his face and across his forehead testified to the fact that he was a man of violence. He was a man of little patience, a temper with a short fuse. Around him, there was always an air of a forthcoming thunderstorm.

Jimmy was another kettle of fish. He was the eldest at fifty years old. The brains, the thinker, the cool calculating head of the firm. He had a slender build. Long blond hair, attractive looks made him a sexy man that women liked. He was charming when in a social gathering. He dressed immaculately and could have been a male model in his younger days. He was smaller than Nick and exercise was never a choice for him, so he just had a slender look. He preferred reading and the finer arts. His quiet and gentle persona could be deceiving. He was not a man to do violence, yet he was very comfortable ordering others to do just that. It was a necessary part of the industry they were in and no one could survive and prosper without the ability to keep order (he called giving love) and most of all terrifying fear (he called respect). Conscience was not a luxury either could afford or even wanted.

Together they were a dangerous combination. Nick, you might expect to suddenly head butt you such was his temper, so at least you knew where you stood with him. Jimmy was a different story. He would put his arms around you as if welcoming a long-lost friend and if he wasn't taking your wallet out of your back pocket, he was stabbing you in the back. Physically, it was hard to figure them as brothers, they were like 'chalk and cheese'. But to be in their presence, you could soon tell, though, that they had a lot in common, pure evil.

The Harkers didn't come from the East End as is commonly thought for London villains. They came from a middle-class family and enjoyed an early life of relative luxury and comfort. Both had been sent to Catholic private schools in Windsor. Jimmy, a dedicated and successful scholar. Nick, good at sports but had no interest in school work, so he made little effort in the classroom.

Nick was expelled from two schools and threatened by several headmasters with writing to the Pope to have him excommunicated from the church for life. This was obviously meant to scare him into better behaviour but it did the opposite as he didn't give a damn. He hated their dogma and the guilt trips the church touted. Fear was religion's driving force and it taught him that people will do anything if scared enough.

Several weeks after he left All Saints in Windsor, a large part of the school burnt down. Everyone knew it was Nick. No one could prove it. This was also the first time he learnt how to create an iron-clad alibi. He had been at the school for only six months. He was then sent to a very strict catholic boarding school in Edinburgh called 'Our Lady of Lourdes', which his father thought would 'sort him out'. He received six of the best canings every day for a full term, many fights and beatings in the evenings and all the censorship for bad behaviour they had. He eventually ran away and joined the boy soldiers when he was fifteen.

He did take the time month's later to revisit the headmaster's home. Dressed in black with a balaclava over his head, he handed out a severe beating leaving the ageing headmaster in hospital for months. He eventually had to retire early, spending his time in a wheelchair. Two of his school mates assisted in letting him in and hiding him until the time was right for the attack. He stole all the money and jewellery he could find to make it look like a robbery. Again, he had engineered an alibi with his army pals that the police could not break, he was two hundred miles away camping in Wales.

Jimmy went on to the London School of Economics to a life of study and envy. He desperately wanted the good things in life. He made friends with people from the higher society and envied what they had. Those espousing to be socialists and communists he avoided like the plague. He wanted to be in the three per cent of people who have the gold and ran the world.

Jimmy got a low-grade banking job and started as a teller in London City. He handled lots of money and daydreamed of robbing the bank and having anything he wanted. Every time he touched wads of money, he felt it was his and felt very powerful. When he did get to go into the banks' vault, he was a 'Rockefeller' in London, this turned him on more than a woman could do. He would laugh at his thought of putting the stolen money back in the same bank under his name.

After several years, he made junior management and had enough money to pay for his flat, modest food and a bottle of his favourite wine a week. Even so, he hated his job and his life, it simply was not enough.

The brother's path split for seven years; Nick progressing from the Boy's Army to the Royal Marines and serving in the troubles in Northern Ireland and Jimmy working in the city as a junior banker.

In 1973, their father died and they were reunited. Their mother, Freda, had left him when the boys were five and ten years old.

They had always thought their quiet, devoted catholic and middle-class father was in import-export, costume jewellery for market 'sellers'. But when they inherited fifty thousand pounds and the Soho 'Dirty Cow' club and a small sex shop in Wolverhampton, they were relieved from their illusions. Turns out their uncle, Harry, had been in business with their Dad.

Uncle Harry was now a retired ex-policeman in Spain. He seemed to have a lot of money and they suspected that he had benefited somehow and helped himself to a large part of their inheritance. He was an ex-detective inspector in the 'flying squad' or as it was known then, 'The Sweeney', specialising in gangs, armed robberies, murder, prostitution and drugs which was a direct connection with their new businesses.

Harry attended their Dad's funeral and later in the local pub, the Red Lion after Harry had a few too many whiskeys, the boys asked him about their dad and the business they never dreamed he would have been involved with.

"Back in the time, your old man was importing cheap jewellery, scratching a bleeding living to keep you boys in luxury and at private schools. The club was known as 'Golden Touch' and let's just say, the owner needed to leave the country rather than do porridge. Your Dad had some cash and I had the leverage, so he got it at a good price."

"Why did he call it the Dirty Cow?" Jimmy asked innocently.

"Think about it, use your noddle! Look at you two guys, brothers? Think about what your Mum did to him."

This stopped them in their tracks. *Did he mean that we were not brothers? Did she cheat?* Both had the same thought but never spoke it out loud.

"So, he called it after Mum as an insult?"

"Right, bloody sure he did and he was right. She was a cow. It gave your dad a new lease of life, although he wasn't good at the darker side of club life. I always had to help out you might say."

"Why Wolverhampton for the shop?" Nick asked.

"It is a waste of time, the woman who runs it worked at the club and was from there, let's say she was his bit on the side and convinced him to start a shop there. She will be shitting herself, now you guys have got it. I doubt if he ever saw a penny from it. You can change that now. I'll get the next round boys."

Uncle Harry was very suntanned from his time on the Costa del Sol. He wore a black suit and his white shirt open at the collar, showing off a big gold necklace and a thick gold bracelet on his left hand and on his right a large silver Rolex watch.

*Mr Bling*. Jimmy thought, Tasteless.

He had taken his tie off after the service. He seemed smaller and weaker than during his police years. The stories about him were a legend in the police force and Dad had relayed them with excitement to the young Harker boys. One was that when he caught up with a villain, he would take his jacket off and give them a chance to have a go at him, never once did he lose a fight.

"He's still getting a percentage of the business, the old bastard. We can cut that out straight away," Nick spouted whilst Uncle Harry got the drinks.

"He knows a lot and can be useful to us in the beginning anyway," Jimmy responded, thinking it through strategically.

A year later Uncle Harry did have a terrible accident at his villa at the Costa del Sol. Seems like he had too many drinks and fell bumping his head and then tippled over into the swimming pool unconscious. His blood-alcohol level was so high the Spanish police called it an unfortunate accident. He was known to get drunk and rowdy most nights and was the subject of many complaints from neighbours. Typical, they thought of this type of British hoodlums who invaded their coast. A last will and testament were found and he did leave sixty thousand pounds and his villa to the Harker brothers and all his shares in the club and shop. The will was dated a week before he died. Unfortunately, for him, he shared the same solicitor as the Harker brothers, Tazewell Javelin.

It was now ten years later and the brothers had turned the business into a multi-million-pound enterprise. They had the clubs as the backbone; however, they had diversified into so many other illegal and immoral activities that when looking back, it even took their breath away. Uncle Harry was indeed helpful and encouraged them to take advantage of opportunities that their world now presented. They kept his contacts at high levels of the police force but also found their own that assisted them greatly, especially in providing protection and information. Even so, the learning curve was tough and steep, mistakes costing dearly, however, the game they played was very profitable money that flowed thick and fast.

Opportunities and contacts came to them initially from local villains and gradually from all over the world. The time flew, one day innocent new owners in a seemingly glamorous world to lords of the dark and seedy underworld.

They had been willing participants in their own corruption. Money, sex and power went to their heads. They could never get enough. It was easy to justify when you look at society today, big business grabbing everything they can, corrupt bankers ripping people off, politicians that had no moral compass, taxes and the whole legal system just as corrupt as the underworld they lived in. There was a big demand for what they offered and if not them then someone else would fill the void. The brothers thought, *Why not get our share?*

# Chapter Four
## Eager

Today his knees were hurting more than usual. The cold damp weather activating his osteoarthritis. Too much football when he was younger and too much weight now. He was walking awkwardly, stiff down Kensington road to his lunch appointment at Celestine's. An Italian restaurant wouldn't help his latest diet. He knew himself too well. *Still I better keep off the vino with the bosses around.*

He had the *Daily Cryer* folded underneath his arm, just in case they kept him waiting, it was crap but passed the time, fitted his working-class street copper image. He enjoyed the star sign predictions. He was a Piscean and felt that the *Daily Cryer's* guru, Miss Janus, always knew what was going on in his life. Today, she had predicted a 'meeting of importance', possible romance for single Pisceans and more interesting information if you rang the special number.

He could do the *Times* crossword in record time and enjoyed the more serious papers for a good read. He kept this always to himself, he didn't need or want to impress anyone, he had always achieved in his own right. *Achieved*, he thought, *detective inspector after twenty-five years and now ready for a small pension and the scrap heap of life. Probably end up doing security for the local shopping centre.*

John Eager was in his late forties, solid build with the start of a beer belly, which he thought, wrongly, that no one would notice with his jacket closed. He had dark brown wavy hair, a brown moustache and solid strong chin. He was still surprised that he still got looks from the ladies in the office. They would often play with their hair when talking to him, pushing the strands behind their ears. His body language course had told him that was when women were interested in you. Well, he hoped so but would never go any further with any of them. Newly divorced and soured by a relationship with his ex and totally committed to his job, which he viewed as his 'vocation'.

His fears always battled in his head, day and night. The drink took them away. He hated the way he always had arguments going on in his head that would never happen. Sometimes, simple things such as arguing with the check-out chick in the eight items only line at the supermarket. *The two cartons of milk should be counted as one. It's the same item! Anyway, why eight, why not six or ten?* Sometimes life didn't make sense to him. *Why would you reward people with a quicker service that are giving you less business? If you buy hundreds of pounds worth, you stood in a queue for ages.*

Other times, it was major debates with his higher-ups. *If we don't go for this one, he will be out and doing in old ladies before tea! I can't go on with a system that fails everyone all the time!* Of course, he had never actually said any of this, just the battles in his head. The real issues in his life always hit him from left field. He had never rehearsed the arguments, didn't have strong well thought out responses, witty retorts. He always thought of those later.

The train of thought took him to those times. When his wife walked out of his life, he could honestly say that he had never had a real argument with her in the last five years of their marriage. She was a cold fish, forever reading books whilst they had sex, always complaining about the hours he had to keep at work, she seemed to just want the money he earned (which was never enough) and to complain all the time. All arguments with her were just in his head, all the things he wanted to say but couldn't. A form of the cowardice of the highest order just between him and his mind. All the communication going on in his head that never escaped into sound. 'Would it have been better and ended differently if he said something, probably not, maybe ended sooner with less pain for all concerned?'

He was such a strong aggressive copper and at home, such a mouse, going along with anything she wanted just for the easy life. That is until it all became too much to bear. The voices in his head had taken their toll. It doesn't matter that you never say something if you think it eventually, your actions spell it out for all to see.

He was early as planned. 12:15 pm for a 12:30 pm lunch. They wouldn't see him limp in and it stroked their ego that he showed respect by being there when they arrived. The table had been booked in the private room at the rear of the restaurant. He handed his raincoat over and was shown by the young male waiter, in a pristine white long apron to the table. He sat with his back to the wall with a view through the small corridor of the front door, the 'gunfighters' seat as he called it. He ordered water, just tap water, the waiter seemed unimpressed but obliging. *Now,* he thought, *before the bullshit starts, I'll see what is going on in the 'Daily Cryer's' view of the world.*

He read his stars again, not always this good. An important meeting that may change his life, possible romance for single Pisceans (what about the divorced ones?) and more interesting information if he called this special number. He was having an important meeting and that bodes well for romance later. Whom was she kidding!

"Anything interesting, John or are you just surveying the bodywork?" It was the chief super of the major crimes squad, Charles Allcock. Tall, slim, silver-grey hair with a long face, big nose and a large mouth covered by thick lips. He was scary looking but had a sense of humour second to none. He was well aware of the banter in the squad room, particularly the twists they put on his name, but it was water off a duck's back to Charlie, as he was known.

"Just tits and bums, sir," John made a small effort to stand up but was stopped by Charlie's hand telling him not to bother. Charlie was always gesticulating. His hand movements were often quick and threatening as he used them to make a point. Many a waiter had floundered as the tray they were carrying is thrown into mid-air by Charlie's flailing arms.

"Glad I got you here early, John, we can draw a bit of a plan. We have some auspicious guests. The ACC and spook named Roger White, Super Jeannie Renshaw, Special Branch South Yorkshire."

"If McAllistar knew he was getting all this attention, he would be embarrassed."

It wasn't so much a plan of action as a briefing. Charlie wanted John to hold his piece, say what had to be said when it came up but not to get into old 'issues of what was right and wrong.' He knew John was emotional about this one and naïve politically, his big downside as an officer, the reason he was still an inspector. Charlie knew that you always needed perspective, choose your words carefully and win the wars, not the battles with subtlety, not emotion and aggression. Proving someone wrong and ramming the point down, their throats never engendered cooperation and support. John Eager would have gone further if he had understood this as a younger copper. Eager by name, highly emotional by nature.

They all arrived reasonably on time, so by 1 pm, they had ordered food and with pleasantries over, they were down to business. The ACC Bill Cartwright was there to listen. He was a smart career policeman, who didn't need to hog the limelight. A small balding man with vivid twinkling blue eyes and a magnetic personality, you knew when he was in the room.

Jeannie Renshaw was a stocky built lady around thirty-five years, McAllistar was now thought to be on her patch. A 'no-nonsense' woman who had battled the glass ceiling to get to this level. Her Achilles heel was always her university degree in law and the fact she was a woman. The general belief that her timing was right and she had been advantaged by the drive for university students giving them a fast promotion track and enhanced by the political need for a woman to join the senior ranks. 'Never worked the streets, never had to collar, a real villain of note in her life' was the criticism levelled, not totally true in Ms Renshaw's case, a tough and determined lady.

The 'Spook' was a young-looking man in his early thirties but looked twenty-five if he was a day. Roger White spoke very politely, obviously a public schoolboy background. He said he was from MI5 and his interest was the international aspect of the Harker brother's business empire. With his long brown hair, glasses, sideburns, wearing a blue denim shirt, black jeans with brown desert boots, he looked more at home in a university or some creative profession. He had arrived by bicycle, which he brought into the restaurant and parked it near the door. He seemed unaware that he stood out as an odd in this very business dressed serious group of people.

After introductions, opening pleasantries and food orders were made, Charlie started, "Okay, McAllistar. I guess you all read the sitrep, so I will be brief. Feel free to ask questions. Inspector Eager here is as close as a 'friend' to McAllistar and the resident expert on the case. Let me get the main points out first whilst you enjoy your food."

John winced at Charlie's little joke about him being a close friend. *Once maybe, not now anyway,* he thought.

Charlie Allcock was true to his word; brevity was his style. They all had files out and were taking notes, except for John Eager. He had everything in his head and his old police notebook tucked in his inside jacket pocket just in case.

McAllistar was out on parole, released early for 'good behaviour' a move that was not communicated and surprised everyone. He had previously refused relocation or police protection in return for his help. Truth is there was neither budget nor particular police motivation to provide either. He was going to live in his father's old holiday cottage in the Yorkshire dales. He had added, "Wherever that is?" as a joke and dig at DCI Renshaw. She let it go or it went right over her head. The cottage had been sold several times over the years and was purchased for McAllistar by a 'friend' recently, he stated in his parole application. The friend's name was on the deeds and it was thought that the funds had come from McAllistar's father's estate. That was what McAllistar told the parole board. The full address was given by McAllistar to the prison service admin and his parole officer.

*Father's estate? He was a poor miner living in a council house*, Eager puzzled.

"We've checked the background of the sale and it all looks legit, the place exists and it looks like the right destination," Renshaw added.

Eagar thought about all his conversations with McAllistar. He had talked about living in a row of semi-detached houses in the steel manufacturing smoggy area of Sheffield and his Dad was a miner. He was not sure he would have the wherewithal to own a cottage in the Yorkshire dales. Better keep quiet about this until it was checked out, he advised himself.

Allcock continued, "There are many things we don't know and some we do. I'll list them. One, we don't know for certain if McAllistar is dirty or not. We know he is a highly trained professional soldier.

"Two, we think that the Harker brothers want him dead for reason or reasons currently unknown. Where and when would be a nice to know? We also know they have had him set upon several times in prison, the worst needing a trip to the hospital section for a few weeks. The fact he's alive tells me something was holding them back from finishing him off. If they wanted to knock him on the head they could have. They want him alive, which suggests that he has something or a lot of things they want and probably we want.

"Three, the Harker's are very busy expanding their empire, ambitious cocky gents and they are going to get too big for their boots and make a mistake one day. If McAllistar has something of importance, this is our best chance to bring them down."

"If I may," the Spook cut in, "what do you mean you don't know if he is dirty or not? He's just got out of prison?"

Charlie realised he had made a slip-up. He felt at his shirt collar to stop his arms getting too animated. A few moments passed as he searched for an easy explanation.

John Eager cut in, "If I may," copying the Spooks high voice and accent as he had taken an instant disliking to the man. Something he knew in life you shouldn't do, being instantly judgmental, made mistakes about people before and will again, he thought.

"In my opinion, there is some doubt and I have expressed this to the chief on a few occasions. I always believed that something didn't add up."

"So, the police, prosecution services and judge and jury all got it wrong?" he came on the attack.

Charlie jumped in quickly, "Let me correct my statement. We have to assume he is dirty and guilty. John has never been able to prove otherwise and he has been the closest human being to McAllistar this last year."

"Too close maybe," the Spook stuck the knife in. John just shook his shoulders and thought he would like to loosen the nuts on the guy's bike wheels or his nuts for that matter.

"So, John," Bill, the ACC interjected, "Let's see how close you are. What do we not know that the files don't say?"

"Lot's sir," John suddenly came to life with zeal and enthusiasm. He knew this case; he knew the main players better than anyone. He lived it, can put it on like a tight glove.

Charlie was a little miffed at the suggestion he had missed something important in his summing up, nevertheless, Charlie Allcock waving his hands around motioned John to get on with it. Charlie then started to eat his minestrone soup, which was going cold.

"We know that the Harkers will soon find out where McAllistar's address is. Like the Super said, I am certain that the attempts on his life in prison were not meant to kill him. They could have done that, no thanks to…" he heeded Charlie's warning about emotion. "They could have killed him easily in prison, but for some reason, they want him alive. I have two theories on this, one: they want to be there, they want to do it themselves. This is personal and their whole underworld is watching. They will want him to suffer badly," John stopped for effect and to let what he said to sink into the combined brains around the table.

"And two?" Charlie hurried him.

"Again, I am certain that he has something they want."

"Why would you say that and what would that 'something' be?" The Spook was interested now.

"Nick Harker, one of the brothers and McAllistar were very close. Ex-army, met in NI and McAllistar saved Nick's life there. That's why they offered him a lucrative deal as a chief security officer at the 'Blue Haven' when he was demobbed."

"What a pity," someone said in a low whisper.

Eager ignored it and continued, "So, what happened is only my supposition,"

He had them all leaning forward, interested, he was for a change centre of attention. He told himself do not start spouting his innocence, just your theory.

"One or two things I know. One, he was very close to one of the girls at the club, I mean very close. She is missing off the radar since just before he was caught in possession. Rumour has it that she was a high-class hooker and Nick boy's favourite. So, I ask myself could she have been the cause of the split, the set up for McAllistar and could he have in his possession something they need to get back? Also, in my conversations with him in prison, he refused to give anything away except 'he knew where the bones were buried'. He also repeated time after time that he was fitted up."

He heard a few mutters in the background "Don't they all."

"Begs a lot of questions like why did they set him up and get him sent down if your 'supposition' is correct and I think it is a stretch, to say the least. Why not get it from him and kill him?" The Spook again was putting Eager down, blasting his theory.

Charlie gave Eager the look that said 'do not bite and do not get emotional for God's sake'.

Taking a deep breath, Eager continued, "Good point and yes, a lot of unanswered questions and of course I could be totally wrong," Eager looked at Charlie and he had a smile on his face as if saying 'that's it, my boy, good work'.

"However, after his serious beating in prison, I visited him in the prison hospital and thought that he might have softened up a bit. I told him he was going to get killed, so his best bet was to work with us and do a deal. He gave me the clear impression that they were just making his life miserable and he was protected somehow."

"So, they found out that he had something they need after he went inside?" Renshaw asked.

"That's my view, ma'am. To add to this, they must have something he wants or he would have worked with us."

"Or he is using whatever he has for protection," Charlie added. The ACC merely watched, not making comments either way.

"Not sure, sir, however, I think he wants it to come to a head and the Harkers do not deal nor let anyone go. So, he needs to get at them first."

"Get at them first?" The Spook was almost sneering. "They run a big and tough outfit."

"McAllistar is a war hero and a tough guy believe me. Depends how important what they have got is to him," Eager continued to stay calm and not be bated.

"War hero?" the Spook snarled. "NI troubles is not a war just a fight against terrorists."

Eager shrugged again. *He obviously never went there*, he thought.

"You mean that this could possibly be their undoing?" the ACC asked quite innocently.

"The way I look at it, sir," John addressed his comments direct to the ACC, "is that the Harkers will work on an ironclad plan but will be pushed by the famous temper of Nick boy and Jimmy's pride or ego whatever we want to call it. Assuming they believe they can force what they want out of him. They will want to do it as soon as possible but will know that McAllistar will expect that. The cottage in Yorkshire will be seen as a trap. Who would move into an old home in the middle of nowhere, easily got at, when you know what is going to happen to you? Only a crazy man. They have to get him out of there, that is a challenge if you want to personally torture him and not knock him off from a distance with a sniper shot."

"Nowhere? Just the prettiest place on earth," Ms Renshaw was not taking the second pot shot on the north no matter how innocent it was and a few laughs could be heard around the table. "So, you think he is reasonably safe on my patch?" she asked.

"No," continued John, "I am speculating. They are a little crazy and could try anything, so I don't want to give the impression that we should do nothing but watch at the cottage. There is also another unknown quantity."

"Okay, John what unknown quantity?" Charlie asked as he wiped the soup off his face and tie.

"His girlfriend, Karlien. The girl who disappeared, sir. If McAllistar believes she is dead he will be out for revenge. He blames the Harkers and it is not beyond belief to think he might have spent the last twelve months planning some sort of payback."

"Good riddance to all of them," the ACC said.

"On a scale of 1 to 10, how real do you think all this speculation is?" Roger White asked as if not convinced that DI Eager was not just enjoying his time in the limelight.

John eyeballed him and held his stare for a few seconds, as, though, he was merely thinking about the question carefully. What was this Spook's real interest in this case? Maybe the Harkers were branching out. One thing was for sure this guy would probably tell him as little as possible in return.

"I spent a lot of time with him. He loved this girl a lot. He has the skills to kill, his medals prove he can and, to be frank, he has little choice. He knows they will never rest until he is dead. He believes the police, the system has let him down. He knows that unless they are taken out completely, he will never have a life. So, I would guess an eight."

"It seems he doesn't want to live?" Roger interrupted.

"He hated prison, dreaded every moment. He had nightmares and never had a good night's sleep. I am sure he wants them to pay and will not rest until they do. But no, McAllistar is not a guy to want to die, take big risks yes, but calculated even if he is driven by revenge," John spoke with passion and showed too much of his emotional involvement.

"You have obviously kept close to him since he saved you," Roger White signed off his questions with a statement that highlighted DI Eager's deep involvement with the case and McAllistar.

"I visited him maybe ten times. Too many unanswered questions, I thought he might change his mind in prison and start talking," John said in justification.

"Did he soften at all? Let anything slip?" asked DCI Renshaw.

"No. He didn't trust me or the system anymore. He was supposed to go to an open prison, get therapy and be out in a few months. The deal was changed at a high level, not sure why and he was put into the scrubs where he was at risk day and night."

"Okay John, thanks," Charlie interrupted knowing he was headed down an old and unproductive track, "good thinking, very helpful, now let's see what we can and need to do."

# Chapter Five
## The Russians

On a special raised mezzanine VIP section, with room for a table of eight, protected by metal rails, was the owner's private table. Tonight, it was ready for a meeting. The table was laden with cigars, champagne, vodka and caviar. Three heavies stood around watching and protecting.

Nick was looking out from the office and he turned to Jimmy, "Our friends have arrived. We better be getting down there."

"Just before we do, let's get our position straight," Jimmy said. "They need to feel confident; we can recover the goods and if we don't, we can pay them back soon. We need time to get the cash and our aim has got to be to keep them off our backs until we do. These are very nasty people."

"So are we," Nick cracked his knuckles annoyingly for Jimmy.

"Nick, these people are in a league of their own, we can't fuck with them. It will not be worth the headache it will bring to our door. Promise me to be cool? Promise?"

"Okay, you're the boss brother."

The guests had been shown the VIP table and were getting stuck into the vodka when Nick and Jimmy arrived. Handshakes and shoulder hugs all round. The 'go-between' and now the Blue Haven Enterprise's corporate solicitor, Tazewell Javelin, appeared from nowhere and seamlessly joined the group. He was known as the unholy ghost, Jimmy being the father and Nick the son creating the evil trinity.

"Welcome, Roman and Leon," Jimmy lifted his glass of vodka, "you are our guests and anything, I mean anything, you want tonight is on the house." A few sneers and laughs. Then everyone gulped down the vodka and Nick refilled the glasses and they all sat down at the same time.

"It's good to be here, tell me, Jimmy, can we talk safely?" Roman asked wanting to get right down to business.

"We feel so, however, for the sake of being a hundred per cent sure, we have a venue tomorrow organised where we can get right down to business without any doubts."

"So, tonight must be purely social eh?" Roman said with a small grunt.

"I am afraid so but not a bad place to socialise," added Tazewell.

"We have some very serious business to discuss and we need to know where you people are with our project," stated Leon menacingly and then standing up, sweeping his arm around the room, "we have better places in Russia and better girls. All these girls, they are too skinny, they need a good feed of borscht!"

Nick was about to say something in response when Jimmy cut him off quickly.

"We value our relationship, dare I say strategic partnership and I am sure tomorrow you will be satisfied with our progress and happy with our vision of the future," Jimmy added with confidence and the delivery of a politician that talks a lot and says nothing.

"That's right these guys are professional and run a slick organisation," Tazewell added to Jimmy's annoyance. *Sounds like we protest too much*, he thought.

The vodka flowed, girls were rounded up and shown to the Russians, until two that Roman and Leon particularly liked were invited to join them. Their lingerie they were wearing left little to the imagination. The Russians seemed to be happy with them.

*They picked the biggest and most voluptuous girls, so maybe the feeding comment was serious,* thought Nick.

The evening went well. It was hard keeping up with the Russians on the vodka. Jimmy made excuses and changed to lite beer, Tazewell never drank anything but cola however, Nick went glass for glass with them. The Russians were also very distracted by and getting a little aggressive with the girls. Jimmy expected a slapped face, which would not do at all, so he eyeballed the girls continuously. His message was to take this well or never work here again.

"When did this happen? How come we didn't get any warning? What the fuck am I paying a scrotum like you for anyway?" screamed Nick Harker down the phone on the back desk several yards from the party. He stood impatient as he waited for the answer. The whole table had stopped to watch him.

"Well, find out right and let me fucking know as soon as you do…yeah, you do that!" he completed the call and calmly put the phone down and then stood by the railing, overlooking the lap dance room. The conversation at the table which had paused for a few seconds continued and no one looked at Nick.

Roman turned to Jimmy with an anxious look, creased forehead, "Problem?"

Nodding towards Nick, he asked Jimmy.

"No, Mr Mattavov, probably bitch trouble," Jimmy dismissed the incident. He did wave the firm's solicitor over to his left ear. Tazewell, an American, around sixty, heavy build, dark glasses always seeming to sit skew on his face and balding slicked-back black hair leaned over. "Taz, quietly see why the theatrics. It is important that our Russki friends see a professional in control operation here. Tell Nick, nicely mind, to cool it."

Tazewell rose, excused himself and went to the top of the table as if he was watching the latest dancer strip, waited a few minutes and then calmly headed for Nick. Tazewell had a limp from a twisted right leg, which made his movements look jerky and as, though, he was moving sideways like a crab. People often referred to this as a cripple's version of John Wayne walk. He was overall a very one of kind individual.

He was disarmingly quiet, courteous and inoffensive, even polite, so you could be fooled into thinking he was a decent guy or your friend. Underneath all of this, kept mainly under control, was a clever but very devious mind. You could almost see the lumps in his forehead pulsate when his mind was working overtime, working out angles, looking for loopholes and putting up 'Chinese walls'. He was not a man of violence but prided himself that he could tie people or corporations up in so much legal mumbo jumbo that they would eventually go broke by drowning in legal fees and a mountain of paperwork.

He thought he was the future of organised crime and these Brits were lucky to have him on their team. To Jimmy, his legal brain and underworld contacts made him a necessary evil. To Nick, he was a yank, Uriah Heep.

"Let's give Randy a big hand and some cash!" boomed the DJ, highlighting the naked lady on the centre stage. "Coming next on centre stage is Amanda, from down under. They don't get better than our Aussie cousins." The Russian's turned and watched missing the interaction between Nick and Tazewell.

After a brief but animated conversation, Tazewell returned and sat patiently by Jimmy. The Russians were distracted a little further. They had better places in Russia, more beautiful girls from the old eastern bloc, Poland, Czech, Georgia a variety of looks and bodies, from Chinese looking to beautiful classic blondes. Regardless, they thought that it would still be worthwhile to watch and fondle the Brits, Australian, American girls that the 'Blue Haven' offered.

"What were your names again, trying to hear above the noisy club?" the large blonde asked.

"Roman and Leon," the Russians both replied amiably.

"Oooh these nice names, are you from Rome then?"

Jimmy rolled his eyes and turned to Tazewell. Whispering and watching that the Russians were engrossed in the girls. He said quietly, "He has it on good authority that your friend was released early. Whereabouts not known at present."

Jimmy stared into space; he was thinking about what he had heard. No one could read Jimmy's face and know what he was thinking.

"Maybe good timing, an opportunity to resolve this and close the case?" Tazewell threw in as his own mind raced working out the options at the news he had just heard.

"Mc-fucking-Allister," Jimmy smiled.

# Chapter Six
## Home

McAllistar awoke with a jolt. He sat upright shaking and holding in the scream he knew would wake the dead. The nightmare never changed, Karlien was shouting, "Why? Why?" at him and bleeding from every part of her body. He sat up for twenty minutes and didn't move. He came around slowly, this was not the cell it was his cottage, it was freedom and it was hope. Carefully, he got out of his sleeping bag where he had lain in front of the big wood fire all night. It was still alive with burning embers, but the room was very cold. The two empty Chardonnay bottles lay on the floor nearby and his ashtray beside them. He checked his Breitling watch, which he never thought he would get back when they took everything from him. It was 5 am – best night's sleep he had for the last year.

He had found the big old door key as arranged under a big disused flower pot around the side of the cottage. When he opened it, he immediately saw the fireplace had been prepared and ready to light, good dry wood carefully stacked from inside with paper and twigs to thinner logs on top. At the side, a box of matches and a mountain of bigger logs were ready to add. He locked the entrance door and took a mental note to fit big new bolts top, centre and bottom. It was a thick wooden door, but the lock was old. "Good old Aunt Bessie," he said under his breath. The windows too had iron bars on the outside and the thick cloth curtains on the inside were drawn tight, no one could see in or get in without a lot of noise. Aunt Bessie had left milk, tea, a mug, some sandwiches and the fire ready to roll, not to mention the two bottles Chardonnay sitting outside the back door in the cold weather. Chilled to perfection by nature and the welcome home he needed. She forgot the corkscrew, but he carried a Swiss army knife.

There were a table and an old brown leather armchair with horsehair sticking out of the holes. A three-legged milking stool sitting in the corner which he didn't understand why. It was as all just as he had requested from the prison public phone, not to bother with furniture, it was probably a waste of time in his case as he didn't intend to stay long. Just enough to work out a plan and get some rest.

He went to the toilet, added some wood to the fire and was glad to see it start to burn, he drank the milk and sat on the floor leaning against the wall to the right of the fire. He pulled his sleeping bag over his legs and lit a cigarette. He had the ashtray on his lap. This was perfect, he felt partially alive again. As the fire started and the smoke swirled around him, McAllistar went over his plans in detail. He then thought of other options and scenarios as he had been taught. *What if this happens, they do this, what about him, what about that.*

He poured himself another Chardonnay. His mind then went into a revenge mode and he wondered if he should include the bastards that had failed him, as well as the irritating prosecution barrister, and the smug fat judge, the wardens and inmates who had beaten him for their crooked masters and John Eager, who he thought was his friend had he betrayed him?

He smoked and drank and thought. He was, though, relaxed and a little happy, even though his mind was full of people he needed to sort out. This passed the time until just past midnight when he decided to get some shut-eye until his day was to begin in earnest.

# Chapter Seven
## A New Business Opportunity – Fifteen Months Earlier

"Guys, I would like to talk to you about a very lucrative opportunity, with little investment and big returns," Tazewell was excited at what he was bringing to the table.

"Go ahead, we are always open to new ideas especially if the money is worthwhile," Jimmy said but with little belief that what he was going to say was of interest.

Nick just sat there at the side of Jimmy's desk tapping his fingers on the desktop and Tazewell was in the visitor's seat facing Jimmy.

"This may not be to your taste."

"Oh, get on with it, Taz. I have an appointment with the Russians you introduced us too in twenty minutes," the impatient Nick blurted out.

"Okay, but be patient just a few minutes. The clubs are profitable and we rake money in from all angles. The gals pay to work there for their tips and we make money out of entrance fees, the drinks and let's say other stimulants and a cut of escort fees which we set up. So, yes, a good operation. However, I ran into someone who has let me say, got a fucking good idea and contacts to make it happen. Imagine hundred's people paying sixty thousand pounds a year plus for membership of a special club we can create!"

"I'm listening." Nick leaned forward.

"Easy money, there is a group of high society people who will pay for let me say certain sexual tastes that we can provide them. Yes, these people are not normal but their bank accounts also are not the average."

"Stop!" Nick interrupted not liking what he was hearing.

"Let Taz finish, Nick, let's not judge until we have heard all of what he has to say," the practical Jimmy intervened.

"My new friend has introduced me to a whole new world I didn't know too much about. It's been done before in the 1700s to the 1800s clubs known as 'hellfire clubs' operated in Ireland and England. These were for the rich and famous to meet and have the opportunity to enjoy their special needs. If exclusive and discrete, I mean even Benjamin Franklin was known to visit the one in the caves at West Wycombe on several occasions as a non-member."

"We'd be closed down," Nick interrupted again.

"Not if it is a very close secret and we have protection anyway as you know. Can you imagine attracting the high end of society and being in the know of their darkest secrets?" Tazewell was getting into his pitch.

Nick started to speak again, but Jimmy held up his hand to stop him.

"Go ahead. This sounds like the Catholic church and confession."

"Like I said, I have been doing some research and using my contacts. Briefly, so you can think about it and Nick can get to his appointment. We have a big area below the club being used for old storage, it has its own entrance down the alleyway and with a big black tent customer can drive in and never be seen. I now have a contact I can introduce you to, who knows certain individuals of high worth who would enjoy this type of club. This guy would help with what shall I say the needs and how to fulfil them. We create a rollicking venue like the old hellfire clubs and rake in the cash."

"This needs to be a hands clean operation from our side?" Jimmy said.

"Yes, I guess so. We can put some safety measures in place and I suggest we test and then find a venue away from central London."

"Taz, thanks. Let Nick and I discuss this and come back to you."

Two days later, he was summoned to the office and given the go-ahead with the proviso he supervises all aspects and delivers on the profit. They also agreed with him on his suggestion to look for somewhere more private longer term in the country, a place that could not be visited easily by the police. The hellfire clubs had been in manors, old abbeys and even down some caves.

The Harkers had just agreed to go a lot deeper into the dark world that surrounded them blinded by money.

# Chapter Eight
## Cocktails at Barney's

Liberty arrived at Barney's a little late. She liked to mix and have a beer with the boys. She liked to think she could drink them all under the table, she was after all from New York and super confident, loud, superwomen. Barney's was an upmarket bar come restaurant. The place was modern, which was a surprise, she had half expected an old boys club like she had seen in many Brit pictures. Sir Richard was seated with an ecliptic group of friends. Friends or sycophants she thought, they were all the same. Gavin was at the bar, holding it up from where she stood, certainly well into his cocktail hour. She joined him.

"Budweiser?" Gavin asked.

"No, give me one of those black beers in a large beer glass."

"A pint of Guinness then?"

"So, how are you holding up?" She looked him up and down.

"I'm okay, do I look okay?"

"Not too hammered yet, but be careful it's still early. Don't want sir to think we are lushes."

"Oh, fuck off, this is part of the business expected. They don't care if I got pissed and vomited all over their table. But let the circulation or advertising drop and they would toss me in the bin without a second thought."

"Your call, I guess." The pint of Guinness arrived and to Gavin's surprise, Liberty just downed the lot in one go.

"Another, thanks," she said to the 'gobsmacked' barman.

"Thirsty?" Gavin said sarcastically.

"Yeah, part New York Irish, excited, I been thinking about the assignment, its big man. Thanks."

Gavin looked serious and concerned. He hesitated for a moment then blurted out, "Look Liberty, I've been thinking, this is very dangerous and maybe I was hasty to put you on it. It is fraught with all kinds of forces we may not be able to control. You could get very hurt!"

"How hurt?"

"Try dead, is that hurt enough for you?"

Liberty took this in for a moment.

"You think I am too young, inexperienced?"

"You have balls, brains and energy but that's not enough." Gavin indicated by counting on his fingers, "one, the United Kingdom is not your territory. Two, you are inexperienced. Three, you stand out in a crowd with your looks, the way you dress, your loud Yankee voice. Need I go on?"

"Okay, why don't I take you to that cold damp room you Brits call an apartment and fuck your brains out? It will keep me warm and could change your mind!" She stared at him. Gavin wondered for a second if she was for real, he felt his penis go suddenly hard. The booze normally interfered with that particular activity.

An arm went around both shoulders as they stared at each other.

"What's this then, you two having a domestic?" Sir Richard did his guffaw laugh that sounded like a donkey in pain to Liberty.

"Come on, Liberty, let me introduce you to some very interesting people. You need to build your profile here and network."

With that, he whisked Liberty away to the table to show her off to his friends and just maybe the table needed a change of pace from the usual boring bullshit that goes on every week.

The table had several ladies in their fifties and sixties, well-kept for their ages. They were polite and welcoming, but it was on surface only, they immediately took a dislike to Liberty. One was an editor of '*Get It*' fashion magazine and the other a well-known freelance journalist and ex-war correspondent. The other, a jeweller named Mr Jones, who had a trendy shop and workshop on Kensington High Street that catered to the rich and even royalty. Tall, blond, casually dressed, handsome. He was interesting, Liberty thought and sat beside him.

He immediately turned to her holding out his hand, "Marvin, please to meet you. Liberty is it?" He held onto her hand a little too long. One of the ladies' harrumphed. He let go very quickly and became very sheepish looking away.

She wondered which one he had a relationship with? Definitely a player, she thought, well the night was still young.

Liberty was also a player, although she preferred to have steady relationships, mostly with two guys at a time with the odd one-night stand when someone turned her on and the opportunity was there or she was travelling and bored. She was not sure how it started, it just seemed that from her early teens, she had had at least two boyfriends at a time. They were always from different backgrounds and never destined to meet.

Her father, an Irish New York police detective and mother Italian. An interesting combination which gave her looks and tenacity. He always had lots of money and spoilt his children and spent a lot of time with them when he could. She remembers him working in the garage with his builder's belt on with all the tools hanging out and the kid's set he had bought her. She loved fixing things with him. He seemed rich but was just a poorly paid policeman.

It happened as suddenly as he had run away one day with a policewoman to Los Angeles. No note, no reason, nothing. Leaving her with her sister and mother a lowly paid office clerk to fend for themselves. Liberty never got over this and it impacted who she was and how she acted from then on.

She got a visit to Los Angeles several times and was surprised at the luxury lifestyle he had with his new family. He had a stepson of her age and the house was filled with toys and playthings. He was very spoilt whilst she and her sister were living just above the poverty line.

He said he was working in the movies as an advisor being an ex-cop and with the experience of dealing with murders and the mafia. Later, she found out he was not totally clean and left before he was prosecuted.

She was sexually active at sixteen years old. She badly needed love and attention of men from then on.

It started, though, with an Italian boy named Atturo at school. A quiet attractive boy, slick dresser and a romantic from his head down to his penis. She did it with him on their first date in her mother's flat on top of the washing machine. She liked the movement of the spin-dryer cycle as she climaxed. She loved to tease him.

"Am I the first man to sleep with you?" he asked.

"I don't know. Where were you two years ago?"

He went quiet and sulked as only Italian Romeos can.

Using her fingers to demonstrate again she said, "Come on. One, you are not a man but a boy and two, you don't think I got this good at it being a virgin. You'd leave frustrated."

She lied. He was her first, but she had the confidence to carry any point.

"I love you."

He was a bit 'wimpy' for her taste, however, due to his dark complexion and extremely good looks all the other girls at school were jealous which was just fine with her, but she needed a he-man like her father was.

Liberty worked in a gay bar at night as a waitress, having faked her ID age. She was straight and needed money. Some of the lesbians who liked to smack her ass and come onto her, however, they were very good tippers and she learnt the skill to play them for all she was worth. She wanted to pay her way through university and become the best policewoman ever with a law degree. So, she took the slaps and touches and even erotic table dancing for tips to save her money for her dream.

That's where she met George, a large twenty-three-year-old African American from Kentucky, serving as a barman at the bar. He was packed with muscles and a big round solid ass sticking out back of his tight trousers. At first, she thought he was also gay until she saw him with one of the supposedly Lesbians in the alley outside. He was giving her a good 'seeing to' and she was screaming with delight. No one could hear inside as the music and the laughter drowned everything out.

She had stepped out for a cigarette and a little peace and quiet plus some cool air. She thought, she must go both ways I must try it one day. She watched from behind the dumpster until the woman collapsed on the floor. George was putting his extra-large 'trouser snake' away. He caught her literally gazing at him and put it away slowly all the time smiling at her.

"Kentucky snake best in New York," he said, patting it proudly.

"More like a river worm. I've had much better!" she boasted.

"A child like you, I would split you in two," he countered.

"Come on then big boy, do your best," she pretended to pull down her knickers.

"I'd go to prison again if I touched a baby like you!" he shouted over his shoulder, as he walked back into the bar.

"Chicken George!" she shouted and the name stuck with her. He was Chicken George from then on and she would have him.

So, it was 'in love' Atturo after class and Chicken George at night. Her mother worked and went to bed early. Her sister was away at college. So, Chicken George would carry Liberty on his back up the stairs, so her mother only heard one pair of footsteps each night. He would leave early taking her down the stairs, so she could come back in the house as having gone for a jog. Her mother was really oblivious as Liberty always did her own thing and cared only that she had lost her man and wanted to find another.

College continued in the same vein, she went to New York City. Many a day she did the 'walk of shame' early in the morning from the men's dormitory with her thong in her pocket and a smile on her face. It was harder here to have two lovers who didn't meet or ask awkward questions but she managed to get away with it. She learned her second skill of telling a lie that no one questioned or didn't believe her. She told her 'story' so close to the truth that it was almost the truth with one or two key elements missing or added. So, Brad, the college line-backer and Joel, a thirty-five-year-old professor, who was married with kids, never connected the dots.

She got a job at *The New York Times* as a junior reporter. Her law and communications degrees helped and she assisted on the crime beat. Her goal of being a policewoman had changed; she enjoyed this work and now dreamed of being a top investigative reporter. Her Dad helped her with contacts; some were his police friends and prosecutors and other underworld figures, who could give her information. Her father's name was McGill and she soon learnt he was a controversial figure with the police. Some loved him and some hated him. She was shunned by many with one sergeant saying, "You should be ashamed being McGill's daughter, get out of here." She changed her name to Bell after that, thinking it was catchy for her career.

She did get some scoops from his friends and underworld figures, even meeting several godfather-type figures. They were using her for other reasons, she was sure, however, the information was good and her reputation was building and promotions came her way.

Her last two relationships that were going on at the same time created a big problem. One married cop and the son of a mafia clan. She met the cop at a murder scene and the mafia guy in his restaurant. It was okay for a while until the restaurant was raided and drugs and laundered money were found. When the Godfather was told she had been sleeping with a policeman, the finger of suspicion pointed directly at her. Leaving town and country was the best option she had, quickly.

"Come on Liberty, tell us all a little bit about yourself."

Sir Richard trying to liven up the cocktail hour. So, Liberty did her routine that shocked and awed the stiff upper lip group. True stories tailored with fiction and the truth exaggerated, funny and very interesting. Men were spellbound by her storytelling and the women aghast with her being the centre of attention, hoping she would leave soon.

Marvin tried not to make eye contact and Liberty just had him down as a weak man of no further interest. She liked the British accent like a lot of American ladies, but there was something about the upperclassmen in the United Kingdom that turned her off. She decided to leave early and go home alone. Hadn't she made a promise to herself to change after a big incident in the United States? Well, maybe. She would go home and read up on her assignment and show these Brits what investigative reporting was all about.

She saw Gavin looking in her direction bleary-eyed and in no condition to speak with the chairman's friends. She grabbed him by the arm and waved goodnight to everyone, took him in a taxi and dumped him outside his flat block.

"Seriously, Lib, come inside and have a nightcap," he slurred.

She could see him on the pavement, sitting down talking to no one in particular as her taxi drove away.

# Chapter Nine
## Aunt Bessie

"Logan McAllistar?" a large lady entered the cottage from the back door. "Logan, where are you?"

"Here, Aunt Bessie," Logan grabbed her from behind and hugged her tight.

"Stop that now, stop it," she laughed. She was almost as tall as him and far wider, she was almost eighty years old and the muscles she had developed working on the farm all her life were slowly turning to fat. She had been a very strong lady in her time throwing sacks of potatoes around like feathers. McAllistar wondered if she could still pick him up and toss him like she did when he was a boy.

"Aunt Bessie, it's so good to see you, you look great!"

"Stop that false flattery now, Logan McAllistar, you were never a good liar."

She stood back and looked at him. He was so much older than the last time she saw him. Was it fifteen years ago just before he joined the boy soldiers? He looked fit and muscular, not an ounce of fat on him, although she noticed his eyes looked tired and weary and underneath dark bags were growing.

"Did you keep it a secret as I asked, Aunt Bessie?" McAllistar asked as his face turned serious and big creases ran across his forehead.

"Yes, Logan, but I don't understand, you are a free man now? No one here will bother you," She could see the concern on his face as the atmosphere in the cottage turned serious.

"What trouble are you bringing to my door, Logan?" she asked.

"None I hope, Aunt Bessie. No one knows where I am and I just need time to recover before I sort things out for good."

She sat on the milking stool and it creaked as, though, to break. It looked odd this bulk of a woman sitting low on a small three-legged milking stool. He knelt to be face level.

"You know I love you like a mother Aunt Bessie, I would never put you in danger," he said with passion and she could see small drops of tears swelling in his eyes.

This was not the Logan that left so many years ago, strong to the point of being emotionally bereft, cocky and self-assured. He seemed a little broken down, but she guessed prison will do that to you.

"Let me get some tea on and you better tell me all about it, everything, right Logan, promise?"

He took some time to consider her words before replying, "Yes, I will. I promise you on my life."

He crossed his fingers; however, he would tell her the gist of what had happened, leaving out some pertinent details and not touch on what he was going to do next. And so, he did. It took three mugs of tea before he stopped.

She sat their mouth open, "Holy Jesus what a mess, what are you going to do about it?"

"Not sure," he lied.

She just hung her head and shook it several times. She lifted it slowly and had tears in her eyes, "Pity Ted is not alive today, he would know what to do."

He held her tenderly by the arms and gently looked into her eyes, searching until he felt he had connected with her like he used to as a kid.

"I promise this will be sorted and no harm will come to you."

"Bah, I am not worried about me, lad. It's you I am worried about; you are all I have left."

He nodded, "You are all I have too. Is it better I leave?"

She stood up, "For God's sake Logan, this is your home. Ted left this to you, yours lock stock and barrel. Been meaning to register it in your name."

"Thanks, Aunt Bessie but don't do that yet, it would be an easy way to find me."

"Oh, by the way, the parcel you sent me is hidden, you know where."

"Thanks. You always came through for me when I needed it."

"It's not drugs, is it?"

"No, I was set up with the drugs, never touched them or sold them, it's something that will set me free and put right a lot. I mean right a lot of wrongs."

# Chapter Ten
## Not Home

"What on earth do you mean derelict?" Renshaw asked over the phone.

"Well ma'am, I mean like it has been partially burnt out for several years, used by local kids for booze parties and drugs."

"Are you sure you went to the right address?"

"I have been on the beat here for twenty years, yes it's the right address."

The constable was a little miffed at her questioning his local knowledge.

"What about the houses close by? Check them out. See if anyone has seen a new guy around. Check all around the village, for god's sake look everywhere you can."

"Nothing ma'am, within a square mile of this old derelict. Yes, I did the necessary in the area, nothing came up of interest," stressing *ma'am* to make the point that he knows his police business and does not want a desk jockey telling him basics.

"Just keep an eye on it over the next few days."

"May I ask what or who am I looking for?"

"A man called McAllister the rest is need to know, I'm afraid," she stated, stressing his place on the food chain.

The old constable was not to be put off by one of these fast-track smart Alecs.

"Beg your pardon, ma'am. I think I need to know the situation, is it dangerous or do I collar this guy on my own?"

"Look, he is not dangerous, just someone to help with our enquiries, although he may not want to. All I want you to do is drive by once or twice a day and call me anytime day or night if you suspect or see anything. Got it?"

"Righty ho then."

*Shit,* she thought, *we've been led down the garden path and I fell for it. Too easy I should have known. This guy McAllistar is no fool, so now I have to call everyone with egg all over my face.*

"Jim." Detective Sergeant Jim Smith put his head around her office door when he heard the aggressive call.

"Bad news, the McAllistar cottage is a derelict."

"What?"

"A derelict. A burnt out. A wreck. Did you not visit it?"

"I didn't see the need once we saw the parole documents. I checked the deed office and it belongs to J. L. McAllistar. I mean…" He could see that the shit would flow downhill onto his head. Until her trip to London, they knew nothing, it wasn't a priority, no big deal but now he was for it.

"He only has one initial sergeant no J, just L for Logan, probably an old relative. We will look like country hicks to those city coppers. Now, I have to tell them that we didn't check it out just assumed that's where he was headed."

"I will go there now and check it out anyway," It was all he could offer.

"No. Constable Dick head has checked it out," she mimicked him. *I've been on this beat for twenty years. No wonder he is still a constable,* she thought.

Looking up, DS Smith was watching for her next instruction. She was obviously much stressed that her degree hadn't helped her here.

"What would you do?" she looked at him almost softly.

"Go back to basics. They always go home. So, I need to find where home is for this guy."

"Okay, check out everything, I mean everything, where he was born, the church where he was christened, local pub, anyone who might have even smelled this guy when he was younger. Been in Boy's Army since he was fifteen, so it's only a short period. I'll get that DI Eager to start checking from that point forward."

# Chapter Eleven
## Billy, the Neck

Billy Garrick was sitting on his swinging broken office chair. It was so broken that he regularly tipped over backwards. Sometimes due to the chair and sometimes related to what he was taking or smoking that day. His work environment was a dirty basement filled with wires and TV screens and video recorders. It wasn't much, but it was his world and he was safe and happy there. No one bothered him, in fact, hardly anyone visited him. That suited him just fine, although he felt like a fox in its lair at times. In fact, he was no more than a rat but thought of himself as a smart fox.

Billy always wore black clothes mainly black jeans and black t-shirts, so it seemed he hardly ever changed. His t-shirt was covered with smoke ash and remnants of carry out meals he gulped whilst watching the video screens. He watched them like a vulture. He had small beady eyes in a big head that was held up by an extra-long thin neck. Billy's neck was adorned by a large Adam's apple that moved up and down when he spoke like an elevator out of control. People often were mesmerised by the movement and stared to the point of embarrassing him. God did give him a profusion of black hair that stood on its tiptoes and waved at passing people in the wind.

He thought of himself as part fox and part vulture. Billy's looks were very distinctive and his mind was messed up with drugs and so he thought he was very clever and had the ability to pick up the lucrative remains that were left like road kill on the club's floor.

To say he was happy about his work was an understatement. He loved his work as the 'security' video technical coordinator at the 'Blue Haven' which he stilled called 'The Dirty Cow'. He got to watch hundreds of naked girls every week, people making out, no one had bothered him since the last security chief, McAllistar was sneaking around. He now reported direct to Jimmy, who only wanted to see him once a week or whenever something special came up.

He was fed all the newspapers and magazines he could read, even if it was for their purposes. He was a night owl working from 6 pm until 4 am. He had a very basic pay, Nick would often joke, "You should pay us to work here." He guessed Nick put a high value on the fringe benefits. Every now and then he spotted someone of note enjoying him or herself at the club and worth videoing. He got cash bonuses for this and maybe Nick would send a couple of girls down to him if he hit the jackpot. He was an insider with the Harkers and read the media carefully to remember the faces and names of the tall poppies, who might get him a windfall one day when they fall. The owl inside him kept him awake, the vulture watching, smelling and waiting for an opportunity and the fox had his own plans for more opportunities.

The hellfire club was a whole new 'kettle of fish' that whet his appetite for unusual and creepy activities. A new world of opportunities and turn-ons.

# Chapter Twelve
## Karlien

Over thirteen months ago…

"Come in, sit down, Karlien," Jimmy was at his politest. Karlien strolled into the office slowly like a lioness going to the watering hole. She found a small chair in the tiny room which was surrounded by Jimmy, Nick and Tazewell. She wore a red mini skirt, red high heels and a white blouse, all were designer named fashion items. Her natural hair was long flowing curly red and her make-up was immaculate. Her skin was a light olive tone that gave her an exotic look when combined with the red hair. She was quite a package. She was classy from head to toe, stunning and she knew it. Tazewell was mesmerised whenever they met. He also knew she was an opportunity for profit if used correctly.

Tazewell, 'Call me Taz', made all the girls in the club's skin crawl, Nick, she feared and Jimmy, she didn't trust one inch. Still, this was her living and it paid well. She had already bought and rented three houses in London. Her houses were packed full of students and immigrants, often two or three to a room all paying rent. Fred, one of the over-weight giant bouncers from the club collected rent for her weekly and ensured the tenants were not sneaking in more people to spread the cost. It was a nice little earner and being in London, she could sell with big profits one day when she wanted to get out of the sex industry or probably more. Which was when she became too old to compete with the eighteen-year-olds.

At twenty-five years old, she had the experience, the stunning looks and great body, so she was at her peak with maybe a few years to go at the top. One thing she decided when she started this work was that she would not end up as a drug and drink riddled slapper. No, she would do this for a few years, then she would find Mr Right and settle down in the countryside or by the sea, maybe move back to her native South Africa and live a charmed easy life. She had a goal and was determined no matter what it takes to make that dream come true.

"Hiya!" she said with a shy laugh and a little wave of the hand. She came across as innocent and that was her biggest asset. Men loved it and wanted to protect her and her bosses often underestimated her because of it.

"Karlien, good job with the TV star. He called and I think gal he loves you," Tazewell said slowly with his Texan drawl.

She just smiled; she didn't need his compliments.

Nick looked at his watch. He was always impatient and he looked angrier than normal. Jimmy picked up on it and started.

"We have a really great profitable job for you and a favour to ask."

"Shoot," she said. She was not showing any excitement. She was now in a position to find her own profitable jobs and any favour could be bad and certainly smells like trouble.

"Next week, we have a really special VIP in town. Needs someone to let's say give him a good time for one night. Needs to be very discrete and low key. No one, I mean no one needs to know or hear his name."

"Okay, my middle name is discretion."

"Really…" Tazewell started and saw them all look at him and shut up.

"And the favour?"

"You know McAllistar quite well?" Nick jumped in.

"Not really, just chat sometimes like all the guys and girls that work around here."

"Really, every time I look, you are chatting to him," Nick had been watching, was he jealous or just stroppy. Nick, she had always avoided; he was trouble.

"What can I say, I think he digs me, but I do not really know him. We just shoot the shit sometimes."

"Pass the time, he should be working," Nick countered.

"Okay," Jimmy held his hands up. "This is the thing Karlien we want you to get close to him, very close and just check him out for us."

"I thought he was Nick's army mate?" she looked confused.

"He saved my bloody life and I gave him a good start here after the army. Now we are unsure about him. Taz has information that leads us to believe he might not be what we think he is. I want to be sure he is not a clipe for the rozzers, which some people are now asserting he is," He looked at Tazewell who gazed away.

"So, what do you want me to do? Date him and what?"

"Suck him, fuck him, get him drunk, we don't care, see if you find anything suspicious. Men talk to women that they 'dig'," Nick waved his hands about. He was obviously frustrated on McAllistar's side if he was clean but clearly not sure that he had brought a cuckoo into the nest.

Tazewell took out his notebook and went through a list of things they would like to know or get. Close friends, phone bills, people who visited his house, people he met, bank and telephone accounts, loose pillow talk, drunken boasting…the list went on and on.

"Oh, Karlien," Jimmy said in a quiet voice, "Can we trust you with this, are you up for this? Please do this thoroughly and do not let us down," He was subtle, however, the threat was clear. You do not cross these guys or you do at your own peril.

Logan, she thought, was a handsome decent guy. He had asked her out several times, so getting close was not going to be an issue. He had never talked about the business or asked for information that might be sensitive. He knew what she did, but she gathered that he would rather not know the details. He liked her too much and probably just tried to put it out of his mind. She better start working him tonight in front of them all.

Men talked to her; all their secrets came out without little effort on her part. She hoped he was clean and what she did would not end up getting him hurt or even something worst. Her policy, though, was Karlien first, everyone else second. If she didn't get the truth and they found out later, she would be on the chopping block. Better be careful if they thought him a 'snitch', then they probably would have others working on this too. She'd bet that technical freak from the basement had already bugged his place, so better be even more careful. *Oh shit,* she thought, *this is not what I signed on for years ago.* Now there seemed to be a special job every month, jobs that left a sour taste in her mouth and a pain in her gut.

Logan McAllistar was having his favourite drink at the bar, Jim Beam and coke. He had done his rounds, briefed the incoming evening security. Everyone was in position and ready as the punters came in. He had organised the cash pickups for the evening. The 'official' cash was collected by the security company three times a night and the other 'black' cash he had to count and was taken away by two heavies. He never knew where it went.

It was going to be a long night. He hated the drug side of the business but put up with it, wrestling with his conscience often. The official 'pushers' were in position and again tonight he had to brief them on how to approach, how to be careful, how to drop the stuff on the floor for the punters to pick up. The 'lookers' needed again to be stressed about how quickly they needed to alert security if a punter was causing nuisance or overdosing, so the body can be removed without disruption or concern.

The toilets had to be checked as some clever customers last night had turned on the cold water. How and what with, he didn't know. Probably a plumber who took his tools out with him. He smiled at the thought and mumbled under his breath.

"Talking to yourself is a sign of madness."

Karlien was leaning over his shoulder and had a sweet smile on her face. She smelled of Chanel number 5.

"Hi," he said, "you're eavesdropping now on my private conversation with myself?" He laughed.

She smiled again sweetly. "Thought we'd say hello."

He really was great looking and with a very attractive physique, she thought, she was picky even with her customers. No fat old guys jumping on you when you were at the top of your game.

She was wearing her Dusty Springfield wig and her friend, a Sandy Shaw wig. These were also their stage and working names.

"You guys could be taken for sisters," Logan was looking at them standing together. Apart from the different wigs, they looked like they could be related.

"Does that mean I am going to get an answer?"

"To what?" Karlien pretended she didn't know.

"To my many invitations to dinner."

"Oh, look it's nothing personal. Doing what I do, I prefer to not mix business with pleasure." He looked down at the floor a little embarrassed.

Sandy Shaw said, "I'll go! I'll go!" jumping up and down and making fun of it.

*Like a baby sister,* he thought.

"It's just that I can't pretend I am not what I am with guys that know. Also, most just want one thing and they think I am easy, you know."

"I understand," He got up and kissed her on the cheek and started walking away.

"You wouldn't go out with him, would you?" Sandy said.

"Not normally but I have to. Direction from the bosses and don't ask."

"Logan, I could make one exception for you. I mean if we never talk work and you treat me like a lady should be treated." He turned around.

"I promise, my Lady Karlien," His spirits had visibly lifted and he looked her in the eyes and felt an electric buzz between them. He was sure she did too.

*Nice,* Tazewell thought watching from the mezzanine, *a quick worker*

# Chapter Thirteen
## Gordon Wright-Pemberton

She was in the foyer of the Trafalgar Gentlemen's club, reading the signs on the wall.

"Goes back a long time," she talked out loud to no one in particular.

The concierge answered from his enormous oak antique ship's captain's desk. "Almost four hundred years, ma'am," he said with a sniff adding, "Longer than the United States has been around." Still smarting about the loss of the colonies she guessed.

The phone rang on his desk, another antique, probably developed by Marconi, she laughed to herself.

"Miss Liberty, Mr Wright-Pemberton will host you in the victory drawing-room."

"The what?"

"Up those stairs, third on the right," he pointed.

"I didn't think these places allowed women in?"

"Hmmm…we had to a year or so ago just as guests though," he sounded regretful.

She made her way through the massive carved wooden double doors that creaked.

Five other men were reading papers, sitting separately in easy chairs enjoying wine, port or Cognac. It was decorated like something out of the 1800s. The pictures were of old sailing ships and battle scenes from centuries ago and looked like they were also painted hundreds of years ago. One of the paintings was an Admiral with a missing eye and leg holding a telescope. *Odd painting,* she thought.

Some of the men eyeballed her for a second, grunted or snorted, rattled their papers and carried on reading.

Her meeting was sitting in a large leather armchair with one leg on a footstool. He had long legs covered by brown corduroy trousers and topped with patent leather brown shoes. He wore a matching jacket with leather patches on the elbows, a yellow satin cravat. He looked about seventy years old but could have been older. He was balding and had a long nose that gave the impression that he was a snooty upper-class type.

Liberty immediately took a dislike to him on appearance alone.

He turned his too-close-together eyes on her, dropping his copy of *'The Times'* into his lap.

It was like a dinosaur had spotted her. His face was impossible to read though and she stuck her hand out towards him. She didn't know what to call him Mr Wright-Pemberton sounded odd in her head.

"Sorry, I can't get up," pointing to his leg on the stool, "old war injury." He took her hand and shook it firmly.

"Miss or Mrs Bell?"

"Miss, but please, call me Liberty."

"Okay, I get it, Liberty Bell. Your father must have had a good sense of humour," He snorted.

Yes, she was definitely liking him less by the second. She gave him a half-smile that said I have heard that one a million times before.

"My mother actually thought it was a good name for a future politician or a James Bond girl," She lied.

"You were probably wondering what to call me with a double-barrelled name. Mother wanted in on the act and I have had to live with this name all my life. So, we have something in common. Call me Gordon and please sit down," he pointed to a rather stiff upright dining chair behind her.

"Can I order you anything? Water, wine or is it bourbon, you American's drink?"

"How nice of you, thank you. Well, not water," pulling a face, "definitely not, wine or bourbon. Do they serve beer here? I mean not the warm stuff."

"Lager, yes, I think they do." She could see a slight smile on his face. With a wave of his hand and a quiet word with the steward and the cold lager in a nice if not dainty beer glass appeared in a minute.

Once she had her drink, Gordon turned quickly to business.

"I want to make it clear that I have expressed to Gavin that I think putting you into this, let's say situation, is definitely the wrong thing to do."

"I have…"

"Please, let me finish. I know you have experience with crime reporting in New York and God knows that city leads the world in crime. Teach us a thing or two, I bet you can. But this makes you a fish out of water working in a country you do not know, a person who stands out and is easily noticed, no personal contacts you can trust. This is all playing a dangerous game. I told Gavin and went to the trouble of ringing Sir Richard to stress I totally disapprove."

Liberty stayed quiet, she had heard this lecture from Gavin and thought that at least he says it as it is. She looked at him with her best 'I understand, but will you help this girl in trouble' look and folded and unfolded her legs twice. The thighs were not working, no effect at all. He definitely didn't even notice.

"Oh, well, they are after selling more papers and seem to think that you will come at this as an outsider with a better chance of getting a result."

Liberty smiled sweetly. "So, will you help me, guide me?" She used her innocent little girl voice. She knew he was an ex-policeman and had been writing about crime for the papers as a freelance for thirty years.

"Yes, I will. But only if you agree to my conditions?"

"Which are?"

"Gavin has offered, generously I might add, a consultancy fee. However, I want the following: You will report to me every step of the way. I want to know where you are and what you are doing, what has turned up every minute of the day. I want to share the byline and have right of editorial on your work. If there is a book in this at the end, then we share the rights. Right?"

"That's a big ask."

"Mmmm, yes, well, let me tell you what I offer."

Gordon went on to describe his police career particularly when he was with the Met police 'collator'. A role that cross-checked and referenced crime and intelligence to share with other divisions and police forces. A role that helped him develop contacts countrywide and inside information on the criminal elements. Prior to the new computer age, it was all manually done in the sixties with card files and keen awareness. In short, he was vastly experienced and connected to both the police and the deep dark underworld. He offered her not only his guidance and advice but inside contacts that took a lifetime to create.

Not just the police he stressed but contacts on the other side of the fence, he had informants everywhere. He would know what information the police and maybe the Harkers both had with much larger resources were getting and doing in real-time.

The phone rang and rang. It was downstairs in the hallway by the front door. A man in pyjamas jumped up as quiet as he could. He didn't want to wake the 'bear' in the middle of the night or he will never hear the end of it. Stumbling down two flights of stairs, he managed to get to the phone before it rang off but not before the 'bear' shouted, "Who is that at this time of the night?" shouting and grumpy.

"No problem dear, I have it, go back to sleep."

"Huh." was all he heard.

"We need to talk." the voice said on the other end of the telephone. A smooth voice with a hint of a Scottish accent, quiet but commanding.

"Talk? Talk? At this time of the night or should I say morning?" he replied gruffly.

"Sorry, but I am out of the country and this is the only time I could call."

"So, what's so urgent?"

"It seems our friends are playing with the Russkies now. I hear from my source that a wheel has come off their car."

"A wheel?"

"They have or had something the Russkies want badly, however, it seems they have misplaced some club videos featuring certain people and acts, secretly recorded and a whole bundle of drugs."

"Misplaced?"

"Who is it at this time of night!" the bear shouted down the stairs.

"Just a business colleague who is overseas and got the time wrong dear."

"Come to bed," the bear commanded.

"Soon, dear." sweating and holding his temper.

"I can only guess that our friends have been very naughty and were diversifying their business interests into a form of blackmail."

"Oh my God!"

"We need to find the videos and get to it first before the Russians, the police or worst still the media."

"You can handle the media and I can sort the police. Let's hope we don't have to."

"Use everything at your disposal, but get this done."

"Wait. Misplaced? Are there any clues, I mean ideas where it has all gone to?"

"Our friends had a security chief for the London club. They were old friends who fell out. He did time for cocaine in his flat and just got out early for good behaviour. He had just enough cocaine to be above personal use. They are after him but want him alive. So, we can only suppose he has all the goods they want badly."

"His name?"

"Logan McAllistar."

# Chapter Fourteen
## The Abbey

It was an old run-down abbey in the countryside, two hours from London. It was being refurbished to be the new 'hellfire club' even better than the original one at High Wycombe caves in the 1800s. It was located outside London in Kent. Roman and Leon were unimpressed at the drive and this old run-down cold place. English countryside viewing was not what they came here for.

They sat in a cold large room, which was probably where the monks or nuns prayed centuries ago. Roman was thinking maybe this is a trap, maybe they were going to wipe out their problem or try. No, that would be stupid. He scratched his back and felt his faithful Makarov pistol tucked away just in case.

"Apologies for the long ride. We think we are being listened to and this is the only place where they cannot get near us for miles."

"Listened to by who?" Leon grumbled.

"A rogue copper, competitors, all comes with the territory. I have the money here for the goods from last month. Tazewell?"

Tazewell stood up cleaned his glasses with his handkerchief and then picked up a case behind him. He handed it to Roman, who opened it, shook it about and looked in at the cash disappointed.

"What is copper?" Leon asked and was told it was the 'old bill' by Jimmy.

"What is an old bill?" he was genuinely confused.

"Oh, for God's sake," the impatient Nick blurted out. "The police. It's the police."

"There's a lot short," he stated without emotion, but somehow the Harkers felt threatened.

"Look…." Nick started aggressively and was interrupted by Tazewell.

"If I may Nick and Jimmy?" They nodded. "We have had a cash flow problem this last twelve months."

"Not our problem. Why do you make your problem now to be our problem?" Leon and Roman said almost at the same time shaking their heads and looking down at the ground. You could cut the tension with a knife.

*Good job we have our guys outside and we outnumber them for now anyway,* Jimmy was thinking.

"You will get the balance of your money within a month with interest. We are keen to develop our relationship and build a long term very big business with you," Nick sought to pacify them.

"This is what you say, how do you say, bullshit, we lend you the goods to make more money and do not ask, how you say a penny and now you say when we get here old mother Hubbard's cupboard is bare?" Leon learned his English with nursery rhythms. "How we know you can find the money in one month?"

"Gentlemen," Jimmy started to shut Nick and Tazewell up as this was not going as planned and was not going to end well unless he could offer more, "It's time we gave Leon and Roman the full story."

"Yes, please do, no more of your nursery tales," Leon almost shouted. Nick bristled and Jimmy was giving him the eye to calm down. You do not mess with the Russian mafia if you don't want to wake up dead with your tongue in your throat and with all your family the same. Jimmy was a down to earth realist as much as Nick was a fighter without fear or thinking beyond his temper.

"We had an employee who we think stole amongst other things a large amount of money and the drugs. We thought he was a police informer but it turns out he was, as much as we know, working for himself."

"What type of business do you run here, a kinder garden? Who is this? Where is he? What are you doing about it?" Leon was still very aggressive.

"He was in prison and this week he got out. We are finding him and we will recover the goods and money."

"In Russia, he would be dead and we would have everything back within days." Leon spat a mouthful of gobby liquid on the floor.

"Why you no get to him in prison? In Russia, we would just walk in and take him."

"That's Russia it doesn't work like that here. We needed information out of him, however, we have only one type in our prison and we could not risk that they would kill the golden goose; whilst trying to get the information we needed. Plus, he's a pretty tough guy, not so easy to scare if you see what I mean," Jimmy explained.

Leon liked the golden goose reference, although he had no idea what a golden goose was.

*Good job, it's a solid wooden floor,* Jimmy thought, looking at the gobbing on the floor. He wouldn't like to think it was his house and his beautiful Persian carpets.

"The police found a stash of your uncut cocaine in his flat before we knew it was him."

"What he does with the rest?"

"We do not know at this time. Hopefully, he has stashed it not expecting to be caught. It is a long story, but he was a friend and had saved Nick's life when they were in the army and as far as we know, he hadn't done anything that had hurt us."

"You too soft, not sure if we can work with you Jack and Jill guys."

Leon and Roman stood up to leave and said, "One month or we will be very unhappy." Nick folded his arms and twisted his neck, getting into fight mode.

"Wait. We can offer you both a share in something that will help you back home with your Kremlin friends and is worth much more than what we owe."

"We are all noddy and big ears," Leon said and they sat down. Jimmy explained what this was and they just whistled together.

"Humpty Dumpty!" Leon tried to express the enormity of what he had just heard.

# Chapter Fifteen
The Fun and Games in Porridge
Nine Months Earlier

A prison is an awful place for an innocent man. It was worse if you have a form of claustrophobia. McAllistar disliked confined locked spaces. When he was a young boy, he had been locked in a small cupboard under the stairway by his drunken mother when the thunder and lightning were full-on, for his own good. This was her way of protecting him. However, he was not frightened of the noisy weather just an anxiety feeling of not being in control. What if she fell over in a drunken state and set fire to the house whilst he was locked inside? She smoked a lot and often fell asleep with a cigarette in her mouth burning the blankets.

Hearing metal doors being locked and bolted every night brought back the memory of the cupboard. The cell had only a small window in the cell near the roof that he could not break or squeeze through and sent his heart racing. A man not afraid of most things in life in his first weeks started to hyperventilate.

He had been allocated a two-man cell on a brand-new floor and he was on his own. The floor was being refurbished and he was in the end cell near the major gateway. The scrubs were overcrowded, however, he figured he had to get a break on something. The cell had a toilet and a small washbowl and one broken wooden chair. This was as luxurious as it gets.

When he returned to the cell a week later, a young man was standing there with a pillow and a blanket in his arms. He looked very nervous.

"I am your new cellmate." He looked up and then down to the floor.

"I see, lad, why are you just standing there?"

"I understand that which bunk I take is sensitive, so I am making to make sure I don't offend you." McAllistar thought it was obvious that his bed was made up on the bottom bunk. The guy, though, was very nervous.

"I have been sleeping on the bottom bunk, however, not sensitive with me, take your pick."

He chose the bottom bunk apparently; he didn't like heights. McAllistar told him that if the screws, came they were to say he slept on the bottom bunk as they got nasty if they didn't personally authorise everything they did, power-drunk like some sergeant majors he had known.

His new cellmate relaxed and after settling in, McAllistar ran through the routine from lights out to shower, breakfast, exercise yard, chores, lunch, personal time to dinner and back to lights out. He told him not to look or stare at anyone no matter how odd. They didn't need any excuse to make your life a misery.

His name was Johnny and he had been imprisoned for a serious assault on his partner. He liked to be called Lucky. McAllistar thought that the name was funny He was a thin and weak-looking man. How could he beat up his partner, who he assumed by his mannerisms was a guy? He didn't enjoy having a company as he enjoyed his own company and needed time to think. He didn't want small talk and there was no privacy when you went to the toilet; it was bad enough in the communal showers although the army had prepared him for this. Still, his cellmate could have been much worse in here with murderers, rapists, gangsters and paedophiles. Guys who just build muscle and have small brains that to him went back to the stone-age men. He kept himself to himself always.

It was the second night that Lucky was in cell 13. McAllistar had a small torch and was reading a historical novel about the Vikings. He loved history. He heard the main gate on the floor open and then the bolts to his door being opened quietly and then the door. Torch out, his body stiffened prepared for fight or flight. In this cell, it had to be fight. No honest warder would open the door at this time of night, no fire bells only the ones in his head. He moved as close as he could to the wall. It was dark with a little light from the moon coming in the small window.

"Areet, be quick lads, bottom bunk," the warder whispered.

Three shadows rushed in. One small, one fat and one tall. They rushed to the bottom bunk and grabbed Lucky and started choking, punching, kicking him and banging his head off the wall.

"Steady were nay supposed to kill the bastard or the guv will be angry!" A Scottish accent.

McAllistar thought that they would stop, but they just kept going. He had to break his rule and get involved as he knew it was him they were after. Diving feet first from the top bunk he aimed at two heads. Thud. He was on target they fell back against the wall. The small one faced him and drew a homemade blade pointing it at him. It was no good with a man trained and superfast like McAllistar, who knocked him aside with one swift movement with a hard punch to the side of his head. Then as he started to go down, he got in four quick combination punches to his ribs. He fell to the floor like a sack of potatoes and didn't move.

The other two were getting up and squaring up. No match for the regimental light heavyweight. A serious of punches to their chins and faces put them both on the floor. He proceeded to kick them all as fast as he could, knocking the fight out of them with his bare feet. Moans, screams, groans and painful cries. He had to send a message and fear was the only respect you get in this hell.

He tried to help Lucky get up. He was too beaten, crying and in serious pain. *Lucky, huh!*

"Howay, quickly he beat his cellmate up, he is an animal!" It was the same voice he had heard before, a Jordy accent.

As he was doing this, the intruders ran out the door. Alarms bells went off a minute later and a team of warders rushed in and restrained McAllistar.

After one night of solitary confinement, he was taken before the governor and chief warder.

"McAllistar, I am disappointed in you. What did you think you were doing? Started off well enough, so far, we took you for a model prisoner. Now, this!"

"It seems we need to call in the police and get you charged with grievous bodily harm (GBH). They say you are gay phobic and you beat prisoner Talbert to a pulp. This will add at least two years to your sentence. What have you got to say for yourself?" The guv was vastly experienced and seemed to worn down and battle weary. This was not an easy job.

McAllistar related the happenings of the evening while the bosses listened carefully.

"Where is your proof, lad?"

"My cellmate will tell you what happened."

"He is in such a serious condition; I doubt he will be talking soon."

*And if they get to him first, he will say what they want him to say.*

McAllistar was quiet for a while, then he said, "There were three of them, a small one with a Scottish accent and probably ginger hair, we called them poison dwarfs in the army. A fat one with what looked like an eagle tattoo on his face and a very tall one who was bald. I hurt them all they have to have marks on them or have gone to the doctor."

The guv and the chief warder looked at each other knowingly. A message seemed to pass between them.

"You could have heard that as there was a bit of a fight that night when three guys meeting, your description ended up in a hospital," the chief warder said.

"Well sir, the warder who let them in had a Jordy accent and as you know, I was immediately taken away to solitary confinement and have not spoken to anyone until now."

The look between the two was exchanged again. McAllistar was sure that they both understood what had gone on.

He was taken back and kept in solitary again for a week. This was for his own good they said and to protect him. He was counselled when he got out to take care, even so, they could have taken him out of the general population but they didn't.

The next time was in the exercise yard. The poison dwarf, a small ginger-haired Scottish guy approached him. He was severely bruised two weeks after McAllistar had administered the beating. The guy was visibly nervous as he approached but tried to not let it show. He stood several yards away.

"Hey Jimmy, the guv wants to see you."

"I don't see the guv?" The guy pointed with his thumb behind him to a bespectacled sixty-year-old sitting on a small wall. He could have been anyone's grandfather. Small in stature, bald, wrinkled and intellectual looking.

"The real guv in here. Now, Jimmy!"

McAllistar looked him in the eye. "Call me Jimmy again and I will send you back to the hospital for a long time." The guy dropped his eyes. One beating was enough and he was on his own.

"Mr McAllistar. Sit down here beside me please." It seemed a reasonable request and he sat on the wall to the side of him a yard away as if he might catch something.

"What do you want?"

"No need to take that tone Mr McAllistar or can I call you Logan?"

"McAllistar is okay," Sharply.

"Okay, I see you want me to get to the point. I have a client who says you have something or some things of his that he wants to be returned. It is a straight forward business deal, Mr McAllistar. Tell us where to find the goods, we leave you alone and let you have an easy time here and what do you know, Bobs, your uncle, Sally, your Aunt, you may even get parole very early," Leaning his head to the side and winking several times. He looked like a parrot to McAllistar.

"And if I don't?"

"It is a very dangerous place in here and we can cause you much pain. It will be a living hell! Now be reasonable, I like your sass. I wish I had known that you were the regimental boxing champion, things would have been different the other night."

"I will think about it." Buying time.

McAllistar got up and walked away. He turned his back and didn't notice the hand across the throat signal made by the guv to the poison dwarf, who in turn waved at a group of guys lifting weights. He thought he had bought some time. He turned the corner towards the latrines when he was hit from behind and dragged inside. It felt like he had been clubbed. He was getting drowsy and being kicked and hit with metal bars on the floor. He wanted so much to get to his feet, a boxer needs to be standing and his fists and elbows in action. He vaguely remembered a whistle blowing and people rushing about.

# Chapter Sixteen
## The Briefing

"So, do we have a deal?"

"Sure do," Liberty said thinking this can be changed when needed but she needed him now. The file Gavin gave her was thin and contained only a few names, a few guesses and no real contacts. Besides she had warmed to him a little. Not such a stuck-up guy as she had thought. Never judge a book by its cover her mother had always told her.

"While I do *The Times* crossword as I do every day," Gordon stopped as if waiting for Liberty to be impressed. Nothing registered with her, so he continued, "I want you to read through this file carefully and then ask questions," He handed her a manila folder, torn at the edges and full of paperwork and pictures. "Can I…"

"No, you cannot take away or copy anything. A few notes maybe, that's it. I guess you have a reporter's pad in that bag. Look at the pictures carefully and if you see any of these people, then run away as fast as you can. The pictures and the information come from police and classified intelligence files. It simply cannot be found by anyone or I will be personally compromised for life."

So, Liberty went through the file carefully. First, the pictures, black and white, most taken from a distance with a telescopic lens and a few police mug shots.

There were ten all marked with names and nicknames in black ink. She knew of the Harker brother's but not the rest of their gang. Looking at the pictures, Jimmy Harker was the only one she would sleep with, her way of counting, maybe Nick if desperate. Tazewell Javelin looked somehow familiar. She took out her pad and read carefully for almost an hour. The beer went warm and flat as she turned into the serious reporter she was and gave it her all attention.

"Ah, did it again," He was happy with his crossword completion. "How are you going, young lady?"

"Ready, done." staring at that silly cravat. Gordon seemed to notice and fiddled with it.

The file had given a broad outline of the Harker's empire. The general feeling was they had grown too quick and too soon and were backed by greater forces. She had absorbed the information like a sponge and every now and then jotting down notes and looking again at the pictures as if to connect them with her notes.

"It seems pretty clear to me," she looked at Gordon in the eye, "Thieves have fallen out. This McAllistar was a friend and employee, fell in love with one of their top girls and became a problem. He was probably pilfering drugs on the side, told the girl, who told them and they got rid of him to jail setting him up as a patsy. Yes?"

"Not quite. Let me show you the last pictures, Logan McAllistar and tell you his story."

He took out another envelope with some press cuttings and an army picture of McAllistar receiving a medal at the palace. The clippings were about saving the general officer, commanding all troops in Northern Ireland and the lives of several other soldiers. 'Our Hero Saves the Day', 'General thanks, Sergeant McAllistar who saved his life and others', 'Sergeant McAllistar receives medal of honour' and so on.

"He grew up in a poor area of Sheffield, which was our city of steel in the north midlands. Father was a miner, died of pneumoconiosis when he was seven. That's from exposure to fine dust down those dreadful mines. Mother went to alcohol and was no help to him at all. At fifteen, he got into trouble and the magistrate gave him a choice of borstal or the army. He joined the army as a boy soldier and graduated to the Royal Marines. That's the elite regiment like your Green Berets. He did two to six-month duties in Northern Ireland during the worst troubles. He was mentioned several times in dispatches for bravery."

"Borstal?" Liberty interrupted.

"Children's correctional centre," he said and then continued, "When he was a boy soldier, he joined the Duke of Edinburgh awards scheme and went through all the awards to the gold medal, which was his first trip to the palace. He worked helping disadvantaged kids throughout as part of the scheme. That was his thing. Helping kids with problems, alcohol, drugs, sexual abuse and all the other ills of society. He has a big passion to help kids. Sound like someone who will sell drugs?"

"People change, hide things. Maybe the girl, you know, love and all that can make a man crazy."

"Maybe. Anyway, he got his medal for saving a general, who wanted to tour parts of Belfast. He had a lead Land Rover and a follow-up Land Rover for protection. They both had Royal Marines as guards. The general wanted to use his Rover for comfort and speed with his close protection team inside. Bulletproof windows, reinforced undercarriage and so forth."

"Yeah, I read all about this in the file."

"Patience, young lady this is where it gets interesting. McAllistar had volunteered to return to Northern Ireland as one of the 'hush puppies'."

"A what?"

"It was a platoon that was not supposed to exist. Working in old clothes, long hair, civilian clothes, they patrolled Belfast and were known by the call sign 'hush puppies'. They were a mixture of a lot of regiments, guys who wanted a little more excitement, I guess. Their role was to be on the streets watching for known terrorists and unusual activities. The local regiment would be informed that they were in their area, however, it was a risky business as the RUC, the PIRA, the UFF or a trigger-happy soldier could mistake them for a threat."

"I know that IRA stands for Irish republican army but RUC, PIRA and UFF?"

"Oh, you are new here. The RUC stands for the local police, PIRA is the provisional Irish republican army the UFF the Ulster freedom fighters, both of these are the para military wings of catholic and the loyalists, protestant organisations."

She nodded her understanding and he continued.

"They were also later accused of being involved in executions; however, nothing was or could ever be proven. They lived in a compound within the Musgrove barracks, County Down. No one had access, not even the MPs. Anyway, the young adjuvant lieutenant was map reading for the general's tour and not being a soldier working on the streets, he took them into the Ballymurphy area and a cul-de-sac."

"The what?"

"Ballymurphy is a Catholic housing estate which was an IRA stronghold and a very violent area. Next thing you know the mob comes out with petrol bombs, stones, bottles and firing starts from the windows of some of the houses. Leaving behind a Land Rover on fire and wounded marines inside. The second Land Rover was trying to turn around and the marines jumped out to return fire but were pinned down around their vehicle. The mob was growing by the second. Back up would take time. Meanwhile, the soldiers in the first land rover were still in grave danger.

"Closest support was a hush puppy's old Toyota Corona with McAllistar driving. He went into the Murphy against his partner's wishes to not to compromise them. Taking a risk, he would be seen as an IRA threat. His screeching tyres and handbrake turn distracted the crowd. Giving the general's close support team time to spin around and get out of there like a bat out of hell. McAllistar jumped out, his partner drove away and he single-handedly pulled one marine and a detective in plain clothes from the burning Land Rover into cover in the gutter, under fire himself now.

"He then stood facing the crowd, disregarding the thumping of the Thompson machine gun bullets flying around him and faced the crowd. He drove them back with several bursts of his machine gun he had carried under his coat on the floor of the Toyota. This bought time for one para to arrive on the scene and then swamped the area. The IRA was dead scared of the paras and the fire halted, the crowd hesitated and McAllistar and the marines from the second vehicle dragged the wounded into the Land Rover. McAllistar reversed the Land Rover with both side doors open through the mob, knocking those over who stood in the way."

"So, he's a real-life Audie Murphy type hero. So, what does this have to do with anything today?"

"You are an impatient young lady. One of the wounded burning marines was Nick Harker. They became good friends after that. Both good sportsmen, football, boxing, rugby, both had an eye for the ladies. Harker left the army to join his brother in business. When McAllistar was demobbed three years ago, he was offered the job as a chief security officer at the 'Blue Haven' club by Nick."

"The other?"

"The contact I am going to give you. He was a Met detective on assignment to assist the RUC CID getting his first tour and taste of Belfast."

"Okay, so you are suggesting that something happened to their relationship and knowing the why is what we have to find out. It could still be as simple as the girl, both loved her, jealousy, the world's oldest well, almost oldest emotional disease."

"Of course, we could be overthinking however if it is just mobsters, drugs and sex, why are MI5 is interested in McAllistar and the Harkers? I have it on good authority that they attended a senior police meeting on the subject and are informed of every development. The police see an opportunity to bring down the Harkers. The girl, Karlien, has totally disappeared. McAllistar suspects they killed her, he wants revenge one way or the other. Harker brothers want McAllistar alive. Russians have been seen with the Harkers. No, something smells in the city of London. Oh, I forgot to mention that the 'hush puppies' were rumoured to have been created by MI5."

"So, where do you suggest I start? I don't think the Harkers will want to speak to me," She smiled knowingly.

"My advice is sincerely to keep a very low profile. You need to find McAllistar before anyone else does and see if you can get him to open up."

"Not sure this type of guy will talk to the press, even if I could find him."

"Ah, maybe but stranger things happen. If he is on his own, facing a lot of enemies, he will need help, friends, money, legal protection, we can offer all that for an exclusive when this thing is over."

"So, where do I start?"

He handed over a corner piece of paper with a name and telephone number on it.

"John Eager, Detective Inspector"

"Now this needs to be handled very carefully. Discreetly." He wondered for a moment if she knew what the word meant.

"Yes, that's my middle name. Liberty Discreet Bell."

"This is no joke, young lady. He has been one of my best contacts for over twenty years. Let's say we exchange information when it suits us both. He is a good copper and I am told the closest to McAllistar during his drug troubles. Call him and tell him GWP said you should meet. That you work with me. Arrange a meeting somewhere…"

"Discreetly?"

"You're getting it now." He smiled. He looked so much better when he smiled.

"Can I ask how did you get that damaged leg, I mean which war?"

"War against the crime of course. People at all levels do not like the media exposing them." He took off his cravat and a thick scar ran from one side of his throat to the other. "Be warned, Liberty. Our cops and crims are only just starting to carry guns, but the streets are still dangerous."

"Why will he help me? Surely this is a sensitive police investigation. Why would he risk giving information to a young yank?"

"Because he wants to help McAllistar. He was the detective he saved."

# Chapter Seventeen
## Sammy, the Squirrel and Dirk Ryder

The room was full of smoke and the smell of beer. It was the cellar at the bottom of the club building. Normally used for 'Come to Jesus' conversations with whoever the Harkers thought had crossed them. A modern-day torture chamber soundproofed with a hidden doorway. All the Harkers motley crew were present. Ten guys ranging from small and wiry to big and muscle-bound heavies. Two women were present, as tough as the guys, rough-looking ex-street girls who were still in good shape.

"You guys have turned nothing up in the last three days. He cannot have just disappeared? This is serious stuff and we are all going to be impacted, so you need to double your efforts and stop wasting damn time. We need to find McAllistar fast and I mean fast. My information is that the police have drawn a blank in Yorkshire. That means he is probably here in London but where?" Nick Harker almost shouted this time. It was obvious he was angry and frustrated.

"Why don't we wait for him to come to us boss?" the big muscle man, Bruce, asked but immediately wished he hadn't.

"What, we do not have time to wait around and why would he come here? Eh?"

"Sorry, boss. I heard he was coming after you."

"Shut the fuck up! If he comes here it's his death warrant. Now, let me divide some duties and I want this to be a day and night job for you guys. Forget whatever you are doing. I want you to report anything to me and if you have nothing then still call twice a day at least."

He divided up the duties. Ladies to work all the girls in the club to see what they might have been told by Karlien or McAllistar himself. Everything get it? No detail is, too small. Places and people they may have talked about, anything. Work the girls hard and work them over if they thought they were holding back. The cellar would be the interview room, very intimidating.

Roland, 'The rat', the new video technical guy, who was called affectionately, he thought, was to review all the security video footage he could find of McAllistar. Who did he talk to? Staff and punters identify them, so they can be talked to. Anyone he was very friendly with, anyone.

The rest were divided to get the message on the streets and armed with photographs. Two hundred pounds to anyone for any information worth anything. One thousand pounds if it helps find McAllistar. All informants whether they be police, druggies, other outfits to be contacted.

"London has more surveillance cameras than any city in the world, thanks to the IRA. He left a trace somewhere. Barry, you and Phil start at Brixton and work guards who saw him out or get our guys inside to find out what direction he headed, how he left, follow the trail. Find out from our contacts who have looked at the videos around the area, surely the pigs have, they are not that dumb."

A little laugher started and it was quickly shut off by Nick giving them all a look that could kill. This was not funny.

They were sent out to check out taxis, train and bus stations for the day of release. They could ask nicely for access to the videos or be heavy-handed if required.

Sammy, the squirrel, a small wiry guy wearing a long dirty raincoat and yellow fingers from smoking cigarette after cigarette, was tasked to go to Yorkshire and work the locals from McAllistar's known boyhood home, work police contacts and coordinated with the 'Blue Haven' teams in Manchester and Leeds.

He would take Bruce, the bodybuilder, with him but keep him out of sight unless needed. He was too obviously a heavy, who would scare average people. Sammy was a whiz at finding people, who were either hiding from the Harkers or had simply run away owing cash. He had a second sense and good intuition, street smart and though he looked like a scruff bag, he was extremely intelligent. If McAllistar had gone to the north then he would find him.

They all left in a hurry.

Just Tazewell, Nick and Jimmy were left.

"We need more options for this search," Jimmy was worried.

"I have called all our contacts and made them aware that we need everything the coppers get or think as it happens," Tazewell added.

"Well, damn well, call them again. They owe us," Nick spurted out.

The stress was beginning to show and his patience was at the end. Tazewell just rolled with the punches, water off a duck's back. You never knew what he was thinking. Jimmy knew Tazewell had his own agenda and didn't trust him as far as he could throw him, which wouldn't be far. Tazewell had that gaze that seems to look either past people or right through them. His mind was ticking and you could almost hear him thinking.

"There is an avenue, Nick, you should explore," He waited on the response as if playing a cat and mouse game.

"Yeah, are you going to tell us or stand around all day?"

"Nick, no need for that tone," Jimmy got between them.

"Well, I hear that he has a friend who has and still is trying to help him. Probably as close as anyone."

"Who?" They both asked. Thinking he was going to say Karlien.

"Detective Inspector Eager. Your antagonist, Nick. He visited McAllistar so many times in goal and was also saved by him when he saved you, so he owes him."

"Okay, it is worth a shot. If he knows anything, I will get it out of him."

"Now Nick, we do not want the coppers all over us. They are watching us now. Looking for cracks. Wondering what we are doing and why. Come from the pal angle, saved your life, fell out over a girl who runs away from both of you and wants to make it up to him. Desperate to fix things before he does anything. Eager is a straight cop so the money will not be acceptable. Get it?"

Jimmy wanted Nick to really understand and not mess this up.

"If I feel he is holding back? We do not have time to be friendly."

"Then we get a professional, not known here to do it."

"Who?"

"Dirk Ryder."

# Chapter Eighteen
## Just Over Twelve Months Ago

They lay together in McAllistar's single bed. They petted, kissed and talked. They always talked and talked. They had a lot in common and a definite physical attraction. McAllistar's flat was very basically furnished, yet she knew he could afford better. It was more of a barracks room than a home. Hence, the single bed they squashed into. He liked it this way. No family pictures on the walls, not even the medals she had been told he had won. An exercise mat and some dumbbells, chest expander, red boxing gloves hanging on the wall and a martial arts nunchaku weapon. One action Bruce Lee poster on the wall in the small living room and a blown-up picture of Henry Cooper knocking down Cassius Clay in their London fight with 'Our Henry's Hammer' written underneath.

He was super fit with a six-pack and a very attractive guy. What she liked most about him was his soft side, a decent guy, so soft-spoken that she often had to lean closer to get what he was saying. Or was that to get her closer? He was a professional security guy in the club and the seediness of that business didn't seem to have touched him.

Karlien was somewhat jaded by her work and she didn't want to be used for sex. She wanted the relationship to develop and see where it goes. Who was she kidding, she thought. This would never go anywhere. He knew all about her, his relationship with the Harkers was diminishing and if she wasn't careful, she would lose her dream of a white wedding to Mr Right who would never know anything about her, maybe a mansion in the Cape near the beach, two kids, a horse, dogs and cats. She had a dream but even that seemed silly today unless she could get one big deal.

They had been seeing each other for several months. Simple lunch meeting or the movies. He liked action movies, she wanted family or girlie movies. She had seen enough James Bond and Rambo films to last her a lifetime. Sometimes she would take him to the ballet, which he had never experienced and a West End show. He had a child-like fascination for live talent as he had little exposure to the finer things in life.

The Harkers and that guy Tazewell were leaning on her for information. She could not find anything that he said or in his flat that suggested he was a police informer. She took every opportunity to search his clothes, answer his phone for mystery callers. She even copied his personal phone book one day when he was called away and she stayed in his flat for the afternoon. If he caught her, she could play the jealousy card. She handed the copies over to Tazewell to check out. At least it was an offering of sorts, showing she was trying.

Today, he was asking questions. "Did you know what happens in the basement room that not even security can enter?" It had a back entrance which had no surveillance cameras. The limos drove into a black canvas tent so that no one entering could be seen. There were parties going on in there. Laughter, giggling and sometimes high-pitched screams. VIPs went in there that only Jimmy and Nick handled she told him.

"Well why, have you, as the top girl, never gone in there or have you?"

Lots of questions very dangerous she thought. He was watching her carefully, scrutinising her every mannerism as he asked. "No, it's just the same stuff that VIPs do not want to be seen doing and they pay big time for the privacy."

That seemed to satisfy him until he asked what type of VIPs. "You know rock stars, DJs, actors, politicians, visiting dignitaries, hell maybe, even the Archbishop of Canterbury. I'm joking," she added.

What about that snake, Billy Garrick, I have to fight to review security videos? He's locked in, why? No one allowed into his video suite. What could he be doing?

*I have to stop this,* she thought, *he is starting to get in shark-infested waters.*

So, for the first time, she made love to him. She could act like no other and he had never had this type of tenderness in his life. She actually saw tears in the corner of his eyes as they lay together afterwards.

In all her years in the business, she had never felt as dirty as she did when the father, son and unholy ghost sat her down and asked for feedback.

They waited and she shivered, trying to make her mind up what to say and not making it sound too bad.

"I don't think he is a police informer. He is, though, starting to ask questions about the inner workings of the club he has no access to."

"How so?" Jimmy asked.

"Well, he is just curious about the back-VIP room and what Garrick is doing. Why is it restricted area and that kind of thing?"

"I guess that is what a security guy will do. I will have a word with him and fill him in. Take away his curiosity and focus him on his job," Jimmy talked as though relieved that McAllistar was okay. This satisfied Karlien as maybe she had not damaged him. She liked him too much.

"Good girl, Karlien. You can forget McAllistar, drop him gently and as promised, this Saturday, I have the biggest call of your life. Worth a fortune for one night at the hellfire club. You go do your job, make John very happy and there are five grand in it for you. Interested?" Tazewell was very proud of his offer. He made her guts turn and she physically shivered, which he interpreted as excitement at the money. He was, though, a necessary evil.

When she left, they looked at each other. Yes, she had done the job and been honest with them.

"Billy's bugs proved she was okay," Nick said, a little relieved as he still had the hots for her.

# Chapter Nineteen
## An Unhappy Customer

"I want to see the manager now!" demanded a middle-aged man dressed in smart business clothes. Balding mid-fifties, red in the face. The big bouncer radioed into McAllistar. It was late afternoon and the staff were prepping for the evenings opening.

"Boss, got a problem at the front door. A man wants to see the manager, what you wanna do?"

"Bring him to the mezzanine office, I'll be there."

The owners didn't come in until later. Logan sat him down and gave him mineral water.

"Who are you? I want the manager," the man insisted.

"I am the chief security officer, sir. What is the problem? Let me see if I can help you."

The man settled down a bit.

"I've seen your face somewhere before, you look familiar."

"What can I help you with, sir?"

"This," He took out a VHS video from a brown manila envelope. "This," he said again and held it up. Logan's look of 'what is it' made the guy continue.

"One of your staff members or all of you for all I know is blackmailing me or trying."

"What's on the tape?"

"Oh, just me having a lap dance, nothing more but very explicit. It's what hundreds of guys who come in here do, have too many of your expensive drinks and do something like this for fun. No harm, right?"

"Can you describe the blackmailer?"

"Yes, a skinny little guy with a very long neck and Adam's apple that sticks out like a boiled egg."

*Billy Garrick, the little video worm.*

"Why didn't you go to the police?"

"Well, I didn't pay him anything as my wife left me a week after the meeting, all over so to speak, so the video can't do any more damage to me. Left me for an insurance salesman out of the blue. Bastard!"

"How did he meet you this guy?"

"I gave the girl my business card, I was a little tipsy, you know, you start thinking with, well, err. He rang me and we met at the 'Horse and Hounds'.

"He handed me a copy of a video and a demand for one thousand pounds. I said I would think about it as I was short of cash. He said he would mail it to my wife if I didn't come up with it in seven days. That I would never hear from him again after that."

"It's still an offence the police would deal with."

"Yes, and have my name all over the papers. People from church, friends and neighbours nodding their heads saying that's why she left him. When in fact she was having an affair for several years it turns out."

He suddenly felt a bit sorry for the guy.

"We take this very serious, sir. This kind of antics could cost the club a lot of business, could, in fact, damage us very badly. Loss of trust and privacy and so no, one would want to come here. This is a rogue staff member probably acting with the girl. I will sort him out you can be assured of that. Thanks for bringing this to my attention."

"Well, all right, I just want him to go away and not try any other angle with me."

He handed over the video copy.

"Now, I remember you, you're that army hero, aren't you? Let me shake your hand."

He shook Logan's hand and left satisfied that he had made his point with a man he now trusted.

Logan rolled the video over and over from one hand to the next. Was the rat Billy acting alone or is this a Harker's scam? Surely not, why would they risk so much for so little? Should he report it or find out what that rat was really doing in his security hutch? He was pretty certain that the guy would go away satisfied, so what to do next?

# Chapter Twenty
## A Bad Day

It had been a long day. John Eager struggled up to his drive to his little two bedrooms semi-detached house with his groceries and booze. He needed a drink badly tonight. It was 7 pm and what a day he had had. Dropping his bags and being careful not to break the wine bottles, he searched for his house keys. Always in the other pocket. Just as he put the key in the lock, a man stepped out from the side of the garage.

"Evening, constable," Nick Harker liked to surprise people and he saw the fight or flight look in Eager's eyes.

John did prepare for a fight by holding the car key in between his fingers, so the metal key end jutted out. A stab in the eye or face could slow someone down but probably not much use against Harker.

"What the fuck Harker are you doing here?"

"Just a friendly visit, John, can we go in to talk?"

"No, whatever you want, let's do it here. I do not want scum like you in my house."

"Ooh, touchy. Well, this scum needs to find McAllistar and sort things out with him as soon as possible."

"Like sort him out or sort things out?"

Harker smiled and self-indulgent smile like only he knew the joke.

"Would I come to you if I meant him any harm? No, listen to me, he saved my life I owe him. He got it all wrong and I want to put things straight with him."

"Oh aye, like what has he got wrong?"

"Well, we didn't plant the drugs on him, they are not ours. His girlfriend is okay. You know he actually thinks we killed her!"

"He told me you sent a message to him in prison saying you were going to hurt her."

"I was angry with him, you know, I blow a lot of smoke. She is okay, I can give him her address, but she doesn't want to see him. See, he is hopelessly in love with a woman that just played him along. That's what the girls in this industry do. Milk the guys for all it's worth."

"What's this to do with me?"

"You are or were close to him from the Belfast times and you have had many conversations with him over a beer or when he was in prison. How many visits did you make?"

"Look, it did me no good. He thinks I betrayed him. No way will he contact me. I don't know where he is."

"He might have given you a clue detective, we both know you are bright and under-promoted. Why do you stay as Mr Plod, you could have done better for yourself by now, you know? I mean look at this place. Talk about basic living accommodation. Look at your old Ford, do they still even make that model? It does not look like you are appreciated much."

"Look, I have had a bad day, a very bad day and I would love to stand here and be insulted all night, but I am hungry and tired."

"Thirsty too by the look of it." Harker nodded towards the two bottles of wine sitting in the bags on the ground.

"I have a friend coming." Eager announced defensively and immediately felt sorry for his remark. He surprised himself for being so sensitive to people assuming he was a lush that he bothered to comment back.

"John, I can make it worth your while."

"Are you trying to bribe me? You know me better Nick."

"Nick? That's more like it. I will help him believe me and then we are even."

"Look, half the country's police force is looking for him. I have been taken off the case today, apparently too close to him and by the way old ties with you. Once they knew I didn't have a clue where he was and that he would not contact me, I was dumped. Put that jerk Samuels on the case."

"A big dick, I agree," Harker stated unconvincingly. "John put your thinking hat on and give me a call if anything pops up." Harker handed him his business card.

"Why would I do that?"

"Well, because McAllistar took something that belonged to some very bad Russians and if they find him…or if they think you know where to find him, well, it may not turn out so good for any of us."

"That sounds like a threat?"

"No John, it is a friendly warning from a guy who appreciates you, who believes we can be friends again. We, despite your view of me, go back a long way and I just want the best for everyone."

*Bullshit, it's a threat play along.*

"Okay, if I think of anything…if you are sure this can be resolved…I will let you know. My best guess is he is in London and waiting on a chance to even scores with you."

Nick visibly winced at that but quickly regained his composure.

"Let me know anything as quick as you can, they know where you live and that family of yours and I really don't want to see that anyone gets hurt in the process."

John jumped forward. Nick held up both hands, arms and elbows in front of his face.

"Hold on, tiger, you do not want to do this."

*I do, I do, even if I lose badly.*

"Just go." John picked up his bags and went into the house. Locking the door immediately behind him. With his back leaning on the door he just said, "Shit," aloud.

He went straight to the kitchen dropped his bags, coat and groceries and found a cold beer in the fridge. Opening the can, he took a long drink. Keeping his shoes on in case Nick came back. *Better than bare feet in a fight,* he thought. As soon as he thought this, his mind said back to him, *or to run with.* He laughed at himself, a long laugh that after a while began to sound like a plea for help from a madman.

Sitting down in the living room he reflected on the day. Called into Charlie Allcock's, the chief supers plush office at HQ. When he went in, there was DI Teddy Samuels sitting to the right of the chief's desk. The chief pointed to the chair on the left for John to sit down.

"You guys know each other?"

*'Oh yes, I know slippery Samuels all right. Smooth light brown Indian looking sportsman, plays tennis and golf with the bosses. Teflon Teddy. Nothing sticks to him even his sloppy police work. How many times have I cleaned up after him, cases written off that I revived and got a result?'*

"DI Eager," Samuels nodded.

"DI Samuels," Eager said coldly.

"No, DCI now. You might want to congratulate him," the chief stated.

They looked at each other. Eager was taken back visibly shaken. He said nothing. *Another fast track for a minority or was there more to this?*

"Down to business then," So, the chief had laid it out to him. Samuel's had got the promotion he deserved and was now in charge of the 'Harker/McAllistar case'. He explained that the ACC had insisted that Samuels get the DCI position and told him also to side-line Eager after he was debriefed. Eager then had to talk to the chief alone. Samuels asked to meet in the interview room for the handover.

Eager had let the chief have it with both barrels. They both went back a long time together, laying out the mess-ups Samuels had been involved in. The chief countered that Samuels had some high-profile arrests in the last twelve months. In the end, the chief had made it clear that the ACC had made all the decisions and they were final. Screaming 'Fuck the ACC' two offices down was not the best thing to do but hey, it cleared the steam inside him. Until the final blow.

"Look, John, there is a promotion in it for you. The West Midlands force needs a uniform chief inspector in Birmingham. Someone with your experience, it is becoming a very bad area. Worst crime stats, next to ours, in the country. The job's yours if you want it?"

"Up north away from my kids. No, sir."

"I am afraid you have a few choices. You are seen by the brass as weak and emotional. You stay here you work under Samuels. Oh yes, I saw the love between you and I bet he has you transferred out within a few months back to uniform."

They agreed he would think about it and take some of his leave which he had not taken for a long time. Then the handover interview didn't go well. He handed over the files and as calmly as possible briefed Samuels on McAllistar and the Harkers. He felt so bad inside, however, he thought he handled the situation very professionally.

*Weak and emotional indeed,* he thought.

Samuels had DS Denise Williams with him. Eager's DS until today. She kept looking at him in an aloof way with sternness in her eyes. They had become good friends and made a good team. Her looks said she needed to be Samuels reliable DS now and any residual sympathy for Eager would damn her career going forward.

*Everyone, in the end, acts in their own best interests,* he thought.

Samuels kept pushing and it turned into an interrogation. He obviously thought Eager was holding out on him. In the end, Eager had enough.

"That's all I know, the lot, amen. I am off now."

"On leave, be sure to let me know where you are in case, we need you."

*So, he knew before that the chief was sending him on leave,* he thought.
*Idiot me, I thought it was a spur of the moment idea.*

Twenty-five years and this is how they treated him. Shipped off to the bush or forced to retire.

"Tell me something," Eager could not help himself, "All the cases you solved in the last twelve months, DCI Slippery, how come none of them was from the other major gangs? Seems you were getting help cleaning up their competition."

DCI Samuels jumped up and got right into Eagers face then relaxed, laughed and walked out.

"No answer then?"

Eager shouted after him.

# Chapter Twenty-One
## Hanging Around

She rang the doorbell incessantly but no answer. She heard something moving inside and a strange muffled sound. Pushing the broken front door, which was ajar and it swung open wide.

"Hello, anyone there?" More muffled sounds. Then she stepped into the hallway and saw him swinging from the bannister upside down with electric wire cord wrapped around his ankles. He was dressed only in boxer shorts and gagged by what looked like a big piece of leather. His face was red and he was bleeding from his torso and head. Her face was opposite to him as he struggled upside down to get free.

"I see you are busy. I'll come back some other time," She could not help herself. He struggled even more and made more dramatic noises.

She pulled the leather out of his mouth.

"For Christ's sake, cut the bloody wire, my feet are going to fall off." She looked around for something to use. "In the damn kitchen get the carving knife...top drawer."

Liberty moved quickly got the knife, ran up the stairs and hacked at the wire. Eager was now screaming and shouting. She thought to herself that maybe she should not have removed the gag; the screaming and abuse were distracting. The thump as he hit the ground made her laugh.

He was incredulous, "Funny?"

"Sorry, I laugh when I am nervous. What the fuck happened here?"

She untied his hands, which had also been tied behind his back with a wire cord. He started rubbing his wrists. She knelt down and cut the wire and rubbed his ankles as hard as she could. The wire had cut deep into his ankles, his bare feet were red as were his hands and face. He eventually lay on the ground, his worst injury seemed to be the bump on his head from the fall. She helped him up and he limped into the living room and lay sprawled on the couch.

*'Fuck, what would he have done if she had not come to the house?'*

He seemed to be coming out of his distress. She went into the kitchen. Eager had obviously just opened his first bottle of Chardonnay before he had been interrupted. The wine glass was half full. She searched the cupboards for whisky or something stronger. No luck. The cupboards and fridge only had a few basics mainly wine and beer. Food was not a priority for him, obviously.

He was tired and was content to wallow in his own pity on the couch. He sat in a daze. She found his clothes on the floor in the hallway and threw his trousers and shirt at him. They just landed on him and he didn't move.

*In shock and his own world,* she mused.

"Put them on I haven't had dinner yet," she laughed. Then she ran into the kitchen and poured two glasses of wine. Handing his over, he just looked up like a puppy dog and said, "Thanks." His hand was shaking so much that she took the glass off him and helped him sip the wine. It seemed the right thing to do. Then he grabbed it and drained the glass in seconds and held it out to her for more.

"Hold your horses, cowboy. I need you soberish."

"Don't worry about me. Who are you?"

"I'm your date smalls."

"Date?" he was stilled not comprehending what was going on.

"Liberty." She stuck out her hand. "I called you today, remember Gordon introduced us?"

"Yes, yes, I thought it was tomorrow night?"

"You said to be careful. So, here I am being careful. Does a lady get a second drink around here?" She took her raincoat off, revealing that short black dress with red trimmings, black stockings and low cleavage. She had come on a charm offensive.

"Beer or white wine?"

"No, red wine then?"

He shook his head. She went and poured him a chardonnay and took a can of beer from the fridge. Opening it like she had a few in her life and drank straight from the tin. *Not a lady then.* Eager thought.

"My God, you look tired."

"Thanks for the compliment. I am feeling better now. About the worst day of my life, but hell maybe it's getting better," He looked her up and down and laughed.

"Always better when I am around. So, smalls are you up to talking? I mean what has happened? Will you give me the full background on the case, as much as you can without compromising your work?" She sat down opposite him. The thighs were definitely working on this middle-aged guy.

"Whoa, a lot of questions. My head is still clogged with blood. It would also take all night."

"Suits me, got a spare bed?" She was teasing him, relaxing him.

"Smalls?"

"A New York term of endearment, believe me. Gordon told me so much about you that I feel I know you," She lied. She took a long gulp and drained the lager and quickly fetched another one.

*She'll drink me out of booze.*

"Okay, I think for several reasons we should go down the George and Dragon, they have a quiet snug room."

"Dragon? A bar?"

"Yes, a pub, just at the end of the street. Got good food there, well, pub food and we are about out of booze."

"Are you fit enough?" He wanted a few minutes to dress and try and sort out his wounds. He went into the bathroom. She simply followed and stood at the door drinking the beer. He turned to say something but was lost for words. Ten minutes later, he was dressed and bandaged. He looked very rough but ready. He wore slippers on his aching feet and a long black overcoat to cover him up as much as possible. He was very cold; a result of the shock.

As they left the house, he reflected that he was lucky to be found by a stranger. Lucky, she didn't follow convention and decided to come a day early.

The force now was the only family he had. The phone had not rung from lifelong friends and colleagues, surely the word was out by now. Surely some of the guys would have called around to sympathise or just called and left a message. Maybe they had made him 'persona non grata' but what had he done?

*In the end, everyone acts in their own best interests.* Eager reflected on his philosophy of life.

The George and Dragon was a very old pub. It had a comfortable feel. Ceilings were decorated with all types of tankards, cups and mugs. The walls were painted in a deep velvet and old cartoon pictures from the last century hung all around. The snug room was small and cosy. No one was there which was a pity as Eager would have liked some of the neighbours to see him with this beauty. Maybe they would even ring the ex-wife, maybe she might be jealous, serve her right.

"Aye, aye," shouted George, the landlord of the pub. "Sweeney's here. Hey, John, you look bad."

"Thanks, George. I have had better days for sure." George was an ex-policeman who had worked with Eager many years ago and played on the police 'A' football team with him. He was very large and tall with a bald head and bulging muscles that kept the trouble makers at bay.

"Nice to meet you, George, so who is the dragon?" Liberty asked with a giggle. She had taken off her raincoat and George was staring at her.

"The trouble and strife, of course," he replied with a wink and a quick look behind him to be sure she wasn't there.

*Good, he will talk about my guest for a long time.*

"Trouble and what?"

"Cockney rhyming slang for wife," Eager pointed out.

*Strange country.*

"Why didn't we stay in, I could have gone out for some food and drink?"

"I am now not sure, after tonight if my place is not bugged."

"Bugged?"

"After today, anything is possible."

'Who would bug you?'

"Not sure. Lots of people have an interest in where Logan is and they think I might know."

"Lots of people? Do you?"

"One question at a time. The Harkers, apparently Russians and MI5, and the police. A long story."

"I thought you were the police?"

"So did I until today. I have been replaced in the case. Too close to the person involved."

"Russians? MI5, I heard they attend meetings and maybe somehow involved."

"The guys that did me up tonight were definitely Russian by their accents. Called themselves Pinky and Perky."

"Pinky and what?"

"Oh, never mind, two kids' TV puppets."

"Strange, did they intend to kill you?"

"No, I think to soften me up. Leave me for a couple of hours and then come back when I am hurting so bad that I would talk. Good job you came along."

"So, they think you know where he is?"

"I do not know anything for certain. All I know is McAllistar has stirred up a hornet's nest for sure."

She went to the bar and brought back white and red wines, big glasses.

"This is all off the record, you understand that I am sure that Gordon made that clear?"

She nodded, keeping a serious puppy face begging trust.

"I can only tell you what I know and to be honest I know nothing that would compromise the case."

She was easy to talk to, which made her good at her job. Throws a line out and then lets them talk and talk, which Eager did. He was more thinking and talking out loud about his life, the force, his ex-family, the Russians who had visited him tonight asking for McAllistar, his boss, DCI Samuels (how could a useless git like him get promoted and takeover any decent case?), what did McAllistar have that was so important? Where was he? Eager realised that he had just let it all out after his ordeal. Much more than he would ever tell anyone never mind a reporter.

George had been leaning across the bar earwigging until his wife came back and assumed he was ogling the girl. She took over and he disappeared into the main bar. Still, the Dragon also pretended to clean glasses whilst trying to catch what was going on.

*Good, the Dragon will certainly gossip, a sad old middle-aged divorced policeman might seem more interesting.* This pleased Eager.

"Sorry, I've been waffling on."

"No problem smalls. So, you seem to know as much as the rest, so why so much interest in you?"

"Good question, want another drink?"

"Does Gladys Knight have the pips?"

"I'll take that as a yes. Doris two more, thanks luv." Doris nodded and indicated that she would bring them over. When she did, she looked Liberty up and down.

"Not often that John brings a young lady in here," Fishing.

"Oh, we are old friends and now lovers," Liberty wanted to see the reaction. Doris bit her lip that you could see her saying wanting to say, "Why he is old enough to be your Dad?" But she didn't and just turned away.

# Chapter Twenty-Two
## Bugged

The door burst open. Charlie Allcock looked up in astonishment. In came DS Williams like a little whirlwind.

"Do you know how to knock? There better be a good reason for this!"

"Sir, I need to know what is going on with DI Eager!"

"You burst in my office and demand…things…Sergeant, have you forgotten any kind of decorum and rank structure!"

"Have we forgotten about bloody well-supporting officers in distress?"

"What the hell are you talking about?" he shouted.

"I got a message to go to the dungeon to room 123. When I got there, I heard screaming and it was John Eager in serious pain. I went in and DCI Samuels was in there with some guys I have never seen before, listening in to what I can only assume was a bug. Eager was screaming and I asked if we had sent help. I was kicked out by Samuels, none of my business apparently, was made to wait in an interview room until he came and wanted to know what I had heard. Well, it is our business when a colleague is in trouble and we do damn all about it but listen in like some radio show. What is going on?"

Charlie just stared and drummed his fingers on the table and thought.

*What the hell was going on? I'm Samuels' boss and know nothing about this? Who could authorise a tap without my knowledge?*

He looked at her, "Sit down."

"I'd prefer to stand, sir with due respect."

"Okay, I am not sure what was going on, but I will bloody well find out. Is that enough for you? Oh, get a car over to Eager's place and have it checked out as fast as you can, also go yourself. Let me know directly if he is okay and what happened, if he is there, of course."

She went straight to Eager's house and met the local unit B policeman, who had arrived quick smart in his little Morris Minor.

"Lights are on, but nobody's home, Sarge. Knocked and knocked no answer. The front door had been damaged around the lock area, a boot mark looks like it was kicked in. The lock funny enough still works. Checked the back door, locked and kitchen lights are on."

"His car is in the drive. Force the door."

"What?"

"You heard me force it."

"DI's not going to be happy," he mumbled but before doing so, he checked under the doormat and then the plant pot by the door side.

"Bingo," he said in triumph, showing her the key.

*The Bobby on the beat uses common sense rather than brute force. Seems like common sense is not so common anymore.* The bobby smiled at his thought and made a bow to let her enter.

She went in. There was blood on the floor and loads of electric wire in the living room. Wine glasses on the table and an empty bottle. One beer can. She shouted his name, no answer. The upstairs bathroom had a blood-stained towel and some of his clothes ripped and covered in blood.

"Check the neighbours," she shouted to the constable. She then carefully walked around trying to work out what happened. The bannister had rope burn marks deep into the wood. It was coming loose at each end at the top of the stairway. She could see the wire and now the carving knife laying in the hallway.

*Has he been killed? Kidnapped? What the hell is going on?*

Denise Williams was a solid-looking woman with a very strong body. Looked like a female boxer or wrestler. Not an ounce of fat on her. She covered her body with a tweed two-piece suit, shoes could have been female work boots. Her hair was short and black and her eyes were a piercing blue contrasting with her dark brown skin. She was thinking and staring when she was interrupted.

"Neighbours next door heard a lot of screaming and shouting. They looked out and two big guys left and then a woman turned up. Sometime later, they left in her car. Young woman apparently."

"Did they have any idea where he might be?"

"Normally, he just goes to a local pub, otherwise no."

"Did they not think to report it?"

"No, Sarge. They say his ex comes around and there have been disturbances before."

"Two big guys his ex?"

Then she remembered the place was bugged. She took the Bobby outside and got him to put back the key. She walked him down the drive.

"Do not say anything about this situation."

"Are you sure? Looks like a torture chamber in there. He could be dead or something. I'll lose my job if I do not report in."

"Can you just say that I arrived and took over, entered the house and told you that everything was okay and dismissed you?"

"Eh, what did you say?" resisting the idea.

"Look, you know John Eager right, he's a regular good guy. This all could embarrass him, undermine him if you know what I mean?"

"You mean he might be into that kinky sex stuff and it went wrong? What about the big guys?"

She just lifted one eyebrow and rolled her eyes. He looked as if to say, 'I get it.'

"The pubs down the street that way," he pointed. No need really, she had had quite a few drinks there with John, celebrating when they had cracked a case and commiserating when they had lost in court.

# Chapter Twenty-Three
## Williams Meets Liberty

DS Williams burst into the snug bar and stopped abruptly. John was sitting with a pretty girl laughing and enjoying his wine.

'What the…' she stopped mouth open. She wasn't sure whether she was annoyed or happy to see him safe.

George came from the back, "Is it a raid then officer?" Looked her over and laughed.

"Denise, what's wrong?" Eager asked as if he didn't know. She looked Liberty up and down and then ignored her.

"Can we talk privately?"

"Oh, this is my new friend, Liberty, she's from the United States, fourth estate you know. She was my partner in crime, DS Williams." The wine had loosened him up a little. Denise gave him that evil stare that she kept for interviewing bad people. Deadly and frightening.

"Outside then," he said and then turned to Liberty, "Do not go anywhere." She laughed the night was getting more interesting.

Outside, the night was cold and sobering. Denise was angry and it showed. She had been so worried about him and here he was in the pub half cut with some bimbo.

"Are you okay?"

"Just a little ruffed up, shaken not stirred," He tried to laugh it off. He was the senior officer and the one she should see as strong.

"I know, I heard."

"Who told you?"

"No, I mean I heard you screaming," She told him what she knew. Eager updated her on his visit and Liberty's rescue.

"What did Charlie say?"

"He obviously didn't know, I am sure. You know he goes red in the face when he is surprised or angry. He said he would find out what was going on. He wanted to know if you were okay, seemed genuinely interested and concerned."

"Call him then and lay it on thick, beaten up badly, see what he says. There's a payphone in the hallway."

Ten minutes later, she was back and beckoned him outside again.

"What did he say?"

"Strange, asked about you, of course, and then told me to drop it and never talk about it again. A 'need to know' type operation directed from above. If I knew what was good for me just move on and that was a direct order."

"Stranger and stranger."

"Oh, and he said to tell John if he knows anything about McAllistar we don't know or his movements he best calls it in and stay safe."

# Chapter Twenty-Four
## Nosey Postie

The postman stopped his old red bike and leaned it against the wall in front of the cottage or gatehouse as he knew it by. He walked the winding weed-ridden path up to the farmhouse whilst sorting letters out of his bag as he did so.

"Morning, Phil," Bessie called from the doorway.

"Morning, my dear. Nice one eh?" thirty years as a local postie, he knew everyone and everything.

"Nice for this time of year. What have you got for me?"

"Sorry, Bessie just bills. I know you been waiting on a letter for years."

"Oh well, no one loves you when your old and grey, that's the way the song goes."

She was looking around and seemed a little anxious.

*Not like our Bessie,* he thought.

"Oh, do you have someone staying in the cottage?"

"No, definitely not!" she reacted too quickly and too strongly.

"Not being nosey, Bessie. I just thought I saw the chimney smoking the other night when I passed. Just want to do my job, if someone was there, they may get letters, so I need to know. Thirty years and the mail has always been delivered to the right doors," He boasted as usual. His claim to fame for thirty years and never a sick day. He not only delivered the mail but distributed the local gossip like the flu.

"Not saying that you're nosey, Phil. Just put on a fire every now and then to air the place out. Gets very damp it does."

"Aye, it would. You need to rent it and make some dosh and the renters will upkeep it."

*Never seen a fire on before,* he thought.

"I like my privacy, Phil, you know that."

*Nosey Phil is not buying this.*

"Come to think of it, maybe is a good idea. I could do with some extra and the cottage is a decent distance from the farmhouse."

"Put a card in the post office and you will get offers in no time at all. Well, bye, Bessie, the post must get through. Ha."

*I pray to God he forgets about the smoke and the cottage.*

McAllistar had been doing his sit-ups and push-ups, part of his daily routine to stay fit. He wanted to run but believed it was too risky even at night. It was a remote area; however, you never knew who was around at night. The local lads poaching and hunting around the place maybe. See him and word would get around. So, he ran up and down the stairway to the small turret room above. Good job he was just doing sit-ups on the ground when he heard the postman's bike being put against the wall. He hid on the stairway and when he heard Aunt Bessie coming in, he knew it was all clear. She told him that Nosey Phil had seen the smoking chimney and her excuse for it.

"I won't light it again."

"You'll freeze at night. I'll bring more blankets down."

"It's okay, Aunt Bessie. Ex-army and all that, used to the cold."

"I'll bring them anyway, tough guy," she laughed.

# Chapter Twenty-Five
## A Lead

Sammy, the squirrel had used up a lot of boot leather around Sheffield. No one had heard of the young McAllistar for a long time. He could find no records of living relatives for his Dad or Mother. The local paper back issues had carried the story of the hero McAllistar. Local boy makes good and it didn't carry any pictures of proud relatives. Just the street he grew up in. One interview with a local guy named Ted, who knew him as a boy, yes, he was a rascal, glad the army sorted him out and made a man of him like me in World War I. *He could not find Ted either, probably dead by now*, he thought.

Most of the neighbours had moved or died, local shop closed down due to new supermarket, the church had closed as well due to lack of support, the local pub had changed hands a dozen times every man's dream to own a pub and then everyman's nightmare due to high rent, changes in drinking habits and lifestyle, long hours, draconian drink drive laws. He had to listen to the landlord's endless complaints but no knowledge of McAllistar.

He was beginning to give up when in totters, an ancient guy with a silver beard bent over using a Zimmer frame. He looked at the landlord and wanted to ask how old is this guy. Instead, he just watched him settle.

"Evening, Ted, the usual?"

"Aye." He found his favourite seat near the fire and sat staring into it.

"Local?" the squirrel asked.

"Been around here all his life."

"Did you say, Ted?"

"Yes, Ted Marshall, old soldier, old miner, old steelworker, now just old."

"Let me get his drink." The squirrel paid and took the drink with his own to Ted. He laid it down and asked if he could sit beside him, cold tonight.

"Ta," was all he said and kept staring into the fire. After a few minutes, he took his ale and sipped slowly and then made a wheezing noise. The squirrel took this for pleasure.

"I have been looking for the McAllistar, used to live in these parts," The squirrel waited but no immediate response. The old guy spat into the fire a lot of phlegm.

Another sip, another wheeze. He was beginning to think that he was deaf when he spoke, still staring into the fire.

"I knew them, used to live down the street. What's it to you?"

"I work for a lawyer, seems like young Logan come into a small fortune, but we can't find him."

"In prison, always said that where he would end the little ruffian."

"No, he is out now, however, no one knows where he has gone."

"I knew the hero stuff wouldn't last. Too cocky for sure. Had a bad life though. Dad died early otherwise the belt would have straightened him out and Elsie, just a drunk."

"Any idea about friends and relatives, I mean anywhere at all he might go?"

"You will probably find him in London, wasn't he into drugs and stuff?"

"You are well informed."

"Not much to do in the old people's home but read and watch TV. He was in the local paper twice, once as a hero and then a crook. Local boy makes good, local boy reverts to form and makes bad."

"I take it that you didn't like him?"

"Bangers through my letterbox, stolen milk, balls in my garden, yes, he was a real pain at times. I was sorry though, not a nasty kid just misguided and left too much alone. So, I called the social workers for him to see if they could help. They took him to some poor kid's events like Christmas pantomimes, got him some holidays outa Sheffield, in the country. He liked it by all accounts and did him some good. Then he cocked up, was sent to the boy's army. Reverted to form."

He spat again into the centre of the fire as if disgusted.

"Outa town?"

"Yeah, Derbyshire dales or someplace there, a farm, I think. Daft bugger said he been to the seaside, no seaside in Derbyshire. Used to threaten me with telling Aunt Bessie when the cocky rascal came home and I had clipped around his lugs."

"Buy you another drink?" Ted actually looked at him with watery eyes.

"Nope, this is all I have every night then back to my prison," Ted turned away and added, "You can put one behind the bar for me tomorrow if you like. Thanks." Then he actually smiled, turned again, spat in the fire and said, "If you see him, tell him old Ted sends his best and to stay out of trouble."

The next day, a visit to South Yorkshire Social Services. Not much help; all confidential and files were probably lost years ago. All lefties, no one there looked like they would take a bribe. He called in Tazewell need to know where McAllistar was sent to the boy's army what court, what location. Police records needed accessing quickly they were most likely with the Derbyshire cops. It took half the day before Tazewell got back. Derby City was merged with Derby county police. The records were moved around and some were lost. Young offender's record was destroyed after ten years.

"What about his army record? Something must have been noted on entry. They keep good records," Tazewell said it would take time. "Needs to be done carefully. Go to Derbyshire and wait."

That was good but where in Derbyshire? A library was the place to start, he would ring Bruce, the muscle first, to pack at the motel and be ready to move.

Reading the maps and information on Derbyshire, there are a few big towns; Chesterfield, Derby, and Buxton. A lot of smaller towns in the countryside. But where would you go to take disadvantaged kids for a holiday? It virtually was all countryside. In the tourist book, two areas stood out; Derby Dales, very scenic and a few country estates of interest to visit and Matlock Bath, an old Roman spa town, touted as the only seaside pier fun area not by the seaside. Interesting! All kinds of interesting activities for kids. They set off to Matlock by number 99 bus from Pond Street station. Approximately one and a half hours drive. Matlock Bath was in the centre of Derbyshire, so if his instincts were wrong, he could get to other points quickly. Find a motel or B&B and wait.

# Chapter Twenty-Six
## A Better Time

He laid on her bed in pure ecstasy. Her hands ran all over his body and massaged his wounded areas with a special herbal cream. He didn't want it to end well only with a very happy ending. She then started on his head. Massaging the sides, rubbing all over, scratching his skull to make the blood vessels come alive and he thought that maybe his hair had grown more. This was the best end to the worst day of his life. He'd drunk a lot but was feeling great. He lay in his underpants under a big purple towel. She had run him a hot bath with low candle lighting before the massage.

He noticed she was reading from a book, 'Sensual Massaging', his hopes were very high. When she bent, her head her hair would touch his body as she moved again up and down his back, legs and feet. Yes, this was great until he fell soundly asleep.

They had decided, due to the bugging and possibility of the thugs returning, to go to her flat in Wimbledon. A small one-bedroom place that she had complained to Gavin that you could not swing a cat in. He told her the rent in London was very expensive. It had taken her an hour trying to find how to work the shower when she moved in. Who would have thought the switch for the heater was on the floor? In England she found everything a little difficult in her apartment. Still, she loved London like New York; full of activity and excitement. Not a bad place to live, lots of life and opportunities for fun. Although one day, she knew she needed to grow up. Maybe a ranch with lots of horses, for that she needed to be very successful, or marry a rich guy; both were good options.

'What did Gordon say that there might be a book on this? That would make money. First, I have to get some lead on McAllistar and get there. All I have is this big Brit teddy bear of a guy, who appears to know zip.' He started to snore, she put both her feet on him and rolled him over, then lay on the far side of the bed and fell asleep.

The coffee cup was put down near her face on the bedside cabinet. "Wakey wakey."

"Go the fuck away! Leave me alone it's too early."

"Oh, you treat me like this after last night," he teased her.

"Nothing happened last night you big oaf. Snorer."

She got out of bed and faced him.

"So, what is it like making love to a mature experienced man?"

She bent over laughing with one hand in the air and the other holding her stomach. Tears of laugher rolled down her face.

"Okay, enough of the dramatics. I only snore when I am plastered. If you stop for a second, I can tell you what Uncle John's brain has come up with, must have been the head massage. I think I have a small clue to where he might be."

She sat back on the bed and sat straight up. "Spill it, smalls!"

"Another massage first," He was fully dressed and joking.

"Come here, smalls." He did and she started massaging the front of his trousers and then she grabbed his balls.

"Okay, do you talk or hurt badly. Spit it out!"

He pushed her off. "You're crazy holding a policeman's balls."

"Is that a joke?"

"Yeah well, not a good one but feel free at any time to cause me pain as it will be the best I've had for years."

She sipped her coffee and looked at him with big eyes saying share we are partners now. Close buddies. "I have helped you and need a reciprocal act." He sat on the bed.

"Seriously, when you were massaging my head a few thoughts jumped in. Logan once said that he had another Mum and Dad and living on the farm was the happiest days of his life."

"That it? Where?"

"Not sure."

"Well, let's just get out the directory of farms and call all of them…how many, twenty, thirty, forty thousand?"

"Calm down, bigs, let me have my coffee and think."

"Did you just call me bigs? I'll help you think." She jumped off the bed and jumped on him wrestling him to the mattress. He didn't resist much. Laying both her knees on his arms she started slapping his face, not hard but in an act of making him talk. She was slapping and he was laughing. He wanted her so much right now.

"Okay, I'll talk enough of the torture, bigs."

She didn't stop for a few more slaps.

"That's for calling me bigs."

"You call me smalls?"

"Bigs is not good on a woman, indicates size."

"And smalls is not saying anything about a man? Huh."

"Enough small or big talk. Think where this might be."

"Got it, has to be somewhere close to there. Aunt Bessie's farm."

"Where? Where?"

"Oh no, you are going have to give something first."

To his surprise, she threw him on his back, opened his fly and started working his penis with both hands. At first slowly, then faster and then she capped it with her thumb.

"Talk or else I stop."

"No, you can't, that is not fair, it's illegal, wait he was sentenced to the boy soldiers in Matlock, Derbyshire. Said he fucked up on his new parents, so they must be close in the court area."

She had a fascination for older men probably due to her love for her lost father. Eager was attractive and different from every guy she had been with. Yes, she was using him and him her, she figured, however, there was some chemistry between them. She could not figure out why but was definitely attracted to him. She said nothing, just slipped him into her mouth until he exploded. Well, she had him where she wanted him now and he is a bit of a charity case speaking sexually, she knew.

# Chapter Twenty-Seven
## In the Past

"You wanted to talk, Mr McAllistar?" Billy's Adam's apple was running up and down like crazy. He had sweat on his brow.

"Thought it might be better to talk here rather than the shop. I hear the 'Horse & Hounds' is your favourite pub."

"Oh, where did you hear that, Mr McAllistar?"

"From a customer, you tried to blackmail," McAllistar took the video out of the brown envelope. "Said you wanted a thousand pounds or you would send it to his wife. Tut, Billy, you know what this means if I tell Jimmy?"

"A slap on the hand?" Billy was noticeably nervous with his Adman's apple moving up and down and arms shaking.

"Try harder, try concreted boots and a long swim in the Thames. Do you know what this would do to the business if this guy went to the press or police? Who would come to the club to be blackmailed? Think Billy!"

"I won't do it again, promise. Can we forget it, Mr McAllistar?"

"I am not sure, Billy. See, if I do not tell, then I might be swimming with you or drowning to be more precise."

"They'll kill me. I just get paid peanuts. I was just trying to get some money to help my Mum."

"Tell me what you do in your hole down there?"

"I video everything that happens for security purposes."

"Don't mess with me, Billy. I am chief of security and not allowed to see what you do."

"Oh, Jimmy would give you any video that impacts security, I am sure."

"And the rest?"

"A record of punters case, they need them. Not sure what they do with them."

"Not sure you are getting the seriousness of the situation." Billy's sweat was dropping down onto his eyes and his Adam's apple was working overtime up and down every time he swallowed.

"They are interested mainly in high profile celebrities, rock stars, politicians and the likes."

"So, there are video cameras down there in the VIP room?"

"Only on certain occasions, we have to be careful as some have their own security, who sweep the place before they do activities. They call it the hellfire club, not VIP room."

"So?"

"Although sometimes we have time to insert the cameras after the sweep. When they fetch the punter."

"Where are the videos kept?"

"I can't tell you that, Mr McAllistar, they will kill me."

"They will kill you anyway. Look, I am paid a lot of money to protect them and the business. I just want to know where the threats might come from. To do that, I need to know everything that happens on the premises. I mean if the police search and find them, I would have failed the bosses, right?"

"They will not find them. I have a false cupboard behind my video shelf, impossible to detect if you don't know it's there."

"Okay, I am going to forget this issue. The complainant thinks I am a war hero and that I will fix it and we may not hear from him again. We need to forget that this meeting ever happened, best for both of us. Understood?"

"Thanks, Mr McAllistar, you saved my life. Oh, I know you are friendly with Karlien, is she okay? Not seen her since that hellfire night."

"What do you mean okay?"

"Well, she took a bit of a beating from the Yank in the special room in the club. Heavy hitter indeed."

"No, I haven't heard from her for a few days. Who was the guy?"

"Some big yank politician, secret service and all. Best we don't know."

"The video?"

"Locked away."

"Oh, I guess it's part of her trade. A bit of rough sex and things like that." He pretended not to be too involved or interested.

"Rough sex? If that is rough sex, I never want any. This was a lunatic beating a woman for fun."

McAllistar went straight to the club. No one was around as it was midday. The bosses would be out at lunch or some meeting and the staff didn't start coming in until 4 pm. The cleaners had done their job and left as soon as they could. Straight down to Bill's grotto. The door was locked; however, he did have the master key. He found the way into the back of the shelf easily, although it seemed to be a brick wall. He tapped it but it felt solid. *Nothing here*, he thought. He searched all around nothing. Then he found a small lever higher up on the wall. Fiddling with it, pushing, trying to pull it and then he shoved it upwards. A section of bricks moved slightly a small gap. Using his fingernails, he managed to pull it out enough to grab it and pull open.

A police search would miss this for certain. There were rows and rows of videos. The red ones caught his eye, they were marked as 'hellfire club' with date and initials. Not sure what the initials were about, maybe identifying the punters. If nothing else, Billy kept a neat video library. He found several for the last week and went to Billy's desk and loaded them. He was shocked and disgusted at what he saw. There were young boys and girls who were being molested by mostly male adults. It was sick, really sick, so much that he really didn't want to watch them, he also had no time to take them all in. He needed to see what happened to Karlien.

The third one showed her in the hellfire club VIP secure room. The room was full of different style beds, several Jacuzzis and water fountains. Old pictures of guys and girls on the walls. Some erotic, some of the naked women and some people dressed as priests and nuns. Each bed was capable of being private by drawing big black curtains around. Chains and all sorts of what he thought was torture equipment on the walls.

The room was private. There was a very big man in his shirt-sleeves and with red braces holding up his trousers. He had slicked-back hair, which was partly balding. They were drinking together. He was knocking back whisky like Scotland was going to run out, she kept pouring them for him. She had what looked like champagne but was probably just running up the bill. She was dressed in a low cut black mini skirt.

She started to strip slowly, provocatively like good call girls do. This was not good enough for him. He started pulling the rest of her clothes off. She screamed and he punched and slapped her down. Then lifted and took her from behind like she was a rag doll. She started screaming and then fighting back, but he was too strong. The rest was a combination of good beating and the guy forcing her to perform perverted acts. McAllistar could hardly look, he started to cry. He never used to cry; always took what came along and was determined not to show weakness, even when Dad took his miner's belt to him.

*This guy is an animal and crazy and I have seen his face before, but where?*

Then the guy shouts to no one in particular, so loud the video picked it up, "Teaching her a lesson to be good next time." Then more and more kicking and thumping even when she was collapsed on the floor. The guy looked at her like he was the one who had been short-changed that she had not been cooperative, not given him a good time. He took a wad of what looked like dollar notes and threw them on her body, grabbed his coat and you could hear him say as he left the room, "Bitch attacked me."

He was not sure what made him do it, but he also took the other eleven red videos, piled them into a plastic bag he found under Billy's desk. He found some unrecorded videos in cases, and replaced the red ones in the cupboard. Locked up and went straight to the local library. Using their micro film machine, he searched newspapers for high-level United States visitors to London that week with no luck. He had probably left London otherwise, McAllistar would have visited him and probably got into deep shit after beating him to death. He was angry very angry.

*God knows what the other videos contain and where is Karlien now?*

# Chapter Twenty-Eight
## The Hellfire Club – In the Past

He asked the librarian if there were any books on the hellfire club. She looked at him through the top of her double-lens glasses as if he was strange. Still, she showed him several books.

"These may help you."

He sat quietly at a vacant desk and searched through the books. He found the history and information he wanted.

Hellfire club was a name for several exclusive clubs for high society people established in Britain and Ireland in the eighteenth century. They talked about persons of 'quality', who wanted to commit immoral acts. Many of them were in politics and other high society positions. The clubs were not easy to join and the members would have had to be very rich. They met in secret in various locations. The most famous was in High Wycombe, it was called 'The Order of the Friars of St. Francis'. The venue was down a series of caves. Yes, he had heard about this place now a tourist attraction. It was rumoured that Benjamin Franklin had been a visiting member.

The clubs were also rumoured to have distant ties to an elite society known only as 'The Order of the Second Circle'.

The 'Order of the Second Circle' he thought about this. Weren't there two circles on the door of what he thought was the VIP area now, is this the hellfire club? Talking again to the lady librarian asking if has ever heard of a society named 'The Order of The Second Circle'. No was the answer. She turned away and began to walk to her desk suddenly she turned back. "Look up Dante's Inferno, he had circles."

*He had circles?*

She was helpful in finding this book. He never read much, so his knowledge of Dante and other poets and writers was limited. He found the second circle and it was called lust. 'Upper hell of the incontinence, where the lustful dwell.'

Seems to fit, does this happen in the Harker's hellfire club? What had he gotten his hands on? What was on the rest of these videos or more to the point what other people of quality? Dynamite could be more like an atomic bomb. He had no video player and no time, so he went to the post office away from Soho and posted all the videos.

After visiting her flat, he found no signs of her. Answer phone, nothing to suggest where she was, just his messages. He then went to the local police station and reported Karlien missing. Then to local hospitals with no luck. He called his police friend, DI Eager and asked if he could put some pressure on to locate her. He never gave the background just she was missing.

"If you have tried the hospitals, I will try the morgues. Are you sure she hasn't just gone off for a few days?"

*Oh my God, the morgue.*

"No, she would have told me, we were very close."

"Is she a hooker?"

He gulped as he didn't like to think about her that way. "I guess high-class escort would be a better term."

"Like Christine Keeler was?"

"I guess."

"I will do all I can. Let me know if she turns up."

That night, he casually asks Tazewell and Nick if they had seen her. Tazewell with his poker face you never knew what he is thinking, however, Nick had a strained look on his face that something was wrong. Both, though, said that they didn't have a clue. Bartenders, waitresses, security no one had seen her for days.

He kept calling her home phone. Just the damn answering machine.

# Chapter Twenty-Nine
## Too Many Questions – In the Past

Lifting the phone, he said, "DI Samuels."

"Can you speak?"

"Yes, but please be quick. We shouldn't talk when I'm in the office."

"McAllistar is asking too many questions about this Karlien girl. Even got one of your colleagues checking things out. We need this to die down and go away."

"Can you put him on ice for a while?"

"You mean…"

"No, not yet, just go away for a while to one of HM's hotels. Give me an hour and then search his place, you will find some items of interest I am sure."

"I will see what I can do."

"Very important, he has no credibility left. Needs to keep quiet, very quiet. This has got to go away. Got it?"

"Understood. I will see what I can do."

Bang the caller hung up.

# Chapter Thirty
## To Matlock

"That's it so far, Gavin."

"Does Gordon know?"

"Yes, I filled him just before this call."

"So, you still don't know what he's exactly got?"

"What am I, a psychic?"

"Well, find him quickly as you are not the only ones. Offer him whatever if it is good."

She hung up.

"Liberty, who was that?" Eager was coming down the stairs after packing his overnight bag.

"Just my editor, Gavin. Spoke to Gordon earlier as he asked me to keep him informed daily."

"Gordon, I never fully trusted him. He was a good source of information and I fed him some stories. But he has lots of connections and a bit of an old gossip. What did you tell him?"

"Oh, just that we are following a lead to Derby, how do you call it, shire," She lied.

"Well, it's a big county and the lead could go nowhere."

"Are we staying for a week, that bag is bulging," Picking it up. "And heavy."

"Just taking a little protection."

"Like what, smalls, a condom?"

"Mmm no, a couple of truncheons from when I was on the beat years ago. One wooden and one rubber, two cuffs and a gas spray."

"No, .44 Magnum? You Brits, you call that protection. Ha. I better look after you."

"Always bigger in America, for lots of cash in America," he sang.

"Please, your singing is worse than your snoring."

He locked the door in a hurry, looking around for any signs of danger.

"Quick, fetch your bags and get in my car."

"Call this a car, doesn't look like it will go far. Why don't we take mine, at least it is from this decade?"

"Do you always argue, want to be boss? Look I will show you later why, got it?"

"Okay, big boss."

They drove up the MI motorway and after thirty minutes, stopped at a welcome break petrol station.

"Can you get the coffees?"

"Yes, sir!" saluting the American way.

Eager searched under the car, under the wheel arches and even lifting the bonnet to look around the engine. Liberty came back as he was under the car on his back near the boot.

"Told you we should have taken mine. How far did we get ten miles?"

"Got it. Eureka!" He came out covered in dust and in his hand was a muddy looking device about the size of a hand.

"What's that?"

"That my dear is a tracker. If they bugged my place, why not be able to follow my car. The thing is look at your feet."

"What's wrong with my…oh another one."

"Precisely."

"They were not taking risks that you might find one. So, why did we come in your car?"

"To trick them. There are different types of trackers, so it could be a safety deal as they knew when I was in NI, the IRA were always putting bombs under cars, so I got used to checking under the car and bonnet before I would drive."

"Or there is another party interested?"

"Well, let's see we have the Harkers, the creep Samuels, those Russian guys, MI5 take your pick."

"Starting to get a little crowded."

Eager looked around in the car park. There were several trucks and the drivers, who had just gone into the café. Sneaking up, he placed one of the trackers under one truck and the other one under the second truck.

"With any luck, they are headed in different directions, south."

"I'm beginning to think you are not a dumb as I thought you were."

"Even better, wait here, from over there at the café and watch as I drive away. Don't worry I will just circle. See if anyone is interested or follows."

He waved her goodbye and shouted, "See you back home."

She watched like an owl. No movement in the car park. Nothing suspicious she could see. Twenty minutes later, he returned.

"Nothing."

"So, let's go."

"Teddy, they are headed to Matlock Derbyshire. Think our person of interest is with an old lady on a farm called Aunt Bessie. Apparently, she took him in for holidays when he was a kid."

"It fits, they all go home, it was just not the home we thought. Who else knows?"

"Gavin, I guess."

"Hopefully, he will keep his mouth shut."

"I think so, he needs a big story. I will call him anyway and stress the need to know the scenario, not even Sir Richard. He has a loose tongue after his long luncheons."

Samuels tapped his desk with his designer pen. Then he called his team.

"No, boss they are headed across country to Taunton direction. Not north."

"What I have it upon good authority…push forward and catch up with them and the tracker and do it quickly."

"But he is a copper, he will spot us."

"Take the risk."

Unless they told GWP a lie? Why would they?

He hated waiting.

"They are going to Matlock, Derbyshire," Tazewell stated.

"We are following them like Bill and Ben," said Leon.

*All those old BBC kid's shows which they had to watch must have screwed with their minds,* thought Tazewell. *Surely, there was a better way to teach them street English.*

"Yes, we are headed to the seaside."

"Seaside? Derbyshire is in the middle of the country, no seaside!"

"Tracker Russian superior technology not wrong, we are going to Brighton."

"Idiots. They are definitely going north."

"Not nice, you call us idiots like…Looby Loo. We no call you Andy Pandy!"

Tazewell realised he had gone too far; you do not mess with these guys.

"I'm sorry, very sorry, just the stress, I want you to get the stuff first."

"If we are to be there first, you must be right."

"I'd bet my life on it."

"You just did, Mr Javelin."

Tazewell gulped. "Look, turn around find the MI and head north and get off left after about five hours towards Matlock and call me when you get there. Okay?"

# Chapter Thirty-One
## Missing Goods – In the Past

"They're gone chief!" stuttered Billy.
"Gone?"
"All of the red ones." Billy sweating and swallowing and his Adam's apple doing swallow dives.
"All?" Jimmy came towards him and bent down to put his face nose to nose.
"All, how for Christ's sake, how?"
"I err don't know...honestly, I don't know."
*Same as the parcel in our office,* Nick thought, *The Russians will kill us.*
"Billy, only three people know about the hole in the wall. Let's count them me, Nick and you."
"Honestly chief, I didn't touch the stuff. On my life...honest."
"Who did you tell? Who?" "No one, honestly," Billy sweat was running down his forehead. Nick thought he smelt urine.
Trying to deflect, "McAllistar has been sniffing around, asking all types of questions. Could be him."

Tazewell, Nick and Jimmy were sitting down in the office.
"Let's find McAllistar and beat it out of him," Nick thundered.
"We are not sure, could be Billy," Tazewell almost whispered.
"No, he would have skipped town. He is a scared little rat."
Then Tazewell's phone rang. "What? Yes, I see," He hung up.
"McAllistar has been arrested."
"Why?" Jimmy asked. Tazewell shook his head.
"We can get to him anywhere," boasted Nick.
"What about Billy?"
"A loose end, better say goodbye," said Jimmy calmly.

"Oh, Billy you have been invited to the executive party, five pm today in the VIP room. Aren't you going up in the world smooching with the bosses?" the security guard said sarcastically.
"Probably need something from me," Billy was though worried.
"Yeah, probably got the best of the flesh down there and expensive booze while we mortals make do with old scrubbers and beer."
Billy looked at his watch at five o'clock and opened the door. Just Jimmy and Nick. Dark no music, no booze, no girls. He was visibly worried.

"There all late, Billy. Let me get you your poison what is it?"
"Whisky and ice, thanks, Jimmy."
Jimmy went to the bar and just poured Billy's drink and handed it to him.
"Not joining me?"
"Next one, Billy, go on down it," He did.

Nick had come close to him and as quick as a flash, he brought out a knife and sunk it into his main neck artery and pushed forward until half his neck came out. Including his Adam's apple. Billy was standing on polished tiles the carpet had been removed. He went white, blood poured out of his major artery and he dropped like a stone.

"That was easy," Jimmy complimented Nick as he would never get his hands dirty.

"Old Royal Marine knife training."

# Chapter Thirty-Two
## The Squirrel Finds His Man

Sammy, the squirrel, was walking down Matlock Bath on what was called locally as the promenade. Well, that's what they call it in the only seaside town not to be by the sea. Bruce, the muscle, was busy in one of the arcades playing games. *A big kid*, Sammy thought, *and about as helpful as a pain in the bum.* What he needed were locals who have lived here all their lives.

He had walked from Matlock itself, where he had drawn blank stare after blank stare when asking about farms in the area that used to help disadvantage kids from Sheffield city of steel.

It had been a long day, his feet hurt. Tazewell never got back to him on the army records that would give a lead maybe. He had called into Nick, who was full of abuse. *Getting a bit scared,* he thought. Well, over the years, he had found most people for them, he was not perfect, nobody was but didn't deserve such language. *This is probably a waste of time,* he mused. It's 4 pm; time for a late lunch and a beer.

He dragged Bruce out of the arcade. "Aw, Sammy, I was just winning," he complained. He was playing a pinball machine and nowhere near winning.

*If brains were dynamite, he wouldn't have enough to blow his hat off,* Sammy thought. Down south parade and he saw an old whitewashed walled pub with seating outside. Inside it was more modern and boasted eight different types of local ales plus they did food. They had their own 'artisanal' bread, whatever that was. He settled for two pints of 'Mr Grundy' and a cheese and tomato sandwich. Bruce had stuffed himself full of greasy chips earlier and was just happy to drink. They sat outside. It was a pleasant day for autumn; the sun was out and there was a small breeze. Bruce was in a short sleeve wife-beater waistcoat, showing off his biceps as usual.

Sammy found a local newspaper inside the *'Matlock Mercury'* as Bruce was not an interesting conversationalist. His sipping of the beer and slopping it back and then burping was getting on Sammy's nerves.

Sometimes in life, you are lucky or is it that there is no such thing as a coincidence and when you focus hard on a subject, the universe eventually helps you. Phil the postie came in with some letters and his bag around his shoulder, bike parked outside on the pavement.

*Why not?* Sammy thought.

As Phil came out, Sammy stood up and asked for his help. Lost, used to come here when he was a poor kid from Sheffield and stayed on a farm with some locals. You know, sent by social services out of dirty old Sheffield, well, it was a smoked filled city of steel at that time, to get some country air. He remembers it with great fondness.

Phil looked him up and down. Sammy was still in his trademark raincoat worse for wear.

"Oh aye, you don't have a Yorkshire accent?"

"Been in London most of my life, so I lost it."

Phil looked suspicious, he needed to smooth-talk him.

"How long have you been a postman?" He didn't realise this was Nosey Phil's favourite subject.

"Oh yeah, thirty years, never a day off sick. You see, I take my work seriously, the post must get through rain hail or snow."

"Wow. You must know this place like the back of your hand."

"Certainly do. The only people I know that took in a kid from Sheffield for hols was Ted and Bessie."

*Bingo, Aunt Bessie!*

"Are they still on the farm, they might know other people who can help me?"

"Ted died years ago. Not much of a farm left, just the old run-down farmhouse and the even older gatehouse. Bessie lives there on her own now."

"Can you tell me her address?"

"You just go up Matlock Road, see that direction," pointing over to the green hills. "Turn right at the roundabout in Matlock and follow the road to Shirland. You will come across a gatehouse, used to be called the keeper's house when there was a manor way back. Now they have a new sign calling it 'McAllistar's Cottage', can't see why they would change it."

*Bingo and full house.*

# Chapter Thirty-Three
## Finding Aunt Bessie

"So, smalls, I mean Sherlock, how do we find the farm?"

"Local cops or post office would be a good start."

They arrived in Matlock and found the local police station.

"Matlock used to host the Derbyshire county police Head Quarters years ago." Eager knew the place from a few visits on official business.

"Better I go in alone," he said, "You're too much of a distraction." He thought about it for a few seconds. He could go in and flash his police warrant card and badge to get cooperation, however, coppers were the worst gossips and territorial, especially in a small town. Someone may wonder what he is doing on their patch and check back with Scotland Yard. Better she goes in. She did. Twenty minutes later, she came out.

"Nothing! Young cops playing computer games, I think. None of them seemed to know anyone. Told them I was the long-lost granddaughter from States on vacation and was trying to look up English relatives. All I had was the last words my Dad said before he died," she said in a teary voice.

"Look up Aunt Bessie on the farm when you get to Matlock."

"Even that didn't work? Couldn't help you look her up?"

"More like trying to look up my skirt!"

"Yeah, since they took the local Bobby off the beat and put them in those little cars, the police have lost grassroots contact. In the old days…"

"Okay I can read your memoirs later. What do we do now?"

Just then a young police cadet came out. He must have been sixteen years old with pimples.

"Err sergeant came in and gave me this for you." He handed over a note whilst staring at Liberty seemingly transfixed.

*Probably the first foreign woman he's ever seen,* Eager thought. Didn't even clock Eager in the driver's seat.

The note read 'Call Scotty' with the telephone number on it.

"Sarge says he worked this area as a dog handler and knows everyone."

They thanked him and called the number. A woman answered. Scotty was walking his dogs in the park as he does every day. The park was just outside the centre of town. He was easy to spot. Big guy at least six foot five inches, the width of shoulders seemed as long, big moustache and two old Alsatians dogs walking slowly by his side.

"Excuse me," Eager began, "Scotty, right?"

Scotty looked him up and down slowly and then Liberty. He didn't seem to register the question for twenty seconds.

"You're the best-looking policewoman I have seen for a long time," Talking to Liberty and then he turned to Eager.

"What can I do for you, inspector?"

He certainly can spot a cop.

"We are looking for local knowledge a while back. The station couldn't help us."

He pointed to a garden park seat. The Alsatians sniffed them both.

"What can I help you with?" He seemed to be very friendly with a big happy smile.

"We are looking for Aunt Bessie who was on a farm here in the '70s."

He thought about it for a while. Took out a pipe, tapped it, filled it with whisky tobacco and lit it. Puffing slowly.

"That all?"

"She took in disadvantaged kids from Sheffield or at least one," Eager commented wondering how much he should tell him.

Liberty patted the dogs, who seemed to take a great liking to her.

"Rex, get down you too, Romeo."

He puffed away.

"Why?" he asked.

"Police business," Eager shot back.

"Not sure if I can help you, inspector, been retired ten years now. The highlight of my day is the dog walk. These two guys and I did our bit."

Liberty was watching him closely. He was holding back, not sure why.

"Look, we are not after hurting anyone we are trying to help someone in trouble. We need to find him before others do."

He put down his pipe on the seat. He was thinking you could see the creases on his brow opening and closing.

"Logan?"

*Wow, he knows,* they both thought.

"Yes, Logan McAllistar. You're well informed."

"You're an American too young for FBI, daughter, girlfriend, what are you?"

"Fourth estate."

"Oh. Apart from walking the dogs, I read all the papers I can find. Heard he got out and was not seen since. What paper?"

"*Daily Cryer.*"

"Mmmm passes my time for sure. The yard and fourth estate working together. Not heard of this type of police work."

*He was milking the attention for sure,* thought Liberty.

"Look, I'll be straight with you," Eager said in earnest.

"That would be nice." Scotty said in a sarcastically manner as if to say, *'Do not treat me like an idiot, I am too old in the tooth for that.'*

"I am not on official business; I am on leave and not on this case. I am a friend of Logan's; well, I was not sure how he feels now. He is in the middle of something bigger than him and we believe it is very dangerous for him. The *Daily Cryer* can help him in many ways from legal assistance to getting him somewhere safe. I can help him unravel this situation and come out okay. That's what we are trying to do. She gets the story, I get to make it up to a friend."

"I always liked Logan. He was a good kid. I used to take him with me on night duty with the dogs. Loved the action. One night, he watched as Romeo and Rex put down a drunken riot in Chesterfield." He gazed into the past, "Trouble is that they brought down five of the cops as well. Bums, legs and cocks were bitten!" he laughed out loud as he revisited the memory of that night.

"They let you take a kid?" Liberty asked.

"Oh no, it was a risk for me. He hid in the back of the wagon and watched. Dogs loved him."

He no doubt was bored and lonely. They retired to a little coffee shop and they thought the best was to let him talk. *He can lead us to Aunt Bessie and then McAllistar for certain.* Eager was sure.

He talked about the trouble McAllistar got into as a boy. The paper shop had been robbed several times at night money and cigarettes stolen. The day he was caught, there was a lot of kids coming out of school in the paper shop. Some were stealing. McAllistar was caught with several chocolate bars on him. The local magistrate was a relative of the shop owner and had no pity. They assumed that he was behind the other break ins. Scotty, Ted and Bessie spoke up for him to no avail. It was agreed that he would go to the boy's army. Made sense as he didn't really have a home. Ted and Bessie wanted him to stay with them, but the magistrate would not agree. His mother didn't even bother to turn up. He kept in contact with him for a few years and then as happens, lost contact.

"Will you tell us where Aunt Bessie lives, I mean is she still on the farm?"

"I can do better than that; I will take you there."

# Chapter Thirty-Four
## The Americans

"Nice of you to meet us at such short notice. Roger, is it? Can I call you Roger?" the biggest man in the room said as he shook hands and sat down around the boardroom table.

"By all means," Roger White replied, shaking the other two guy's hands and wishing he hadn't. Strong, very strong handshakes crushing his hand, maybe to send him a message.

There were three Americans. *Big guys,* Roger thought. Long raincoats, short slick haircuts, big black shoes more like boots. All wore red ties and white shirts. *I am betting they are carrying. Definitely an ex-military, heavy-duty dudes for sure,* he thought.

If he was honest to himself, he felt a little bit intimidated by them. These were field operatives and he was an office jockey, mainly no 007.

"So, what can I do for you gents? All I know is my boss asked me to meet you. No idea who you are and what this is all about?"

"Well, let's get you cleared up on those points," the same big guy spoke with a large sweep of his arm as a friendly gesture pointing to the other guys in turn. The others just stared at him like they were taking in everything, reading his body language. They were all intense, focused and if he could admit it very scary.

"This is Sam and Gary. I am Harvey. We are in the same line of work as you. Helping keep the world safe." He flashed a badge and put it away before Roger could get a good look at it.

*That's clearing things up? Bullshit. Sam, Gary and Harvey my ass,* Roger thought.

"You mean that you work for the United States government? CIA? FBI? Secret service?"

"You could say that we work for the United States government, a specific branch and we do not advertise who we are if you get my drift? There is no need for us to be specific at this meeting. Need to know," Harvey said while touching his nose. Sam and Gary shifted a little in their seats but still maintained the intense staring.

"We have been directed to you by one of our sources. The Russians seem to be chasing a guy err," Bringing out a little notepad and flicking through, "Named McAllistar. You also have been at meetings about this guy. We want to know why?"

"Well, that's the big question," Roger said flippantly and then regretted the cold stares he was given.

"I mean no one for sure knows. Everyone is just guessing that he has something important. I was asked to sit in on police briefings because of the Russkies, let me say friendship with some local villains."

They just started, so Roger while clearing his throat gave them the whole low down on the Harkers and McAllistar situation. It seemed a waste of time as he didn't believe he was telling them anything new. Still, his common sense had told him to assist.

"His girlfriend, the escort," looking at his notepad, "Karlien, do you think he has something of hers, something important?"

"I can't imagine what she would have which is so important or that he would have it. Unless she kept a diary of pictures or even a video of herself in action with her clients," He laughed and then it hit him and the others.

*If she had a high-profile client and evidence, the Russians or even the Harkers can use it for leverage, blackmail and influence.*

They all leant forward, the big man rushing his fingers through his balding hair.

"Is it possible that Harker's filmed, let me say, special activities at their club?" He now needed to be careful. Wasn't Karlien working at the hellfire club and then disappeared.

"It's possible, yes. They have a lot of high-profile clients and seem to be untouchable. I guess it is a scenario…"

"So, why has he waited until now?" Gary actually spoke.

"Look, I do not know. If you could find the girl you might get a better idea. I mean…"

"That's no longer an option," said Sam assuredly.

*Wow, they both can talk. He is so sure that she's dead then.*

"I can only surmise that he went to prison so quickly that what he may have he does not know the value or he kept it to use on the Harkers for revenge or as leverage to find out what happened to the girl."

"So, the best place to start is with the Harker brothers?"

"Well, they may know more than anyone, I guess. They are tough guys surrounded by their enforcers, not an easy job."

They all leaned their heads to the same side and twisted their necks making a cracking sound. Like they were choreographed. It was funny but no time to laugh for sure.

Roger got the message it was very clear,

*'We fucked up tougher guys. That's what we do for a living!'*

"We then need to know about this cop, Eager. His pal, right? Where can we find him?"

"I'll have to check with the boss and get back to you."

"You do that!" It was a command. They exchanged telephone numbers and left.

# Chapter Thirty-Five
## Top Brass

The commissioner had his full regalia uniform on. He was pruning himself in front of the mirror in his luxurious office.

"Off to the palace, Charlie. Big event coming up," he said proudly.

Charlie Allcock wanted to get to business. He was upset and when that happened, his heartbeat was faster than normal, he started to sweat on his brow and he tapped his chair arm constantly.

*The chief is a bit of a show pony.*

"Sir, I need some answers, not sure what is going on?"

"Sir? Charlie, we are alone, you never call me sir, we go back too far. It must be bad." Still looking and adjusting his uniform in the mirror.

"Michael, the ACC is dealing around me with a DCI Samuels, who reports to me last I heard. No line of command. Told me I didn't need to know what they are doing. What the fuck is that about?"

"No need for profanity, Charlie. Tell me quickly I have to be off by ten. Hey, Samuels is the guy he just promoted right?"

"Yes. Look they bugged a fellow officer and listened whilst some Russian guys tortured him!"

That got the chief's attention.

"They what?"

Charlie went into as much as they knew whilst the chief sat down and nodded.

*Did the chief know, not sure,* he thought.

"Got to go Charlie. I will look into it. Meanwhile, keep your ear to the ground and do nothing until I can clear this up."

*He doesn't have a clue. He smells though some bad PR not what he needs if he wants to get his lordship,* Charlie thought as he left.

# Chapter Thirty-Six
## A Bad Turn

They used a crowbar and the crack of the cottage door breaking must have been heard a mile away. New locks had not been fitted yet. They burst in with guns in hands ready for action. There was nothing inside the cottage. Just a stool and some cigarette butts in the fireplace.

"He is not here. Maybe wrong information," said Roman.

"There's a farmhouse at the back. Shall we check out?" Leon said while looking out the side window. There was no need; Aunt Bessie arrived at the doorway.

"What are you doing!" she shouted.

"Looking for our friend McAllistar," Leon answered calmly.

"You bloody well break in to do that?"

"We didn't break-in, the door was broken when we got here."

"Liar. I just heard the crack and you still have the crowbar in your hands."

"Okay, old lady, we go easy on you. You tell us where our friend McAllistar is or we help you remember."

"You what? I am going to the police." Roman stepped forward and tried to punch her in the face. She was quick to move sideways and a big slap from her huge farm hands landed him in a heap on the floor.

Leon laughed, "Wait until I tell that you were beaten by an old lady."

"Shit, she hits like an old MacDonald farmer."

She moved towards the door when Leon caught her with a sweeping blow with the crowbar to her back. She fell like a sack of potatoes. Roman stood up and kicked her twice in the head.

"Teach her to bitch slap me."

"Look what you have done, she is dead, I think. No good to us now," Leon growled.

They left quickly as the pool of blood from her head spread around the floor.

A quick check of the farmhouse and they were gone.

Outside, Sammy, the squirrel and Bruce, the muscle, sat in a small hire car, a hundred yards down the road. They watched the Russians break and then a few minutes later after the big lady had entered the cottage rush out, then down to the back and then quickly back to their car and drive off.

*Strange*? Thought Sammy. *Maybe McAllistar is in there? No, the Russians would be carrying, not likely to run away.* He wondered where his back up was, they were taking their time and the Russians were ahead of them for sure.

# Chapter Thirty-Seven
## Meeting McAllistar

Sammy waited and watched. Soon a car pulled up followed by an old Volvo estate with two dogs in the back. *What have we here?* he thought, *getting busy around here.* Out of the first car climbed a young woman and then, yes, it was DI Eager if he wasn't mistaken. The two Alsatians jumped out of the Volvo and seemed to get very busy or more like excited. A really big old guy was with them. The dogs made for the house and he could hear them whining right down the street where he sat. "They had found something." He hoped the Russians had not done for McAllistar as he would be in serious shit if anything happened to him.

Aunt Bessie lay in a big pool of blood. Eager got into action to check her out. Scotty phoned from the farmhouse 999 for an ambulance. Liberty watched Eager, it's the first time she saw a lot of blood. Eager ripped Aunt Bessie's pinafore off and started making a head bandage to stop the bleeding which was coming from her temple. *Not good.* The hospital was not far away and Scotty's years of authority got everything into action. He asked for a doctor to come with the ambulance, he sensed resistance to this request so he was not sure if one would turn up.

The ambulance arrived with a junior doctor and the paramedics who got to work on checking her out and making her comfortable. The young doctor was uncomfortable in moving her. Indecision, what if they did more damage than good? Was the back broken? It looked bent and badly bruised. The new bandage had stopped the bleeding, moving her was going to make it worse, but they had no choice.

The old ambulance man looked at Scotty, they had worked together over the years, shared the same pub. He raised his eyebrows at Scotty.

"Look, lad, she is going to die if she stays here. So, let's be on with it and do our best." Having made the decision Scotty and the ambulance men moved her slowly onto the stretcher and it took four of them to wheel her and lift her into the ambulance. Soon it was gone with sirens blaring. The young doctor was sitting in the back shaking a little and hoping they were right.

Sammy told Bruce, "Get me to a telephone quick." It all seemed to be coming to a head as he saw McAllistar entering the cottage.

Liberty looked around the cottage. Definitely, someone had been living here. Sleeping bag, cig ends in the fire, some rubbish lying around. An old army bag in the corner neatly stashed. *So, we are close to McAllistar for certain.*

"What the fuck!" a big voice boomed from the doorway. The dogs growled and Scotty had trouble controlling them not to attack McAllistar. His fists were clenched and facial expression even tighter. They say a man is either ready for fight or flight, this man was ready for a fight. He wore a brown beanie and dirty army old fatigues clothes. He was unshaven for days and apart from his height he would not be easily recognised. He had walked across the muddy fields, the back way to the farm and then the cottage.

"Steady, Logan," Eager put his hands up. "It's Aunt Bessie, she has been brutally beaten and is on her way to the hospital."

McAllistar eased and looked around him, the girl, Eager, a big cop and his dogs, it was like Paddington station at peak hour and he had thought that he had cleverly hidden away. Eager explained what they had found. McAllistar looked in disbelief and muttered something like, "He had brought trouble to her door." Liberty said nothing for a change. She was reading the mood and high tension in the room. It was not her time; she would just throw a spanner in the works.

They stood in a circle, dogs had been taken outside, however, Scotty had returned to lend support to Eager if required.

"Eager, if you think you are arresting me you will need more than this old man and a couple of dogs."

"What about…" Liberty almost said she was not going to be dismissed if there was a fight but thought better off it.

"Logan, I'm on your side, always have been."

"Oh aye, that's why I got hard porridge."

"I am not on duty. In fact, I am in between being in the force and being out. I came to help you. Believe it or not."

McAllistar nodded to Scotty as his boyhood memory had come back and he regretted the 'old man' jibe as this man had been his friend.

"And her?" pointing at Liberty.

"Her is a girl named Liberty, Mr McAllistar. I was thinking I could help as well as I represent a major newspaper that has the wherewithal to support you through all this."

"For what?"

"Obviously for your story when this is over." She was almost saying this like he was slow or dumb which didn't help.

"When what is over?" playing dumb and frustrating her.

"When the fucking bad gangster guys, the Russians, the police, the spooks and God knows who else wants a part of you or what you have are gone! You didn't see what they did to Aunt Bessie, these guys mean business," She lost it. He went quiet as it seemed to work.

He turned around, "I need to know if Aunt Bessie is okay."

It was agreed they would leave. The police would have been informed and surely must be on their way. McAllistar grabbed his army bag and attaché case hidden under the stairs and jumped in the Volvo with Scotty. Eager and Liberty followed.

# Chapter Thirty-Eight
## Murder

The highway patrol car phone rang.

"DCI Samuels."

"Are you there yet?" the ACC's voice boomed out of the speaker.

"Yes, sir, a bit of a mess really. His old aunt's in hospital beaten badly. McAllistar was at the hospital and left. It seems that a man fitting description of Eager was there as well. Looked and talked like a policeman, the nurse said. Plus, a young American lady."

"Local cops know anything? Eager's a fool; now he is aiding and abetting a criminal, we got him too dead to rights," the ACC seemed stressed.

"No, need to know, we just want to talk to these guys about an ongoing investigation. If sighted, do not approach, call me."

"Good. Well, we can add murder to McAllistar's crimes! Put me off the speaker."

"Yes, sir, off now. Murder?"

"This video guy from the club turned up dead in a sewer a year ago, pretty well decomposed. Killed through the throat with an old Royal Marine knife a Fairbairn-Sykes fighting knife, according to the ME. Easy to make a connection with McAllistar as this is the guy who got the videos off and is an ex-marine. So, he cleaned up so he would not be able to tell the Harkers. Right?"

"So, all 'points' bulletin?"

"Not yet, let's get him and the tapes first. If we can't find him in the next twelve hours, we go public and flush him out."

"Does not sound like McAllistar, sir."

"Not the point. He is a wanted very dangerous murderer, I can authorise you to carry a weapon. In fact, I will send one to you. The chief will sign off, no issue. Do you understand me?"

*Yes, loud and clear,* he thought, *once we get the videos, perfect reason to shoot to kill a dangerous murderer or a liability witness, I am getting in too deep for sure.*

# Chapter Thirty-Nine
## More the Merrier

"I can tell you roughly where they are."

"Roughly? How is that helpful?" demanding voice of Sam the American.

"Listen, they are up in Derbyshire, a lot happening and the net is closing in on McAllistar."

"Derby what?"

"Derbyshire, it is in the Midlands."

*Rude, caveman*

Roger explained the situation and gave clear directions by road and give or take, depending on the traffic, it could take say five hours.

"No, we going by chopper, ring us back with map references."

"Look, you are walking into a lot of people chasing them. It's going to be a zoo up there if this keeps on."

"We are patient people, Roger, we know when to pounce like a crocodile."

"Righty ho then, do not say I didn't warn you."

"Yo, though we walk through the valley of death we fear no evil because Roger, we are the most evil people in the valley!"

*Moron. I better tell the boss that they have released Rambo and his gang, they think they are in Vietnam, not Derbyshire countryside.*

# Chapter Forty
## Three's a Crowd

McAllistar didn't have much of a choice. He had no transport, money was getting low, stupid to use his bank card and it seemed everyone now knew where he went to. He would go along until he had a clearer plan. Scotty offered his house, however, all agreed it was too dangerous for him as his car had been seen at the cottage and hospital. Better for him they thought if he goes home alone. He gave them directions to a B&B way out in the Derbyshire moors on the way to Buxton. A bleak area of stone walls and sheep cuddling each other against the walls to stop from freezing and old farmhouses, which were never maintained. Not many individual, old school farmers took on the capital cost of rebuilding, they never understood as a need from season to season.

Ned was virtually a hermit but a good guy who kept himself to himself. Scotty had seen him through rustling, fires and his wife's untimely death.

"Tell him I sent you and he will look after you. Very discreet guy, hardly talks."

It was easy to find as apart from the pub they passed in the middle of nowhere, nothing else. But fields and sheep were in the area, just his B&B sign and an arrow pointing down a dirt road.

"Ah do mi ducks," Ned nodded to them when they arrived. He was a small wiry guy with old farm clothes, a flat cap and what looked like an old hanky around his neck which was supposed to be a scarf. His face was reddish and lined which represented a hard life working outside all seasons on the farm. He was very happy to see customers arriving, means cash coming in.

The farmhouse needed a lot of work; however, they were presently surprised at the outbuilding containing the two B&B rooms. They were very clean, warm and with own toilet, bath and showers inside. Even a jacuzzi outside.

"Ave yer eat owt or nowt?"

"What did he say?" Liberty was puzzled at Derbyshire slang. Almost sounded like another language certainly not English.

"Do you want to eat?" McAllistar translated.

"Oh, do you have a menu?" Liberty asked.

"Pie, we just have pie. In fact, always have pie these days." Giving her a small smile as if she would be impressed.

"Let me see then. Mmmm I think we will have a pie then," she answered with a little sarcasm that went right over Ned's head as he seemed pleased at the answer.

"Yer reet pie," Ned was unfazed and answered like she had made a choice.
"Oh, you don't have a beer or a wine, do you?"
"Mmmm the devil's work alcohol."

The rooms all had bibles. Downstairs at the entrance, all kinds of religious signs like crosses and quotes from the bible replacing pictures, the only picture left was of his wife and kids outside a church that looked fifty years old.

Eager just shook his head at Liberty's naivety. This was a religious fanatic, she was chancing her arm with him.

They had hardly washed when Ned called them to supper. They sat in the front room of the farmhouse next to the kitchen. A big shepherd's pie, fresh peas and Yorkshire pudding arrived together with a devil's chardonnay bottle.

"What's that?" Liberty said, pointing at the puffed-up Yorkshire pudding.
"It is Yorkshire pudding." Ned replied.
"I thought this was Derbyshire and how come a pudding is served with the entre?"

"This is the main course," Logan told her, understanding that in the United States entre was used for the main course, "and the Yorkshire pudding is a national dish. You can have it as a starter, with your main course or add a bit of sugar and currents with custard as a sweat." Longest sentenced Logan had said for a while.

Eager just shook his head. Logan didn't want to drink, so they all tucked into the food and Liberty shared the wine with Eager.

"Mmmm this is good for Brit food." Liberty was impressed with the Yorkshire pudding and the pie and peas.

"Let's talk," Liberty was ready for business, time to do a deal.

"If you do not mind, I have had a long day, I guess week maybe even a year. I would like to turn in. Used to being in bed really early if you know what I mean?"

"With locked doors," Liberty added which was not well received.

"I tell you what, let me clear my head, we can talk and make a plan first thing in the morning. Who has what room?" McAllistar asked, not really wanting to share with Eager or anyone for that matter.

"We'll camp down together the room with the double bed," said Eager, sweeping his arms towards Liberty.

Ned was listening in the kitchen and was surprised that Eager and Liberty were taking one room together and McAllistar the other. He guessed it the other way around as Logan was far younger than the other guy.

*Be devils,* he thought.

"Oh aye, are you two an item then?"

"No, just know each other longer. We are not getting married after one blow job if that is what you mean?" Liberty asked innocently as if it was of no importance. Logan was lost for words and Ned was confused.

*What the devil is a blow job?*

"Good, then let's get to bed and start again in the morning," Eager added, a little too enthusiastic.

"Hold 'em cowboy, you on one side and me on the other. No touching!"

"Oh!" a little disappointed. He *should have not to worry,* he thought, *the danger and excitement of progress of the adventure could make her very friendly to him later in the night.* He slept in hope.

# Chapter Forty-One
## A Plan and Deal

Eager awoke but could not move. His right wrist was chained to the metal bed head with his own handcuffs. He struggled and struggled, but she had put the cuffs at the strongest point of the bed head. No chance of getting them over or pulling them out. Rattling the bed would get Ned coming and he would wonder what the hell was happening, they needed to at least stay another night.

Had they been caught up with? Was he a prisoner? The Russians? The Harkers? He started to imagine all kinds of scenarios and to top this, he would soon need to pee badly.

Logan was sitting in the jacuzzi. It was warm if you kept your body under the water. The cold autumn winds were sweeping down the alleyway between the farmhouse and the outbuildings. It was 6 am, no one around, quiet, peaceful, a chance in safety to think and plan. He tried to throw revenge off his mind as it clouded his thinking. Was Eager for real? This cocky little yank lady, could she help, could a newspaper be the answer. How does he find out where Karlien is if he gives away his trump cards? What about Aunt Bessie, will she make it?

He went down the road in his mind to Nick and how had their friendship deteriorated? Yes, he was happy about the job when he was demobbed. It seemed good at first. Good money, nice enough lifestyle compared to the army, easy work and in command of the troops. Was it the fact that, as he learned more about the Harkers and their various enterprises, he started to feel dirty? What about the kids vomiting with their drugs or completely in a coma? The dirty old men that hung around and what about the young boys being sneaked in. He had expressed his concerns and feeling, maybe too much, as Nick had changed to the devil reincarnate, he loved these businesses, the easy money, being feared across the country. Could he still appeal to Nick and put things right again? Well, back on some sought of a track? Maybe not.

"Hi, mind if I join you?" It was Liberty with a big towel around her. He didn't have time to answer. She dropped the towel and, in a G-string and bra, she jumped in opposite to him and sat down. She went under for warmth. He had seen some incredible bodies at the club but this was as good as any of them. She noticed him looking.

"This is all I have."

"Mmmm you know, I have been away for the best part of a year."

"I assume you are a gentleman, Mr McAllistar. I have come to do a deal nothing else."

"Where's John?"

John, that's better, not Eager, she noted.

"You might say he is tied up at present," she laughed, "I was not sure you trusted him. After all, he is a policeman, who could revert to form to save his job."

"I think he is in too deep. You might have to help drag us both out of this."

She pitched him on handing over what he had, duping the videos, which seemed to be the centre of all this. Working with her on the whole story. Big payment, safe house, solicitors and that the truth will set him free.

He talked about Karlien and how he could find out where she was if still alive. If not, who killed her. He told her about the video of her beating, described the American who seemed familiar to her.

The bottom line, after he went quiet for a while, was he would think about it.

Back in the room after she released Eager, he ran to the toilet and then came back and wrestled her on the bed and locking her up with his handcuffs. He turned his back and two arms took him from the neck behind him throwing him onto his back.

"How did you escape?"

"Look how thin my wrists are, smalls." Sure enough, he had not wound the cuffs too tight not to hurt her.

She climbed on top of him and said, "I guess you deserve this."

# Chapter Forty-Two
## The Crooked Spire

Folklore has many stories on how St. Mary's All Saints Anglian Church's spire got so crooked. One theory is that when the Devil flew over Derbyshire, he got tired and landed on St. Mary's Church spire in the middle of Chesterfield town. He slept with his tail wrapped around the spire and when rudely awoken by the ringing of the church bells, wrapped his tail tighter and gave an almighty twist creating a very crooked spire. Others including a blacksmith fixing the devil's hoof put a nail in his foot and the resultant pain made the devil twist the spire. The unkind version was that the devil saw that the bride in the church was a virgin and was so surprised that there was one in Derbyshire that he banged his tail against the spire. A landmark for miles around and visible reminder to all that the devil can do anything he wants, even bend a holy church spire. It is located in a very public place and with many tourists around the perfect place to meet McAllistar's own devil.

Nick was outside on a park bench in front of the church. His guys, all four of them including Sammy, the squirrel, Bruce, the muscle, Fred, the gunman and the newly arrived Dirk Ryder, were spread out as inconspicuous as possible. Sammy had a two-way radio to Nick and the others. Nick thought that McAllistar would be daft not to spot his guys. Still, he said that it would be a fair meeting and he could bring support as well. Both wanted to talk not fight and that was a good sign unless the questions get too difficult or the deal goes south.

Nick reflected on the past, his story, his questions, what he would say about Karlien, who planted drugs on McAllistar? Looks like he stole the drugs from them. How could he smooth this all over and get the tapes and drugs and his business back on track? Any kind of revenge can come after this. He needed the Russians off his back for the drugs that were stolen, the tapes to guarantee ongoing protection and McAllistar to go away for good.

Jimmy had wanted to handle this but McAllistar was his mistake, his to sort out. He needed to stay calm and not be bated by any threats. He wore blue jeans with brown cowboy style boots with steel toe caps, a denim shirt and flat cap. He had no weapons but his fists and his steel toe caps. A fight would be close, however, McAllistar had been in prison with time to muscle up and he had regular workouts but was growing soft with the good life. His gang would intervene if he was losing.

"Boss, I think he's here walking towards you." the radio fluttered.

Sure enough, McAllistar walked up with a newspaper in his hand as cool as anything and sat at the opposite side of the bench. Nick could see an unshaven face, beanie covering his head, old army combats and a very weary face. His blue eyes shone out like steel looking right into his own eyes. They sat and looked at each other up and down. Silent as both waiting on the first to speak.

"Thanks for meeting Me." was all that Nick could say. McAllistar grunted and said, "You called me, you start."

"I called you to understand a few things and see where we go from there. I have questions that need to be answered."

"So do I!" Nick started to get stronger in his tone. If McAllistar smelt fear and possible aggression the meeting would be all over.

"Okay, in no particular order. Why did you fit me up with drugs? What happened to Karlien? Where is she? Is she dead?"

"Mine is what happened to the Russian stuff that you received? Where are the videotapes you stole?"

"Mine first."

"Okay, we didn't fit you up with the drugs, not us. Karlien had a bad evening and beating from some American client and we sent her home to recover. Didn't want to see you or us ever again. Got her to see the doc and then when fit to travel, we sent her first-class home. Cost a fortune."

"And I'm supposed to believe you?"

"Yes. I want an end to this and I am sure you do. I admit there have been times when I wanted to kill you for the position you put us in. I really have no idea where the drugs they found in your flat came from, except it seems from our Russian delivery; same cocaine uncut from Afghanistan. So not us, it doesn't make sense, does it, why would we want you in prison out of the way? Our modus operandi is to deal with it ourselves. That's how we would recover everything. They found the stuff in a jam jar in your flat, three thousand quid high street value, so either you were going to sell or use it, but where is the rest?"

"What do you mean?"

"Think about it hard, Logan. You received the drugs. Only four of us can access our office where you said you put the parcel. You were found in possession of some of it. We needed you on the outside to recover the goods?"

"You tried hard enough inside!"

"Well, we got desperate. The Russkies want the cash for the drugs. We needed those tapes back, so we hired a few guys to see if they could get some information out of you."

"They didn't ask nicely."

There was silence for a few moments. Nick looked down at the floor and McAllistar kept scanning the area to be sure the two heavies he spotted were not moving in.

"Sorry about that," although he made a nervous laugh, "if it makes you feel better, we had to pay extra for the damage you did to three of them."

McAllistar didn't look impressed, just a hard stare behind which his mind was racing.

"You guys are rolling in cash. Just pay them and sought out who took them later."

"That stash had a street value of ten million pounds. We don't have that type of money sitting around for Pinky and Perky. It looks like you took the drugs and sold them and just kept a bit for yourself."

"Pinky and Perky? Nick you know I have never taken drugs in my life. Hate the stuff. Hated it in the club but put up with it as where else would I get a job and pay you gave me."

"Everyone has their price huh? It looked bad although who would give the Sweeney Todd the information for a search warrant, it bothers me."

"I didn't take the drugs. Those Russians walked in with a big brown paper parcel for you and Jimmy. If Karlien was here, she'd tell you I went straight upstairs to your office and put it on your desk. If I'd known it was hard drugs, then I would have hidden the parcel. I mean who would walk into the club with a heap of drugs in a brown paper parcel? It is downright, stupid. In fact, contact Karlien, she will tell you. So, whoever took the parcel and planted the stuff tipped off the coppers."

Nick thought about it. He had known McAllistar for a long time and what he was saying did hit his logic bank. If it wasn't him then who?

"There are only three keys to our office and you have the master key."

"So, you Jimmy and Tazewell have access."

"So, are you suggesting that Tazewell did it? He is an integral part of the team and at risk also if we do not anti-up to the Russians. The videos?"

"Yes, I have them stored away my insurance policy. I watched a few, what kinda shit are you guys into?"

"Sick right? How do you think we have so much protection from the authorities? We were almost closed down years ago with your mate, Eager, making our operations his target. He was driven to destroy us, probably his way to get a decent promotion."

"He's not my mate! You guys dabble in this and that, however, I never even guessed that you would get up this type of sick activities."

"You watched them all? Why did you take them?"

"They were enough to make me vomit. I was trying to find the beating video of Karlien that Billy the neck told me about. Ask him and he will tell you. He let it slip to me."

"That would be hard."

Another silence both staring around.

"Aunt Bessie, why did you guys hurt her. I could kill you just for that!"

"Aunt Bessie, oh the farm lady. No, not us, not my style, Sammy saw the two big Russian mafia guys leave the cottage."

"Russians?"

"Looking for their drugs and tapes. We had to buy time and tell them about the American politician and they told the KGB too quickly. I can only guess they owe the KGB for the drugs and protection. So, trying to beat us to it, I guess. But definitely not on our orders."

*It didn't hurt to get McAllistar on their backs, might even help,* Nick thought.
Another uncomfortable silence.

"So, where do we go from here?" Nick broke the silence. He was not sure they could beat it out of him, although Dirk Ryder had ways. Would he cooperate, strike a deal? This was not the place nor time to pick him up, too public. Sammy, the squirrel, could follow him.

McAllistar's forehead was covered with creases like he was thinking too hard.

"You can find out from Karlien that I didn't take the drugs."

# Chapter Forty-Three
## Dirk Ryder

Dirk watched from inside as he had climbed to the windows just below the church spire. You could see for miles around, however, his focus was on the men sitting on the bench below. No sign of an argument, they looked from a distance like strangers just saying hello. Nick did look a little wary and restless. He could read body language; one of the skills he had been taught. Nick definitely looked nervous.

*Brit gangsters, more like little old ladies,* he thought. *Not like the apartheid era at home. Now that was real tough stuff. Real Afrikaner men. No wonder we gave the Brit Empire's army such a hard time in the Boer War.*

He was a big powerful man, could have been a prop for Springboks rugby team. Tall, six foot six and at least 250 pounds – all muscle. Easy to spot in a crowd and a daunting site.

Dirk had been working for Apartheid Government. He was an integral part of a secret group known as the 'death squad' or C10, later to become C1. He preferred working on his own for the real dirty work as you never knew how this all would end and who would talk. The government paid well and in US dollars outside the country.

His speciality was torture, getting people to talk. He liked the real tough guys, *ANC terrorists my foot,* he would think. They all talked in the end or died, either way, it didn't make any difference to him. The Afrikaner god was on the side of the chosen people, not the blacks, who wanted to ruin his country that they had built. The only first world country in Africa, what he did was totally justified in his mind.

Now McAllistar. He couldn't wait to get his hands on him. He would cry like a baby and give everything up. He watched what looked like a priest in a smock, who came up to McAllistar and they walked together inside the church. Nick got on the radio. His instructions were very clear. Sammy only to follow McAllistar when he came out, no one else. He thought that he could hear running from the other side of the church and called it in before moving to the windows on the other side of the spire. He saw McAllistar running fast across the road to the car park.

McAllistar had asked the vicar, pre the meeting with Nick, to come out in fifteen minutes and ask him to come in for the confession he had asked for. The vicar was taken aback when he forced the twenty pounds in his hands and ran through the back door of the church to station road and jumped in a car in the car park opposite to the church and it took off at high speed.

*Maybe tomorrow*, Dirk thought.

# Chapter Forty-Four
## Jimmy

"They what?"

"Cut one of his fingers virtually off, the ring finger."

"Who the fuck did this?" Nick shouted.

"Some Americans trying to find the videos or McAllistar or both," Tazewell said unemotionally.

"I'm coming back now. Is he okay? Where is he?"

"With our private doctor, shocked but okay."

When Nick got back to London by train, Jimmy was home in bed. He looked pale and shaken, not his usual cool, calm self. He had a big bandage over his ring finger on his left hand. He told his story.

Three big Americans had come into the club saying they wanted to offer him a deal. The barman had shown them up to the office.

"So, gentlemen what deal do you have for me?" mistaking them for some US mafia types. There was just one security guard downstairs missing in action, the rest of the gang were all out searching for information or with Nick.

"This, my friend, is our offer. You tell us where McAllistar and the video of our client are or we cut your fingers off one by one until you do."

"I see no airs and graces, straight to the point, I like that," He tried his cool unruffled composure.

"I like the stiff upper lip bit smart ass."

Two of them grabbed him immediately and the big guy severed his ring finger with what looked like a large hunting knife.

"Shit," he screamed, "No foreplay then?" At least they laughed.

"Second one then, I think a thumb this time or would you like a big toe off? Hard to peddle your bike then, no balance, understand?"

"No need, I will tell you what I know." He did but it didn't seem to satisfy them, so he thought he was in for more pain.

"Okay, Mr Smart guy. If you have told us a lie, be prepared to walk and eat funny the rest of your life. You call this number with any further information or when you recover our video and our man."

"To walk like what?"

"I need you to understand, we'll be back if we do not get what we want and be sure we always complete our mission. Understand?"

He told them that Nick was meeting McAllistar in Chesterfield right now and was going to get the tapes back and they could have their client's video, no problem at all.

He also mentioned DI Eager and the reporter to add a little more confusion and offer other sacrifices. They also asked about Karlien and were told she was back in South Africa recovering. He didn't know where exactly.

"They seemed to think that she had been taken care of. I mean they were surprised that we thought she was alive."

"Who the fuck was their client?"

"I think the guy Tazewell set her up with. The guy that beat her, stupid. Some Yankee big wig politician."

"And they are cleaning up," Nick made the statement they both knew. "Could anyone who has seen the video also be a target?"

"They'll be after you next and Nick, they are all well-armed for sure."

"The finger?"

"Severed, bloody sore, but the doctor says it should be okay. Told me to go to the hospital to be certain not his office. I told him he better be certain. I think he got the message. Get the boys back here and Dirk. Ensure they have some toys of their own. These bastards are going to pay."

Nick then told him what happened with McAllistar.

"Did you believe him?"

"I think he could be telling the truth, so we may have another problem inside."

Jimmy pondered on what he had been told. Sometimes in between moaning a little at the pain of his severed finger.

"You lost him?"

"He said he would be in contact, needed time to think. I told him we do not have time. He said we needed to find the person who took the drugs and he will as well. Seems genuinely bitter guy now, lost a year of his life. He had set up an escape route, typical NI stuff with the priest. Luckily, Sammy was around the back and he and Bruce jumped into our car and followed. Can you believe they parked next to our guys?"

"I can believe anything now. Look we need to check out Tazewell. He could he have taken the drugs and blamed it on McAllistar? Call our man at the yard and see what he can do, also a bit of bloody protection from crazy yanks roaming around with guns would help earn his keep. Could anyone else here have done it? We need to find Karlien quickly; she is our trump card to get McAllistar to hand over the tapes. If the yanks get them all, we could lose everything. Who arranged her trip home?"

"Tazewell."

# Chapter Forty-Five
## The Report

"Where in heavens name are you? Why have you not called in? GWP is saying you are breaking the deal, ringing the chairman, awful having to cover for you every day," Gavin was mad and frustrated.

"I have some good news and bad news, what do you want first," Liberty said coolly.

"Fucking good news, of course. Tell me you have McAllistar."

"Sitting right across from me drinking tea."

"What? Are you joking 'cos if you are…"

"Now, now cowboy, calm down. Not joking, promised we would use our considerable resources to help him."

"Can you talk without him present? So, what is the bad news?"

"Not at the moment. Gavin, you can't tell anyone, anyone, at all. Understand? Gavin, we will lose him if you do. This is a big deal please do not talk about this it is crucial."

"You mean not even GWP or the chairman? Are you on a train?" He could hear a train rattling by in the background.

"No, but almost. Trust no one, this is dynamite stuff and as you said, very dangerous. Just understand this is bigger than Ben-Hur and anyone we know could be implicated or know someone who is. Get it?"

The station public phone was held close to her ear and McAllistar sat in a wheelchair covered with blankets with his Beanie over his head and half his face. His kitbag under the blanket held close. Liberty was wearing an old duffle coat which she had got from the farmer. It was dirty and smelled of cows and dogs. It covered her completely, from top of her head with the hood and right down to her ankles. She had never felt so dirty and badly dressed. She would stand out too much with her normal attire. Her overnight bag had gone with Eager, all she had was a purse and some lipstick on her.

*I can't wait to have a shower and get out of this garbage.*

Eager was driving back as they were probably looking for his car. Sure enough, Sammy and Bruce were following.

She could almost hear Gavin's heavy breathing like he was having an orgasm or his lips were being licked heavily with his tongue wetting them and smacking them together. This was his life and maybe the biggest story ever as every journalist prayed for.

"Tell me, tell me for Christ's sake!"

"We are coming near you. Need to tell you somewhere private. No, don't say where who knows who is listening in."

"Okay, Miss paranoid, I'll play your game."

"Meet near where the top man sat down after being at Barney's."

"Bloody crosswords, I hate crosswords, particularly cryptic ones," He thought for a while.

"Got it! What time?"

"Three hours before he sat down about."

# Chapter Forty-Six
## Meeting of the Chiefs

"So, Bill I had a visit from Charlie regarding," he thought about it, "well, a complaint, really. In short, he says something smells in the kingdom of Denmark."

The ACC Cartwright was seated in front of the chief's big desk, fiddling with his pen, changing it from finger to finger on one hand. This was below the desk, so the chief could not see.

*Quoting Shakespeare does not make him look smart. Where is this going?*

He lifted his big eyebrows and stared with his electric blue eyes.

"Something what? If he had a complaint, he could have come to see me, line of command and all that," He was indignant.

"He said he did and was told it was a need to know, even though one of his direct reports seems to know?"

"Oh, DCI Samuels. Well, it is a delicate situation and we were sworn to secrecy by MI5. Samuels was approached to provide intel on the McAllistar guy."

"McAllistar?"

"In my last weekly report, Sir Michael, just out of prison, worked for the Harkers, seems they must have fallen out. Anyway, it is thought that he may have something the CIA wants. They have leaned on MI5 and they have solicited our help."

"Need to know even for me?"

"I alluded to it in my report." It was obvious that the chief had been too busy hobnobbing at Downing Street to have read the report. That was good for the ACC.

"Alluded?"

"Well, at the time we knew very little still, so it was sketchy, to say the least."

"And now?"

"Well, it is confusing. Some videos were taken from the Harkers club which seems to be of interest to our American friends. McAllistar may have murdered the club video guy. Well, it seems to point that way. My best guess is someone of high value is on those tapes and they want the video recovered before it is made public."

"High value?"

"Just guessing, maybe a senior Russian they can turn or could be a high-ranking US politician or something like that."

The chief was not amused and made it obvious with a sideways nod of his head and a furrowed brow. He leaned forward.

"I am not happy ACC, not happy at all. This has all the makings of a PR disaster plus I should have been contacted by the chief of MI5 first. I will speak to the minister and have him hauled over the coals. As for you, I am disappointed. You know how many pieces of paper across my desk a day? How many calls on my time by everyone in any kind of authority? This was worth a visit and personal brief!"

"Yes, sir, sorry. I thought I could handle it and not bother you too much as I appreciate how valuable your time is. I was wrong. I will book an update every day and call you if anything breaks." Head slightly down, looking at the desk, playing the scolded employee, who has realised the error of his ways.

"What about the phone tapping of one of our own? Him being tortured and us standing by."

"MI5 did the bugging, the Russians were torturing him."

"The Russians?"

# Chapter Forty-Seven
## Blue Lights

*Oh no*. The blue lights came up behind him. The police car wanted him to pull over. Eager was on the M1, just outside London. The journey had been boring as he had got used to his sidekick; she was a company he had missed, a pretty interesting girl and a bit of fun. In fact, his boring life had been turned upside down since he met her, even if his career was in the toilet. He pulled over, one of the officers strolled over to his car.

"Can I help you, officer? I do not think I was speeding."

"Inspector Eager, I have been asked to escort you to HQ."

"Well, it's not convenient at the moment."

"I was told to escort you and or bring you in, sir."

"Are you serious, you been told to arrest me?"

"Not in so many words, sir, just if spotted, don't come in without him whatever it takes. Strange I know but ours is not to reason why. I can drive you as it is a blue light job apparently and my colleague can drive your car." He looked at the old car like he was glad he was not the one to drive it.

"On who's orders?"

"Your gaffer, I think Chief Superintendent Allcock."

The lights and siren were switched off a few miles from their destination. The constable was a good driver and tried to make light conversation. Eager was deep in thought, *what now? What do they know?* He had to prepare himself as this could be the end of his career, maybe even a charge. He was not sure. The car slipped around into the staff car park at the back. DS Williams was there waiting, she was anxious and seemed to be dancing as she moved from foot to foot.

He got out and waved to her.

"I'll have your keys delivered, sir." He thanked him. Williams was shaking her head as she approached.

"John, John what have you done?"

"Me?" Looking innocent.

"Yes you, sir, they seem to be very upset. Chief's gone red in the face again and seems arms flapping to be flying around the ceiling!"

"Well, he's ruined my vacation!"

"John, come on in the back fire stairs, let's get up there before he has a heart attack."

"Mmm, I'm not so lucky. Ha."

"You're the cool one." She was walking fast and he was hobbling a bit today trying to keep up with her.

He walked into the chief super's office. Charlie immediately got up with the surprising speed and closed the office door.

"DS stay, John, sit down." He was in a clear and commanding mood today.

Just then the door opened and DCI Samuels came in.

"Not now." Charlie blurted out, "Not now!"

"But sir, he has knowledge on the case I am working on. He has been helping a criminal."

"Out," Charlie pointed, "Get out!" Samuels left in a hurry. Charlie did look like he was about to have a heart attack. Red in the face and sweating. He sat down, took several deep breaths. Surprisingly, his next words were, "Coffee?"

It was good coffee in the chief's office, so they both said, "Thanks," at the same time. He got up and said nothing just poured the coffee with the usual questions milk and sugar? He then sat down with his.

"John, have you got something to tell me?"

"Well, I was having a good vacation until I was brought in." DS Williams almost spat her coffee out as she tried not to laugh.

*This is not the John Eager I know. He seems not to care. Lighter. He will make Charlie explode if he plays too many games.*

"John, look me in the eyes and don't be a smart alec, I am not in the mood."

"I am not sure what you want me to say, sir?"

"John," his voice beginning to lift, "Don't fuck with me," turning to Williams, "Sorry sergeant. John, I am trying to help you here. Out with what you know."

"I am at a loss, please tell me what you think I know?" and then added, "Sir."

"Okay, let's talk about mixing with a criminal and breaking his parole."

"Who?"

"McAllistar, we have it on good authority that you have been with him. All that you didn't know where he was giving us all the run around. You're a policeman for God's sake and part of our team."

"I was not part of the team since the last time we met. I was thrown out after twenty-five bloody years of service and as for McAllistar, who said I had seen him?"

"Samuels got a tip-off."

*Samuels and the Harkers getting me out the way.*

"Ever thought who tipped him off? Even if I did, I am on vacation and not on duty. I am not a parole officer, let them find him."

"Well, try mixing with a person wanted for possible murder!"

"A murderer, Logan?"

"They say he might have killed the video guy at the Harker's club."

Charlie realised that Samuels was on the way to find the ACC and he would have a call soon asking him to handover Eager to Samuels.

He stood up grabbed his coat and told them to follow him. He walked briskly for his size, a man on a mission. He had given Eager something to think about. Out on the street, down a few alleyways, left then right then left then right. Eager was wondering where Charlie was going and for that matter where his life was going. He finally stopped at a small coffee shop in a back street. He walked into a cosy little room, four small square tables with red plastic table cloths, moving between them and nodding to the big lady behind the coffee machine. He continued through a small kitchen to a room at the back. One big kitchen table and four chairs.

"Sit down," he ordered. "VIP room for special guests, we will not be interrupted here."

They all sat down. Charlie sat opposite Eager and DS Williams sat to the left of the super. Eager felt like he was being interviewed. In came the big lady with three cups of coffee and a big meat pie.

"This is Sally, my big secret," Charlie actually gave a small chortling laugh and she tapped him on the shoulder. When she left, he said, "Put her away twenty years ago. Not a bad sort really, just got in with the wrong man, been here now a long time. Best pies in town and always has some information for me."

It was not a pretty sight watching Charlie tuck into the pie, but they waited for him to finish. He seemed to have calmed down and the redness on his face had subsided.

*Bet Doris doesn't know this is where he puts on his weight. Unfaithful with meat pies.* Eager laughed inside his head.

"Now come on, out with it all. I'm on your side John and I cannot help you or anyone until I know exactly what is going on."

Eager was thinking fast, weighing up the pros and cons. How much should he tell him? Did McAllistar kill someone?

"Come on, John. The super is straight and on your side. Don't throw everything away for that American floozy," Williams spoke up.

"Floozy?" *Was she jealous?*

"You know what I mean. You like a teenager around her from what I saw."

"I was in shock, been hanging upside down for too long!" As he spoke, he realised he was being too defensive. Anyway, Liberty was a small fling in his otherwise miserable life. She was too young and would move on once she had the big story out and he would go back to being a middle-aged loser. She was using him, however, that was fair enough as he was enjoying it all, so he was using her as well. Fair is fair.

"John, I've been doing this longer than the two of you. I can smell when things are not right, not right at all even in the force. So, off the record tell us what you know?"

Eager's head went from side to side as he did his final deliberations in his head.

Finally, as he drained his coffee cup.

*Off the record, he was joking for sure.*

"Okay, I will tell you what I know."

The big lady came in and filled their coffee cups singing *'Anything Goes'* before he started.

*Right,* Eager thought, *it is not over until the fat lady sings.*

# Chapter Forty-Eight
## Gavin

They had kept the disguise and the clumsy ancient wheelchair that used to belong to Ned's wife. She walked and pushed after the taxi ride from the station, which she stopped four blocks from Gavin's flat ensuring the taxi driver didn't know where they were going. Pays to be cautious.

*Was he sleeping? Having a good time and he is dam heavy. Whose idea was this? Oh, mine, of course,* she mused as she struggled along the pavement.

The flat block was old and the front door never worked. Gavin was not a high flyer with material possessions nor the lifestyle where he lived. He didn't spend much time there was his lifestyle choice, so why waste money on a fancy flat?

As soon as they got inside, she said, "Rides over, cowboy." McAllistar grunted and jumped up dumping the chair and the blankets to one side of the entrance lobby. Liberty threw her duffle coat on top and made a 'yuck' kind of sound. Rubbing her clothes up and down to get all the filth from inside the coat off her. McAllistar watched in amazement at the frenetic hand movements.

Gavin lived on the fourth floor, his penthouse he used to joke. Liberty saw that the front door was ajar, obviously, he was expecting them. She knocked several times and then she pushed hard and the door swung open.

"No!" Gavin shouted in fear. He was laying half on the couch and half off. He seemed in agony.

"Oh, it's you," Relieved, "Check the street, see if they are still around. If they are, we are all in trouble!"

"Who, what, why?" Liberty wanted to know. Meanwhile, McAllistar went straight to the window after locking and bolting the door first. He knew danger didn't wait for questions. This guy was obviously stressed and very scared of some people out there.

"The fucking Yankees, that's who!"

"You are not making sense." She went to him to check what was wrong.

"They were going to cut my fingers off one by one if I didn't tell them where you are."

She checked him out. Badly beaten, worked on his stomach the way he was holding it. He had a few bruises on his face, no blood.

"Gavin, Logan McAllistar," introducing them and they nodded at each one, "What did you say? Out with it."

"Just that you were both in Derbyshire in a B&B and coming back in a few days."

*Good, the big story was more important than his fear.*
"Did they buy it?"

"They were coming back and I had to find out exactly where you were pronto. Or I would be called stumpy for the rest of my life!"

"Who were they?"

"How would I know? Big guys like an army or navy seals. They were really going to cut my fingers off, how the hell would I type then? What are we into?"

*That would be the least of your worries,* McAllistar thought.

It was quiet. They both looked at McAllistar. He opened a pack of cigarettes and offered them both one. They all needed some nicotine and lit up. Gavin was still very shaken, so Liberty had to hold his cigarette in her mouth and light it for him.

McAllistar took a long drag and blew out the smoke.

"I can take a guess. Some big shot US politician is on tape beating the hell out of my Karlien. Not sure who he is, Nick Harker told me he was a big shot."

"And they have come to retrieve the tape and cover it all up." Gavin added.

"By covering it all up that might be cleaning up anyone who has seen the tape and Karlien as well," Liberty added.

McAllistar visibly jerked at the mention of her name and he thought they may have already cleaned that part of the mess up.

"So, the police is after you, the gangsters, some lunatic Americans, anyone else?" Gavin was not expecting anyone else.

"It's a cluster, fuck, I know. Oh, and some Russians are involved." McAllistar added.

"Tell me what you have got that is so interesting to just about everybody?"

"Not yet. We need to get out of here pronto. It is no longer safe. Where to go?" Liberty said with a real sense of urgency.

# Chapter Forty-Nine
## Olga

"Priduroks!" They sat in front of her desk hands on knees like school children in the headmaster's office. They were in the back office of a so-called 'commercial attaché' in the Russian embassy. Olga had flown in and was in a foul mood.

"You have not got the money for the drugs, you have told us that you can get compromising tapes of a big American politician, you do nothing, get nothing, you beat up old ladies. You are both an embarrassment to the mother Russia."

Olga was a colonel in the KGB, a woman not to be messed with. Her arm muscles bulged out of her jacket and the thigh muscles were stretching her skirt. Her dark hair was cut short in a basin style. If it wasn't for big breasts, she could be mistaken for a man.

She grabbed Roman around the neck with one hand and lifted him into the air as far as he could stand on his toes. He was coughing, choking and spluttering. She dropped him back into his seat. His face was beet red; he was visibly shaken.

"Old lady beat him up too," Leon offered.

"Shut up, imbecile! Now, this is what you do. You get this Tazewell guy and bring him to me."

Roman and Leon looked at each other.

"Now!" she commanded.

"Okay Colonel, we bring him here quick smart." Roman could speak again.

"Not here at one of our safe houses. Somewhere quiet where I can talk to him."

"What if he doesn't want to come, Colonel?"

She turned and knocked Leon off his chair. He rolled over and hit the wall with a thud.

"That is your answer."

They both nodded enthusiastically.

# Chapter Fifty
## Meetings – Bloody Meetings

"You let him go!" the ACC sounded totally disgusted.

"Yes, no reason to hold him." Charlie said calmly.

"Sir," the ACC turned to the chief, "DI Eager is of high interest to our investigation, he has been consorting with a possible murderer, a man who broke his parole, a drug dealer for God's sake."

"He is working this case with me now and has access to some very valuable information. He is a career officer, a great career I may add and he knows what he is doing. Not flapping around on 'tip-offs'," Charlie Allcock said firmly.

"What do you mean by that?" The ACC was angry.

"Need to know," Charlie touched his nose.

"Need to know. I am your boss," turning to the chief, "This is gross insubordination. I request that Mr Allcock be relieved of his duties immediately and tell me all he knows or lose his pension when I prosecute him."

The chief stood up, he had enough.

"Stop this right now both of you. Charlie, tell me what is going on." The chief and Charlie go way back to Police College.

"I'd rather do that in private, sir."

"In bloody private! I am your superior and one of the highest-ranking officers on this force. In bloody private indeed." The ACC was going red in the face.

Charlie had planned to be calm.

"Why? The ACC is right, he should know what is going on."

"Well sir, he is close to DCI Samuels, too close and I think Samuels is dirty. Also, the information I have is the videos do contain a lot of paedophiles, pervert or both. Maybe even a ring of them at high levels."

The ACC coughed.

"DCI Samuels dirty! How can you say that? Blacken a great officer's name so that you can play games. You know Eager is jealous, so if that's your source, a bitter officer passed over by a high performing younger one. Are you accusing me as well?"

"No sir, definitely not," Charlie emphasising sir, "I have promised Eager some space and time to get back to me with the evidence. Then we can all look at it together. I just need some time to work out fact from fiction. Eager trusts me and DS Williams, he will not work with anyone connected to DCI Samuels. If I break my word, we have less chance of pulling this off."

"We could throw him out of the force if he doesn't co-operate with the investigating officer and that is Samuels." The ACC seemed desperate not to be cut out of what Eager had. The chief noticed and was silent for a couple of minutes, deliberating what to do in his head.

"I think he believes he is out already, so nothing you threaten would change his mind." Charlie cut in as he knew the chief was doing his thinking pre his decision. This was his way, even so, Charlie had planned not to give anything else away regardless of his determination.

"How much time?" the chief asked quietly.

"A week should do it. He needs to find McAllistar again."

"Don't you mean McAllistar and the reporter girl?" The ACC smiled as this would put the chief over the top. Bad press equals to no lordship.

"They all split up according to Eager."

"Well, then why would there be three bags and lots of clothing in the boot of his car?"

"You searched his car?"

"Yes, Samuels did. So, what do you say now?"

"Stop! I will give you five days without interference from anyone," the commissioner said looking at the ACC. "Charlie, you must get these videos before they go public. Vital Eager understands that this will compromise the met if the media gets them first. We cannot have trial by media and God only knows what they have got. Bring him and McAllistar in and let's sort all this out before it becomes a bigger mess. It also could be a big case for us to bust along with the Harkers, who may have allowed this on their premises."

The ACC coughed again.

"Samuels, to my office, now!" the ACC commanded.

*What now, he sounds very mad. Samuels, indeed what happened to my first name or rank?*

Samuels was updated on the meeting with DCS Allcock and the chief.

"He's given him free rein. That is very dangerous, sir."

"I told DCS Allcock that he could have Eager's broken-down car back if it helps him get around and meet up again with the other two reprobates."

"Good sir, I have put a tracer in the car and one in McAllistar back pack."

"Concealed well, I trust?"

"Yes sir, might find one, very lucky if they find two."

"We have to do this subtly but the hard way, I mean the very hard way. We cannot play softly. Also, the Harkers better assist in sorting this out. Get your hands dirty if you have to get my drift?"

# Chapter Fifty-One
## Gavin

"Thanks for coming, Sir Richard. Can I get you anything?" GWP gestured to the immaculate Chesterfield armchair. Sir Richard sat down.

"Mmmm sun is over the yardarm, I guess. A claret would be nice." He sat down on the edge of the chair. He felt he had been summoned by this upstart.

One of the staff rushed across and the order was made.

"I thought it would be better we meet here, Sir Richard as it is private and I have this gout thing in my legs. So, I appreciate you making it easy for me."

Sir Richard looked around uneasy. *Not a patch on my club, old fashioned and worn out,* he thought.

Looking at his watch, Sir Richard was impatient and said, "I only have thirty minutes, so can you get to the point of the meeting quickly?"

"I have two major points." Holding two fingers up, "The deal I did with this American girl is she would keep me informed of her progress, so I could advise and so forth. Gavin has made no effort to answer my calls and complaints about her. She is a wild card operating, I guess on her own and God only knows what she is up to! Two, there is a rumour around this club that some compromising videos are at the centre of all this and some members are uncomfortable."

"Why?"

"I can only guess that they know it is connected to the Harkers club and some, I dare to say, may have visited the place."

"You mean they have been naughty and want us to squash anything connected with them?"

"Well put, Sir Richard."

"Who approached you?"

"I cannot say as it was the manager here who mentioned this on my oath to not try to find the names or ask him."

"So, how would we know if they are on the tapes? By the way, this is the first I know about tapes." Sir Richard was now indignant as well as impatient.

"See, this is the way Gavin operates even the chairman is cut out of the loop." Trying to work Sir Richard up, which was easy as he had already been to a long lunch and his nose was turning red.

Sir Richard stood up, swallowed the last drop of the claret and stared down at GWP.

"I will talk to Gavin and have a 'come to Jesus' meeting with him and the girl if we can find her. As to interfering with the freedom of the press for unknown people for unknown deeds, I am not sure that I can do that." He was firm and now putting his foot down.

"I was told that the person or persons unknown would be willing to put considerable advertising in your way. I mean considerable."

Sir Richard's eyes lifted to the roof, he thought for a few seconds and said, "How considerable? I need to know?"

The Americans were sitting outside a coffee shop in Soho. Heads down, huddled together, busy discussing their next moves. A big shadow came over them. They were big guys, but this man was a mountain right in front of them. They all reached inside their raincoats,

"I wouldn't do that if I were you." Dirk Ryder wagged his finger. "I have shooters watching you and if needed, I will kill you with my bare hands if I see a weapon."

He lied about the shooters but not about his physical capabilities. He pulled up the fourth chair, turned it around with the back facing the Americans.

"I come in peace and this is London, more CCTV cameras than any city in the world, IRA and all that. So, no need to become high profile."

"What do you want?" Gary asked irritated at not picking up this big guy's approach. All his life, he prided himself on his awareness that kept him alive. How come all three didn't notice this giant coming on them?

"First of all, my boss sends his greetings and thanks to you for not severing his finger right off."

"Your boss?" Sam asked.

"How many fingers have you cut lately?" Dirk thought that they were being awkward.

"A few." Sam butted in.

"Mr Harker and you picked the wrong guy to mess with on his turf."

They all looked around as if bored but mainly looking to see if he did have shooters around.

"You have a point?" Sam was gaining confidence, now he was sure this guy was on his own.

"It seems you are after the same thing that we are. So, we offering you a deal. We can work together and pool resources and information. When we resolve this, you get the video you want and we get what we want."

"Why would we?"

"'Cos, for one thing, this is Mr Harker's turf and we know our way around. He has many informants plus the police in his pocket. What have you got?"

*A few terrified people who could cough up information and a useless it seems MI5 agent. In fact, they were lost with a poor plan of revisiting this paper guy* Sam thought.

"Okay, it works for us. Tell us what you know and we will tell you about our adventures in the cold and damp God-forsaken country," Sam was being the ugly American.

They exchanged what information they had and agreed to touch base daily. Dirk told them that when they got the whereabouts of McAllistar or the tapes, they would be the first to know and their talents would possibly be needed.

"So, Mr Harker has no hard feelings?"

"He always puts business first and does not want to make any enemies if he doesn't have to."

*He is keeping his enemies close and will get revenge when this is over. If he doesn't, he will lose lots of street cred,* Dirk thought, looking forward to making these guys pay when the time is right.

"Smart man."

*Not smart enough, he will lose more than a finger when we have recovered the goods,* Sam mused.

# Chapter Fifty-Two
## Javelin's Bad Day

He didn't like it at all. Meeting the Russians in a deserted terraced house in Islington. Leon welcomed him at the back door and took him into the back room. It was empty except for one chair and a hanging light bulb over it. The walls were dirty and bare. Yes, he didn't like it at all. He was even more concerned when not only did Roman and Leon come in but this big woman. At first, he thought it was a man.

"Zdrah stvey," the woman uttered in a gruff voice.

"She is our boss, say hello," Leon offered and got a scowl from her for his trouble.

"Howdy." Tazewell tried to cover up his nervousness.

"Sit." She pointed at the single chair. It was an order to be obeyed.

"What is this all about? I am a friend; I should not be treated this way like a dog."

"I do not treat you like a dog unless you do not tell me the truth and then you would wish you were one." Olga stood over him.

"Woof," said Roman to add effect. She was not impressed.

"Out both of you. Make some tea," she ordered.

She sat on him facing and straddled her legs on each side of his. Her sheer weight was hurting him and particularly his bad hip. Her skirt pulled up around her waist, not a pretty sight. Her nose almost touched his nose. She smelt of cheap perfume, a musty smell, definitely not Chanel number 5. His mind was working quickly, he had never been treated like this before in his life, always had a chance to talk his way out of problems. He tried to move but her weight was too much and she flexed her big thighs creating real pain. He knew he was in trouble.

"You sit still or I break you in half, no problem to me. You will not walk again."

She had his attention. Her breath was bad and blowing right in his mouth as he tried to appeal to her. Her teeth were yellow and crooked. He had a monster on top of him.

"I do not know what I have done? I have been a friend to Russia and I am treated like this!" Tazewell was desperate.

"Friend that takes our drugs and loses them and not pay for them. Promises to help us with information on big American politician and give us nothing. Friend, no you are not a comrade."

"Tea?" Leon entered and when she looked at him in disgust, he quickly ran back out.

She got off him. He was visibly relieved and tried to catch his breath.

"Okay, we do not play games any more. I have my comrade's story and need to check it with you. I think if you tell lies." She went behind him and put her arm all around his neck and then pumped her arm muscles. He went red and started choking and then not breathing. She counted to five and let go.

"See, I will break your neck if I hear one lie, just one lie."

She questioned him for thirty minutes. She knew Leon and Roman were listening at the door. He told her nearly everything he knew from the drugs going missing to the big American politician who he named to much more on the videotapes, more people to turn or blackmail and a goldmine for the KGB. She listened carefully and wanted to know how they could find the tapes.

"The Harkers have contacts in the police and everywhere else, while I am sitting here, they could be finding McAllistar and I will not know a thing. I need to get back as soon as possible to see what is happening."

"I need to talk with the Harkers."

"Okay, okay, I will arrange it," Tazewell said to appease her and he saw his chance to get away and buy some time.

"Okay, dasvidaniya." She walked away as if they had had a friendly meeting and the interview was over.

"She says until the next meeting," Leon offered when he walked in the room.
*I can't wait.*

When he got back to the club, the security guard waved him across.

"The bosses want to meet you in the dungeon right now. I'm to tell them when you arrive."

Tazewell got a feeling his day was about to turn worse.

# Chapter Fifty-Three
## The Next Step

When Eager got to his house, he drove around the area a few times. Looked for suspicious parked cars. *I'm getting paranoid, no one knows I am back.*

Although he rationalised that the police did and that meant Samuels would know and who else would he tell if his theory on him was correct? No, better grab a change of clothes quickly and find Liberty and Logan. The note on the door said:

'The dragon's husband wants to meet you.'

They said they would let him know where they were somehow. That was easy to work out. He slapped the clean clothes in a plastic shopping bag and when he was outside, he looked at his car. Should he go by car? He had already been picked up once. No, he would walk and grab a taxi once he knew where he was going.

"Ah, James Bond, welcome back! Nice to see you back, lad," George nodded at Eager to go into the backroom behind the bar area. He followed with two pints of an old speckled hen.

"Been busy here, lots of people asking about you. You are very popular, I'm jealous."

"Like who?"

"A DCI comes by regular, local Bobby comes in and orders a pint and digs around about you and then the hoodlums. Enticements and threats. Not interested I say and I have not seen you for ages."

"Good, thanks."

Just then the dragon walks in, looks at them, gives Eager a 'I know what you are, a baby snatcher' stare, turns and walks out.

"Here, this was left for you." George produces a small piece of folded paper with several staples holding it closed.

The note just had an address: '221 Notron Street, Greenwich'.

"Ever heard of a Notron Street, Greenwich, George?"

George shook his head and fetched his London street map. No Notron Street listed.

"Maybe it's a code like a crossword? Doris is good with them." He called her and she came in with a tea towel in her hand, unimpressed that George was loafing around; whilst she was holding the bar down on her own. She looked at the address. "Try the name backwards." Rolled her eyes and walked back into the bar.

"Norton!" they both said at the same time.

*God, I think she thinks I am smarter than I am.* Eager laughed thinking of Liberty's code. After swearing Doris and George to secrecy, he got George to call a taxi to the back door and left.

There was no 221 Norton Street, so he took a leaf out of Doris's book and reversed the number to 122 and found an unassuming terraced house with a red door. He walked by to the next street pretending that he was still searching and to be sure he was not being followed. Eventually, he walked back and down the side alleyway to the back door and knocked. There was a lot of movement inside and then he heard a voice from the bedroom window above.

"Hi! Smalls, what kept you? Come in, Logan will open for you."

Seeing her even after a day apart made his heart jump. Then as he entered the house, the talk with Charlie Allcock came back to him. He had to understand that the force was his life and hopefully if things work out, a brand-new future. In from the cold, Charlie had said, probably a promotion, hell who knows even his replacement when he retires. Logan would be state witness and a free man. All he had to do is ensure the tapes were taken to HQ and deny the media, which meant Liberty, to see them and use them. Her big story gone and she would never forgive him or want to see his face again. He would be a hero maybe, even a commissioner's recommendation and lonely.

She ran down the stairs and jumped up at him, wrapping her arms around his neck and legs around his waist. Gavin and Logan watched surprised at the familiarity.

"Hi! Big fella, I missed you." He felt dirty and conflicted on what he had to do.

"What's wrong?" She immediately picked up on his energy.

"Oh, nothing," He looked around the house, "Pretty well set up, nice pad."

"And you should see our room," she added. He felt worse and looked pale.

"Are you sick?"

"No, it's just been a long day, week!"

A few minutes later, the four of them were sitting in the living room with tea and coffee. Eager was introduced to Gavin. Logan just nodded, but Eager noticed that it was a friendlier nod, not a cold one from when they started this adventure.

"Betty has been with us a long time, very discreet," Gavin said, noticing Eager watching the tea lady carefully.

"She has been looking after this place and our guests for eight years. Competition is fierce and this is where we hide our special guests or informants as the Americans say, 'keep them on ice' until the story breaks and we are exclusive." Gavin was proud of his fake American accent. Liberty just rolled her eyes upwards.

"Right," Gavin started, "What is our next step?" There was silence for a few minutes as they all were thinking.

"Easy," Liberty broke the silence, "We get the tapes, dupe them for safety insurance and see what we have. Right?"

"No. They are my only leverage on the Harkers to find Karlien. My insurance."

"How do you intend to do that?" Eager asked.

"I met Nick Harker, I just got to get back in contact with him and give an ultimatum to get me her contact details, have the call with her to ensure she is okay and then double-cross the bastards."

"What about us? Our story? Making them public will protect us all. I mean the Americans almost cut off my fingers, we are playing with fire here until we break the story."

It was the first Eager had heard about Gavin's interrogation and the Americans. It went quiet again.

"Look, Logan, if I, I mean we," looking at Liberty, "can break this story, I guarantee that you will never have to work again. You can go to South Africa and find Karlien, I will even fund a private investigator there. We will get the best lawyers to fix your police troubles, you can totally be free."

"Nope." Logan McAllistar was a man of few words and stubborn as a mule.

"I have a plan that might work for all of us." Liberty stated and they were all ears.

# Chapter Fifty-Four
## MI5

"Your team operating on my territory on enquiries seem to be a hit squad." the head of MI5 was saying to the head of the CIA London office on a conference call.

"No. Not true, Phil, not true at all. We have no legal or illegal ops going in Britain at the moment," she said assuredly.

"I got a call from my minister today asking about an American hit team for God's sake running around London threatening people."

"Not ours, Phil. I got a top-down request, I mean top-down, to introduce some independent operatives on a run of the mill enquiries to get you guys to assist as you know the landscape. Not a hit team, just a follow up on some leads they had for terrorists. What do you have on them?"

"Just three guys, big guys ex-special, forces I guess."

"That all?"

"That's what we got so far; we are checking into it. My guy followed instructions and didn't ask too many questions."

"Call me when you have shit!" Bang! The connection was cut.

*Now I know that they are involved.* He knew it.

Roger White was working late in his cubical at MI5 head office.

"Roger, a word if you don't mind."

Phil sat on the edge of his desk looking down on him. Roger leaned back on his chair to move away to regain his space.

"Sir?"

"The minister had the Met commissioner complaining that we have been helping the Russians and wire-tap on a policeman?"

"Well, not quite the truth, sir. If you remember you sent me to a police meeting on the Harkers and this guy McAllistar to see if the Russkies were involved with the local mob. I was an observer. Anyway, the ACC and DCI Samuels said that they had a signed off warrant and asked me to assist in placing the bug and listening in. They don't think it was good to have their own bug. So, I helped."

"And?"

"Well, the target had just got home and the Russians barged in and started questioning him for information on McAllistar's whereabouts. They got disturbed and left or something like that. Not sure."

"Did you see the warrant?"

"No, sir, it was the ACC. I didn't think I needed to check him."

"What has McAllistar got that is so interesting to everyone?"

"Some drugs and compromising videos, I think. No real details."

"Anything else you want to tell me?"

"I gave you the heads up on the yanks. They have been on the phone again wanting more information. I don't know what the status is and can't help them."

"I want you to get back in touch with everyone. Find out what the hell is happening and where this McAllistar is and the detective. I want a full report on my desk tonight no matter how late. Take some help if needed."

*So, why is the commissioner complaining about us, his own second in charge could have straightened this out?*

# Chapter Fifty-Five
## Clubbing

"Now, welcome on centre stage for the first time in the club, straight from New York's top entertainment venues, the lovely Annabelle!"

She comes to the middle of the centre stage swaying her hips with both hands on them. White wig, cowgirl mid-calf boots and a cowgirl brown leather waistcoat, underneath a laced-up chemise and string set outfit, G-string also visible.

"Give her a warm welcome everyone and do not forget good old British pound appreciation."

The customers clapped and gasped a little at this sexy vision before them.

"Welcome to London." some guy a little drunk shouted and then tried to get on the stage. She bent down and gently shoved him back. He laughed, at least he got some attention and a bit more was coming his way in the shape of a large bouncer.

"Be nice. He's okay," she said in a whisper, the bouncer warned him, dumped him back in his chair and left.

The music started with *'All My Ex's live in Texas'* by George Strait, then *'You Can Leave Your Hat On'* by Randy Newman and she slowly slid up and down the pole in the middle of the stage. Then she danced to the upbeat *'Hips Don't Lie'* by Shakira. She was making all types of suggestive moves and the crowd loved it. So much so the customers left the other stages and crowded around Liberty's to see what the commotion was about. Then she started to dance and strip down slowly to her G-string. Wolf whistles, shouting remarks and clapping.

"Who the hell is that?" Jimmy asked from the upstairs VIP area.

"New girl, boss. Came in tonight with about five others." The new chief of security for the night, Bruce, the muscle guy, ventured.

"Quite a looker. Check her out and then bring her up to me."

"Be a pleasure."

"I mean see if she has an ID and ask a few questions. Get a feel for her and take that look off your face, you know what I mean."

"Sure, boss."

Liberty had gone to the club to talk to the other girls to see what she could find out about Karlien and recent activities of the owners. This was risky, although she was sure they had not seen her face and would not expect her to turn up on their doorstep, even if they knew about her, which they probably did by now.

She needed to be there through the night and make as many friends of the old hands as possible, they might know something that could be helpful. McAllistar had been insistent that someone would know where she was and given her a few names to talk to. He was crazy about her for sure. They may talk after the customers buy them a lot of drinks, although most landed these guys with an exorbitantly priced bottle of champagne whilst they drank water. Still, the older sops seemed to drink to be able to put up with their lives and declining career. If you are twenty-five plus, how could you compete with the eighteen-year-olds?

"Hey, you darling," Bruce, the muscle, called her over. "Boss wants to see you." Using his big thumb to point up to the VIP area.

*Shit!* She pretended not to hear him and casually walked away carrying her clothes and headed for the dressing room. He was having none of it. Moving quickly for a big man, he was in front of her and in her face in seconds. Face to face; too close for her.

"Hey, cowgirl, are you deaf? Boss wants to see you now and what the boss wants, he gets."

"Have you been eating curry?"

"What?"

"Your breath smells." She moved away wafting her hand across her face.

"You do as you are told or I'll bend you over and use you as a piggy bank! Now move."

She had no choice, no way this gorilla was going to let her go. She had no back up as both McAllistar and Eager were known faces. Gavin would be hopeless, anyway, he was on his way to convince Sir Richard, he needed body guards like retired SAS guys. Good luck to him as he had sworn not to give away too much.

"Piggybank? I'd like to see you try," Liberty said gaining some composure. Bruce started to laugh.

"ID?"

"Do you think I have room," showing her body off, "for ID? Imagine where would I put it?"

"Just move, luv. That's a good girl. Make the boss think that you enjoy it here. He likes the look of you and I wouldn't mind a bit of you too."

"Well, only if you're the last guy in the world. No correct that, if you were the last guy in the world, I would become a lesbian first."

He laughed again and scratched his scalp. *Maybe she is playing hard to get.* And laughed again. *Hard to get! In this place, I am funny.*

She walked a swanky sexy walk to the stairs and climbed slowly and deliberately as she was trying to work out what was going to happen. He followed her on the steps but got a signal from Jimmy for him not to come up.

Jimmy was sitting with several girls who got up and went downstairs passing Liberty on the way. Giving her dirty looks as if she had interfered in their good deal with the boss.

*Good, he is on his own, I can hit him with the champagne bottle if I have to and run.*

"Hiya!" she said in the most confident voice she could find. To her surprise, Jimmy stood up and shook her hand. He was though giving her a thorough, once over, in a professional way, this guy was not a drooling customer.

*He's pretty good looking for a gangster.*

"Quite a show you put on. Not seen that response for a while. Sit down, drink?"

"Thanks. A beer would be good, I mean a cold one, not like the Brit warm beer. Thanks." He pulled a bottle of lager out of an ice bucket on the table, held it up so she could feel it. Once she nodded, he screwed the lid off and poured it into a beer glass very carefully. She noticed the bandage on his hand a bit like the one Gavin now has. Otherwise, he was immaculate in a light blue suit, blue tie, white shirt, very expensive brown brogue shoes.

*This guy is really smooth, smells nice too, just watch out, girl. He is so smooth that he could slip under doors backwards.*

"Tell me about yourself?"

Thinking quick she told a story about being from Texas, working in New York clubs, fortunately, she remembered a few names of similar type clubs from her younger days. Liberty believed that to tell a good lie you had to be close to the truth, so it was believable and never questioned. So, she added in parts of her younger life that made sense.

"Why London?"

"Oh, I wanted to see the world, never been out of the States."

"Really?"

"Well, also boyfriend trouble. Didn't like what I do, except for the money, of course, love for his drugs. Anyway, after a few beatings, I ran away from them all."

"Them all?"

"Oh, there were others, men all the same, trouble."

"Made a lot tonight?"

"I got a lot of these dollars, I mean pounds. They're worth more than dollars, right?"

"Right, it is still early, I will get the DJ to give you more spots. Stick around and talk to me after. If you are interested, I can help you make really good money. I take it you are up to giving high-value customers a good time?"

She nodded, "Kinda, except beatings, I prefer now to administer the pain if it gives pleasure to someone."

Jimmy laughed and indicated the interview was over. He handed her his business card and told her they needed to talk later and he meant late afternoon he would not get to bed until early morning due to the hours the club was open.

*Brits, even the mob bosses are polite. This is closer than I hoped or wanted.*

Jimmy signalled the security chief to come up.

"ID?"

"Says she hasn't got any space for ID."

"She didn't come here dressed like that. Her next spot, search her locker, find anything, copy and bring to me. Then when she leaves, get one of the guys to follow her carefully and report back to me any time. Everything right?"

"Right, boss. I'll do it myself if it is after closing time."

"You're six foot six, yeah? You are also about six-foot-wide with your muscles, how the hell will she not notice you at 3 am in the morning on the deserted streets of London?"

"I'm like a ninja!"

"Go get Sammy." laughing.

*Sometimes, this dumb ass is really funny,* Jimmy reflected.

# Chapter Fifty-Six
## Plan in Action

"So, that's where we are. Crazy, I know, but we are very close to getting the tapes," Gavin stated with confidence.

"How close is that?" GWP was not impressed that he had been left out of the reporting loop promised, he was angry and 'hunting bear'.

"I am hoping the next day or so. McAllistar does not want to give them up, as I mentioned earlier, until he finds out what happened to his girlfriend. She was flown into the country via British Airways, first-class and went off the radar. He has checked all known family and friends and found zip."

"So, you believe that these tapes have some let's say, high profile people, doing naughty stuff eh?" Sir Richard had been to lunch.

"How do you know if anything worthwhile is on them?" GWP pushed.

"McAllistar has seen some of them. He is not very good with recognising 'high profile' people as he has had no interest in the news for years, however, it looks like at least a paedophile ring. He is certain the videos were filmed by the Harkers for blackmail and or protection or both. My newspaper man's nose tells me these are explosive."

"Your nose better be right." Sir Richard added.

"Their video guy was brutally murdered as part of the cover-up."

"Haven't the police got McAllistar down for that?" GWP suggested.

"What about protection?" Gavin changed the subject and held up his bandaged hand.

"Oh right. Expensive, these ex-SAS guys. Let's use our normal security guys."

"Sir Richard, these Americans are top pros, dangerous, maybe CIA or a rogue group. Rent-a-cop won't be able to protect me," Gavin appealed.

"Mmm, get the costs for two guys and let me know, until then use our guys," Sir Richard ventured.

*Some fucking use they'd be, thanks a lot,* Gavin thought.

"I know someone who can help, owes me a favour. I will call him and let you know when to meet. At the office or your flat?" GWP was hatching a plot to get closer to McAllistar.

"I don't know. I am going to move around a bit. I'll call you later."

*I am going to make myself scarce.* Gavin thought as he took a deep breath.

# Chapter Fifty-Seven
## Copy Cats – Step Two

"Police," Eager said holding up his badge in the face of a teenage girl sitting in the video shop.

"What have you got in the backroom?"

"Just videos, just videos and a kettle," she replied nervously.

Eager went past the desk and into the back office. As he had assumed, they had four video machines connected for copying illegally.

"What are these?"

She was dumbfounded and was starting to cry.

"Err shouldn't you have a warrant or something?" she blurted.

"These machines are for copying videos, right?"

She nodded and was shaking.

"It's okay luv, we just want to use them not arrest you," Logan consoled her.

"Use them?"

"Urgent case, need to make some quick copies." They then took out twelve red videos and got her to show them how to use the machines with the shop's blanks.

A big fat bald and bearded guy came in full of tattoos and biker pants and wife-beater t-shirt.

"What the bloody hell is going on here?" he demanded and he lurched forward at the seated Eager. Logan had him on his face in seconds with his arm reaching the top of his neck. He couldn't move.

"I will tell you what's going on here," Logan stopped him struggling. "It is illegal to breach copyright. Understand?" Logan let him go.

"Now be a good boy and get up." He stood up trying to get his arm moving.

"You the pigs, don't you need a search warrant? You are going to arrest me?"

"We are the police and need to copy some videos for an urgent court case. You help us and we will overlook what we have found. Got it?"

"No further action. Nothing?"

"I promise you will never see or hear from us again." He was visibly relieved.

They had taken the Edinburgh flying Scotsman train to Sheffield, buying two return tickets for the full journey. Eager had drawn out cash in London and their only worry was the CCTV cameras. In Sheffield, a visit to a back street 'rent a wreck' and they were on their way back to Matlock and the cottage. Logan insisted on going into the cottage himself to his priest's hidey-hole, so Eager would not know where they were hidden.

The door was not fixed and easy to open, just police scenes of crime tape around it. Someone might be watching, so Eager had the car ready to gun and kept his keen police eyes all around. Nothing out of the ordinary.

Logan returned at a fast pace and jumped in the car.

*Trust is hard-earned,* Eager thought.

Step two in Liberty's plan was, whilst she was checking out the Harker's club, that they would go and get the videos. It was Eager and McAllistar that decided to secretly copy them, no one else but they would know as it was too risky for the rest of the team. It was insurance, although one set had been enough trouble. Too many people were after them and God knows what might happen if the originals were found. McAllistar had resisted this, however, eventually after much persuasion had agreed. Eager had to promise that he would not turn cop and grab the videos. Also, Liberty could not use or have them until he had found out about Karlien. She promised, although Logan was happier with Eager being with him, he was not fully trusting Liberty and the media yet. The deal was to hide the second copy in a place of Logan's choice. He would be the only one to know where and the originals back in the priest's hidey-hole in the cottage.

Eager was totally conflicted, although he went along with the plan. Logan had gone into his cottage and had come out with his kit bag full of videos. He had not told Eager where he had hidden them. Eager was standing, looking for any sign of the cottage being under surveillance. He had watched bits of some of them and Logan also let him see Karlien getting beaten.

"Look at this?" It was the tracker in his kit bag.

"Shit." They will know where we are and will be coming in fast.

"Never thought to look in the bag until I was packing the videos. Do not worry." He threw the tracker out of the car and saw it bounce and smash down the road.

Eager drove off quickly anyway. "Not very environmentally friendly."

"Did you put this in my bag?" accusingly.

"No, but I bet I know who did. My car was in the Met car park and the keys were left inside for me."

"Who is he?" Eager didn't answer straight away as he was thinking hard.

"Who?" Logan demanded.

"A major US politician."

"How big, how big?" Logan sensed that Eager was holding back.

"Big enough to be a president one day."

They took a quick look in the video shop. Eager watched closely. The sound on the video was very low unless he shouted.

She made him a drink at the bar in the room with her back to the camera. He drank it in one go and asked for another. They talked a little and then she started to strip down to her G-string. She was gyrating sexily and was talking to him. Little sound, so it was hard to figure out what she was saying. He seemed to flip moods and turned so angry, he was drinking heavily for sure, however, she was in his face with words that seemed to make him mad. He was not sure, certainly odd.

"Who exactly?" Logan persisted.

"The Republican leader of the House of Representatives."

"It's like getting bloody blood out of a stone!" Logan was getting frustrated.

"A guy called Travis Preston, a southerner, tipped to run for president. Well, he comes from big oil money, so he is probably buying it."

They both stared at each other, the same thing was going through their minds. This accounts for the Russian and American interest for sure. It confirms they are in a very dangerous game.

The other videos which he caught flashes of were definitely sick, very sick. Being a reader of the tabloids and *The Times*, he recognised many faces. One made him stop dead in his tracks.

# Chapter Fifty-Eight
## Sorrow

Logan insisted on seeing Aunt Bessie in the hospital. There would be no police guard as they assumed the assault was being treated as an old lady being beaten up by robbers. The believed the local detectives would not be in the loop regarding the McAllistar connection, so they didn't have a clue regarding what really happened. They would believe the villains had no reason to come back to her. Even so, Eager went in first and checked where she was and searched around. He passed Logan his police badge to help him just in case he was stopped. Looked, though, more like an ex-soldier than a police inspector. Logan picked up his bag with the tapes and left.

*Yes, trust is hard-earned,* Eager thought as McAllistar left.

Logan followed Eager's direction right to the intensive care ward. A junior nurse came up to him and asked what he wanted. He explained he was a relative and had come down from Scotland to see her when he heard. The nurse was not happy but could see genuine sadness in his face and tears forming in his eyes as he looked through the window into the ward and stared at Aunt Bessie with bandages and tubes sticking out of her.

"She has not come around yet, still in a coma. They say she will, though."

"Can I just say hello and hold her hand, we were close and it might help?"

She looked around to see if the sister or a doctor was in sight.

"Promise me two minutes and if the sister comes, tell her you just went in. Promise?"

He sat with her for five minutes and held her hand and talked to her. He was sorry so, very sorry as he had promised he would not bring harm to her door.

He thought he heard her say, "Logan." She squeezed his hand. He swore revenge to himself and told Aunt Bessie that he would come back and stay with her forever and ensure she is looked after very well.

"Hmmm," The junior nurse was at the door pointing the way out.

"Sorry, I lost track of time," He jumped up and left.

"Who was that?" the sister arrived as he disappeared down the corridor.

"He was sitting with Bessie when I found him. Just been to the toilet for two minutes."

"God girl, don't you read briefs. We have to inform the security and the police if she has visitors! He looks like the guy wanted for murder!"

Logan was out of there quickly in the car and off. The calls were being made rapidly from hospital security, the cops would be here soon. The CCTV cameras would record their car make and number. But it would take time for them to review. Sure enough, halfway down the road, they were passed by blue light with sirens blazing and then two others. They had underestimated the understanding and communications system of the local police.

"Where to now?" Eager asked.

"Let's go back to the B&B. It's halfway to where I want to go to hide the copies, plus it's in the country, not many cop cars and I am tired and hungry."

"Bit risky?"

"Scotty knows him so we can trust him."

"So does Gavin and Liberty. What if they have been picked up?"

Logan laughed, "Gavin I would worry about, but Liberty would have to be hung drawn and quartered to get anything out that tough cookie."

"Off to Ned's then, meat pies and the devil's work!"

# Chapter Fifty-Nine
## Suspicion

"Leon, what the fuck did you do?" Tazewell Spear was irritated. He just had the worse meeting of his life. Made the Russian monster women's treatment look like child's play.

"Beat up an old lady who not help us. We do this for you guys as if we do not find the stuff, our bosses will not be so nice."

"Beat her up, you almost killed her. The jury is still out if she will live."

"Serves her right for bitch slapping. We took car numbers that passed us on way to cottage. Also, one sitting down the road watching. One old car with two dogs at the back, a cop?"

Tazewell took the plate numbers and promised to get back to them quickly.

"Stay by the payphone?"

"No payphone, pub phone," Leon corrected him.

Sure enough, Tazewell called back with the owners. One was Eagers, one a hire car (probably Sammy, the squirrel) and the other, a Scotty Thomas from Matlock.

"Check this Scotty out. He probably knows where they are if not with him. Be subtle and careful this is not the Wild West."

"Be like John Wayne, right?"

*God helps us,* thought Tazewell.

The meeting called by the Hawker's was in the dungeon. Soundproofed and where most violence took place if required. Jimmy, Nick and Dirk were there. Only one chair in the middle of the bare tiled floor. He would need all his wily legal skills to get out of this as it bodes very badly. Thoughts of 'Billy, the neck' crashed across his mind. He was visibly shaken.

"What's this, a firing squad?" He shuddered at the joke he had made. They were all serious, glum faces.

"Sit down," Nick said and he did.

"What's up? Why treat me like this? I am a loyal member of this team." They ignored him.

Jimmy started first with a serious of questions. Did he enter their office when the drug parcel went missing? Did he set up McAllistar? What was his relationship with the Russians? Where is Karlien? Did he know about the videos? Who was the guy who beat her up? He answered them calmly and smoothly. They were guessing and testing him to see if anything slips.

Nick was walking around him intimidating, Dirk was standing with arms folded looking into his eyes and Jimmy standing with a level calm voice, cool as a cucumber.

He answered no, no, just doing the clubs work with the Russians, Karlien left London in first-class, two seats and entered South Africa, they can check.

"We have," Jimmy pulled out a piece of paper, "50,000 US dollars put into your offshore account what for? Why?"

"You searched my home? After all that I have given to your ventures, you don't trust me anymore? This is my home now; you guys are my only friends," He started to play his 'poor me' card. "When I was a kid, I was always the last guy they picked for the teams. Me standing there alone, sad, they even picked the girls first. So, when you guys gave me an opportunity to be part of this team and bring my contacts and skills with me, it was the best time. I would never do anything against you!"

"Answer the question," Nick demanded. He was now frustrated. "It was a week after Karlien left?" Nick prompted him.

"Okay, I was contacted by my fellow 'Americans' regarding Karlien. The guys who asked me to arrange the trick. They now wanted things tidied up as they put it or else, I would pay with my life. Really, I didn't know he would beat her, stupid. But the crazy thing is they blamed me, wrong girl, they said, so sort it pronto. Then this money drops into my account. I never gave anyone my offshore account details. I was pondering what to do when all this trouble with McAllistar popped up. Check the account, there are two payments of five thousand US dollars to ABSA bank in South Africa."

"Who did the dirty work?" Tazewell hesitated and then thought he better tell the truth.

"Dirk."

# Chapter Sixty
## Scotty

Scotty came out of his house through the side gate with his dogs taking his morning walk. Both dogs were on leads with mussels until they get to the park. The two guns were in his face as he turned the corner of the house. The dogs went berserk snapping at the two men facing, although they were powerless. Scotty held them tight, he had faced guns and danger before in his career. He was looking down on the two guys and tried to work out what was happening.

"You tell us where McAllistar and the policeman are or we start by killing your big bad wolfs." Roman threatened.

"We little piggies like killing wolfs," Leon added. Roman rolled his eyes upward.

"What the fuck do you mean? I don't know where they are, I just gave them a lift to where some bastards had beat up an old lady." He spat on the ground in front of them.

"Which one first?" Roman waved his gun around.

"Or maybe we kill your old lady inside the house. Do you a big favour, am I right?"

"Last when I saw them, they were going to a B&B. Really that's all I know. I just gave them a lift," Scotty pleaded.

"You lie, big guy. Cops lie!" Roman was getting aggressive.

"What's a B&B?" Leon asked.

"A local farm where you can stay for the night and have breakfast."

"Address? Where?" Roman asked.

Scotty thought they would be long gone, so what was the harm and gave them directions and the address.

"You tell the truth?" Leon said.

"Yes, it's all I know. Just ran into them and they wanted to find out where Aunt Bessie lived. I took them and after she went to the hospital they left for the B&B."

The shot was loud, very loud and Rex fell over in an instant. Scotty went for Roman's neck, picking him up and throwing him around like a rag doll. He had a rage that he had never felt before in his life. The pounding of Leon's gun butt on his head left him half-conscious.

"You no tell truth, we come back and your other wolf, your old lady gets the same," Roman shouted as he left. He then turned and shot Scotty in the leg.

Scotty fell down still conscious, thinking about Rex and the long time they had been friends and companions. The times when Rex had saved his life. He was gone forever life would never be the same. Bastards!

Romeo laid at the side of Rex moaning and whimpering. They had also been together for a long time. She was bewildered. Scotty heard her and jumped up quickly to chase and fell over. Blood running down his head, face and leg. He got back up just as his wife ran out.

"Oh my God, oh my God!" She screamed. "I need to dial 999." She turned to run back in the house.

"I gotta get going right now."

"What, look at you? Scotty, you've been shot for God sake!"

"No bones or arteries hit, I am okay it's just a flesh wound, meant to scare me. They killed Rex and they are going after my friends."

He sat down besides Rex and lifted his head in his arms and kissed him. Tears ran down the big man's face. He didn't now have time to say goodbye properly. He needed to follow them quickly and the police would be there soon.

He went inside and took his shotgun out of the arms cupboard which was only ever used for shooting rabbits and foxes. He loaded his pockets with twelve-gauge cartridges. She stood blocking his way.

"At least let me bandage your wound," she said trying to delay him.

"Just a little blood, no time. Come, Romeo, we are going hunting!" He pushed passed her. Romeo jumped up and they got in his old Volvo estate just as sirens were closing in.

"Scotty, don't be stupid and don't get hurt! Where are you going? Don't be stupid let the police do this!" she screamed trying to stop him. She knew he had been a great policeman in many dangerous situations, but she had never seen him cry and act so aggressive. He was out for revenge.

# Chapter Sixty-One
## Not a Safe House

"Eric, hi! GWP here, I have been searching for Gavin for two days."

"Haven't we all? He rings in constantly for the editorials and layouts. Strange, he never shows up?"

"I have something urgent for him, can't wait, I am afraid."

"Not at home then?"

"No, nowhere at all. I need to talk to him really urgent."

It was GWP, a legend in the industry.

"I think he is at a safe house. Not sure. It is only Gavin who knows where it is. I have the house number though, maybe you could call him on that and find out?"

*Perfect. He would teach them to cut him out of the story and the credit.*

"Hi! DCI Samuels?"

"Speaking."

"Gordon here. I think I can help you find McAllistar, Eager and the reporter girl."

"Where?" very interested.

"You will owe me a big favour and I expect it to be returned when I need information?"

"Sure, sure, no problem. Shoot I am listening," Samuels said with excitement.

"I have the telephone number of where they might be staying. Papers safe house. Do not tell anyone that I gave it to you."

After checking out the number and getting the address. Samuels ran into the ACC's office.

"I think I have it, sir." Proud. The ACC gets up and closes the door.

"What do you have?" He blurts out what he has found from a very reliable source and has it on good authority. There is a fair chance they are there.

"I need an armed team and search warrant, sir."

The ACC thought about it for a while with his blue eyes twinkling.

"Who else knows?"

"I came straight here. No one, I want these collars myself."

"I see chasing super already eh? Rank means a lot to you. Power, more income, more opportunities to make money, am I right?"

"God yes, sir."

"What would you do for it all right now?" His blue eyes seemed to turn dark, he was talking to the devil. The ACC walked over to his safe in the wall, used the combination and took out a box under a lot of paperwork.

"This is a .44 Magnum gun with a suppressor. Got this as you might say a gift when I was seconded to the RUC in my earlier days. Used by the IRA to kill our soldiers, lured to houses like lambs to the slaughter." He held it up. "In perfect working condition, lots of bullets. Dirty Harry uses it in the movies, very powerful weapon, once hit you do not get up again."

DCI Samuels was getting nervous for where was he going with this?

"If a team goes in there, the chances are the tapes will be put into evidence and they, shall I say the 'suspects', may have seen them and will talk. Get my drift?"

"You want me to kill them all?"

"You do get my drift. I mean they have some evidence of a silly thing I was doing. I need it all tidied up. If I go down, we all go down for shall I say our protection activities."

Samuels felt the blood drain from his face. He needed to think. The look on his boss's face told him this was real, he really expected him to kill these people. He also instinctively felt that now was not the time to show any kind of fear.

*Because seriously, I can't do this!*

# Chapter Sixty-Two
## Kisses

3 am and leaving the club, Liberty put her arm in Candy's, who was a little worse for wear. The ladies being tipsy or drunk was not allowed in the club. She was risking a total ban, probably had a bad night money wise. She whispered that she would take her home knowing that she would probably be followed and Candy had mentioned that she knew Karlien well.

She was slurring badly.

"Had a good evening, ladies?" The cabbie was leering at them.

"Address?" Candy finally remembered and slowly spat it out.

Sammy was watching and immediately called his car up and followed.

They arrived at a small two-story block of flats in Hoxton. Candy fell out on the pavement.

"Five quid, luv or you can pay by other means," the sleazy cab driver offered.

Liberty took ten pounds from her pocket and threw it at him.

Helping Candy up the three steps was a trial, however, she could see a car way down the road with lights off. She was certain that they were watching. At the front door of the entrance, Liberty took Candy in her arms and kissed her on the lips. Candy responded. They looked like two lesbians living together, she hoped. They went inside. She watched the road carefully without flat lights on and saw the car slowly drive by. When it got close, she turned on the lights so they would know where they lived and maybe go home, job done.

Candy had started to get drunk with the customers, being thirty she was miserable about the dwindling offers she was made. Drinking to drunkenness was not acceptable for the girls at the club, so she knew soon she would be kicked out or would have to keep doing favours for the security guards.

She was given several cups of coffee and seemed to be better.

"Tell me about Karlien?"

"You mean Dusty?" still slurring a little.

"Dusty, her stage name?"

"Oh, did you see her before she went back to South Africa? I mean after she got beat up?"

"No, but I saw her the other day."

"What! What do you mean you saw her the other day?"

"Couldn't miss that bitch. She has a black wig now for her jobs."

Candy had met Karlien coming out of the Ritz hotel where lots of rich international visitors hang out.

"Are you sure it was her?"

"Absolutely, bloody sure. I spoke to her. She asked me to not tell anyone as she wanted out of the Harker's clutches. Oops, I just did!" Hiccupping.

"Did she tell you where she lives now?"

"Nope. Meets rich guys in fancy hotels in the area. I am tired now and want to sleep."

And she did on the settee straight away like she had been knocked out.

Liberty slept on top of her bed until 5 am and then after checking out the street for that car, sneaking out the back door and down the alleyway. She headed for the safe house by underground. She was certain no one followed her, even so, she walked around the block once and then went down a neighbour's drive and when out of sight, jumped the fence at the safe house's backyard.

Gavin was asleep and throwing stones at the window took time for him to come around and peeking out of the corner of his bedroom curtain, he realised it wasn't the Americans coming to get him. He let her in and she brushed past him a bit annoyed and tired.

"What happened?"

"Too tired, but I need to sleep and sleep a lot. Can you wake me at 11 am and can you get Betty to cook me something like biscuits and gravy? Thanks." And she ran upstairs to bed.

Gavin was scratching his head, biscuits and gravy?

# Chapter Sixty-Three
## Revenge of Romeo

"I'm off then lad," McAllistar shouted to Eager.

"Off where?"

"To hide the dupes. Be back in forty minutes or so."

"Oh, be careful regarding my friends with the blue lights spotting the car."

"Not a chance." Then he was outside the B&B, into the old car and the car wheels screeched as he sped down the farms, dirt and pebble road. Eager watched him turn right at the end of the drive going north.

*Lad, now is it. Slowly, slowly, we are getting back to where we once were as friends. Still not trusted fully,* Eager thought.

He asked Ned if he could use his telephone. Ned wanted to know where he was calling and then negotiated a price.

"Leave yer change at the side mi duck." He then walked off with his very old sheepdog following him outside. The phone was ancient. Very dusty from not being used, he bet for a long time.

Eager got through to Charlie Allcock, who immediately knew who was calling.

"Sir, the tapes are hidden in McAllistar's cottage. Must be a hidey-hole somewhere. Get DS Williams to check out the history of the house and if nothing turns up, then take it apart brick by brick."

"Are you sure?"

"Watched him go in and then bring them out with him. He let me watch some. After showing me bits, he had second thoughts and put them back in the cottage. I was outside, not privy to exactly where."

"I'll get the Derbyshire guys to seal off the cottage and chopper there with our team."

"Better tell them to be armed as a lot of nasty types are looking for the tapes."

"Wilco."

"Oh, by the way, I saw bits of them, you wouldn't guess who was on one of them?"

He told him. Gasps came down the phone.

"You might want to warn the chief."

"No, no, tell no one. Hold our gunpowder at least until we have and can verify the tapes and then we need to think carefully how we launch this information. It is dynamite and the biggest bad PR for the Met ever. We have to be careful it doesn't blow up in our faces. John fully understood, right?"

"You're the boss. I cannot call when McAllistar is around and this has to look like it was a police search, not a tip-off from me."

He put the phone down and then a gun came to the back of his head. Eager stood very still and lifted his hands in the air.

"Do good Mr Plod," Leon said, "Now plod, outside, no funny business or I will put a big hole in your Humpty head."

"To the barn." Eager did as he was told at a slow pace, not to panic his assailant and to give him time to think.

*Definitely the Russians again. This will not be fun.*

He entered the old tumbled down barn that had pieces of the walls missing. It was typical of the old farmers who never saw a reason from generation to generation to invest in capital upkeep. He noticed two cars hidden at the back a Rover with normal plates and a brand-new black Mercedes with blacked-out windows. He took note of the number plate '2 RUS'.

*A Russian diplomatic vehicle.*

Ned had been lifted onto an old tractor and sat there silently, not moving. He was not tied up, just scared to death and shaking. He was muttering, "Ye be devils."

*No help there then,* Eager thought as his mind was working overtime on how to get out of this mess. Hanging upside down was not the worst of his worries. A big lady or a man, he was not sure at first, and another Russian guy watched him carefully as he was brought into the barn. He or she was not armed, but both the guys had sidearm lifted, probably cocked and pointed right at him. He knew she was the boss by the way she stood and commanded the men.

"You can lower your arms," she said, "so no heroics as you can see, we can kill you both at will, so be nice."

"Oh heck." he heard Ned say.

"Be quiet, little man!" she shouted and then turned back to Eager.

"Look, he just runs the B&B nothing to do with all this. He knows nothing."

"He now knows us and that is enough."

"What do you want?" Eager wanted to play for time maybe Logan would get back, see the cars and rescue them. *His only chance*, he thought, *but he had only been gone ten minutes what did he say forty? Oh hell, keep them talking.*

"Detective Eager, do not play games with us. I can torture and break the man you are is my training. So, why not co-operate and save you a lot of pain. No?"

*I wonder how long the torture lasts,* Eager thought in his head, this was a private joke. He did laugh out loud. He wasn't sure he was losing his mind.

*Laugh and the world laughs with you, wasn't that a true saying?*

His head exploded as the big woman lifted her foot and with an amazing quick movement hit the side of his head. So, he was thinking no one is laughing with me. His laughing had confused Olga, so much so as he was falling, she kicked him in the side of his body with her other foot. He felt his ribs explode as he hit the floor.

"Not laughing now Mr Plod," Leon could not help saying.

"So, Mr Funny, you want it the hard way. Get up!" Leon had to help him.

All he could think off was how the hell could this big, fat woman lift her foot that high so quickly? He didn't have time to see it coming. Another foot slap to the side of his head as he stood up in front of her. Not fat but pure muscle.

*I actually feel good. Kinda interesting dizziness. How long can I last out?*

It reminded him of the old thatched cottage, which he moved into the way back. The people five hundred years ago were much smaller and the black beams inside the house were low and four times he banged his head taking furniture in. After the fourth, he had a dizziness but contrary to what he expected, it gave him a buzz.

He was shaking his head and giggling. He thought about hostage negotiation training, what was it? Stay cool and don't antagonise. Well, this was a real situation and they are going to kill him and poor Ned. He also hoped for Ned's dog, poor thing, as he wouldn't last a day without his lifelong master.

Leon and Roman seemed to be amused at Eager's response. He felt they could almost be on his side. No, he realised, that was the bang on his head talking.

"Leon, give me your gun." she commanded and she placed it right in Eager's crotch.

"Big funny man with no balls or scrotum. Imagine how funny that is?"

"Okay, you want the tapes I can help you."

"Now that is better. Better to have no balls than really no balls." It was her turn to laugh and she looked at Roman and then at Leon, who got the message to laugh too.

"Now where? No more games!"

"I can show you where they are hidden."

*That's it. Brilliant! Take them to the cottage, Charlie and half of Derbyshire constabulary will be there.*

"How far?"

"Ten miles or so."

"Okay, you play games with me and you will regret it forever. Kill the little man and dog and let's go."

*As if dying is not forever. Shit, Ned!*

There are times that you hope the cavalry will come at the last minute and rescue you. That happens only in films and rare occasions. He prayed for the first time in years for divine intervention, his last resort.

He had got Ned killed by his cleverness, but what else could he do?

"No! Kill him and the dog I will not take you to the tapes," Eager shouted. "Bring them with us," he demanded.

"I'm the boss here. Roman kill them now use a silencer." Roman pulled out a silencer and started screwing it onto his gun.

A roar of a lion came from the barn doorway. It was a terrifying screaming roar. They began to turn, but the speed that Romeo entered the room was so fast that it was a blur. She went straight for Roman and at his throat, ripping at it; whilst seeming to hold it tight. She knew who killed her friend and was getting her revenge. Normally, police dogs, particularly Alsatians, are trained to bring down felons by the arm. They also went for the legs and in a riot situation where they got very excited, the crotch. Romeo had never been trained for the throat, it was her wolf animal genes and it came naturally. Leon dropped the silencer he had been messing with and lifted his gun. The boom of a shotgun inside a structure, albeit deteriorating, was deafening. Leon was lifted in the air as Scotty gave him both barrels. He went halfway through a hole in the wooden walls, laying on the hole with his head outside.

Olga grabbed Eager around the neck in a stranglehold and faced Scotty, who had no time to reload.

"No. Do not even try to reload! Dog first, then you and while I am doing this, I strangle this bastard with my bare hands if he does not help me."

She pointed the gun at Romeo and then she shuddered once and then again.

Little Ned had been forgotten and he got his other friend, 'Pete', the pitchfork and ran it into her back, first it went in two inches and then he pushed it all the way through.

She fell to the floor having difficulty breathing, one lung holed. Blood gushed out of her mouth.

"I'm a diplomat with immunity. You get me an ambulance." she was gasping.

"No. We get you a box," Scotty was firm.

"Oh heck," Ned said.

# Chapter Sixty-Four
## Calls

"Samuels just called and gave me the address of a house, where he believes some of our friends are." Tazewell rush into Jimmy and Nick trying to retrieve their support again or at least negate anything they might be thinking of doing. He handed a piece of paper over to Jimmy. He looked at it and smiled.

"About time he paid for his keep," Nick said sarcastically.

"That's all Tazewell." Jimmy said formally and dismissed him, which was not a good sign. Tazewell decided he had to accelerate his plans quickly otherwise he would be a toast. When he left, Jimmy nodded to Nick.

"Let's get Sammy to check it out."

"Why don't we just go in there and grab them?" the impatient Nick uttered a little confused.

"The game is afoot, my dear Watson. We need to be careful, very careful now. I do not trust Tazewell nor the cop in his pocket."

"The game is what?"

"Sherlock Holmes, never mind, get Sammy and Bruce moving and throw Dirk in there just in case. Not to do anything unless I say so."

"I'll call this in." Eager told the others. Leon and Roman were dead. Olga lay vomiting blood and trying to breathe. Ned was comforting his sheepdog, Rebel and wiping blood off the pitchfork. Scotty was stroking Romeo and watching Olga die as he hoped or he was considering putting her out of her misery quickly when all the witnesses had gone.

"Can you patch me through to DCS Allcock please?" he told the dispatcher. Several minutes later holding onto the dusty big ancient phone and being watched by Ned, who had followed him back to the house. Eager assumed he was watching to charge him money for the call. Tight these farmers.

"John, a total farce. The tapes were all blank. The commissioner is going to go crazy I spent a fortune on the chopper!"

"He didn't trust me I guess, he tricked me."

"What now?"

"Well." Eager was thinking how to break the news as an international incident that had just occurred without sending Charlie's blood pressure through the roof.

"Well, sir I want to tell you that I need help right now, here where I am." Charlie knew something big and not nice was coming his way when Eager called him sir.

Eager dropped the neutron political bomb and it was agreed that he should bring a senior officer from the Derbyshire police and that Eager was to get out of there and stick with McAllistar to get the evidence that justified this bloody mess.

Eager didn't mention that an ambulance was needed, just the coroner's crew. He needed time and a police position to be formulated otherwise, the press would be all over this in a few minutes, cameras and all. This would be big news. He hoped and banked on Olga dying before the troops got there.

"The commissioner, MI5 and 6, the minister for the foreign office and even the PM would have to be notified and involved. God only knows, is the Queen not meeting the Russian president later this month?" Charlie's last comments.

"Jimmy?"
"Yes, Annabelle?" recognising her accent.
"You said to call for some extra big bucks work tonight."
"I did, indeed. What is your real name?"
"That's a secret, but you can call me Feather."
"Feather, really?"
"My mommy told me not to give men my name and address until I knew them well," she said this in a mock young teenager's southern accent.

"We have what you might say a show in a different location tonight, in the country, high worth individuals just coming for a good time. I need beautiful, playful, discreet, make them happy no matter what ladies. Is this you?"

"Big bucks is me and I can fit all your other categories. How much for the night?"

"I will guarantee you five thousand pounds minimum. If you do not get it in what we call tips, I will make the difference for you. Normally, the ladies get much more, especially from the Arabs."

"Sounds great."

"Be at the club at 8 pm and we will chauffeur you and the other girls to the venue. Do not mention this to anyone, its hush-hush."

"Thanks, see you then, Mr Harker."

"Oh, by the way, we need to look at your ID."

"No problem. Are you checking if I am underage?" she joked.

Jimmy laughed too.

*Shit!* She thought as she put the phone down. She had to go outside into the back garden and have a cigarette and think.

"Sammy."

"There are three of them in the house. A man, not McAllistar or Eager, an old lady probably the housekeeper and guess what?"

"I don't have time to play games!" Jimmy was irritated with being told to guess.

"Annabelle, the girl I followed from the club if that is her name."

"Are you sure?"

"Yes, certain. Walking in the garden smoking large as life."

Jimmy asked, "Who owns the house?"

"The *Daily Cryer's* holding company, Carlton Investments. A reporter, I guess. Should we grab her?"

"No, she is coming tonight to the new 'HC', so she will be in the country with us. We need to watch the house to see when the others return, hopefully, with the tapes."

"Got it, boss."

"Oh, by the way, get Dirk to go to the address you followed her to, see what this Candy knows. I want everything they both said right away."

"Sure, boss."

"And Sammy, if she knows too much, tell Dirk no loose ends."

# Chapter Sixty-Five
## McAllistar

He had driven out of the farm towards Buxton on the only road in the area. He didn't intend to take a forty-minute drive back and forth as he knew that Eager would be able to work out roughly the distance he would travel there and back and so would have an idea, if worse came to worse, the hiding place within a radius. Telling him he would be away forty minutes meant that the radius would be much bigger and harder to pin down a hiding place. He knew he was paranoid but still didn't trust Eager, even though he desperately wanted to. He had few friends left. His army mates had reunions every year, but he would not go back and live in the past and frankly, as now he had been convicted as a drug dealer, he was embarrassed to face them. Eager was still a cop and would revert to form. He was unable to help him with the frame-up that sent him down.

He saw a tall, thin, red brick building in the middle of a field just before the road turned to cross the moors. It was about six-foot square and odd thin building. He parked just off the road and crossed the field to it. There was no one for miles around, no cars on the road. It was old and obviously not being used. The lock on the door was easily broken with a big rock he found. It was full of dust, cobwebs and rat droppings. It looked like an old water pump inside. McAllistar was unsure why a water pump in the middle of nowhere. That didn't matter as no one had been in the building for decades. No houses for miles and then only farmhouses, so no kids anywhere around who might play there. Stepping inside, he looked where he could hide the dupes. He had to turn around to see a dusty ledge above the doorway. The tapes fitted and were out of sight, even so, he went outside and dug up some grass and dirt to cover them. He patted the dirt on the plastic bag he had the tapes in and put the bits of grass on top.

He sat down on a big rock at the side of the car to have a cigarette and spend some time, so it looked like he had driven further. Reflecting on where he was and if he would get what he wants and get out of the position he was in. Sometimes, the universe works in mysterious ways and shit happens and you do not immediately see the silver lining.

He thought about being sent to the boy's army, it was a change in culture and very hard for the first few months, however, he began to enjoy it and the best years of his life was his time in the Royal Marines which the boy's army led to. He had a home, a family of mates, structure and everything found, clothing, food and money guaranteed. Then there was the excitement of danger and the feeling that you were doing something worthwhile. He enjoyed the recognition for bravery, the medals, the admiration of your mates and the fact that his community, where he was born, would know he made something of himself.

If he had not gone away and went through another sliding door of life, where would he be today? Working down the pit like his Dad? Yes, he felt he was given a wrong sentence again, but it worked out. The silver lining, he guessed, just takes time.

Now things were messy. Did he love Karlien? If she was alive, wouldn't she have visited him in prison if she loved him? So, she must be dead or doesn't care. What attracted him so to this woman? The only home life he had known was the few week's holidays at Aunt Bessie's. His home was not happy and not really a family. Brutal father and mother, driven to drink and drinking to death. No real love. At Aunt Bessie's, they would all sit around the table for great breakfast, lunches and dinners. They would play games, work the farmland and animals. A simple life and he adored the way Ted and Bessie loved each other, always chatting and laughing. Yes, he wanted that simple, clean, happy and beautiful life with Karlien.

He also wanted a family so much, kids he would love like he was not by his Mum and Dad, a smallholding and a loving wife, friend, lover and partner. He didn't want to work in an adult entertainment club. He wanted to save Karlien from her life and take her away to a serene country environment where she would never have to sell herself again, where she would love the simple life of a loving family. Save her like a knight in shining armour, who was he kidding!

Would he have taken the easy life at the club and gone on for years? Easy money, easy life. Helping disgusting activities by osmosis, really. Turning a blind eye, looking the other way. Easy to do, no hassles, no standing for anything. I told them I hated drugs but allowed the kids to get them from the pushers, organised it within the club.

Did his friendship with Nick bring him down the dirty path with him? He was a good guy in the army, a good mate and sparring partner. The sleazy, easy life must have turned him bad. "Therefore, the grace of God is where I would have ended up. Bit by bit, they got me to do things that were not right, a slippery slide to hell. Nick knew that I was a bit old fashioned, so he was breaking me in slowly. The job was easy after the army, he was trusted and respected, the money was good and this was a way to lower my morals without me even knowing it or recognising or denying it for what it was?"

*So, what will be the silver lining if I get through this?*

He returned to the chaos at the farm just as Eager was completing his phone call. A quick look around at the barn and the bodies, blood and Scotty seeming mesmerised standing over this big lump of a person, who was gasping less now and bleeding more. He has seen plenty of bodies before and the scene interested him more than repulsed.

"They did Bessie," was all Scotty could say. McAllistar looked at the bodies of Leon and Roman.

"Saved me the bother then."

Eager came rushing out and told them the force was on the way. He told Scotty to hold the scene. They had to get their stories one hundred per cent right. Especially about Romeo and Ned's pitchfork attack. He was in shock but had to stress that he did it as she was about to kill Eager, not the dog. They only attacked when they knew life was in danger. Stress that they were in the process of killing them all and had threatened so. Also, they needed to make it look like they were helping the woman not letting her die. He stressed this was an international incident and dealing with the Russians was not easy, so someone up high may want scapegoats.

Then Eager and McAllistar took off in the Russian's Rover, an unknown car to the police with normal, not diplomatic plates.

# Chapter Sixty-Six
## Found

"So, last chance to tell me where she is?" McAllistar was firm. He was on a payphone at a motorway stop.

"Good news. She didn't go back to Africa. Do not ask me why. She has been seen in London and my guys have her identified in a certain area. We are watching some key places where she had been seen on regular occasions and should pick her up soon. Tends to go to these places in the evenings," Nick replied, hoping McAllistar would understand why she goes to the Savoy and Ritz on a regular basis.

"Are you playing me, lad?"

"No, we are as gobsmacked as you must be. But the key is that she is alive and we will get her and swap for tapes and then this is all over. We can all move on."

"What about drugs?"

"We are following up some other options. I am tending to believe you some."

"Some?"

"If you have fitted up, then the finger points in a couple of directions. All I am saying is the jury is still out."

McAllistar was thinking about this news. If true it was great. Was the universe working in his favour and the silver lining is starting to come his way?

"I thought you were sure she went back?"

"I have the invoices for two first-class seats to Joburg. She was in a wheelchair and my guys took her to the airport and watched her be wheeled through. She was so bad that she didn't even talk to them and was bandaged up. We had to get a doctors certificate to say she was okay to travel."

"She came back then?" He was hurt if this was the case, she made no attempt to contact him at all.

"Possible."

"Next steps?"

"Call me tonight and be in London so we can exchange if needed. Right?" Nick said anticipating they would go back to the papers safe house.

"Oh, by the way, you do not have to worry about the Russians," McAllistar offered.

"Why not?"

"They are both dead."

# Chapter Sixty-Seven
## Truce

It was the same café they had been to before when Dirk Ryder surprised them. The three Americans sat inside this time and spread out a little. They were not going to be caught off guard again. They were ready for anything and assumed, though, that the Harkers would not do anything foolish in a London café after all, this was not Chicago in the Al Capone years. Regardless of the situation, being careful was their nature and business. This was London which has CCTV cameras monitoring every street and police on every corner. No one was going to do anything stupid in their own backyard.

Harvey sat at a table for four on his own, facing the door in what he called the gun fighter's seat. Sam and Gary on each side of him on tables set back. The staff thought it was funny but assumed Harvey was a rich American and these were his bodyguards. They had been in regular and tipped really well. Harvey asked for a free refill. He was told they needed to bring another coffee and charge for it. "Not like the States unlimited refills." he complained to the manager. All he got was, "Well this is not the States. Brits!"

Dirk came in first and looked around and nodded to them. Next Tazewell, Nick and then Jimmy finger bandaged.

"Gentlemen, we meet again," Jimmy said in a friendly voice.

"Please join us." was Harvey's reply, equally calm and almost as friendly. They did as Jimmy sat opposite Harvey. Dirk sat with Sam and Nick with Gary. They seemed uncomfortable by this, but they were the professionals. The waiters came and asked if they needed anything. "Later," was the response. The manager was getting very uncomfortable as the atmosphere was electric, Jimmy could see this and didn't want him calling the Bobbies.

"Here," he asked the manager to come across. "We are not hungry, however, take this and the staff away while we have a private meeting." He gave fifty pounds in notes. The manager's eyes lifted with surprise and he immediately withdrew with the two waiters to the other side of the room. Their faces were familiar, but he could not place them.

"You have something to say, then say it." said Harvey, the impatient one.

"Right down to business then. We can work together and you get what you want and we get what we want. You take yourselves back to the United States and never come back and we live in peace and harmony."

"Never come back?"

"We can have a truce," holding up his bandaged hand, "to resolve this mess we have and go our different ways in peace. If and when you come back to my turf, the truce is off. Understand?"

"Gee, he's got a lot of balls," Sam said from the side.

"Be quiet." Harvey had turned around to eyeball him to stay out of this as planned. He was thinking that they would be all part of his clean up and Jimmy was thinking this would last until the Americans helped, became the fall guys for the murders, which must happen, of course, they would be the dead fall guys.

"And what do we want?"

"Your boss, employer or whatever wants no trace of his little indiscretion, so it would not harm his let's say reputation. Right?"

"Why would we need you?" Harvey asked.

"Well, you have been here for how long? Choppered up to Derbyshire and back and been running around like chooks, pardon my Australian, with your heads cut off. Not to mention cutting a few fingers! This is not your territory and your contacts have been unhelpful, am I right?"

Harvey's body and fists tightened visibly.

"Do not take offence, listen to what I am offering."

"Speak then and it better be good." The aggressiveness came out of Harvey and a bit of a show for his boys.

"We will have the people with the tapes soon. You take your original if it exists and go. We also will have the girl soon."

"What girl?"

"Karlien or Dusty as she calls herself."

What happened next, if you blinked you would miss, not Jimmy or Nick, though. There were glances towards Tazewell from the Americans, Tazewell to Dirk. All seemed surprised, it was subtle but unmistakable messages were being sent back and forth.

"The girl has been neutralised!" Harvey blurted out.

"Not true, she seems to be very much alive and back in London."

"Prove it!" Harvey was louder than he wanted to be.

"We will. If you want to partner up, we need your help tonight."

There was a minute of silence as the Americans consumed the information and processed it. It was true the local CIA office MI5 had been useless. The people they beat and cut had no information. Even the cop guy in Derbyshire was missing during their visit. This was the best offer and a chance to achieve their goal.

"How did you put a camera in that room that night?" was Harvey's question.

"Not us, we never authorised it, that room has never had video surveillance, too sensitive for our business. This is another mystery."

"The secret service would have swept that room earlier and just before he entered and anything electronic, bugs and such would have been found."

"True, but it wasn't us, we have not even seen the video and have no idea what or who is on it. And we do not want to know. We saw the girl afterwards and what a mess."

"It could only have been brought in by the girl or connected to power and switched on just before they started."

"Are you suggesting Dusty did this?"

"She was the only outsider allowed to enter. They stood guard on the door after the last sweep."

This had been bothering Jimmy and Nick for some time. Billy must have been involved from the technology side. The room was not an authorised room for video, strictly forbidden. Was Karlien involved? If so, why? And was she and Billy friendly? This was a big risk for them and how would they use the video later without getting caught? There had to be a mastermind involved. The plot thickens.

"Okay, is it a deal?"

"Deal," all three said.

"Okay, this is what we need to do," Jimmy laid out the trap plan.

On the way back to the club, Nick drove Jimmy and the others were sent back in cabs. They needed to talk.

"So, if Taz is telling the truth, he and Dirk did some extra activities for the Americans. Taz sending her to South Africa and Dirk being there to bury her like his other apartheid victims," Jimmy was talking it through. Nick listened intently.

Jimmy continued, "If you had to guess who set this up, who would you pick?"

"Tazewell for sure. He has dubious contacts in the United States, is American, wily like a fox, greedy and I never trusted him. When he cleans his glasses and gazes down whilst talking to me, I figured his brain was working on some scheme."

"Right. What about Dirk?"

"Just muscle, torturer and paid assassin. Free-agent, really, can do work for anyone, I guess. Not bright enough to plan this all nor would he have the relationships or contacts."

"Can we trust him?"

"Yes, unless he fears some sort of retribution and then he will turn on us."

"Both have to go?"

"I guess so," Nick was clear about it.

"The drugs?"

"More we know, more it points to Tazewell. The Russians bring the drugs and deliver to McAllistar, so he is holding the baby. It never made sense that they delivered in broad daylight in a parcel."

"If there were drugs inside?"

"Possible."

"Then plant the drugs in his apartment and call Samuels to raid. McAllistar out of the way looking guilty as hell. He thought we would have him killed in prison but didn't figure on the videos being taken by him and hidden."

"The Russians come down on us and Tazewell is free to sell them and to others, what games is he playing or who is he playing with?"

"The game is definitely afoot," Jimmy quoted his favourite line.

"Afoot more like a bleeding yard!"

"Fuck! You said she was dead!" Tazewell was desperate.

"The girl is as dead as a dodo. I do not make mistakes. I met the wheelchair girl at the airport, checked her passport and ticket and told her that I was a limo driver sent by you to take her to a place of rest."

"A place of rest?"

"Well, you know a little pun. I told her Grand Kruger Lodge at Kruger National Park. Three months rest and recuperation on the house. She didn't have a clue what was going to happen."

"How come she is still alive and back here?"

"No way, she looked like the photo you sent. No way, eeeish."

"You better be right as one of them or the other are going to kill us. We need a plan."

"You need a plan? I just execute assignments as ordered and paid for and I did my job on the girl you sent to me."

"Tell them that."

# Chapter Sixty-Eight
## Preparing the Way Forward

Eager and McAllistar entered the safe house. Gavin was on the phone with the next day's editorial and layout giving direction. Two uncomfortable 'rent-a-cop' guys were standing near the front and back doors with not a clue what was going on. They were not armed.

Gavin got off the phone as soon as he saw them arrive. Liberty had been shopping for more outrageous outfits on Gavin's credit card.

"Have we got news for you!" Almost the same words came out of them all at the same time.

"You first." Gavin said having already heard Liberty's news as a newsman, only the latest was of interest. Eager gave them a rundown of the day's activities at the B&B. Gavin took notes. Liberty's mouth was wide open as she recognised that the dark side of life, an angel of death, had descended. It was no longer a fun game but very serious. She shuddered.

"Your turn." Eager said to Liberty. She gave them a blow for blow report on her evening at the club and her interface with Jimmy Harker. She turned to McAllistar and related her conversation with Candy about Karlien. He screwed his face up.

"This is what Nick Harker told me today, says he will have her by tonight."

"Can we start looking and find her first?" Liberty asked looking at Gavin.

"I'll get some reporters to go around the hotels and see if we can find her first. Description? Picture?"

"Here." McAllistar pulled out a crumpled picture he had kept with him all the time in prison. Liberty put in that she maybe be wearing Sandy Shore or Dusty Springfield wigs or may have moved on to another singer. Either way, she would stand out.

"Where is Candy's flat?" Gavin asked.

"Hoxton," Liberty replied.

"Funny, a woman hung herself in her flat today at Hoxton. In the copy, I have for tomorrow's addition."

"Name?" Liberty asked.

"Let me see," checking his copy, "Pamela Holder."

"That's her, saw it in her bag when I searched it."

"Searched it?"

"I took her driving license to use it, as they are asking for ID and I can hardly go with mine."

"Go! You are not going anywhere!" Eager screamed at her.

"I'd like to see you stop me!" she screamed back.

"Oh, you would, would you? You will get yourself killed for nothing. I will arrest you now for theft and put you away until this is over."

Liberty went ballistic. "Come on and try, old man. You and who's the army? My story, my big story and no one is getting in the way. Come on arrest me." Putting her fists up in a boxing position as if to fight him.

"Okay, I will, it is about time you were taught a lesson." Eager went for her slapping her punches away. Her kick to his groin was painful and not expected.

*Our first fight,* he thought.

"Chuffing Eck." McAllistar got between them. "Come on. Lass, calm down and listen." He was holding her around the waist in the air as she was still kicking.

She stopped struggling and McAllistar let her down. He didn't like this type of personal confrontation, heard his Mum's head being banged off the sink too many times.

She went to the floor to Eager, who was still holding his private parts in obvious pain.

"Sorry, sorry," she said bending down and holding his free hand in hers.

He was amazed that the pain only made him giddy. Same as Olga's kicks. He had avoided pain all his life, walked a mile from any fight, no violent sports and now he was finding out that he actually didn't mind it.

"Well, I am not going to marry you with that temper!" They all began to laugh; the bad mood was broken. So, they talked. Yes, he didn't own her but he was an officer of the law-bound to protect her and he thought that he was a friend as well.

"We are, we are so close, let's not give up now," she pleaded.

"You don't know how bad these people we are dealing with are. This is not a game, Liberty. They will kill you and all of us if it suits. To go there is suicide."

"You're the policeman, let me go and protect me."

"You are insane. We are operating outside the mainstream law. If I get help, everything would be compromised. We just left two Russians dead and one badly injured. Now an innocent woman has been killed. We will all be brought in and McAllistar most of all."

Silence for a while as they thought about it all.

"More bad news," Gavin interrupted, "GWP knows our telephone number here. The assistant editor asked me if he called me, which he didn't, so I assume he has passed it on or am I paranoid?"

"Come to think of it, I thought I was just imagining it but I felt someone watching me in the garden today."

*Maybe we are all paranoid. But if we are, this is the time,* Eager reflected.

The decision was made to move right now but where and how?

They grabbed their bags and jumped the back wall into the house behind the garden. They then ran two different directions, Gavin and Liberty went south to the tube station first. McAllistar and Eager did linger for several minutes to see if they were spotted and followed. No movement, so they went several streets over to wave down a cab.

"Evening, George. Have you got three spare rooms for the night?"
They all walked and met at the pub. It was quite late afternoon before the drinkers come in after work. The dragon walked in and looked at them all with her dark eyes.
"I mean four spare rooms," Eager corrected himself.
"Only got three, but they all have two single beds."
He showed them to their rooms. Gavin and Logan in one each and the other Liberty and Eager. As long as the dragon didn't know. He was glad the neighbours would know about the pretty American young lady he was with, but sleeping together in this village would be severely looked down on, although it was not uncommon, just kept literally under the covers.
"We can push these together," Liberty whispered to Eager. His face lit up.

"Sir, I need your help today," Eager pleaded on the telephone.
"You need my help, I am hoping to keep my pension with just a few months to go, I think I'm on the edge!" Charlie was stressed. Eager could only imagine his red face and sweat running down his forehead. Eager hoped he was not going to have a heart attack before he could help.
"This is life or death vital, you hear me out, sir."
"Go on make my day, any other corpses you have stacked up. How about a few Americans, the PM would love another crisis? They want you to come in or be brought in. Spent most of the day with the chief, foreign secretary, MI5 and God knows who else."
"Yeah, I am sorry but unless you help me, more will stack up and it will be me, McAllistar and the reporter, not to mention the editor."
"Okay, tell me what you want."
"I need authorisation for two weapons, automatics if possible and a very small bug with a good radius."
"I will have to go to the chief for this and he is not in the best of moods. So, tell me exactly why?"
Eager told him about a possible hand over of the tapes for the missing Karlien. He would be outgunned and if he had any chance of recovering the tapes, this was the time. They debated over bringing in a specialist team and Eager resisted. He didn't know when or where. The people he was up against were on high alert and a black ops team spotted could ruin the whole thing and bring lots of casualties. The second gun was for Logan. This presented problems for Charlie, who would rather position it as he gave Eager two, in case he didn't have time to reload. They agreed on a radio direct to himself and that Eager would keep him informed.
"Will the commissioner approve?"

"He can see his 'lordship' wandering down the Thames if this is not cleared up. Plus, I had to use our ace card, didn't want to but he insisted you be brought in as the committee wants."

"Our ace card?"

"What you saw the ACC do. The commissioner will want those tapes badly, I mean really badly, before anyone else sees them. This is his biggest nightmare. You got to get them and get back! So, call me in thirty minutes and give me your location for the delivery."

"Wilco."

"Oh, by the way, a scared manager of a café described the Harkers meeting with three big Americans. He said they sat around like it was the start of the gunfight at the O.K. Corral and then they seemed to all leave as friends."

"So, they have teamed up?"

"Watch your back. MI5 finally came clean, they are sure there is a rogue unit working with or for the CIA."

They met in the empty snug lounge. A few drinks on Gavin's credit card again. He had been on a payphone to his office. The dragon served some sandwiches and ugly looks.

"Well, we are on our own. The chief would not approve any weapons, just the bug and radios. If anything goes wrong, they will deny pre-knowledge. He has insisted that I tell Charlie, sorry, my boss, the chief super, where we are going for the handover as soon as we know. Apparently, he has a very bad migraine. Ha, serves him right."

George much against Eager's advice had become part of the planning team. He was interested as, apart from throwing drunken yobs out after hours, this was the most exciting thing that had happened to him since he left the force. A pub is every Englishman's dream until you work seven days a week until 11 pm and then back for cleaning and deliveries early morning.

"So," Gavin said counting on his fingers which he liked to do, "let me get this right. One, we are up against the most dangerous mob in town maybe the United Kingdom and two, we now have an American CIA or whatever hit team with them, highly trained professionals maybe ex-Navy Seals or Green Berets. Three, we do not know if the Russians are out of the game and/or planning revenge. Four, we have no weapons and if we did, we only have two guys capable of using them and five, Logan still refuses to give up the tapes for our security, even though he has been assured from two sources that she lives. Six, our great police force abandons good honest citizens when needed the most. Did I get this right?"

"You have run out of fingers on that hand, however, putting it in plain English, seems like you guys are fucked." George added his two pennies worth not making anything better.

"I can shoot. All good old Americans can," Liberty added, trying to lift their spirits.

"Good evening all. I see that everyone is present, that's great." DS Williams had walked in. They all seemed to jump back a couple of feet.

"Can I talk with you outside, John?"

They went outside into the car park where her police vehicle was parked.

"Charlie thinks that you do not trust him. Ask Williams to come to 'where the old dragon resides'."

"He's right, the less he knows the better chance of keeping his pension."

"I have the gear for you. I guess you know how to work it all?"

"Yes, pity he didn't get authorisation for weapons."

"John, you do not have to do this. Walk away, we can arrest McAllistar and put the hard word on him. He would not want to go back to prison."

"You do not know him like I do. He is like a cricket ball on the outside very tough and on the inside, a marshmallow, however, never push him as it all turns hard and nothing will come out of it. We have a chance to see this through and bring down the Harkers and a lot of sick people. You didn't see all those videos; I saw enough to make me sick of the fucking human race!"

She folded her arms. Denise had a soft spot for Eager and a major loyalty towards him. He had helped her in her career and never once underestimated her as a woman, unlike a lot of those big dicks in the force did. 'Get me a cup of char luv that's a good girl'. Condescending dicks.

"I want to come with you."

"No, definitely not, why risk your blossoming career for an old warhorse over the hill and probably out of the force after this, especially if it goes wrong."

"I am not risking it for the old horse. I am a police officer and we are embroiled in a situation that needs to be resolved and sorted. I want to help sort it!"

"No."

"Well sir, I will not give you my extra presents."

"Extra presents?"

She pulled a bag out of the car boot. Her sports which bag she used for the gym. She opened it. Inside were two weapons, a bowie knife and extra ammunition. A Glock 19 and a Sig Sauer P226 with double stack magazines.

"Did Charlie send these? I thought the chief had stopped it?"

"In a way."

"In what way?"

"Well, he signed off on me retrieving two weapons from the last armistice for checking again for an old cold murder case."

"If you play straight with Charlie, I mean tell us where you will be, time and so forth, he has agreed for a three-man special ops team to be available just in case things go wrong."

"Lead the team then, I trust you and your instincts. You can be on our channel that will involve you and keep you clear of whatever legal trouble we get into."

He needed to think about taking the weapons. He was trained to carry arms but not the best shot. McAllistar was a marksman and could kill. The old double-tap to the head. But did he need to add more complexity to the already dangerous situation? What if we use or lose the weapons? Denise would be in big shit. A bowie knife, really, did she think they were hunting bear? Maybe this was the best she could do, she knows McAllistar can use a knife effectively. Hard to conceal, though, a big bloody knife for sure.

They chatted about some prep work he needed her to do and then tested the radios and with that, she left with hers tuned to the right channel they would use.

# Chapter Sixty-Nine
## The Best Laid Schemes of Men and Mice

McAllistar would call and arrange a public meeting to get Karlien and pretend to handover the tapes. Eager would cover, backed up by the police team and DS Williams. If things turned bad, they could swoop in. This meeting needed to be early as Liberty had to leave for the 8 pm pick up at the club. If they hadn't found Karlien by then and made excuses, then he would postpone to the next morning saying that he wanted it to happen in broad daylight.

Gavin would be communications officer and stay at the pub with George listening in. Gavin would also record the situation blow by blow for the newspaper and the book. Eager knew Gavin was best out of the way and George was being held prisoner by the dragon. He so desperately wanted in some action to spice up his life.

"You are going nowhere, George Whittaker or else!" was her command.

DS Williams was researching properties owned by the Harkers or their company. If it was a new location, then it must be owned and kept secret they guessed. If the bug failed or the shadowing, then they would have options.

Liberty would take the bug and hide it somewhere. No one wanted to know where as long as she got through the searches at the club. After she needed to make sure that it was transmitting.

Eager started to think through the holes in his half-baked plan:

Flaw 1: they needed to know where the Americans were in this as they have teamed up with the Harkers it seems. Why would they let the star witness against their boss live or any of them for that matter?

Flaw 2: When they followed Liberty, how would they get inside without a warrant and a bigger backup team? How would they know when she was in trouble? If the hanged lady was anything to go by, then she was in trouble and this was a trap. But what would they gain by Liberty? Silence the press? Information on where they were? A kind of full disclosure on what they had been doing and who else knows what before killing her?

Eager was very worried. This would not be the case if McAllistar was not so thick-headed about the girl. Take the tapes in, get a big team together and take down a lot of people. Big bust no big risk. He needed those tapes or the dupes in fact both.

Denise needed to zoom in just after they were handed over. Arrest the ones carrying, which he assumed would not be the Harkers; they always kept clean hands, although this was big and they might not trust anyone else.

He knew he always got nervous before a police bust, this time, though he was positively neurotic, so much rested upon what happened next. Liberty's life, his job, his life maybe and others and to top it all, he could face prison time if this all goes south.

"What, you can't find her?" Nick was agitated. They were so close to getting this right and moving on.

"Trouble?" Jimmy asked.

"They haven't found her yet. Watching the three hotels and no sign. Even the squirrel sniffing around has only come up with a girl fitting her description popping in from time to time to the Savoy."

"Don't worry, we have other options like the reporter girl tonight. Dirk will make her talk."

"I think we should let her go with the bishop first, that's punishment on its own."

"Good idea, soften her up a bit!" They both laughed.

Tazewell came in. He was nervous and they were now always quiet in his presence.

"Who did we send on that plane, Taz?" Nick asked.

"I can only believe that it was her."

"No detective then? Her friend Sandy was very similar in looks and body height and other features. She disappeared at the same time, wrapped in bandages, she would pass for Karlien. Right?"

Tazewell lowered his head thinking and took off his glasses and started cleaning them as he does when thinking hard.

*God, we killed the wrong girl.*

"The plan," then Jimmy started. "Leave the guys watching the hotels. Call in the rest of the team so we can be prepared for any eventuality."

"Even Willie, the wanker?" Nick asked.

"Yes, we may have to cover a wide area as McAllistar will choose the playing field where we meet. Willie has his uses."

"Can't we demand where we meet on our turf?" Tazewell butted in.

"He is far too clever to accept that. No, he will decide where we do the exchange for sure and it will be a public area," Jimmy rebutted him like a child. No patience left for him.

So, they discussed the next steps. If McAllistar rang and they didn't have her, Nick was to play for time, make an excuse but keep the meeting if possible. Escort girls visiting clients normally, go later in the evening, although she had been seen around 6 pm on some occasions. They needed people ready on foot and at least three vehicles on standby. They had brought in ex-getaway drivers, who were highly skilled and obtained similar vehicles to cover a getaway.

Nick would have a shooter shadowing him ready for action near but far enough away that if there was a trap or bust, he would not be carrying. They would have four shooters around, only the guys who knew what they were doing, mostly ex-army. They doubted McAllistar and Eager had weapons, although they always had the 'be prepared' boy scout motto in mind. The main goal was to get the tapes, the girl and McAllistar could be dealt with later if needed, although they were beginning to believe that he had not taken the drugs. So, why fight a war that was not necessary? The general feeling, though, was that he needed to be part of the clean-up.

"Samuels?"

"He claims that they were still moving around, whereabouts unknown. Not directly involved or supported by the police yet, although Eager had been given a week to bring them in by his sympathetic super," Tazewell replied.

"The Russians, Pinky and Perky?"

"Not heard from them. Tried to call. No response. Left messages at the embassy. Nothing. Maybe they have gone away?" He didn't go into the horrible meeting he had with their boss, the lady monster. He shuddered at the thought.

"McAllistar told me they were both dead," Nick added. Tazewell was surprised but thought this was good for him.

"How?" Tazewell asked. Nick just lifted his arms up in the air enough to say he didn't know.

"The Americans?" Jimmy asked, feeling his bandaged finger that hurt and hurt. This was personal with him.

"Waiting on our call. Do we give them, their bosses, the tape or kiss them goodbye?" Nick asked.

"Kiss them goodbye, of course. They didn't do this to me and walk out of here achieving their goal." He was holding his hand up and very bitter.

"More will come," Tazewell ventured. He was thinking that maybe they could help him as they intended a clean-up, which he felt that would involve him also.

"No, they will pay up tens of millions of dollars and then there is no need to follow up."

Tazewell gulped, his big deal they had now was taken over and he would see nothing of the payoff.

"Once we have the reporter girl talking, we get them to come to the abbey and sort them out there after the evening's entertainment," Jimmy added.

"The black hogs?" Nick asked.

"All eight thousand pounds of each of them are at the farm at the abbey."

"Feeding time then," Nick said almost excited.

"Feeding time?" Tazewell asked, even though he thought he knew what was coming.

"The hogs eat, when kept almost starving, human bodies' bones and all. Nothing left. No bodies, no murder. Come down and watch," Nick replied happy to see the impact on Tazewell. Tazewell had visions of being eaten by the hogs, he sensed that he was being set up for a big lunch for them. The mood of the Harkers towards him was subtle, however, he could feel a cold chill. He had to get out and away, but how?

They discussed the Americans as they all knew that these guys were professional and would not walk into a trap and if they did, they could still cause a lot of damage.

*Especially if they are warned,* Tazewell was thinking and formulating an escape plan. They needed a hook.

"The girl and the tape will bring them," Tazewell started his planning.

"The girl?"

"Karlien. They want her dead. They paid me before so I will have to tell them we got the wrong girl but it will bring them on us like wolves."

"So, we need to get them all there. Karlien, McAllistar, Eager all of them." Jimmy grimaced as he thought how much the hogs would have to eat. Maybe he needed more hogs and how would they round them all up? Tazewell would be a full day feed himself alone. He laughed out loud. No one knew what he was thinking.

# Chapter Seventy
## Monster on the Loose

"She's what?"

"Gone, sir," Chief Inspector Fenwick said nervously, his pencil-thin moustache twitching.

"Gone!" Charlie's stress level was rising.

"How?"

"Came in with five Russian security people and told the constables that she had diplomatic immunity and they were sending her to Russia for proper medical treatment."

"So, they walked her out of the Derby Royal Infirmary with no resistance, no call to me?"

"Sir, I attended and they were very insistent and had all her diplomatic credentials with them and one of our foreign office officers. They moved very quickly. They did sign her out properly."

"Bloody good help that is! What about her treatment?"

"One punctured lung and a very bad incision to her back that missed the other lung. She was on oxygen, drips and had a blood transfusion. Not really right to take her."

"She is under investigation for the attempted murder of a police officer."

"Sorry sir, but she does have diplomatic immunity."

# Chapter Seventy-One
## The Bait

It was 5 pm and Sammy was starting to get bored. High tea at the Ritz was expensive and he had been inside the hotel for two hours. The bosses would gripe if he spent a lot with no result. The stuck-up waiter, doorman and concierge had all looked down their noses at this little guy who was in an old raincoat and brown desert boots. It was like he was dirtying the pristine hotel foyer and turning guests away. In short, he stood out and didn't fit their customer profile.

*Fuck the stuck-up assholes. They are only low paid snotty servants; I earn more than all of them put together on a good day.*

He took a wad of twenty pounds notes which added up to a 'monkey' in cockney slang or five hundred pounds. Letting them all see he had a lot of cash. His bill was twenty-eight pounds and he called the waiter across. He put fifty pounds on the silver tray.
"I need some information and you can keep the rest."
The waiter looked around, "What type of information, sir? Are you a private detective?"
"Something like that. I am looking for a lady, very attractive, probably wearing a dark wig, calls herself Sandy or Dusty?"
"Why?"
He threw down another fifty pounds adding up to a ton.
The waiter was licking his lips and looking around nervously. The money was very attractive for his low pay. Sammy knew he had something to give but was holding back for some reason.
"I am not going to hurt her. A friend of mine uses her services shall we say and lost touch. I want to put some business her way."
"Oh. The escort business lady," He looked around again and grabbed the notes. "She has an appointment very soon. Guy has rung down twice to see if she has arrived. Her name is Sandy." He then ran off.

*She probably pays them all something so she can get the calls from the concierge or be allowed in to give room service. The hotel managers of these fine establishments would have heart attacks if they knew what their staff were doing*

He saw a young woman come in and start showing what looked like a picture to the staff. They all shook their heads after looking at it. He was sure it was not the police, he could recognise and smell them a mile away. Someone was looking for someone and it was too much of a coincidence that both were looking on the same day. She left soon after, so maybe given up, he hoped.

Sandy arrived five minutes later, shook the concierge's hand with a twenty-pound note in it, partly hidden but not from the squirrel's eyes. He said something, probably the room number and off she went to the lifts.

Sammy moved quickly, he needed to round up Dirk and Bruce and some transport outside and call the bosses. He figured that he had thirty minutes to get the trap in place as this was not an all-night job, he was sure.

# Chapter Seventy-Two
## Double Traitor

Tazewell was very nervous. He had booked a ticket to New York, packed and sent money from his bank accounts to his other offshore accounts in the British Virgin Islands. He thanked God that he had kept all this information in his head as they would have found the documents showing money paid in for the drugs after they disappeared. Now, he needed to set a trap to keep the Harkers busy. Surely dealing with McAllistar, Eager, Karlien, the reporter and the Americans would keep them busy while he slipped away?

"Thanks for meeting me," he said again whilst he was looking down and wiping his glasses. They were at a small café on Paddington station. A busy place and somewhere he doubted that there were eyes to spot him. He had an espresso while he waited.

They sat around him on the small four-seat table arms folded.

"Spit it out," Harvey said as he was tired of meetings and no action.

"Okay, I have some good news and bad news for you."

"Oh, get on with it," was the terse response from Sam.

"Some things don't always go to plan." He placed his glasses back on his face and looked up.

"Like fucking what?" said the normally quiet Gary, getting annoyed.

"Like the girl is not dead. Before you all jump on me, let me tell you that she switched with a look-alike friend who was the girl killed. I had no idea why other than with the bandages it was mistaken identity. Dirk is so careful normally."

There was just silence as they absorbed all this. Uncomfortable silence for Tazewell. He had to break it.

"I have come to tell you that I will pay back the money and give you some information to make up."

"Let me just sum up the experience we and our client have had with you," Sam started in a very aggressive tone. Tazewell was chosen to give their client a discreet good time on his visit to London due to some of his contacts in the States. The client had told them that he was drugged that night and he cannot remember much.

Tazewell had reported the girl's medical condition and asked for money to pay for it in a private clinic to shut her up, included plastic surgery, which was very expensive. The response was to ask for a way of taking out the evidence for one hundred thousand dollars, so the only person that could stop their client becoming president would not be around anymore. Why would they want to pay for plastic surgery for her silence and not just have her taken her out? Then they are called in to clean up properly as blackmail attempt had stated that videotapes were made at the hellfire club and this event was or could have been recorded. The discreet good time happens to be a big shakedown and I am sure that you and the Harkers are responsible. So, a 'cluster fuck' all-round was his final comments.

Tazewell shook his head sideward several times violently in denial.

"Not true, not true! The video guy was working his own deal. The Harkers just use videos for protection. The whole hellfire club, which is very lucrative, works on the members never being compromised."

"The video guy?"

"Billy, once they found out he had told McAllistar about the videos, he took a long swim in the Thames with concrete boots."

"He must have been working with someone?"

"Not sure, he was a loner. Look, now it seems that the Harkers blame me and I need to get out. I was not involved in any way apart from trying to carry out your client's wishes in the night and requests post facto the incident."

"You get out when this is fixed and clean," Sam said but he lied. Tazewell knew too much and for all, they knew that he had pictures of the girl's injuries and maybe even a sworn statement that can still be used. He was known when they checked him out in the States to be a wily untrustworthy lawyer out for himself.

"Well, it can be sorted for good."

"All ears." was the reply.

"They are planning to use you and then kill you all, leaving you as the fall guys. Jimmy has not forgotten you for cutting his finger almost off. He needs to get back his street cred. Others are moving in from Eastern Europe and Jamaica trying to take his territory."

They were silent again absorbing the information.

"How, where and when?"

# Chapter Seventy-Three
## London Bridge

The plan was to meet at 6 pm and do the exchange at London Bridge in central London, which was always busy. The poet TS Elliot in his masterpiece poem *'The Waste Land'* wherein he refers to shuffling commuters across London Bridge to hell-bound souls of Dante's 'limbo', which, unbeknown to McAllistar, fitted right in with the two circles of lust used for the motif of the hellfire club.

He had chosen it as it was so public, CCTV cameras and lots of police around. It had an A3 five-lane road running across it and plenty of room for pedestrians. The underground monument station was at the north end and London Bridge station underground at the south end if needed.

When McAllistar called, they said they had Karlien and agreed to meet at 7 pm in the middle of the bridge. Just Nick, Karlien and McAllistar for the handover.

"Where are the tapes?" Eager asked.

McAllistar patted his army kit bag.

"You mean that you have had them in there all the time?" Eager was gobsmacked.

"Yup. Well, not all the time. Did they find the blanks?"

Eager looked surprised and guilty.

"Thought so," McAllistar rammed home the breach of trust.

"I am a policeman, Logan. These are horrible, horrible people that need to be stopped. If they get the originals, I need to know where the copies are now? Imagine the kids that are going to be raped and sexually abused, they will be scarred for life, maybe even do the same, 'sins of our fathers', a vicious circle. We know the girl is all right so we can get her free with support."

"Need to finish this laddo. Chuffing Eck! They owe more than the girl. Part of my life wasted, abuse in prison, reputation destroyed, most of all what they are doing to the children and if not stopped it will continue for a long time. They didn't do this without protection." It was then that Eager realised that Logan may do something drastic outside the plan.

"Liberty is risking her life for this story and may end up with nothing. This is a crazy ride and if you do something crazy in public, we all go down with you. Live to fight another day, please Logan, listen to reason."

"If the Harkers get the tapes, they won't be found and I am betting the same with the police. Be covered up. Best Liberty gets the copies."

"If anything happens to you, then we have lost all we have worked for."

He thought about it for a while.

"Best she gets them. I'll make a plan."

"That's all you will make a plan? Not telling me?"

"Yup."

It went like clockwork. Nick was there at the middle of the bridge and Karlien also. She was all dressed up to party with the Sandy wig on. McAllistar walked slowly from where Eager had dropped him off at the beginning of the south side. The bridge was only 269 meters long, so it was only a few minutes before they all faced each other dead in the middle.

McAllistar looked around, only tourists and office people trekking across the bridge. Some standing and looking up and down the Thames, taking in the sites. Mostly couples and a lot of foreign school children visiting London. Traffic was reasonably light for London, but it was coming to the end of peak hour. He was very alert; however, he could not see or sense anything wrong. Nick had come dressed in jeans and a long sleeve shirt open at the neck. Nowhere to hide a weapon and he doubted that he would do anything stupid on the bridge. How would he react? Not getting the tapes was unknown.

McAllistar looked at Karlien with mouth wide open. Almost just as he remembered her with what looked like some plastic surgery to cover scars on her face and forehead?

Nick nodded, "As promised, the amazing Karlien. See reports of her death have been overrated, just as I told you. So, let's get this over with and all go our separate ways forever. Peace man."

"I need to talk with Karlien first," McAllistar insisted.

Nick pushed her towards him.

"I need to verify the tapes are real, so I need to look at them," Nick countered.

"Talk first." Nick shoved her back again more to move her towards him. It was awkward, she seemed cold and hesitant to him.

"You okay?"

"I was. Do not give him the tapes! Hit him, Logan and let's get out of here."

"I missed you," Logan was distracted and wanting to tell her how he felt even in these circumstances. This was frustrating for Karlien.

"No time for that. The tapes are worth a fortune, hit him and let's go."

He was taken aback. The girl he loved was cold and only interested in the tapes. What was going on?

"A deal is a deal."

"I was hurt badly by that guy and I want lots of cash for it, he has to pay. If the Harkers get my tape, they will cash in and cut us out. That's their style."

"Do you know who the guy is?"

"Yes, a billionaire politician, Tazewell told me. Come on, you can take him. His guys are on the other side, we can make it to the underground and lose them. Come on!"

"Enough!" Nick shouted, "Hand over the tapes so I can check them."

McAllistar was not being pushed.

"How are you going to check?"

"There they have a portable video machine inside." Pointing down the bridge.

A black truck was coming along the bridge and abruptly stopped on the kerb beside them. McAllistar walked forward to hand over the tapes when the side door slid opened and he was faced by men with guns pointed at him. He was then pushed from behind by the bridge cleaner he hadn't paid attention to, he was Bruce, the muscle. Inside he was coshed and tied up, so was Karlien. It happened in seconds and they were on their way into the London traffic. Two more black identical trucks followed and they all went different directions off the bridge causing confusion.

Eager radioed Denise, who was on the side of the bridge they were coming off. He had been at a distance, so he didn't have a number plate of the truck that took McAllistar even if it had one. There was a myriad of streets coming off the bridge and Denise's team chose one of the trucks, the best guess. By the time Eager got back into the traffic, it was too late, they were all gone they were too fast and he was too late. He banged his car horn several times in frustration. They were all top getaway drivers and knew London like the back of their hands. The only way to stop them was a police broadcast, which he agreed to with Denise. Although they were masters when doing robberies of changing vehicles several times in minutes, ruining the trail.

She had chased one van around the busy streets, it moved quickly, however, using the siren, lights and pavements where necessary, they managed to catch and pull over.

"Good afternoon, Sergeant, can I be of assistance?" The driver was an old man dressed in a tight black suit and white shirt, blue tie very dapper. The ops team was out in a flash and the side door opened with guns all facing it. It was empty.

"Willie, you will have to come with me." Denise recognised 'Willie, the wanker', stooge, police time waster, never been broken down and admitted anything. You could watch him do an illegal act and he would deny it to your face.

"Oh, that's the best offer I had in, let's see, fifty years!"

*Smart-ass!*

# Chapter Seventy-Four
## The New Hellfire Club

"It was a big cock-up! They got them both!" Eager shouted out loud as he entered the pubs back room.

The team had their mouths wide open and eyes wide.

"Why?" He was handing the tapes over. "They got what they wanted, so why risk picking them up in such a public space?"

"If it was the Harkers?"

"What? Nick set them up, gotta be on CCTV," said Gavin.

"That's the thing, the CCTV according to it, Denise checked, showed Nick trying to help them, banging on the door, screaming until it opened and he got a punch in the face, flooring him as they drove away. He actually made a complaint to the officers attending."

"Bloody play-acting. That's how they did it in broad daylight."

"Not sure, George. Could I have a beer, please?" Eager needed a drink or two.

Liberty had come downstairs in a big raincoat she had bought to help her cover up for the journey. Underneath, she was ready for the hellfire club. Small purse, bug hidden on a pack of condoms. New sexy lingerie all red. Red high heels and stockings with stocking belt, G-string, nipple tassels and a lightweight red dressing gown. This was not visible to the team assembled. The dragon would die if she took off her raincoat, Liberty knew it. George would have a heart attack for certain and Gavin would get all friendly again as it appears that he has been drinking all afternoon. Eager would disapprove the old prude.

"Make mine a white wine, smalls please." She was up to date with the happenings and not too concerned it seemed.

"So, you can't possibly go there tonight." Eager passed her wine to her.

"You want another kick in the balls. You simply don't learn your lessons, do you? No Logan to save you this time," She started to laugh.

A couple of gulps and they were getting refills including Gavin. George was not allowed to drink when he was working, which he was later.

They talked it through over several more drinks. She believed it was their only chance of getting the tapes and Logan back. If they wanted her, it was her theory that they would all go to the same place. Denise had come up with a few premises owned by their company or privately and was pressing the button on search and rescues. It had now gone too far and too serious and Charlie was taking charge. Eager reluctantly agreed that they should stick to the plan, even though his stomach was turning over and over. He would drive her to nearby the 'Blue Heaven' club and be prepared to follow. Charlie had agreed to the team with Denise being on standby and following at a very long distance.

Eager had asked her to do a search on ownership by the crooked solicitor, Tazewell Javelin, which was underway by a detective constable at HQ, no results so far.

"So, we gotta go boys. Wish me luck!" Liberty said at the doorway. They all looked up at her.

*Yes, she has big balls,* Gavin reflected in awe of her. Eager got up and crossed to go with her at the door.

"Oh, one more thing, boys, a sneak preview." She dropped her raincoats and light dressing gown just as the dragon walked in and stopped dead in her tracks. George and Gavin were just staring totally with tongues hanging out.

A smack to the back of to the head sorted George out.

She got to the club and Bruce was the one chosen to search her. This was good, she thought as he was a bit of a sleaze bag and she could work him. He looked at her ID.

"Pamela Holder. Should I call you Pam?"

"You, my big boy," touching his abs gently, "can call me Feather. Are all your muscles as big as these?"

Bruce was searching the small purse. He had just taken out the packet of condoms to look into.

"You will need the extra, extra big ones for me!" Boasting but distracted and he replaced the condom package in the purse without checking it properly.

"Well, you buy them and we will see after the show, big boy. By the way, where are we going tonight?"

"New location, luv. Hush-hush, not to tell anyone. But don't worry, I will be there for you at the end of the night."

*Dumbfuck.*

She saw a minibus leaving full of the girls and some children. Then Jimmy came over and directed her towards a white limousine. She had lit a cigarette and put it out on the pavement away from the limo, hoping that Eager would spot her. Jimmy helped her in and there was Nick.

"You're travelling with us in style. Feather, this is my brother, Nick."

"Hi! Why am I getting the VIP treatment?"

"Because you are special my girl, star turn. Would you like a drink?" The limo had an impressive bar. *Better to stay sober and aware,* she thought. *Oh, bugger it.*

"Do you have vodka and lemonade?" The windows were blacked out, so she saw nothing of the journey, not that she knew her way around London. They were definitely leaving the city. It was getting late now, although the peak hour traffic was over but being London the roads were always busy. She had turned the bug on before she left the club with Bruce drooling behind her. He was sat in front next to the driver in the gun fighter's seat. The speakers were not turned on, so he could not hear and better still not speak; if he said something out of place, they might smell a rat. They would know she had been playing him and want to know why. He kept looking back like a love lost sheep.

"So," Nick said keeping the conversation as light as possible, giving no signs that would scare her. "I have heard about cowgirl success. Is that what you are wearing tonight?"

Liberty swallowed her vodka and stood up slowly taking her dressing gown off. She had to play the part of a loose woman making up to the bosses. She exposed her outfit and spun the tassels around her nipples.

"Stunning!" Nick said.

"The bishop will be pleased," Jimmy said and they exchanged grins. Bruce was looking back, almost twisting his big neck to do so.

"Eyes front, soldier," Nick had picked up his microphone.

The brothers drank slowly, Liberty swigged a few vodkas down and then changed to wine.

"Big bear, come in." Eager answered the radio while following the limo at a safe distance.

"Big bear? What is it?"

"We have been shut down. All have been stopped, searches, you, I and the team have been recalled."

"What? Did I hear right? By whom?"

"Next to the top."

"Can't our friend talk to the top?"

"Trying out of circulation, not contactable. Number two is in control. CA is suspended."

"You are to return right now or be arrested."

"Can't hear you? Bad reception."

"Oh, big bear. The lawyer has a run-down farm in Kent with an old abbey on it."

"Still can't hear you!" He pretended.

"You will if you lose them, little dove. Over and out."

Was he now on his own against the Harkers mob? The location sounded right for the 'hellfire' club and they were headed south into the county of Kent.

"Who did he know and trust the Kent police," he asked himself. "Maybe he could call in favours? Oh, that would be right. Hey, I'm on the run from the Met and would like you guys to come with me with firearms and bust a big London mob. The first call would be to the Met and they would hold him in a second."

They pulled into a big motorway stop. It was packed with cars and people. The limo stood outside the shops and he could see Nick and Liberty going in. *Probably a toilet break,* he thought. Then there were four limos three white and a black one all at the petrol pumps.

*Oh no! Not again.*

His vision had been obscured by moving traffic in front of him and a guy peeping him to get out of the way. He had to move, the honking was drawing attention.

All the limos started to move at the same time. Jimmy came back and got in the black limo and all of them moved off. When did Liberty come back, he missed it. The beeping of the bug was headed back to London. Who did he follow, he didn't have a clue.

*Cock-up number two.*

"Little dove, need an address."

"Oh, big bear. Lost them, yeah?"

"Give me the address, little dove or I will take your feathers off."

"This channel may be compromised."

"I'll take the risk. I didn't lose them, they lost me with lots of limos."

"So, may I introduce you to the bishop?" Nick had his hand on Liberty's back.

"My, yes. What a beauty! Does she talk?"

Liberty had been stunned by this mountain of a man. Fat wasn't the word and ugly like she had never seen before. Suddenly, the tough New Yorker disappeared as she realised what she was in for. Yes, she understood that she might have to play around a bit, dance and tease, but this was serious stuff.

"Yeah, hi. I prefer action over talking."

"Oh my." He seemed very interested and grabbed her hands in his. Two of his fingers were missing, the rest had rings, one with a big amethyst stone, gold with a fish symbol and sterling silver with a cross. He could hardly walk with the weight which made him wobble. She almost started to vomit on him.

"Nick, my son, can I have a private word with you?" the bishop nodded to move to one side.

"Sure."

"Run along, my girl, we can have some good times later." *Thanks,* she thought, *let me get out of here but where and how?*

Nick took her to one side after asking for a minute to the bishop.

"Go down to the main hall, there are two bars. I will meet you in a few minutes. By the way, the bishop likes them younger, so you are off the crook." He laughed at his own pun.

The bishop wanted to know if there was any truth to the rumours that they had moved as they might be raided and he was not impressed with the journey time, which cut short his fun time. Nick assured him that they were creating a real 'hellfire' club of the past and as they developed here, it will get better and better. He also had new pretty-faced twelve-year-old for him tonight, a virgin. The bishop smiled with glee he hadn't seen before.

*He will have to put his hand into the donations box more for this one.*

The abbey had been transformed since their last meeting there with the Russians. Rugs and carpets covered the floor of the main hall and two bars had been set up near the fires at either side of the room. Massive draping's unfolded from the ceilings to form partitioning and privacy for a myriad of sitting areas and lounge beds. The walls were adorned with the phallic symbols, pornographic paintings and religious and devil symbols of all types.

The people were dressed in all types of religious outfits and some as devils with red horns on their heads, dark face makeup, tight one-piece leotard outfits and long tails. It was bizarre looking around. Dominatrices walked around with their whips and sexy outfits. Most of the customers wore masks that made it even more odd, almost a carnival atmosphere in hell. It seemed to add to the fun as people greeted each other like old friends, even though they probably didn't know each other. Maybe some did, she thought, as she watched the interaction.

Music played in the background was a combination of religious hymns and classical music. The real action happened down the stairs where the monk's cells had been turned into bedrooms fitted out with all types of sexual equipment to suit all tastes. The rooms that had once hosted the hard life for the monks, who got up in the cold at 3 am to pray on their knees on the hard floors, now had the feeling of sheer luxury, although very small.

The barmen were stripped to the waist, all boasted a perfect body with six-packs. They had no hair on their chests. Long hair and boyish features. They had a Freddie Mercury body style and they too wore masks. The bar ladies were either topless or dressed as nuns, all were well endowed and heavily made up. The sign at the bar had the original hellfire club menu: Holy Ghost pie, devil's loin, breast of Venus and hellfire punch.

*No women come here then. Just all types of guys and big bar women,* she was thinking when Nick came back and said, "Come now and make some money."

It all seemed okay to her they were treating her well and nothing seemed out of order or so she hoped. He introduced her to five Arab men lounging in their own area and smoking their hookah pipes. Nick pointed out a small CD player.

"You like *'You Can Leave Your Hat Off'*, yeah. It's loaded. Go get 'em, girl." There was a pole to every seating area and she knew what to do next, at least she wasn't humping the bishop.

# Chapter Seventy-Five
## The New Hellfire Club Continued

The room was upstairs at the back of the Abbey with a private outside entrance via a stairway attached to the sidewall. It was previously the Abbot's private area. Not a simple cell but a living room or office, small bedroom and toilet and shower. The big open fire was burning and the first thing McAllistar saw when he woke up was flames and he could hear the crackling of a fire. He thought he was in hell.

"You idiot!" Karlien shouted at him. They were both tied to thick old high back wooden chairs. They looked like they belonged to the abbey a hundred years ago.

"Idiot?" he said, shaking his head to clear it. "Idiot?"

"Yes, idiot. The video was my big hit, the chance to change my life for good, to have my dream home and live happily ever after and you had to steal the tape!"

"Dream home, big break, live happily ever after." He was still coming around and not understanding.

"I took a hell of a beating for that video, had to fuck that ugly smelly Billy. Then you waltz in to steal it. Now they have it and we are both toast!" She was shouting. The walls and doors were very thick, so no one could hear.

"But we loved each other?" McAllistar was not getting the picture.

She threw her head back and laughed. "Love, I don't know love, just money and men who give it to me."

This was not the Karlien he loved or knew. He had gone to hell and back for her. What a fool he was, what a fool. He stared at the floor trying to understand fully, his head was still throbbing from the blow from the cosh.

"Why didn't you hit him and escape when I asked if you loved me? 'A deal is a deal'," she mimicked him.

"You set up the beating and video?"

"He is a billionaire, family man, big politician and tipped to be the next president, how much do you think he would pay for me to go away. Taz said at least fifty million."

"Taz?"

"He helped me set it up, it was his idea. All I had to do is get stupid Billy to film it and take the beating."

"How did you know that he was going to beat you like that?"

"I didn't think he would go as far as he did, drugs, whisky and insults worked."

He thought about her talking to the guy on the video that had poor sound. He had assumed she was teasing him into sexual activity, but she really was goading him into violent action.

"They don't have the tapes."

"What?"

"I am not that stupid. I knew they would try something, so I was going to tell them where they are after the swop."

"So, we have the leverage to get out of here?"

"Maybe. They will try and beat it out of me first."

"No, not true. Well, not a beating, much worse." Nick had entered the room with a very big guy behind him. Both were wearing monk's hassocks with large wooden crosses hanging in front. They both put back their hoods.

"Let us know where they are and we let you go," Nick said in a matter-of-fact manner.

"Like on the bridge? I wouldn't trust a scum like you again. So, let us go and or I will kill you both."

Nick and the big guy behind him were laughing.

"Let me introduce you to Dirk Ryder." Ryder had entered the room with a big black sports bag.

"Evening," he said in a polite friendly way.

"Dirk is a resident expert getting information out of terrorists in what they call apartheid South Africa. He has one hundred per cent success rate in terrorists talking using his cruel but necessary methods."

"Eeeish a few did die in the process before talking," Dirk added for effect, looking like he was trying to be modest.

It was getting dark and Eager had found a spot overlooking the abbey and farm. He had infrared binoculars that George had given him, which he said he used for bird watching at night.

*Right!*

It was the right place. Security gang members everywhere, limos and top of the line cars parked in the yard. He had brought the two guns and the knife from where he had hidden them in the wheel compartment in the boot of the Rover. He never intended to use them, the mess was big enough but what choice, did he have? He was dressed in a pair of black jeans and zip jacket he got from George; a size too big for him. He hadn't quite gone the full commando with a blacked-out face.

*I am too old for this shit!*

"Stay still. Do not move!" a male voice gave the command. He was laying down on his stomach viewing the abbey area and he froze completely not moving a muscle.

"Sir, it's you," Denise Williams's voice came from behind the gunman.

He turned slowly, looking up at four faces. Three police officers dressed in black with body armour and flat black caps all staring down at him.

"Thank God! I thought I had been caught."

"Reinforcements," she said proudly.

"I thought support had been called off?"

"When I told the guys what was going on, they wanted to help. I will cover them as they can say 'only following orders' and were not told of the stand-down by me."

"You could lose your career on this if we don't get the tapes and prove what we are claiming."

"So will you."

"I am deep in it; you have a chance to get out now and retreat."

"Not on, boss. What do we do next?"

He was at a loss. There was too much security surrounding the old abbey. The abbey was blacked out and if it wasn't for the cars outside and a couple of dim lights on the pathway, you would not know what was going on inside. No noise, probably soundproof.

He explained that he was sure McAllistar, Karlien and Liberty were inside. McAllistar and the girl as prisoners and Liberty, he wasn't sure if she was compromised. They knew the ACC was now in charge and would not order support or help get a search warrant. In fact, just the opposite; he would get them caught.

"Where were the commissioner and Charlie?" he asked.

"Rumour has it that the commissioner is on sick leave. Something like serious food poisoning all of a sudden. Charlie has been suspended pending an investigation by the ACC and is out of it, although he had asked to be informed on the quiet."

"The bad guys are running the show then."

"Those pigs?" They thought she was talking about the crooks until she pointed to the left of the old abbey at two great big dark shadows in a pen next to the old barn.

"Pigs, more like cows," one of the officers noted.

John Eager turned his binoculars on them. "Nope, humongous black pigs."

They all looked at each other knowing what the pigs could eat.

"Do we have a camera?" Eager asked. It was affirmative the camera had been left in the police support vehicle hidden below behind some trees. One of the officers left to get the camera. When he returned it was a small camera with a flashlight. "No much use at a distance unless we get up close but better than nothing," Eager murmured.

"Sir, what next?" Denise asked.

"I have a plan."

# Chapter Seventy-Six
## Leverage

"You will have to excuse me, I have guests downstairs. So Logan, just spit it out and we all can move on. I owe you my life and promise we will let you go. I can't bear seeing you tortured."

"Me too?" Karlien asked.

"Afraid not."

"Why?"

"I think our American friends want you out of the way."

McAllistar started twisting his hands around trying to loosen the knots and rocking the big chair whilst all eyes were on Karlien. Her head had dropped to her chest.

"They do look alike, don't they?" Dirk added.

"Sandy?" Karlien asked in fear.

"Enough," Nick said and left.

"What happened to Sandy? Tell me!"

"Let's just say she is having a very long stay in South Africa."

Karlien started to sob, realising what her game had wrought on her friend.

"You bastard!" she started to scream and shout at him.

"No point, luv soundproofed, the old top monk didn't want anyone to hear what he was doing to the young monks. Ha."

She was thrashing around sobbing, crying and the odd scream. McAllistar continued to work on his ropes, twisting and turning his wrists, which were being cut and bleeding, the chair was moving slightly. It was very old and he had more of a chance of falling heavily backwards and trying to smash it. It was creaking badly, however, Dirk was too busy to notice, laying out his portable torture tools.

"Now, let me see, Mr McAllistar. You want it the easy way or the hard way?"

McAllistar spat on the floor.

"I am going to kill you!" He spat out at his torturer with confidence. "I'll take that as the hard way." Torture excited him.

"I'm going to kill you!" Logan repeated.

"See here, boy," Dirk rolled back the floppy hassock sleeves and pumped his big arm muscles, "I would love to teach you a lesson, however, I am pro and need to do the torture thing first. Even if you tell me the location, the torture still goes on until they get them. Give me the information quickly about where the tapes are and after they find them, I will give you a shot at the title. Sharp." Holding his thumb up towards McAllistar.

Laughing he turned around to the fire with what looked like a long iron poker with a knob on the end.

Karlien was sobbing and muttering something moving around in her chair like she was possessed.

"One eye first, I think, that should do the trick," Dirk said as he was turning the poker in the fire. He eventually lifted the poker into the air, came it was glowing red hot.

"Mmm yes, this will be quick and I would like to say painless, but I would be lying." He laughed to himself like he was a very funny part of his overall approach. Make it fun to you and they know you will enjoy torturing them. Although he often had not to leave visible marks, this was different. McAllistar was going to be killed, so he was starting with the eyes. When he was dead, being blind didn't matter, although they all hoped it would end before this and he talked.

"Look, I was going to hand over the tapes for Karlien but I knew that they might double-cross me, so I hid them. I don't want to keep them. I can take you to them."

"Too late for that, my bru. No trust left, you see. Tell me where we can find them and Nick will let you go. You will only be half-blind, I will change my approach and hold until he lets me know. I can't be fairer than that eh?" He laughed again to himself. He was a man who enjoyed his work.

*Some hope of that.* McAllistar knew. Nick had changed a lot and gone over to the darkest side of the dark side.

"That's your plan?" DS Williams queried incredulously.

"Best I got. Anyone with a better one please speak up."

One of the officers had to release the big hogs just as a distraction and chase them towards the abbey. The other two had to start a fire in the field that was visible from the abbey gate but far enough away so that the Harker security would take time to get there if they wanted to see what was happening. The officers should disarm and arrest these guys to even up the odds, only if it was safe to do so, no heroics and big risks. DS Williams had to stay on the hill and keep radio contact with George and Gavin. Meanwhile, Eager would sneak around the old barn and to the back of the abbey to see if he could get in unseen somehow. He was taking the two guns, the knife and camera.

"And if it goes wrong and you get caught, what then?" DS Williams was not impressed but could not offer a better plan. She knew he had dodgy knees which he had hidden from the service for a long time. So, he was not a Rambo by any means. He wanted to keep her and the guys out of as much trouble as possible, which was heroic but maybe stupid. She was younger and fitter than him and her boxing gave her an advantage in tight situations. He had simply said 'not on'.

"Okay. Any questions?" Eager asked, taking a deep breath.

"Lights?" the tall officer asked.

"We don't need any torches here."

"I mean sir matches to light the fire."

"Oh, sorry." He dug into his pocket and pulled out an old gas lighter. His smoking had got worse since meeting Liberty.

The red-hot poker was getting very close to Logan's right eye. Dirk was laughing to himself and taunting him.

"Going half-blind McAllistar."

"Did you know the joke about the loonies in the loony bin trying to get out?" Karlien had come around and was trying to distract him hoping that McAllistar could somehow get free and this nightmare could end.

Dirk dropped the poker down by his side getting interested in her story.

"Go on then, but it better be funny or your nipples will feel this poker," He laughed again.

"Well, there are two loonies seeing the doctor for a discharge. One goes in first and the doctor says to him, 'What would happen if I poked one eye out?'

"The looney says, 'I would be half-blind.'

"'What if I poked both out?'

"The looney says that he would be totally blind. The doctor signs his release paper and as he goes out to the waiting room, he tells the other the answers are half-blind and fully blind."

She coughs. Dirk is facing her with his back to the fire and McAllistar, who is struggling with the ropes and chair. She plays for time as much as possible.

"Well?" Dirk was getting impatient.

"Well, in goes the other looney and the doctor asks him what he would be if he cut one of his ears off? 'Half-blind,' he answers, 'What if I cut both off?' he asks and his answer is 'fully blind'. The doctor asks how does he figure that out? The looney says his hat would fall over one eye and then when the second ear goes over both."

No laughter now. Just a look that says she was wasting his time.

"Now shut up."

"Did you kill Sandy?" Karlien asks.

"Sure did, it was painless believe me she didn't know what was happening. Now shut the fuck up!"

He turns and warms the poker again in the fire and then turns back to McAllistar.

"Enough wasting time, let me get on with it. Oh, blue eyes love them."

He leans forward, McAllistar leaning back on the chair trying to get away from the poker. They hear a piercing scream. "You bastard!" Karlien had tipped the chair forward enough so her feet were firmly on the ground and ran at him using the high wooden top of the chair as a battering ram. He was pushed back towards the fire touching the edge and the poker dropped. In her anger, she had gained some enormous strength and lack of fear you get when, you know, the alternative is death.

McAllistar had made his chair fall back with a hard thud on the ground hoping to break the base of the back where his ropes held him. Dirk was holding a burnt arm screaming African's obscenities, red-faced with anger. He went and washed cold water over it in the bathroom. She also fell backwards onto the hard tiles and was free as the chair which, completely smashed to pieces and the ropes fell off her small frame.

"You bitch, now you will know first-hand what happened to her!"

"She was my friend, my lover, my new life!" Karlien shouted back. McAllistar was learning things that he didn't want to know. Dirk lifted her up with both his hands wrapped around her throat.

"See, slowly you will stop breathing and kicking and then you will join your Sandy."

The outside door from the steps that came up the side of the building was rattling; someone was trying to open it. Dirk dropped her and picked up the poker and went across to it. The handle was turning but the old door was not locked but stuck in the frame as it had been so for many years. He heard, "One, two, three" and then a shoulder hit the door. It hardly moved. "One, two three" again and then a kick. It shuddered. Dirk thought he better help whomever this was and after the next 'one, two, three' He yanked the door open when the kick came. Eager fell into the room at his feet.

"Well, welcome to our little English tea party." Dirk kicked him and Eager rolled over holding the Sig Ruger towards him from the floor. Dirk just hit his hand quickly with the hot poker and Eager dropped it and rolled over again. Out popped the Glock from the back of his large pants onto the floor followed by the bowie knife and camera.

"What the fuck!" Dirk was laughing at this one-man arsenal sprawled across the floor.

Eager scrambled for the Glock rolling on the floor. Dirk lifted the poker for the kill.

"I think I would like a shot at the title now," McAllistar was standing up trying to get the blood running around his stiff arms.

Dirk kicked Eager in the stomach. He lifted both guns and the knife. He thought for a moment and dropped them into his bag and zipped it.

"Okay, come on, why not? I've got fifty pounds on you and bru, you are going to feel it." He stretched his neck and cracked his fingers together.

McAllistar hit him at least five times in the chest very quickly which didn't seem to have any effect. Dirk swung a quick but wild windmill punch that McAllistar easily dodged back in left and right like a man hitting a big punch bag, again no real affect. Dirk turned and kicked him in the stomach and then followed up with a double-handed axe blow to McAllistar's back flooring him. Dirk had to run and kick Eager again as he wriggled towards the sports bag and guns. Then he came back for McAllistar, who was up and moving slowly. He came in but too close. McAllistar feigned to the right and then down a little very close to him, coming up with Henry's hammer the left-hand hook right on the chin. That shook him, so in he went pummelling away. Dirk was tough and came back at him. His right cross knocked McAllistar against the hard-stone wall. He was sliding down it when Dirk started kicking him. Then it stopped. Dirk dropped to the ground and Karlien stood over him hitting him on the head with the poker now red hot again.

"Stop! You will kill him," Eager shouted.

"Too late, lad, he is definitely dead."

McAllistar took the poker off Karlien and threw it in the fire. "No blood, no fingerprints."

"We need to move," Eager said holding his stomach and stumbling around.

He pointed down the stairs behind the barn and up to the mound overlooking the abbey. McAllistar recovered the guns and knife and handed one to Eager.

"Where's Liberty?" Logan asked.

"She's down at the hellfire club below, however, I think they are onto her just using her until the crowd goes. I'm going after her."

"Nope. I am," Logan said without hesitation and with no room for argument.

"Help me get that cloak off him." Eager helped pull the hassock off the big body and Logan slipped it on blood and all.

Eager watched him slip out the door to the stairway. He knew he was younger, fitter and trained for this sort of rescue plus, he was literally knackered from the kicking he had taken. They then left the way he had come and hoped it was still clear.

# Chapter Seventy-Seven
## Hell

Liberty had avoided the three on one offer from the Arabs for five thousand pounds. They seemed to think that she could take all three in different positions as a natural thing to do. Still, they tipped her well for the dance and all of them fondled her again several at a time.
*I'd make more money here than reporting.*
Nick had then thrown her in with a big fat woman, who just wanted to, "Play with you, my dear." She thought there were no women here but they obviously were. Play she did. This was okay, better than the bishop and bought Liberty sometime to think as the fat lady rolled on her making all kinds of guttural noises. She left the exhausted woman and put her lingerie back on and walked past the other cells trying to avoid Nick and find a way out. Eager had better not have cocked this up as she was half-dressed and had no idea where she was. One consolation, she had lots of cash. She walked by the line of cells, the sounds were awful, crying of children, screaming of either pleasure of pain or both. Men were swearing a lot as they climaxed.
*The smell was the worst. Incense and sweaty bodies. Yuk.*
She knew she was in hell and needed to get out. Just then a cell door opened and for a moment, she saw the fish on a bed with two young boys who were screaming in pain. Minister Bill Stephens! She hoped he had not recognised her, fat chance, too busy the fucking paedophile!
She found a big wooden door at the end of the corridor. It was bolted but with a bit of effort, she managed to open the three bolts. All were rusty but had been recently opened for the refurbishing exercise. She peaked out, it was a quadrangle garden area surrounded by cloisters, where the monks, she supposed, walked and sat not talking to each other for years. She slipped into the garden and was about to close the door when she heard a cry, "Mummy, help!" It was one of the boys. She couldn't go without them try as she may and she realised that this could be life or death to her. She looked around and there was a piece of wood that had been used to keep the door open when they moved the furniture in. It was like an axe handle, hard solid wood. She ran back in and opened the door of the cell and the fish was on top of the boy who was sobbing, "Mummy, help." She had no qualms hitting hit right in the middle of his back and then back of his head. He slumped over, knocked out or dead, she didn't know.
*God, I have killed a minister of the Crown!*

She grabbed the boys, threw some clothes at them. They were scared and slow to dress no matter how much she hurried them. Pulling them along, dressing as they went, she headed for the door just as she saw freedom, Nick jumped out in front of her barring her way.

"Where do you think you are going, Liberty Bell?" She still had the wood in her hands and was considering to attack him when he just grabbed it. The boys hid behind her sobbing.

"Oh yes, we know all about you, nosy little reporter and a yank to boot. Well, we are not going to be more of your headlines for sure. Maybe you will become a headline on your own, 'Reporter missing. No sign of her, believed to be eaten by hogs!' You see, you went too far. Now you know everything, not just finding alleged tapes to prove your story. First-hand experience and boy, you are a waste of a good body."

"Let the boys go!"

"No position to give orders."

"But I am." Logan stepped in front of her with Sig Ruger in his hand.

"How the fuck. Dirk?"

"Dead as promised," Logan said casually, regretting he was not the one to kill him, "Now if you do not want to join him, lead the way out."

"My guys are everywhere; you can't get away."

"Pity, then you will be the first to die. Now go." Pointing the gun at the door.

He led them out into the quadrangle, down the cloisters to a garden gate that was the way to the old gardens that the monks used to work. The garden was overgrown and the walls around it were mostly fallen. McAllistar could see and smell a fire in the distance, some shouting. Then some gunshots of low calibre. What was happening?

The big hogs frightened came running across the garden and barrelled into McAllistar with a knock-on effect on Liberty and the boys, who were walking behind him but too close. Nick was off like a flash.

They then ran over the field, jumped the broken-down wall, headed for the barn and up the hill that Eager had described. The hogs bemused by all this followed like dogs.

Nick was shouting for help but something else was happening which they were not sure what. They just kept going. More gunshots, shouts and screams. The boys were slowing them down, although the hogs had them scared, which at least kept them moving to stay with Liberty.

They made it to the hill. Eager and the police team were there. Eager was watching the goings-on through the binoculars.

"Seems like a black Merc arrived and armed men got out. Bit of a barney going on." He handed the binoculars to Logan.

Eager thanked the team and asked them to leave as they were in enough trouble already with the goings-on here. DS Williams agreed that the gunshots would bring local police in good time and they would be out of their jurisdiction and in serious trouble.

"What about the two louts we handcuffed?" the tall officer asked.

"Let them go." Eager ordered.

"As far as I can see, the big misshapen guy with his glasses over his balaclava is Tazewell Javelin, their lawyer with some blacked-out professional-looking special ops guys using automatics with suppressors. He seems to be checking the people as they leave." Logan was scanning the area.

Lots of people poured out of the abbey running for their vehicles to get away as fast as they can. The shooters disregarded them as they were not of any interest.

"Do they have the tapes?" Eager asked.

"No I have them hidden away. We need to get out of here right now." Logan said taking command.

"No! We need to end this with you handing over the tapes." Liberty was livid, so was Eager standing in front of him with arms folded, Karlien behind sitting on the floor with the boys.

"No, we have all risked our lives for you and you are still playing games. You have Karlien back so you need to hand over the tapes and we can all be done with this!" Eager was strong and angry with it.

"If we live." Liberty added.

Logan lowered his head. "I will bring them to you."

# Chapter Seventy-Eight
## Too Hot to Handle

"There is only one way out of this." Eager had them all in the snug bar of the George and Dragon. It was passed the 11 pm, closing time. "That is to surrender the tapes to the police, me, and I get them to the top brass and we get a deal going for everyone."

"What about my story, smalls? Did you forget little me, who has been driving this adventure? Did you know what I had to do in the club to get my story? Any idea?" They were all quiet, probably their imagination was running wild.

"I didn't think so," Liberty was making her case in the strongest terms possible.

"No, your story has got to be part of the deal," Logan said to appease her somewhat.

"Yeah right, they will just hand them back and say newspaper people go for your life, have a terrific time bringing down half of the London knobs and more. Oh, and while you are at it, ruin our relationship with our American cousins. Freedom of the press we all support. Right!" Gavin gave his diatribe.

"I need the one of the ACC to get Charlie, Logan and Denise Williams out of big trouble not to mention my wrecked career. So, why don't we get that one at least and negotiate with the rest?"

"What about mine?" Karlien asked in a demanding way.

"Young lady," Eager started, "You have drugged a major US politician and set about a blackmail act. If the Americans don't shut you up permanently, then you will probably be locked up with this Tazewell guy. Do I make myself clear? Forget it as it has already cost the life of your friend, so do not be the next casualty. We need to negotiate a new life for you somewhere."

She went quiet. She had also killed someone in all this. Could life get worse?

"Well, I want the one on fish. Those boys were screaming and screaming, he is a bleeding, moron paedophile," Liberty demanded.

"Now the new junior minister at the foreign office, PM announced it today. 'Well deserved promotion for an accomplished manager of good governance.' What a rot," he said. "Imagine if the Russians got this tape, blackmail him and we do nothing about it?" Gavin added.

"I am not worried about the Russians, it's about those two boys and others he has abused. He is part of a ring of paedophiles we need to bring down."

"They are still not sleeping, poor things, just crying and crying. I've tried coco, hot chocolate, biscuits, chips but they will eat nothing." The dragon entered the conversation.

"They need professional help. We need to resolve this and take them into care as soon as possible," Said Eager, stressing the urgency. The discussion went on and the late-night drinks flowed. Eventually, all agreed on the two-tape strategy to be enacted first thing in the morning.

Logan and Karlien were left alone. She was a little tipsy. Logan didn't drink and had stuck to water, she had mixed wine and liquor.

"I'm sorry, I liked you, I really did. I am what I am driven to it by my lifestyle, I guess. Sandy was so close and loving, fun and understood what we were and how we felt doing what we do. Do you understand?"

"You led me a merry dance by eck."

"It was my big break, my escape from the sex trade. You have to understand. Do you understand?" Logan was cold and hurt and not really talking to her.

She repeated her comments several more times as drunks often do and then walked across too him stroking his hair, kissing him on the forehead.

"Sorry, I going to be…" She ran off to the bathroom.

The morning came and Logan appeared with a plastic supermarket bag full of tapes.

"Where were they?" Eager demanded.

"Well, after I swopped the tapes in the cottage for the blank ones, I didn't know what to do with them, so I kept them in my kit bag. When we stayed here, I put them in the roof of my room. Small attic access, probably never been opened since George did kill the dragon."

"You had them all the time? The unbelievable risk you took," Liberty said holding out her hand. He looked inside and knew Eager had marked the police chief's video and the minister's.

"One for you and one for you." He handed them out like Christmas presents.

Liberty and Gavin got ready to run off with their big story.

"Didn't you need protection?" Eager asked.

"Bugger that, this is a big story," Gavin blurted out as he left in a taxi very happy.

He had inside information on the hellfire club, his own undercover reporter and the shoot-out plus, he could tease the minister's story for a few days and boost circulation. This could bring the government down. Gavin, the slayer of bad governance. Good job. Liberty could not read his mind at this point in time as she was too busy in the taxi writing several big stories.

Eager rang Charlie.

"You need to come here with some other senior officers and the internal affairs, human relations other chiefs right now. I have the tape. DS Williams can bring you to us. We need action right now on the ACC. Oh and bring some protection as we are dealing with some heavy stuff."

It seemed a lifetime as Eager sipped coffee, awaiting the cavalry. The TV was set up to play the video in the snug bar. Logan had re-hidden the other tapes in the roof and was told to make himself scarce. They heard the sirens of several police cars plus others in unmarked vehicles arrived at the pub.

DCI Samuels had seen a lot of senior people rush out. He was asking what was going on around the office. One of the secretaries told him that DCS Allcock had been ringing in and got her boss to rush out to meet him she presumed. He understood that it must be Eager and the tapes. His ally and supporter was done and dusted. He had the nerve asked him to commit murder for him. Yes, he had promoted him and they had provided protection for the Harkers for some good underworld leads and a bit of cash. But murder no. He had better tell him.

The neighbours of the pub looked out beneath their nets and curtains at the drama unfolding, the most interesting thing to happen around here for a while. What was going on? All that top brass going in and policemen surrounding the public house.

The old lady muttered, "Bet they are drinking early, breaking the law. Coppers always do that."

The video ended and the room was silent. You could hear a pin drop.

"Let me see it again to be sure it is him," The chief of human affairs asked.

They all shouted that it was definitely him and if he wants to see it again, he was on his own. It was too sick to watch him with an under-aged girl. They were completely shocked and disgusted. This was a fellow senior officer they had worked with for years. He was efficient and had a great sense of humour and dedication to his calling. When this hits the fan, the 'old bill's' credibility will be demolished and they would all become a laughing stock and murdered by the press.

Charlie asked about the commissioner and was told that he was in the hospital with severe poisoning. He had his gut pumped and they were testing to find out what was the poison, apparently not food. He had gone to dinner with several of the other senior people including the ACC. They shook their heads. Could he have tried to get him out of the way? It was a good thought and in police work, there is the position that there is no such thing as a coincidence.

"Who is the next in line then?" Charlie asked.

"That would be me. Since the commissioner has not appointed a deputy, still debating with the mayor. I would have the seniority as the DAC. But what are our next steps? This is dynamite stuff, I will need to go to the commissioner, sick or not sick and inform him and get direction."

"Meanwhile, he might poison us all or get us locked up. He will become desperate if he gets wind that we have the evidence to send him down," Charlie stressed.

There was a lot of muttering in the room.

"Okay, Charlie and DI Eager come with me to the hospital. This must be kept secret, does everyone understand? Vital, it does not become gossip and as you all know Scotland Yard is the gossip centre of the universe." A few laughs in the background.

"The tape needs to be copied and secured, without it we have nothing," Charlie added.

"Right, you and DI Eager get two copies. I want the original one in my safe pronto and the other two in the evidence locker, separate cases numbers and secured. I will meet you, let's see," looking at his watch, "In one hour at Guy's and St. Thomas Hospital."

# Chapter Seventy-Nine
## Headlines, Readership and Revenue

"What is all this about ordering me in here?" Sir Richard burst into Gavin's office. Liberty and Gavin were pouring over a few headlines and articles on the coffee table smoking like chimneys. No one answered Gavin, just lifted the first headline.

"Well, your back, that's good. Circulation has been dropping and you know that revenue follows. You simply cannot run a newspaper over the phone." He hadn't quite looked at the headline as he was huffing and puffing around. He then noticed the first one: 'Shoot out at the old abbey, a *Daily Cryer* exclusive.'

"Or do you like this?" Liberty held up one: 'She'll have to fire him! Newly promoted minister at the secret 'Hellfire club' a perverted paedophile!'

"Or would you prefer this headline, Sir Richard, 'Fish caught in the paedophile ring, a *Daily Cryer* exclusive.'

"Or this?" Gavin was having fun now. "London drug lords run underground pervert club! *Daily Cryer* reporter went undercover. Read what she saw and lived to tell the tale. A *Daily Cryer* exclusive."

Not all creative headlines make the actual newspaper, just the one that can sell the most copies.

He sat down wiping his forehead with his hanky. It was lunchtime and being called in made him angry, some good sorts waiting on him plus, his glass of wine.

"You have had it in for Bill Stephens there, better be airtight evidence!"

Liberty held up the videotape, "It's airtight all right. Do you want to see this pervert in action with young boys?"

"No, but legal need to go over it with a fine-tooth comb. Is that all you have? A video could be tampered with."

"Well, I am a witness and I have two nine-year-old boys he assaulted last night, who have blood coming from their asses and will identify him."

"Oh, that's where you are wrong, young lady. See you have to be careful. Stephens has an airtight alibi. He was assaulted last night badly and is in hospital. Found near his home dumped in the garden. Some yobs or druggies looking for money."

"That would be me that hit him," Liberty said proudly. Sir Richard's mouth dropped and he was trying to talk but couldn't.

"Better tell you the full story rather than bits and bobs," Gavin cut in.

So, they did and related to what had happened since they last met. He remained very quiet with the odd cough and blinking of his eyes, a nervous trait.

"This is like a movie or a nightmare," was all he could spit out.

"We still need the lawyers involved. I think senior to ours like a Queen's council and GWP."

"Not sure, that is a good idea. One GWP we are certain of that he compromised us and gave the safe house number to one of our enemies that could have killed us and the rest of the tapes have let's say some of London's finest involved with this paedophile ring and we do not know until we have looked at them all who was involved. So, if a QC was, then he will pooh-pooh our evidence."

"That's crazy, a QC, never!"

"Would an assistant police commissioner be involved, do ya think?" Liberty let that cat out of the bag as she needed him to get what was going on.

"What?" confused, this was all confusing and out of his comfort zone.

"Think of it, this way we have enough dynamite stories exclusive to us. Imagine the circulation increasing, the revenue, selling to networks all over the world. We get to milk this for months and then maybe a book, TV rights and on and on."

*As Neil Diamond sang, money talks, he is getting it.* Liberty and Gavin knew.

He was silent thinking and they left him to it, working out risks of being sued against the big cash and growth that would come in. Also, whilst the PM had not called since just before the last election, what would she say, being blindsided by this catastrophe, reading about it in the *Daily Cryer*. She had complimented Stephens twice in several days from his rising star promotion to supporting him against the crime against him and vowing more police on the streets. He would look stupid with a poor ability to judge character. She could even lose her job. The *Daily Cryer* was right-wing paper supporting the current government, although the crime is hideous.

"Okay, make sure legal do their job. Get some outside legal you trust if needed. I would like to see the copy and legal advice before it goes on the press. Not interfering, just for my own comfort as I have the most to lose if this goes south."

"And the most to gain," Liberty reminded him.

"Huh, by the way, well done you guys. Amazing result," He was totally back onside.

"The ex-SAS guys for the next week or so, we are not popular with a lot of people?"

He waved go ahead whatever as he left the office, his mind was still working out numbers.

# Chapter Eighty
## Live to Fight Another Day

Nick had escaped into the abbey and locked the main door. Most of his guys were either dead or still having a gunfight with attackers outside as he could hear the bangs as they fired, however, it was more sporadic now. Losing he assumed as these were trained professionals with night scopes and state of the art weapons with suppressors as opposed to a mish-mash of stolen weapons they had. He guessed it was the Americans and they had not expected much resistance or the loud bangs of his guy's weapons.

He saw Stephens starting come around in his cell. Bruce was running like a chicken with its head cut off. He had an old army submachine gun in one hand. Nick knew this weapon well from his army days, so he took it. He called him to get Stephens out in the back garden and back to London. Bruce lifted him and virtually ran out of the quadrangle to the girl's bus that was leaving. Dumping him inside the door, well, he jumped over him and dragged him inside. They laid on the floor motionless. The girls were screaming and standing up waving at the attackers to not stop them getting out.

Tazewell came to the bus with a support guy and checked out the girls.

"Not here," he shouted. Noticing Bruce on the floor with a dead-looking naked guy, he asked him where were McAllistar and Karlien. Bruce told him that he thought they had escaped as Nick was shouting that they had.

"Where is Nick?"

"Inside the abbey."

They were let go of no interest now.

Tazewell told Sam, who wanted to at least finish the job with one Harker.

"Never leave an enemy wounded or they will come back at you with twice the force," Sam told Tazewell, who was getting nervous. They had made him bring them here and he had little choice as he was certain that he would be fish bait like 'Billy, the neck'. With McAllistar out of the way, he could forge a new alliance with gangs like the Jamaican Yardies, who had just started moving into poor disaffected youth in predominantly black areas of London. The guys who bought the stolen drugs off him.

The sirens in the distance told them it was time to leave very quickly. Nick had set fire to the abbey, which was mainly stone, however, the dressing up of flowing curtains, carpets and wooden furniture and beams were all highly flammable. If it didn't hide all the evidence, then at least it was a distraction. The walls had burned, torches down the corridors to light where there was no electricity. He took off his monk's cassock and grabbed a torch, burned it and ran around all the draping's and curtains.

He went outside and gave the attackers a burst of the submachine gun. "That should keep them at bay for a while." Nothing in return, they seemed to be running away.

He shouted to the guys left to come to the abbey back. One was wounded, it was the squirrel.

"Can't take you with me, Sammy. You lay here, the police will be here soon and you will be okay. Just say you were asked to come to a private party and these people turned up and attacked. Admit nothing. We will look after you inside or out. Be sure none of us was here, okay?"

They laid him on the ground safe from the abbey fire which was gaining momentum.

"Right guys, how many of you did cross country at school?" No answer.

"Try and keep up with me and be careful not to break an ankle. We need to put as much distance between us and the abbey as possible."

Nick was super fit and had been his school's cross-country champion. The rest followed but were soon spread out and lagged behind in a long line. Nick kept to the edges and tree lines and headed north towards where he thought the motorway was or at least a major road. He stopped when he thought that he was out of sight and had made some headway. He let some of the stragglers catch up.

"Boss, this is exhausting, I have the stitches," said the biggest holding his side. It was not the same as beating people up or doing robberies with short bursts of energy. This was hard work in the dark through hedges, ditches, small streams and small copses.

"I am going ahead and getting some transport and help. You all need to keep moving, walking, skipping or running, I do not care. See that light in the far distance, head for that but do not come out from cover until you see me. Tell them all to keep the code or else." With that, he was off like he had not been running. He was the prize, not these foot soldiers.

A myriad of blue lights was flashing at a distance. The abbey was blazing away and he knew that it would take time for them to sort out the mess and make sense of it. They would put out an all-points bulletin, he guessed but not for men on foot nor did they have vehicle types to report, he hoped, except it would be good if they ran into the attackers.

He turned around one more time as the abbey was exploding in fire, he could smell it from several miles away. The flames were high.

*A real hell and fire club now. Sanctum sanctorum*, he thought to himself and started running again.

# Chapter Eighty-One
## A Lot to Understand

The commissioner was not good at all. He laid in bed with tubes coming out of, it seemed, every part of his body. Guy's and St. Thomas Hospital was a toxicology hospital, one of the best in the world, so he was in good hands. He looked very tired and so much older than the chief they knew. He was unshaven, again not the pristine guy they knew, but he told them that he just couldn't be bothered with anything right now. He didn't care about how he looked; he was going through a nightmare. He admitted that he couldn't think straight which was not good for the discussion they were about to have.

"What couldn't wait that you have to be here right now?" irritated.

The DAC came close to the bed. Charlie and Eager stood against the walls.

"I am going to give you this in a synopsis and as quick as I can. We need to arrest and charge the ACC with paedophilia."

The blood pressure machine had a conniption. The DAC went into the background as much as they knew. The commissioner's face screwed up with pain or stress or poison or all of the above. Even so, he was still sharp when faced with a crisis.

*Shit, what a PR nightmare on my watch. Could this be the end of my Lordship? Could this be possible?*

"No, send him on leave awaiting a full investigation, make sure he is cautioned properly, no slip-ups or technical hitches. Could it get worse?"

"Well, yes, sir," Eager was hesitating whether to tell him or not, but it was all going to come out now and he would be seen to be totally disloyal.

"Worse, worse?" the blood pressure machine was going sky high.

"Yes, there is a minister of the crown involved as well. I have seen the tape." His mouth was wide open.

"A what?"

"Bill Stephens, sir."

"He's just been promoted?" the commissioner was shocked. Thinking about it he said, "Keep this very quiet, only us and no one else."

"Too late, sir. The *Daily Cryer* has the tape and story from McAllistar and the reporter who has witnessed him in let's say action," Eager said as plainly as he could and watched the blood pressure machine start recording very high numbers.

The commissioner was shaken out of his apathy from the poisoning.

"This must be done as quietly and quickly as possible. Go to the PM's office and get a meeting to inform her. The ACC is on the next list for a knighthood and Stephens has just been promoted as a shining star. This is very embarrassing for the PM. The government could fall for God's sake! Then to Mary at the prosecution's office. She needs to allocate a team that can keep their mouths shut and work with us. Charlie bring them all in?"

"All?"

"The Harkers, their lawyer, the press lady, McAllistar everyone involved, leave Stephens in the hospital and await the PM's instructions. Get a task force together. I don't care if it takes working twenty-four seven. You are authorised to draw everyone you want. I want all those tapes! DI Eager, do you understand?"

He nodded almost sadly. The commissioner picked up on his reluctance.

"Do you understand?"

"Yes, sir." There goes his relationship with Liberty.

"We have a theory that your poisoning may be connected. He wanted you out of the way. He immediately suspended me and sent a task force to pick up Eager and the rest. It was life or death to him," Charlie added.

The commissioner thought about it and remembered several cocktail sausages the ACC had passed him at the reception, the night he fell ill.

"Search warrant office, cars, houses you know the drill. Get teams of SOCs out pronto." With that, he turned over and tried to vomit in his bedside sick bowl. They all left pronto as well.

Samuels had weighed up his options. The ACC promised to take him down with him. Now the rumour has it that it is about paedophile ring at the 'hellfire' club involving the ACC, nothing is secret or sacred at the met. Unimaginable that this could be the case, however, he was now very scared it added up the ACC had asked him to murder people. He reasoned that it could not be the protection they had provided for the Harkers as it would be hard to prove and would not warrant murder. Still, he had carried messages back and forth to the Harkers, asking them to help to recover the tapes.

His logic told him that all was not lost. He could turn state witness for a deal if worse came to worse or if something happened to the ACC, maybe it would all blow over.

He walked into the ACC's office with the Magnum still in its box. He looked up as he has been too busy with paperwork. He had not even noticed that the fifth floor was almost empty of the top brass.

"I've brought this back."

"You let me down, you ungrateful turd. I will sort you out, no more promotions, maybe even a demotion, yes, that's it."

"Well, before you do that consider that the top brass is returning and I think they are going to arrest you? They have the tape, I assume."

Looking out the big window he said, "Yes, there's DCS Allcock, rushing in from the car park with a group of detectives. Be here soon." The ACC went red first and then ashen and started to hyperventilate.

Samuels laid the gun box in front of him.

"There's a good little pervert, do the right thing for your family. They will hush it up. Overworked ACC takes own life."

He turned as he got to the door to face the big Magnum pointing right at him. He had loaded it himself when he was considering doing the dirty work.

"I'll take you with me, you little traitor."

"What's the bear going to say, interfering with little girls? Do you think she will stick with you through the trial, the media and time in prison, what about your daughters and grandchildren? Laughed at work and school. Top cop a pervert."

He walked away holding his breath in case the shot came. As he was walking out of the secretary's office, a very loud ear-piercing bang came, blood and brains splattered through the door.

DCS Allcock and the team were now rushing in.

"I think he just saved you the bother," Samuel's said sardonically as he passed them.

# Chapter Eighty-Two
## Publish and Be Damned

"Lock all the doors, turn the lights off, all non-essential staff to go home right now. Security as well!" Gavin was shouting in a panic.

"Switchboard as well, turn it off." he continued. The production and editorial team were wondering if he hadn't gone mad with the pressure of the last few days.

"Bill, find out if we have started to dispatch, if not, put a bomb under them. Everything must go out and hit the streets right now and then lock the warehouse doors as well."

Gavin explained that he just had a call from the chairman, who in turn had a call from the PM to stop the publication. He refused and the PM said they had no choice but to get a gagging order from the high court. This has an impact on the country and needed to be investigated properly for fairness to Stephens, who was still in the hospital unable to speak for himself. The chairman had told him that he had seen all the evidence and it had past the most stringent legal minds and it was in the public interest to know how senior government officials acted. He then got a threatening call from the 'bulldog', the PM's communications executive. No more access to Downing Street and other ways of cutting out our reporters. He told them that they will publish and be damned and left for his country estate so he could not be served as well.

There was a big cheer for Sir Richard when they heard this early in the morning, so it may take time to get a judge out of bed and bring to order to us. So, they needed to move quickly and then lock up tight until the paper is on the streets. London distribution first, it was normally last as the papers needed to get out to the distant locations to make the morning deadline. He wanted them to see the paper everywhere and know it was too late. He needed the times when each truck was dispatched. Bill, the production coordinator, was running back and forth like an athlete and for his body size that was impressive.

"The police are setting up roadblocks. We got two trucks away, but I think they sent the others back. Told them a terrorist scare!" Bill was panting.

Gavin was thinking hard. This is not a third world country and dictatorship suppressing the media.

"Fill your car boots everyone and distribute them around free if necessary. We need to prove that they were on the streets before the order. We can get around the blocks if we move quickly. They can't stop normal citizens and we can get down side streets where the trucks can't go or if you haven't got a car, take the tube. Take a billboard each and pin them up outside the shops, better to still find the street sellers first at the tube stations. Do not accept anything from anyone and if asked, you do not work for the *Daily Cryer*."

Eight of them rushed off with Bill to pick up their stock and then hit the car park or local tube station.

"Jerry, get the photographer out of bed and tell him to go around taking pictures of people selling the papers. Better still inform as many the paparazzi and say there is a good pay-out if they get a good pic catching the police or anyone closing down the sales on the streets. Use my direct line, the switchboard is closed."

"On it, boss."

After that, he next called the BBC, ITV and Sky News to tell them a big story was breaking and they needed to get on the streets and look at the *Daily Cryer*. So, big the PM had the police acting like Gestapo stopping distribution. He knew how to set fire to the media.

There then was banging on the front door. A lot of banging, although the lights were out, they just kept on banging. Then they went around the back to the warehouse but found it closed also and no lights in the inside.

*We published and we will see if we are damned!*

# Chapter Eighty-Three
## Task Force

Charlie was at his best in front of a big group. His arms were still flying around as he made his points. "A bit of a 'Joe Cocker'," someone mumbled.

This was a big task force and included prosecutors attached to each team. He then divided up the workload:

Organised crime department got the Harkers and their solicitor, Mr Javelin with the full backing of senior management, no more protection for them. They would be led by DCS Freddy Trowbridge, a well-respected veteran.

The first step, a thorough search of the club and any other houses they live in, cars, the lot. Collect what evidence they could, do not interview the Harkers until all the pieces are in place. All exit points in the United Kingdom to be sent photos to stop them if they tried to leave the country. All other forces in the country as well. They would have specialist teams to follow them if needed. DI Eager suggested Javelin was in the group that attacked the abbey, so maybe a split in the group and Javelin is a possibly a bigger player than at first thought.

Internal affairs got the ACC suicide and DCI Samuels, known protégé and according to DI Eager, 'dirty'. He was the last one to see the ACC alive. What was their deal? They would get warrants to search their houses, offices, cars and safes. They would stick to the story that he was stressed and were trying to find out if anything major was worrying him. The tech department would look at his computers at home and work.

DS Williams got her small ops team back and was charged with bringing in McAllistar, Karlien and the other tapes. Eager had told them the hiding place in the pub, however, he cautioned that McAllistar was canny and could have moved them. He always neglected to say that there was a second copy of each tape.

Charlie would be the only one to watch the videos when they were recovered for top secrecy reasons.

Both were to be treated as star witnesses and McAllistar's breach of parole to be ignored. Her next step was to review the McAllistar's drug case from start to finish with a fine-tooth comb. Was he set up?

DI Kathleen Kearns from the child protection unit got the abused boys working with social services. They had been allowed to stay with the dragon as they were severely traumatised and it was thought best not to move them just yet. Plus, they had to find out where they came from probably a sourcing ground for the paedophiles. She needed to take an array of pictures, which included one of Bill Stephens that she could show when the time was right to see if they can pick him out.

"Kathleen, can you give the team some idea where and how these boys got here?"

"Certainly, the minibus was filled with young women and children. What most people do not know is that human trafficking is the biggest illegal industry next to drugs, however, it is growing faster. Multi billions of dollars are involved each year globally. It is highly organised and another fact is that women seem to be the majority of human traffickers."

"Why women?" a young detective asked.

"The children and young women are often acquired, if that is the word, by improper means such as fraud, force or deceptive means. Some children are sold to the traffickers by their parents due to abject poverty, some women are seduced with job offers, education, romance, living in a free safe environment without conflict. Women are good at this and are trusted. Back to the point, these children are from Nigeria. Nigeria has over five hundred languages and we think that they speak Yoruba, although the interpreter is still not sure. Not that they are speaking much. We need to find the rest of the children and women, some teenage boys I am told as well."

"Are they all from Nigeria do you think?" the same detective asked.

"No, they can come from all over the world. Afghanistan, India, Albania, Sudan, Iraq, Romania, the list goes on. One connecting factor is abject poverty countries. In the United Kingdom, it still happens. Runaways, orphan homes and so forth. So, no one is removed from this modern-day slavery. Around thirty per cent are used for sexual activities, the rest from forced marriages, domestic and farm work, running drugs, a whole range of activities. Some get false passports; others are hidden in trucks. The Czech Republic is a favourite place to start illegal entry into the United Kingdom. It is highly organised and the people taken are scared and threatened. I am told that a child taken from say a shopping Mall is South Africa changes hands eleven to thirteen times from person to person in five minutes. Now that is a highly organised crime."

"Most of these were young children, so we are dealing with paedophiles, not just forced prostitution. I do not understand why sick people want children for sex?" a lady prosecutor asked.

"Sexual abuse of children is common. Ninety per cent of children are abused by someone they know. This ten per cent of children are being used by monsters to make money. No one quite knows why people are attracted to children. Sick, yes. Some say that their brains are wired wrongly and some that in their past, this happened to them, 'sins of the father' syndrome. There are two types: 'hebephiles', who like children on the cusp of puberty and 'ephebophiles', who are attracted to children who have just reached puberty."

The team made noises in disgust.

"Okay. Thanks, Kathleen, most enlightening. Kathleen and her team are working with the boys and other contacts, previous offenders and so forth to try and track down these…people. Meanwhile, we need to shake down who we can to get a description or name. Maybe they were paid by cheque or bank transfer, not just cash. The videos will help us find the customers; however, we need the traffickers. These poor people are being held against their wills somewhere and we need to find out who and where," DCS Allcock added.

DI Eager had to go on trips to Kent regarding the happenings there to be interviewed with Karlien, McAllistar and Liberty. All now key witnesses against Nick Harker. The Kent police wanted to get the full brief on what was happening there as they called it, 'The shoot-out at the OK abbey'. They would also pick up anything of interest SOCs had discovered. They would be required to attend the post mortems on the dead bodies, four in all. A visit to the hospital and see if they recognised the wounded person.

They then had to go to Derbyshire and meet the local police and MI5 and MI6 representatives as Russia was kicking up a big fuss about luring and murdering their commercial attachés. Ned and Scotty had already been grilled and made statements. They wanted to do it at the scene of the crime. It all needed tidying up.

*Maybe he could take Liberty as well,* Eager thought. Then he knew that she would be pissed at him about handing the original tapes over her ongoing big story. If McAllistar would not hand over the dupes of the tapes to Eager, he could try and work out how far he drove to the moors and back in forty minutes, fifty miles per hour and have a look around. The good news is that he could get more of Ned's pies as this was definitely an overnight job.

"Any questions?" a few muttered.

"Yes, who gets Bill Stephens?" a young detective hoping for a big career break.

"Off-limits for now." There was a noise in the room as they were thinking another cover-up for this government.

"Go, I need regular reports the DAC and the commissioner want timely blow by blow on our progress. By the way, this is hush-hush. If you want a long career, tighten your lips. Let's get it done!" End of Charlie's motivational speech and he nearly poked one eye out in the process.

# Chapter Eighty-Four
## The Next Big Story

"I have been trying to ring you for hours." Liberty was worried.

"They tried to stop distribution by a gagging order. I beat the order and got enough copies on the street to justify, it was too late."

"I've finished the hellfire club story and can you send a courier to pick it up and drop off a paper?"

"Yup, however, you need to get in here, all the TV stations want interviews, you are about to become famous!"

"Has Eager called?"

"Yes, lots of information. The abbey was burnt to a crisp. Four dead bodies and one injured in hospital. Listen to this, the police are calling it 'The shoot-out at the OK abbey', a great headline, don't you think?"

"What else?" Not impressed.

"The ACC at the Met topped himself!"

"Topped?"

"Blew his bloody head off. They are saying it was work-related stress, just another cover-up."

"Can I write it up?"

"We do not have the tape and I got someone else on it, you can't have everything, greedy girl. You know the official story and an inside source said blah blah blah."

"That it?"

"Oh, you need to call him as they want statements and trip to the abbey and maybe up north to the B&B, local police, everyone is involved."

"Maybe not."

"Think, young lady. He is the best source we have. Bringing down the Harkers is big news and you need to be at the centre of it. That means cooperating with the police while they are making out charges and being nice to Eager whatever."

"Can I use your SAS guys then?"

"Not here yet, not sure what they are doing. Do you think the Harkers would want to put you on ice?" She hated his phoney gangster accent, too many Humphrey Bogart movies.

"Wouldn't you? We are all witnesses, the three of us plus Eager, at the abbey. I can identify Stephens, Nick Harker trying to kill us, lewd activities going on, drugs, prostitution, pervasion, need I go on."

"I think you have *The Full Monty*."
"The what?"

The day was busy for Liberty. Plenty of interviews and demand for more. She played coy on the details, "You will have to read tomorrow's edition of the *Daily Cryer*." Even the chairman called her and told her that she had 'hit a home run', which for a change she understood. She demanded the next edition, which was up one hundred thousand copies, it was called the 'hellfire' edition. This could be milked for days, maybe weeks. She still had the Russian episode to write and try and push that edition.

US networks wanted interviews and she had a range of job offers come in from competitors. 'Kick ass reporter from New York' was one headline getting in on the act and hoping to boost circulation.

There were negative interviews set up by the 'bulldog' to try and say that she was mistaken or lying for cheap publicity.

"So, the minister is in hospital after being mugged that night and you try and make this hard-working minister look like a pervert. Shame on you!"

"Really, you weren't there. I hit him in the hellfire club whilst he was fucking a little boy, who was bleeding and crying 'Mummy'. I know him; I have interviewed him several times. So, do not try a phoney cover-up story as I thought your party was for law and order. Just for a few, I guess the party people can do what they want and you protect them by trying to bring someone else down. Shame on you, you little pathetic spin doctor!"

He was coughing and trying to cut in but, her attack was so quick, loud and surprising that even the BBC arbitrator was shocked.

The phones started ringing off the hook in support of her. As she left, she turned to the bulldog and said, "I hope you guys get put out of power soon."

He was, though, the wrong guy to cross.

# Chapter Eighty-Five
## Daily Sit Rep Day Two

From: DCS Allcock
To: DAC, Commissioner
Daily Sit Rep – the 'Tapes Affair' Day Two Private & Confidential
Sir,

1. I will bullet point the progress as the teams are working around the clock and information is very lucid.
2. Eleven tapes recovered from McAllistar, thanks to DI Eager. I am watching them now and noting who I can recognise and the activities being carried out. The tapes must have been left on for the evening as more than one person is on each one. So far, a lord, a bishop, a pop star and a member of parliament I have been able to identify. Definitely, an organised paedophile ring extending across upper society.
3. I have the United States' sensitive tape in my possession. What is the next step?
4. Harkers club, homes and so far searched. All clean as if they were prepared. The video cameras in the downstairs club, previously used as the first 'hellfire' club, are not there nor is anything amiss. Looks like a receiving and storage area.
5. Their solicitor, Tazewell Javelin, has not reappeared since he was recognised on the abbey attack night. We will search tomorrow his house and so forth.
6. Statements have been taken from the key witnesses: DI Eager, Liberty Bell, the reporter, Karlien Steenkamp, the protagonist in the US politician case. A case against Nick Harker is building.
7. Searches of the ACC's house, safe, office and car have only brought up a small purple bottle in the safe. Contents unknown, now being tested by toxicology at Guy's. Otherwise, nothing of concern has turned up. Computers are still being checked by the technical team.
8. The abused boys have identified Bill Stephens; however, they will not be good witnesses unless protected. Liberty Bell is the strongest witness. She was cautioned for the assault she admitted, however, due to the circumstances I doubt if we will want to prosecute.
9. The boys came from a local children's home, which may have been the suppliers of under-aged children for the club. Once I have completed my

review of the videos, I will get the technical team to take out as many pictures of the children and abusers so we can trace both.
10. The abbey shoot out – DI Eager visited and identified the four dead as from the Harker gang. The wounded person is known as 'Sammy, the squirrel', a chief henchman for them. He refuses to say anything other than that he was attending a party and all hell broke loose with these guys attacking. We are awaiting fingerprints from the weapons to connect him and then go back to re-interview.
11. Bullets recovered in the walls of the abbey are consistent with the American state of the art special ops weapons. The rest of the weapons found were a mish-mash of handguns and even a Thompson machine gun. The theory is these belonged to the Harker's people. This is consistent with the editor of the *'Daily Cryer'* statement that three American guys who visited him to find out what he knew about the tapes and severed one of his fingers. He described them as either Navy Seals or some sort of special ops. MI6 have been informed and asked what they or the CIA know. Trying to recover the sensitive US tape and/or get rid of the key witness to the event.

Yours truly,
Bill Allcock
DCS

# Chapter Eighty-Six
## Only the Lonely

The ride to Derbyshire was a quiet and lonely affair. Eager still had the Rover which was a much better car than his and it was the one thing the Russians had never asked about. He guessed he would have to turn it in some time. Liberty sat beside him sieving about the rest of the tapes the police had found, her big ongoing story as she took apart the perverts one by one, one headline after another, which would establish her as an international top journo, investigative reporter and celebrity personality. Not that the exhausting interviews today had not gone a long way to doing that. She blamed Eager and was not sure that part of her anger was that she had lost control over him. Was her charm working off? McAllistar had said that they went straight to the hiding place, so it must have been Eager.

*Reverting to true cop form, the bastard!*

Karlien and McAllistar sat together in the back. They were much the same cold and distant and no conversation at all. McAllistar was still hurt but he cared enough to put her under his wing and take her with them as she was still very much at risk. She had told him that he was like a big brother to her. Not the words any guy would want to hear from a lady he loved. The abbey situation had scared her and the knowledge of what happened to her friend still haunted her. She had refused police protection, preferring to be with Logan for safety.

Eager tried to make conversation, but she simply looked away and shook her head. He guessed he was for it later that day when she calmed down but had enough venom to put him straight. The only answer he got from anyone was his request for a pit stop. They all needed a break and coffee just north of Northampton on the M1.

McAllistar wanted to visit Aunt Bessie who was still in hospital and he could now use his bank card without fear of being traced. So, he could take her some nice fruit, chocolate and a card. He had come in at the end of the trouble at the B&B, but they still wanted to interview him and get a detailed statement. She was responding to treatment and had come around with a bit of amnesia. "Logan, what trouble are you bringing to my door? I love you like a mother…" His promise that fell through and these words haunted him. Why did he go to McAllistar's cottage and wrought so much pain on the only mother he had ever known?

The rest of the journey was the same until Roy Orbison's *'Only the Lonely'* came on the radio. Eager thought he heard Liberty sing along and had part of a smile. She, though, was thinking how lonely he was going to be from now on, certainly tonight.

They got to the B&B at 2 pm as planned and were met by officers of the security services and a local DCI named Ian Fenwick and three other CID detectives. Fenwick was a trim guy, immaculately dressed with a pencil-thin moustache. He had been in the training and human resource departments most of his career and was a go by the book guy. The place had been marked out where the bodies were found and sealed off with police tape. They had been told to tell what happened but not why if asked and claim 'official secrets act' only if it got too difficult or close to the truth.

Ned fetched tea for all. He kept muttering, "They cautioned me." His eyes lit up when they said that they were staying the night, all four of them, a few more pounds for him.

"About time you guys came. This is a murder enquiry and it has taken you almost a week."

"Well, we have been a bit busy," Eager responded.

"Yes, I see it all on TV, certainly the lady has been busy, quite a personality, swearing on the box," He had a look down on you sneering style. They all immediately disliked him.

"DI Eager." Roger White stepped forward to shake his hand. This was the guy who was smart at the first meeting. Now he wanted to get close.

They shook and Eager introduced him to McAllistar, Liberty and Karlien.

"Quite a stir you all have made."

In came a little fat guy with a big moustache and a brown suit which looked too tight and brown heavy shoes. He had been smoking cigars and he stunk as the nicotine stuck to him.

"Why did you kill Russian commercial attachés?" was his first words.

They didn't answer as they knew that he was programmed to attack and lie to his yellow back teeth. He didn't like being ignored. Fenwick was by the book he was in charge and let them all know it. He was his guest, he was suffering. They told their story and showed the positions they were all in. He kept interrupting, however, they continued to ignore him but he was getting under their skin deeper and deeper.

They went to the farmhouse with the CID detectives and wrote out their statements which they were sure would match what Scotty said but Ned, they were not one hundred per cent sure what he might have said under pressure.

The big question was, "What did the Russians want that made them try to kill you?"

This was met by the 'official secrets act' due to national security and a major ongoing investigation by the Met. Fenwick was not impressed, lifting one eyebrow as they all repeated this line. He had had the word from the Derbyshire chief constable that even the PM was involved. "So, do what you have to do, but do not go too far. These were known Russian agents after something very sensitive."

"See, she is CIA and he is from secret service. They bring them here to torture information out of them and then kill them." The little guy was persistently annoying. They tried not to bite.

"Bring the big fat lady back then and make her sing. Then this can be over." Eager couldn't resist.

"She was hurt badly by this little *idiota kusok!*"

Ned has just come in and turned around like a frightened rabbit and ran into the kitchen.

The police wrapped up and left. Not very friendly, just professional courtesy. Roger White hung around in the yard.

Eager followed the little Russian to his car. Another embassy car with Russian diplomatic plates.

"Hey, Colonel?" The little guy turned around automatically. You could almost hear him say what the fuck! Eager pointed to the Rover. "Ever seen this car before?" It had normal plates and when Eager had checked a forged road license and number plates, they belonged to a written-off car.

"Does this car belong to you?"

He looked at it and spat out a bit gob of cigar yellow spit. Shaking his head, "No. We have better cars."

"So, it's not yours? Or the embassies? Never seen it before?"

"No." turned around abruptly and left.

Roger had buttonholed McAllistar in the yard. Liberty was on Ned's phone calling Gavin. Karlien was having a cup of tea with Ned in the kitchen.

"I was just apologising to Logan here. I was totally wrong about you and McAllistar. Hell of a job you all are doing. The tape of what can I say the American politician has been handed over to the CIA and they have promised to call off the rogue team they denied existed and send them home."

"What about Karlien?" Logan asked.

"Well, that is part of the deal. Forget her and move on."

"Did they buy that?"

"Apparently so. Especially after the 'shoot out at the OK abbey' fiasco." He laughed at the headline.

The two secret services guys had a car to take them to Derby railway station. Logan and Karlien left for the hospital and to show her McAllistar's cottage. Eager and Liberty were left on an outside table, sipping Chardonnay, the devil's version.

"Fancy a jacuzzi?"

"Smalls, you are not in good books right now!" She let him have both barrels. It went on for some time and he found himself sipping harder and slipping under the table.

"Finished? What would you say if Logan and I had a second copy of all the tapes?"

She looked at him with suspicion, eyes narrowing, drilling into his head trying to find the truth.

"If you are lying to me."

"Not." He just didn't know where they were and afraid to tell her.
"The full twelve?"
"Yes, we decided to copy for safety."
"Well, if that's true smalls, you may not be lonely tonight."

# Chapter Eighty-Seven
## The Truth Will Set You Free

"Phil, you tricky guy, our deal is off."

"What you have the tape?"

"Yes, but guess what? It's been copied. Our technical guys just confirmed it." Gina the aggressive London chief of the CIA spat out a lie.

"I was told it was the only one in existence."

"Not true. Where do we start to find the copy?"

"Are you sure?"

"They say ninety-nine per cent."

He thought about it for a few minutes.

"I guess we have to trace it to the beginning follow of the trail, which starts and almost ends with McAllistar except for when the police got it. Although this lawyer guy apparently started this and maybe he took out some insurance before McAllistar got a hold of it."

"Where is he?"

"On a road trip to Derbyshire to sort out the other Russian shoot out at the B&B with DI Eager."

"Where is the B&B?"

"Oh no, Gina, no more morons shooting up the countryside. I will send some people. Roger will be back soon; he has been there all day. I will send him back with some support."

"Roger White?"

"Okay, get back to me quick." No thanks at all.

Her first call was to the rogue team. She told them about the potential duped tape first.

"Get this straight to Langley, they are already starting to ask questions lots of Brit contacts other than me and they do read all the papers. You have limited time. Clean up this mess and be out of here in twenty-four hours or I can't protect you or your boss anymore. Clear?"

"Understood," was the only answer.

She said she had feedback that this solicitor they now know well and started all this may be the one that copied if not McAllistar's group. She told them that Roger White knows where the McAllistar et al. were.

"Oh, by the way, be good boys and do it with finesse. No bodies, no gunfights at the OK abbey, no witnesses and noise that brings the whole world to our door. Pick up your shells and do not leave bullets in walls. Clean operation, got it?"

No answer as they were too macho to take this from a woman and thinking maybe she was part of the clean-up required, they would check.

*If they know the meaning of the word finesse,* she reflected.

He was getting in his car when Nick jumped on the other side.

"DCI Samuels, I believe?"

"Nick, what are you doing here? This is Scotland Yard's car park for God's sake."

"Visiting someone I hope is still a friend."

"Look, the ACC topped himself and I have had two days grilling by internal affairs."

"I want McAllistar and Eager. Where are they?"

"Look, the police have the tapes, it's all over."

"Not the tapes, I am interested in just revenge. They have ruined everything. The club is closed, hellfire club burnt down, four guys killed, the reporter woman opening her mouth. Yes, her as well. The Americans and Karlien. Where are they?"

"Everyone? I heard they, Eager and McAllistar, took a trip to sort things out up north."

"Where!" Nick's knuckles were going white.

"I'll find out. Some B&B, where the incident happened. I go back in and research."

"Whilst you are there, find out when the Yardies started selling coke on the streets and where is Tazewell Javelin?"

"Not heard from Taz for a while, only calls when he wants something. He was photographed way back with some Yardies in a back street café, a year or so ago. We thought that he was liaising for you guys to shift stuff and we pulled the pics."

"I bloody well thought so."

It didn't take him long the Russian killings and venue were common knowledge now.

"Roger, you have something to tell us?" The three Americans were stretching their necks again as if preparing for a fight. He had just got back from the north and had made his report and was unlocking his bicycle from a stand at the side of the building. They were all around him what you call 'monstering' a person.

"The tape has been handed over; however, they made a copy. We want the copy and the girl. Where are they?"

Roger had been briefed by Phil on his conversation with Gina, so he knew but couldn't believe that these guys got the information so quickly.

"I have no idea," he said casually. The punch came into his gut, it was very hard and he fell to the ground and completely lost his breath.

"Hard way or just tell us and we go."

"You bastards, I hope you have a quick way out of the United Kingdom as I will see you go down for murder. I don't care who you are working for."

They laughed and kicked him a few times. No one was around as most staff had knocked off at 5 pm. Even security was not on the ball, although he assumed that they had picked this place away from the cameras.

He told them that he had left them at the B&B and gave the address. He was not sure they were staying there due to the general knowledge about the place.

"You're coming with us."

"Why?"

"We don't want you talking until this is over and we are gone."

"Add kidnapping to your offences." They all laughed and picked him up by the collar and dragged him to their blackout Merc.

"Tell me the truth. Is there a copy of the American tape? The American techs say it has signs of being copied." Charlie was shouting down the telephone at Eager.

"Not to my knowledge. Why would there be? McAllistar is happy to be rid of them and wants to move on with his life, already planning to live in his cottage and look after his aunt. Why would he copy them?" He lied.

"Them?"

"I assumed you meant that he took a copy of all of them?" he lied again, very close to piquing Charlie's interest and nose for something amiss.

"Maybe this Javelin guy, being a crooked lawyer, took an extra copy for insurance. McAllistar has hardly been out of my sight and there are no copying machines where we have been. The farm has only an old TV from the dark ages. The B&B rooms don't even have a TV, videos are 'The devil's work' according to Ned."

"Heads up then, this came from CIA chief and our guys are worried this rogue hit team is still operating and coming for the dupe and the girl. We are sending a SAS team, these guys are beyond normal ops, it will take time for permission and for the team to assemble, be briefed and get there by chopper. So, you need to move quickly to a new location and let me know."

"Maybe send them to the B&B, they can put them out of play. We need to move now. I will follow up with McAllistar if it was him, he needs to tell me and will. I do, though, not believe it." He was crossing his fingers and knew that telling lies to a boss and good friend would definitely not set him free.

# Chapter Eighty-Eight
## Flight and Fancy

Ned was watching Liberty as she was for a long time on his phone. He was worried about the bill and when she would pay.

"Really, why would you do that, Gavin? Every pervert in the country will be after me!" Gavin had explained with excitement that some punters had taken pictures of her in the cowgirl outfit when she did her first strip against the club rules. He had bought them and they had gone out in today's edition.

"Big stuff, bigger circulation than we could dream of. 'Undercover beauty gets inside knowledge of sleazy gangster club operation'. Our readers love the tits and bums and you have ample in these pics. You're famous, this will make you more famous, and I can see awards coming your way. Sir Richard has already agreed to double your salary. Ride with me on this, Liberty."

"Pull it…"

"We have got to go right now," Eager was shouting. Ned was still watching the phone, although this took his interest.

"Not staying?"

"We will pay you for the night, Ned, but we have to move, some bad guys are coming." Ned's face fell and fear took hold. "What about me, Rebel and Nelly?"

"Nelly?"

"My cow needs milking every morning or it hurts her."

"Anywhere you can go for the night? They will come, not find us and go."

"No. Well, I could go over to Jean's, but it is miles away."

They agreed to drive him. So, Rebel, Ned, Karlien, Logan, Liberty and Eager squashed into the Rover and they drove towards Bakewell and dropped Ned and Rebel off at his old friends. Eager was happy that Nelly wasn't tied to the back of the car and gave him cash for the night and taxi back. He didn't talk in front of Ned, best for him.

He parked in the Peacock Pub's car park in the centre of the town and started to explain his conversation with Charlie. They were all quiet.

"You took copies?" Liberty was covering for Eager.

"Yes," Logan's reply

"Great, I still have my big stories. Where are they?"

No answer, he was thinking the tapes were poison. Why not leave them to rot.

"Where are they, Logan?" she demanded.

"Not sure if this is the time and place to have arguments. We have to get through this and then fight over the tapes later," Eager said trying to get back onto the emergency at hand.

"So, you can hand them over," was her snide reply.

*She would never quite forget and forgive,* he thought and maybe he would be lonely tonight.

*They are still after Karlien and maybe all us to clean up is my guess,* Eager's sombre thought.

"Three?" Logan said quietly.

"Three? Oh, you mean this rogue team? That's what we have been told but who knows more may have been added."

"Let's take them out?" Logan said as if it wasn't a big deal.

"Let's get a drink, I definitely need one," Liberty's suggestion, so they all marched into the Peacock. Logan told them his plan. He was tired of running and hiding, just tired of it. He would take the guns and knife, go to the B&B and leave them a message. Like if you want the tape copy, come to the Dark Peak and moor and I will hand it over.

Eager gulped his beer and it ran down his shirt. The others sat silently with mouth's wide open.

"That's your plan? You are worse planner than Eager," Liberty broke the silence.

"Nay, it happens to be a good plan. Let me explain," Logan had made his mind up.

He talked about the Dark Peak and the dark moor. The peak wasn't really a mountain; it was a high hill and was mostly covered in mist especially this time of year. The moors are a combination of sphagnum peat bogs and gritstone. You go up and down and up and down every few steps sinking into the bogs. The sphagnum moss holds up to twenty-six times, its dry weight in water, so it is slippery and very wet. There are areas of steep slopes and cliff-like edges which are very dangerous in the dark and mist.

It was a mystical place where folklore had it that many walkers had been consumed on the moors. The locals looked on it as satanic area, it was desolate and difficult and they say voices and screams had been heard by walkers. The Dark Peak area was the choice of the Moors murderers in the 1960s, who killed and buried five children there and maybe more.

Most of all, he asserted, it was his playground. He had joint training exercises on these moors with the boy soldiers and police cadets several times a year for three years. Many times, he was lost all night, exhausted with no sense of direction. Even the instructors with them didn't help. Police lights flashing up and down on the Snake Pass road was their only direction out of the moor when the authorities realised they had not returned to camp.

Then over the years when he was looking to get away from day-to-day worries or the stress of Northern Ireland, he went there with a bivouac and lived for several days on his own, exploring and enjoying the most dramatic outdoor life he could find. He then knew this bog ridden, beautiful and mystic area like the back of his hand.

"These are top professionals from all accounts, well trained under all conditions," Eager butted in.

"Don't get flummoxed, John. I bet they have never been trained in these conditions, desert, jungle, sea, snow, forests, urban areas, even mountains but not like these conditions not anywhere else. This is my advantage."

"They have state-of-the-art weapons."

"True but no good if you can't see your target. Even night goggles do not work properly in the mist there."

"I'm coming with you then," Eager volunteered.

"Nay with your knees and you are overweight, first hundred metres of bogs and you would be exhausted. You would then be a liability. Thanks but no, I can do this on my own."

"Nothing wrong with my knees or my weight, a little bit over my fighting weight." They all laughed at him being in denial. The way he walked gave him away like he was walking on bones alone.

He needed a good compass, some wet gear, thermal underwear, gloves, torch and chocolate bars plus the weapons. They let him eat a good meal in the pub while Eager went to the camping stores that was a feature of Bakewell being a hiker and campers centre for the Peak District.

McAllistar wrote his directions on a pub napkin. Liberty copied it in her reporter's notebook for the SAS or police.

"Go on A57 to Doctor's Gate, then walk from Lady Clough to Hern Stones and I will meet you at Bleaklow head with the girl and tape. No weapons. Watch out for flashing light or a whistle." Right at the bottom of the napkin, he wrote in small print, "It's no use to water anymore."

McAllistar wanted to look at what Liberty wrote and then he checked if she had added 'it's no use to water anymore' on the page.

"Meaning?" she asked.

"All in good time show it to John when he comes back from dropping me in case I don't come back."

"They will know it is a trap and will laugh at the no weapons point," Karlien said.

"Yes, I know. I am counting on their egos and time pressure. They can't keep running around and shooting people. They need to clean up and move on quickly."

"What if it is a clear day and you have no cover in this bleak moor?" Liberty was worried.

"Less than a hundred hours of sunshine a year. The summit is higher than the clouds plus, we are entering winter; it is always bad up there, always."

Eager had come back with the equipment he required.

"You are very brave or stupid and they say there is a fine line between both," he added, not liking this plan at all. Would they fall for it? Chances are he will freeze to death before they find him.

# Chapter Eighty-Nine
## The Dark Moor and Dark Peak

McAllistar and Eager had been gone for thirty minutes when they heard a helicopter fly low over the area and the pub. They rushed out to look it was a small and black one and was flying low and slow as they must be checking out the area to get their bearings.

"That must be them. I hope they dropped off the note and got out in time." Karlien was very worried as a lot of this she knew Logan was doing for her.

Liberty was on the pub's payphone to Charlie on Eager's request. She gave him the rundown of what they were doing.

"That's crazy!" he said.

"Can I quote you on that in my book?"

"Reporter! Just spell my name right eh."

"Crazier as a helicopter has just flown over us."

"SAS team has not left yet. So, it is a real, serious situation we have."

"He doesn't want the SAS on the moors, it would make it difficult for him in the mist and dark to know who's who."

"You have the directions?"

"Yes."

"Tell me where you are and stay there, I will send the troopers to you."

They had pinned the note to the front door, which was under cover of an awning so rain, if it came, would not be a problem. They hightailed it up the Snake Pass towards Buxton. As they went around a large winding corner, McAllistar looked at the pump house in the middle of the field.

"Interesting place, in the middle of nowhere," he said.

"What is it?"

"Oh, an old water pump house that hasn't worked for decades."

They went over the plan to pick up the next morning. Eager wished him well and McAllistar was off to Bleaklow Head following his own directions. It was getting dark, raining and cold.

They identified the farmhouse and landed several fields away, pretending the helicopter was just flying over. They disembarked quickly, weapons check and spread out heading for the farmhouse. They were cautious as is their training but had confidence that they were going to surprise them. Eventually, they checked out the farm and barn. Harvey had rushed into the barn weapon held high and Nellie jumped up and mooed. He nearly shot her. "Fuck!"

They found the note on the door.

"It is obviously a trap," Gary noted.

"Obviously," Sam repeated.

It was agreed that he was playing toy soldiers with them and trying to get them on his own turf. Maybe he wanted the situation to end, or had help or was brave enough to take on three battle-hardened veterans. Or he was playing for time and sending them on a wild goose chase. Probably he didn't count on them having a chopper.

The pilot checked his maps. This is a dangerous aircraft country; many have gone down and a lot of wreckage lying around. "Flying over is bad enough but landing is not possible. Not in the dark anyway. If we land in a bog, we will never get out. What am I to do with him?" Nodding at Roger White tied up and barely conscious in the back.

"In daylight, I will call you in if the mist is better. I have an idea about what to do with him."

They agreed to land on the A57 at Doctor's Gate. Even that was risky at night on bad roads with sweeping bends. They had max ten seconds to get out and away, which they were used to.

After they had walked in the dark, cold, wind and mist following the map by torchlight and compass, they stopped for a quick drink of water and double-checked their bearings.

"I am going to enjoy killing this bastard," Sam said who was already exhausted with a swollen ankle from standing on and bumping into things.

# Chapter Ninety
## Follow Up on the Harkers

"So, you see, Detective Trowbridge, you have no reason to impact my client's business and should allow it to open right away. You have searched and found nothing illegal or untoward," said Dave Badlock, the Harker's new solicitor. He was known to be a top solicitor for the underworld and when he went into court against the police, they used to say 'bad luck' as he seemed always to get his clients off.

"Detective Chief Superintendent." a detective informed him. Trowbridge just waved his hand at him to not bother, the jibe was meant to unsettle him. He wanted villains behind bars and rank was not an issue to him.

"I have cautioned your client and he, with your support, prefers to say nothing. Nothing that will take away our concerns and allow us to release the club back to shall I say normal business. We are looking for his brother and again, he prefers to not be helpful. We are building a strong case here with witnesses and I will be back for sure." A good shot across the bows doesn't hurt.

"And the club?"

"I will consult with legal and let you know this afternoon if there is any change. By the way, I see Mr Javelin no longer represents them?"

"Mr Harker now prefers experienced English lawyers with knowledge of the police, courts and overall system. We are not aware of Mr Javelin's whereabouts at this time. As we explained, he seemed to be running his own deal at this abbey."

"Thank you for your time, gentlemen." Trowbridge said as he stood up to leave.

"This afternoon or I will be forced to file an injunction to release the club."

"This afternoon."

*We need to get rid of the witnesses.* Jimmy was sure then the case will fall apart. He was more worried about what Tazewell was now doing with the Yardies.

# Chapter Ninety-One
## The Peacock

Nick had taken the bulk of the team left, leaving Jimmy with two security people. They needed to act quickly and decisively. So, Nick took seven heavies in three cars and he ducked down in the back until they were well out of London as he knew they were on high alert looking for him.

DCI Samuels had given them the B&B address, so best they head that direction and see if they can pick up a trail. They had brought some firearms and toys like pickaxe handles and baseball bats. The arrived around 9 pm and found the place deserted. They had no need to break as the place was all opened. They looked around for clues to Eager and co.'s whereabouts. Nothing. When they were leaving Bruce, who had a habit of looking downwards, noticed the bar napkin screwed up on the ground outside. The Americans had taken the directions, all three of them, by marking their maps with a crayon type pencil.

"The Phoenix, Bakewell." Bruce said.

Nick grabbed it and read McAllistar's instructions, his brain was working overtime. He knew it hadn't just blown there, it was all screwed up and thrown down. Was it for him or someone else? It had to be the Yanks. So, why the moor? His territory for sure, he talked about it a lot. In friendlier days, he wanted Nick to 'come and taste the real outdoors'. Water under the bridge had seen their relationship changed for the worse, however, he could only admire him that he had guts.

So, that accounts for McAllistar and Karlien, so would the rest be at the Phoenix Pub? Maybe the Yanks will do his job for him and he just needed to get Eager and that damn reporter out of the way. But what did the PS at the bottom mean? It's no use to water anymore? A code or clue for something?

"Off to Bakewell for some tarts." he shouted to the gang elated, he had a good lead to follow.

"Tarts?" Bruce was totally confused.

"Can I have some more coins for this money eating machine?" Liberty asked, frustrated at the public phone running out all the time.

Dave, the overweight publican, was washing glasses behind the bar.

"Look, luv, you are hogging the phone, other customers are getting angry plus, you are very noisy even in the corridor."

"Coins," Liberty held her hand out unfazed. "I am ringing in my story and it is late for the deadline."

"Wait a minute are you…are you…you are, aren't you?" He picked up today's *'Daily Cryer'* from behind the bar and there she was in all her glory skimpy cowgirl outfit and stripper lingerie.

"Wow, I haven't had a personality in here forever…well, David Attenborough came once. Well, he came to the door and sat outside. I think it was him. Guys look at this!"

"Coins!" He gladly handed them over only if she autographed her picture which she did and he gave her the coins for free. The locals crowded around him.

Then in came DCI Fenwick in his off duty smart but casual clothes. He went to the bar and looked at what the locals were pouring over. His pencil-thin moustache was twitching.

"Ian, have you seen this?" holding the paper up to his face.

"I had the dubious pleasure of meeting her and others today."

"She's here." His head jerked around and immediately spotted Eager and the other girl drinking at a table.

The SAS team landed their blue thunder 'dolphin' in the local football field. The team leader went with two members and one was left behind to guard, the chopper with the pilot. Four-man team, all different weapon specialists. They were so busy in the pub that no one even heard the chopper fly over and land.

Fenwick walked over to Eager's table. He wanted a quiet night with no issues on his turf and was surprised to see them in Bakewell.

"DI Eager, considering to start a shoot-out in Bakewell?" It was his little sarcastic joke. Then in walked one SAS soldier, no signs of rank or regiment, combat clothing that on a normal person in this camping and hiking area would not look, too out of place. This wiry little guy, though, had a big presence and was unmistakable army. He also had an earpiece, which was obviously used for communication. He had left his weapons outside, not to alarm anyone and walked straight over to Eager as he had pictures of them all.

*My God, he is starting a war here!* Fenwick thought as he had come to know that trouble followed this man.

They wanted to talk outside, which was very cold but sobering for Eager in minutes as the cold air got into his lungs. Liberty had re-written the directions Logan had given and Eager gave them a rundown on every event he could. He seemed satisfied and went to leave, however, Eager told them of the chances of a mix up that Logan feared and the poor visibility, so he didn't want to shoot or be shot by friendly fire.

"Don't worry, sir, this is what we do. Leave it to us."

Fenwick watched from the pub door. The soldier stopped and was holding and listening to his earpiece, one of the team was talking to him. "Mr Eager, how many terrorists did you say there were? We were told three."

"Three as far as we know but not counting out that there could be more."

"We have three vehicles incoming with maybe eight guys. They have just passed the soccer field and look suspicious."

Fenwick heard, "My God, terrorist! I will call for some backup."

"I wouldn't do that, sir." The little soldier was firm and used to command, "If these are the people we think they could be, your guys will be killed."

"Armed response then?"

"Who are you, sir?"

"DCI Fenwick and this is my turf."

"We are authorised from the highest level to track these people down and kill them if necessary, which is nearly always is," he said like he was just giving directions.

"Track down, kill, highest level?" Fenwick seemed to be starting to hyperventilate.

Eager stood up and took him aside. He gave him a short pitch on letting this go and a wink and nod as to who these people were, got some ambulances and armed support on standby but clear of the area. He ran to the pub phone and Eager bet he was calling the chief constable for directions.

"Rude man," Liberty said as she came out the back. He had knocked her off the phone and pushed her aside. "Police business."

"Get me the landlord out here." a soldier ordered her and before she could buck the command, Eager gave her a look of urgency. She bit her lip for a change.

The soldier was talking and giving directions to his team. They had zeroed in on the Peacock and two of them were checking the cars out. They had not made a move to come in the pub yet, just sitting in their cars in the car park in three separated places, front, left and right sides.

The soldier made a plan. His fourth guy was called in. Each one was to watch a car out of sight but ready for action. They had flash bombs if necessary, to blind in case of an open attack.

The landlord arrived all a fluster. "We have a situation here, sir that could be dangerous for staff and customers. I need the customers to leave orderly and without fear and go home. Nothing to create suspicion. Very important. Can you make this happen right now, a few at a time? I stress they need to act very normally after a good night in the pub. Can you do this?"

"What do I say?"

"Make something up. DCI Fenwick has ordered you to close early today. So last drinks."

"They will not be happy! Staff?"

"Cellar?"

"Yes. I get it, hide down there. What if they come in while searching?"

His eyebrows lifted as in shock. "I will guarantee they will not be coming in."

The landlord went away and you could hear mutterings from inside. Slowly they started to leave. Most headed for the other pubs in the town centre leaving the landlord regretting the financial loss.

"Right. When all is clear, I need you guys to step outside into the car park together. Just to the doorway and talk casually looking toward the main street."

He was looking at Eager and Liberty.

"So, we are the Judas goats," It was a statement not a question from Liberty.

"Right, so trust us. They either want to capture you, kill you or they are just a gang of robbers who have come to take the nights takings. Either way, we have you covered."

"What do we do when if the shooting starts?"

"I would move as quickly as you can to the side and move out of the way or get behind me, a long way behind."

"Not lay down?" Liberty asked.

"You mean lay down, put your head between your legs and then kiss your ass goodbye," was his answer. It was not well-received humour.

They waited inside the pub nervously.

"So, I know where the tapes are," Eager was trying to keep her calm.

"It was a clue to the tapes?"

"Yes, in case anything happens to him. He gave me a hint at the second clue on the way to his drop off point."

"So, tell me."

"No, too dangerous for you."

"You tell me or else!"

"No."

"Okay, we can do thumb war, best out of three."

"No."

"Okay, you guys walk out slowly, then stop so they can recognise you, continue your domestic, makes it more real." The soldier was behind them. They went towards the middle of the car park and the cars burst with activity. Three from each jumping out with a variety of weapons. The soldier put on a balaclava.

"You bastard, you have ruined my business! You deserve this, Eager." Nick started to lift his weapon and aim.

"He's mine, you kill that fucking whore."

The SAS soldier appeared from behind small arm with semi-automatic browning hi-power held by his side. He shouted very loud for such a small man.

"The first person to lift a weapon will be killed. We have you surrounded with professionals."

"Fuck you!" Nick shouted and pulled the trigger on his revolver. He missed Eager by a large margin. Then all hell broke loose. The soldier lifted his browning hi-power so quickly and fired twice. He was so fast that Nick could not get a second shot away. It was not ready to aim fire but fire. He hit Nick twice in the chest. He fell with face forward and his weapon spilt onto the car park.

The shooting started other shootings, which lasted for only a few seconds. There was no automatic fire just clinical single shot, targeting the ones with weapons. His team had brought down four. Two dropped their weapons and lifted their arms high up. Nick's driver tried to get away, he was stopped with a bullet through the windscreen into his forehead.

The two left now were disarmed and made to lay on the floor legs and arms spread. The five-shot were dead. Nick was still breathing and alive. The team medic came forward and administered some emergency care and morphine shot to kill the pain.

Eager and Liberty had done the opposite to run away. The shot didn't make them run, they dived down and hit the gravel car park at the same time, both picking the same spot. Eager landing on top of Liberty and her face was pushed into the gravel. Spitting out pieces when she got up face and nose bruised and bloody.

"Well, thanks, my hero. Now tell me."

"Shit, you never give up."

"So not the ones we are looking for?" The soldier asked.

"No, these are London hoods that have a beef against us."

"Not very popular, are you?" the little soldier stated laconically.

"I guess not." Eager lamented.

"Cover for us, we are off for the original task we came for." He whistled and the team came together and moved on running together.

Fenwick then called in two ambulances and four police cars, which he had told to wait outside the town. He had been in the cellar. The whole town was awake now and started to gather at a distance trying to work out what was going on.

The landlord came out of the cellar with the staff and Karlien. He saw the crowd and the mayhem in his car park. Rubbing his hands together he knew this was good for business. The pub would be packed tomorrow and people would come from miles around to look-see and get first-hand stories of what happened. It may even become a tourist attraction. Yes, good for business.

"Oh my God!" Fenwick surveyed the scene. The paramedics checked out the dead and two were with Nick. He needed to get to the hospital as soon as possible as; he was close to death. They loaded him in one ambulance and off they went. Fenwick nodded to a police car to lead with blue light and stay with the injured person.

"Well, where are the soldiers?" The helicopter had just flown overhead headed north. Eager nodded in its direction.

"They can't leave, what about this mess? We need to interview them, take their weapons for testing and sort this mess out!" Eager doubted that they would ever get their weapons and he noted that they had picked up their used shells before they left.

"Gone to save a friend on the moors."

"What! More killings? You have to be kidding me, right?"

"No."

# Chapter Ninety-Two
## It's Not Over Until

"Scotty, some people are coming down the path to the side gate with a person in a wheelchair, must be collecting for some charity," his wife Doris shouted from the front parlour.

"I'll get it, dear." Romeo went to the door with him growling and then barking, so he went outside and locked her in the house. Romeo was not happy with this and kept growling and barking. They were knocking on the side gate. He shouted to them that he was coming and opened the gate.

The big Russian woman, Olga, was on the wheelchair and stood behind her was a man with an automatic weapon pointed at Scotty.

"Do nothing silly, my comrade best shot in KGB."

"What do you want?"

"You ask what should be obvious to you." Wheezing in between sentences, "You don't think that killing my two comrades we wouldn't come back to avenge them?"

He stared at her stuck for words whilst his brain wanted to find something to fight with. Should he duck and try to slam the gate door. No, he would be dead in seconds. Romeo continued to growl and bark.

"Let him out! The dog needs to die too."

He backed up and they followed him.

"Shoot the dog as it comes out and then him," she commanded.

"Romeo, go down," he commanded. The dog stopped and lay on the floor of the kitchen as trained.

"Not smart, now we have to go in the house and kill any witness, your wife maybe?" Olga was not kidding.

That moment the door opened slightly and the shotgun appeared. Doris had come to see what was happening and had heard Olga. No one was going to kill Scotty, never mind Romeo. She had never fired a shotgun or loaded it, she was in a frenzy and could not get the cartridges in, so she decided to bluff.

"You will kill no one, drop your weapons and go or you will get both barrels!" she shouted. Scotty stepped sideward, out of the way of the Russians, however, he knew he would also be hit at this range. She hesitated and the Russians also.

"It is not loaded," Olga guessed.

"*Packen!*" Scotty shouted.

"What?" Olga asked but too late. Romeo, a police dog, trained in Germany to German commands, answered the attack/bite command and immediately pushed past Doris and through the door and jumped high in the air over the wheelchair to the man with the gun. She knocked him over and grabbed his gun arm.

Scotty grabbed the shotgun off Doris and started beating Olga with the butt as she was reaching inside her handbag for a weapon.

"Get me cartridges," he shouted to Doris. She was in shock but brought two out. He loaded them.

"Go inside, dear and call the station." He then retrieved the weapon that the man had dropped, held it in the man's hand and fired it in the air.

"Fuzz." Romeo came to heel. The man still lay on the floor holding his arm. He was not sure about Olga; she was still conscious swearing at them in Russian.

"I will come back and kill your family and anyone connected to you. This is not over!"

"I am afraid it is." He looked around and fired two shots. Doris was inside on the phone so he went inside and took over.

The sergeant passed the information to Fenwick after dispatching a vehicle and calling for armed response.

"DCI Fenwick?"

"A shooting, sir in Matlock. Two dead. Ex-policeman is involved."

*Fuck, it is raining bodies.*

# Chapter Ninety-Three

"More coins," she demanded. The landlord complied.

"She ever going to get off that phone. It's 3 am," he asked Eager, who had reported to Charlie and made out his statement for Fenwick. So, now he was having a nightcap and worrying about McAllistar. Liberty was phoning in the latest incident, another exclusive they were coming quick and fast. Gavin was elated and stayed up to read and process. He never got his ex-SAS security and looked like he didn't need it now.

The landlord offered rooms for the night and Karlien had gone to bed. The police scenes of crime units were outside with big lights and tents. A large group of media were assembled but kept a long way from the car park, trying to get information, TV included. This was a big thing in Derbyshire.

"I have got to go, another double killing in Matlock. A friend of yours is involved. It never rains until it pours," He was saying how important he was.

"Not Scotty? Is he okay?"

"Apparently, he likes killing Russians."

"Can we come with you?" Eager asked.

"Not on. This one is locked uptight and I don't want you there."

"I'm hurt." Eager pretended. Fenwick left; this had been his worst night off ever.

"And do me a favour, get out of my turf before anything else happens." His moustache continued to twitch.

"As soon as our friend returns."

"What's wrong with the twitcher?" Liberty asked as he passed her on his way out.

"Oh, just another exclusive for you. Scotty has been involved in a double killing at his house. Got his number, shall we call him?" She was tired and was hoping to take Eager to bed and force the location of the dupes out of him one way or the other. Her adrenalin was now running again.

"Yeah, smalls, let's do that. Get me a wine first while I call his home number."

# Chapter Ninety-Four
## Sod's Law

As luck would have it after a very cold and wet night, dawn came with sunshine and the mist lifted on the Dark Peak and moor.

*Sod it,* McAllistar cursed as it only got one hundred hours of sunshine on the moors a year, mainly in spring and summer, winter is nearly always misty and now he could see from the peak for miles. It was a beautiful day, just what he didn't want. He could see them coming his way like stickmen in the distance. To walk in the right direction at night was amazing. He had seen some lights go up and down at some stage, although it was intermittent. The up and down every few yards into and out of the peat bogs must have exhausted them. Yes, they were definitely highly trained professionals, very tough guys.

He sat on top of the black Bleaklow gritstone edges. Strangely shaped stones positioned around the summit of the hill, which was the second-highest in the dark moor. He wondered if the early man sat here and why after so many centuries the stones didn't fall over. He liked the gentle breeze at this height, which helped him think and his view was as high and wide as he could get.

He had chosen Bleaklow as it had no footpaths approaching and was difficult to get too. Its peat bogs were not the biggest in the area, however, they were the wettest and crisscrossed each other making it even more tiring and difficult to transverse. The only people that enjoyed this area were hikers known as 'bogtrotters'. *A strange lot,* McAllistar reflected.

They were in the desolate area, coming towards him more of a boggy track now with rocks and some broken fields that sheep used to graze. One was limping badly as far as he could determine. In came a chopper and landed in an area that must have had a flat enough landing zone that was safe to do so. They all got on board and it took off his direction.

He guessed that the unusual and unexpected clear weather got them to call in the chopper and cut short the journey, although they must have been kicking themselves after such a strenuous night. No weather forecast could have predicted this weather here, so waiting until morning was probably not an option for them which was good for him.

They were coming on the land again, the only spot closer to him they could find that was safe at least three hundred metres away. They hovered first over a peat bog and then a body fell out of the chopper, probably fifty feet. It fell with a crack on the side of the bog. They landed just behind the body, checked it and moved towards him.

*What the hell was that about?* He wondered. *Hopefully not one of the team they had captured.*

The SAS team had decided to await the morning and see the lay of the land if it was possible to fly. They figured that McAllistar had set a very difficult course for the terrorists and that it would take them all night to find their way, maybe longer. They would be exhausted and that was his game. Bleaklow and the High Peak were famous for many aircraft crashes and were littered with broken machines, so taking a night flight was not a good risk. They had done many exercises in the Peak District so were very familiar with the terrain. They had landed in a field just off the highway, got some food going and reported to HQ as the soldier was sure the phones were running hot from the higher 'yens' as they called them.

In the early morning, they saw and heard a helicopter go towards Bleaklow and guessed that it belonged to their opponents. The soldier decided since it was so clear this day to circle around and land on the other side of the hill away from where he guessed the other helicopter would have landed. There was no land flat enough for them to put the chopper down, so they abseiled down the ropes. They would have dropped on the top of the peak; however, they were being cautious of what they might encounter or scare McAllistar into a shooting. They thought it would be better to climb up from the back.

McAllistar needed a new plan. Leading them in the mist into a bog ridden area and taking them one by one was now not an option. These heavily armed guys were now heading his way and his stomach was turning over. He looked around and saw in the distance another helicopter to the rear of the hill. He was now worried as they have two teams after him, not just the three guys. No chance in this weather with two handguns and a knife beating them. He was dead meat if he stayed around.

To his right in the crisscrossed peat bogs, he saw at least six people jumping up and down racing through the bogs. You just saw them for a second as they jumped up and then over and down. They were moving towards the peak and were laughing and shouting at each other. Day trippers made the most of the clear weather. *Bogtrotters.*

They had the full attention of the three Americans, who were trying to work out who or what are these people and were they a threat. Crazy in winter, half-dressed going through the bogs like it was easy and fun. He took his opportunity to move down from the big rock and scale down the rocks on the side to a large rock shelf at the bottom of the hill. He thought that this could be a good hiding place and was within a hundred yards from the bogs to his right. At least he had a chance there if he was able to drag them into the bogs and split them up. They must be very tired and were carrying a lot of weight. He had at least a few cold hours resting.

He had a stick with him with which he was going to check the depth of the bogs to see if he could hide under the peat if necessary. Not the best plan, he admitted to himself but the best he could think of at this stage.

He could also let them pass and try and make the helicopter and the pilot to fly him away. Another not the best plan but at least he was having ideas as his brain worked overtime. It's times like this that you think 'What was I thinking coming out here'.

*Oh, fuck it. Fuck Murphy's Law or Sod's Law.* If the mist was here, he would have the advantage.

He took himself as far under the rock shelf as possible and awaited his fate. A sitting duck if they looked under. Maybe they were waiting for him to appear with the girl and talk to them. They obviously had ignored 'do not bring weapons' but who was he kidding, they all knew the game or so he thought.

He just had to wait, hope and pray for a break.

# Chapter Ninety-Five
## Everyone Has Their Price

The meeting was a small affair, the PM, her communications chief, the bulldog, McClements and the commissioner. They were at number 10 Downing Street in the PM's private office. The commissioner handed over a one-page report. It had the names of the high-profile members of the 'hellfire' club.

He was still not well but had been summoned as the only person allowed to attend from the Met. His recovery had been accelerated once the bottle of poison from the ACC's safe had been analysed and an antidote administered. Still, he was tired, weary-looking and with a short fuse.

"This is the only copy of the list," the commissioner said proudly.

"Who compiled it?" asked the bulldog.

"DCS Charlie Allcock. Lifetime policeman. Very efficient and reliable."

"Discreet?" the PM asked.

"Of course." The commissioner was not happy with such a question and the PM saw it.

"Sorry, Sir Michael. This is such dynamite stuff; we need to be sure that it is not gossiped or leaked."

"I understand, PM, however, we have handled a difficult situation in the best and most private manner. That is the only copy of the list, handwritten, not on any computer."

"Yes, yes, but can we be a hundred per cent sure that apart from Minister Stephens no one else has been named?" the bulldog persisted.

"The tapes were recovered by DI Eager and handed directly to DCS Allcock. They have been locked in his safe and he has not allowed anyone to access them."

"Did Eager look at them?" the bulldog continued.

"I believe he did scan a few."

"Is he reliable?"

"A good copper, been looked over several times for promotion. The ACC didn't like him very much, Charlie, I mean DCS Allcock is very big on him."

"The reporter girl, has she seen them?"

"It is my understanding that McAllistar only gave her the Stephens' tape." Sir Michael replied.

"Minister Stephens you mean?" the bulldog jumped in.

"Yes."

The PM's eyes rolled around as she read the list. The bulldog leaned over her shoulder and whistled.

"I will be frank, Sir Michael, I need time to think about this as this could impact the government a lot. Not only us but the confidence in the police, judges, royalty and society. These are debauched people that need to pay but how is the question I am struggling with."

*General election nine months away is also a consideration, I bet.*

"What about Fish, sorry, Minister Stephens." The commissioner was showing his distaste for him and using the nickname DI Eager had proffered.

"Let me update you. The children were interviewed by top social workers and psychoanalysts. It seems they cannot recognise Minister Fish at all, they were led a little by the policewoman and the reporter. The *Daily Cryer* have lost the alleged tape and will publish a retraction and then all we have as a witness is a publicity-seeking reporter, who had it in for him. It will not fly in court," the bulldog said confidently.

"So NFA?" the commissioner was not buying this cover-up and it showed.

"Minister Stephens is resigning due to ill health from the attack, so best leave it at that," the PM said, searching the commissioner's face for a reaction.

"The ACC?"

"Overworked, the stress of a policeman's life was too much for him," the bulldog jumped in again.

"So, we should give him a medal? A knighthood maybe? Maybe a degree in science," The commissioner was becoming sarcastic.

"We will need all the other tapes brought here as soon as possible." The bulldog ignored the comment.

"There is an assertion from our American friends that their technical people said the tape we handed over was duped," the PM asked.

"I have no information to that effect. To my knowledge, you can only tell a dupe because it loses definition slightly, not the original."

"I see, maybe testing the waters just in case we took out some insurance. Langley says they know nothing about this case," the bulldog put in.

"They would." The PM had bad experiences with the American activities on British soil.

"What about all the other paedophiles on the tapes?"

"Hard one, Sir Michael. Fewer people who see the tapes the better, so you will have to trace them some other way."

"If any of this gets out, then we will all go down. It is a big mess to cover up. We have the Harkers in our hands. Now we will have very little and life goes on for them."

"Collateral damage, I am afraid," the bulldog said.

*The self-serving little Scottish prick. Tell that to the people they have damaged, the druggies and the little kids.*

"I think that the two officers should be well rewarded for good work. This McAllistar also, maybe some compensation for false arrest and prison time. All should sign a new official secrets act. I mean well rewarded," she stressed.

"Very well, PM." The commissioner was being dismissed and stood up to go.

"Oh, Sir Michael, some good news. The New Year's honours list has been approved by Her Majesty. Congratulations your lordship."

"Thanks," he said, tersely turned and walked out.

*Bloody politicians!*

# Chapter Ninety-Six
## Change of Luck

Liberty had been summoned urgently back to London to meet Sir Richard and Gavin. She got a taxi to Derby station and train to London.

Karlien had opted to stay at the pub and wait on McAllistar getting back if he did.

Eager was sitting in the Rover at the spot he dropped McAllistar off from 6 am. He had a flask of coffee and some Bakewell tarts, better than doughnuts. He watched the SAS chopper flyover. He was left wondering what had happened to Logan. The weather was so good that he feared the mist would have lifted and taken away his cover. Still, the SAS troopers were on their way to help. The weather was a double-sided coin he guessed.

The Americans had not noticed the SAS chopper as it had circled well around to get to the back of the peak and as luck would have it, the Americans had just boarded their chopper as the SAS chopper approached the peak, which was very noisy, so they couldn't hear the second one.

He heard them shouting his name and using a whistle. So, they did expect him to come out to talk. He laid still trying not to breathe too hard. A mountain hare dropped into his cover. It was starting to turn white as it did every winter to meld in with the snow and protect it from predators. He didn't move an inch, the hare though smelt him and then bolted out. He now thought that he had been given away. It was a big white Hare and very visible and noisy as it ran. They would know it had been disturbed. He understood one burst of an automatic weapon and he would be cut to pieces under the shelf. He did assume they wanted him alive to make him talk and then kill him. So, stay here and hope for the best or make a run for it?

Then it started to rain very hard. A cold wind started to blow and this all would bring the mist down. England can have five different types of weather in one day, so he was not that surprised but now very happy.

He crawled to the edge and slowly popped up from the side of the rock shelf. Listening first the name shouting was a distance away. Lifting his eyes just above the shelf's edge, he looked around. Sure enough, they were still heading for the peak and his direction with heads down as the rain beat against them.

He looked to his right and the 'bogtrotters' were sitting, resting for their journey back. Black all over with peat, they were still playing, laughing, drinking water in the rain.

Chancing he popped up again and crawled out enough to look at the peak. He saw soldiers on the top, they looked like British soldiers but he could not be sure. Could be hired mercenaries. They started to lay down in firing positions he assumed.

Now was the time or never. He ran as fast as he could and made the crisscross bogs where the 'bogtrotters' were. No gunfire yet. He knew if you heard the gunfire you were not shot and then a loud burst of automatic gunfire in his direction. He was okay then. The young 'bogtrotters' took off and in seconds were bopping up and down the peat bogs on their way back, quicker than they came. He followed them as fast as he could.

He heard several high-velocity single shots. 'A sniper?' Then nothing until he heard the rotors of the chopper flying away. He stopped; it was not coming to his direction. Still, he kept moving up and down until he was exhausted.

Then rotors of the Blue Thunder chopper, it was hovering above him. He could hardly hear but, he thought an English voice was saying, "Fancy a lift?"

*There is a God.*

# Chapter Ninety-Seven
## Sold Out

Liberty had gone to her flat as she thought it was safe to do so now. A good shower and a complete change of clothing, she looked better than she had since this adventure began. She knew immediately that the place had been thoroughly and professionally searched. A woman knows when the little things are not put back perfectly. Curtains askew, which would drive her crazy with her need for things to be straight and neat, underwear ruffled. *Not the usual suspects,* she thought, *as they would have trashed the place.*

"Let me get this straight, you are printing a retraction for that bleeding paedophile! Why?"

Sir Richard was coughing very uncomfortable.

"Don't you realise what that will do to my credibility as a serious reporter?"

"Calm down, Liberty. That is not the worst," Gavin with eyes down on the floor mumbled.

"No, the fucking worse, what could be worse? Tell me!"

"They rescinded your work visa. You have fifteen days to leave."

"They what? Our lawyers can fight this and delay it for years."

They were both looking down.

"Can't they?"

"Listen, we did a deal as the tape is missing, they say the children are not good witnesses and were led to pick out Fish and that you had it in for him. So, in order not to be sued, we do the retraction and life moves on."

"And I am sacrificed, with all the risks I have taken and the great stories I have brought. Circulation is up, up because of me and this is what I get!"

"The board has approved a very generous package, first-class airfare home and I can help with contacts in the States. You will be home, this all behind you, with a great job. Your career is just starting, my girl," Sir Richard said sheepishly and as if he didn't believe it himself.

"How did the tape go missing?"

"It was in my safe, only three of us know the combination."

"Who?"

"Well, I, Joan and Sir Richard."

She blinked in disbelief.

"The other tapes and paedophiles?"

"Police have them under investigation, we believe," Sir Richard explained.

"Right, I will believe that one when I see the prosecutions."

"I need to think." She jumped up, slammed the office door behind her and walk through the main news office. All the staff jumped up and gave her a standing ovation to show the respect they had gained for her.

*I am not going to let them see me cry.*

Outside she waved a cab down and jumped in.

"Where to, luv?"

She was thinking and holding back the tears.

"Meters running, luv."

"Errr take me to Barney's."

"Sir Richard?"

"No use, Gavin. They threatened to stop all public and party advertising and double it. You see the carrot and the stick approach. That damn McClements, do you know that they call him the bull dog?"

"Yes, but can't we fight this? It is a big story the government supporting a paedophile?"

"I fought it at the board meeting and they had got to every member. Not sure, maybe the extra advertising, bigger dividends or they have something on each one. Anyway, I was outvoted after fighting for three hours."

"But…"

"Sorry, Gavin, I really am. Gotta go, lunch appointment. Drown my sorrows what."

When he left, he walked through a silent subdued office. His popularity at an all-time low.

Gavin felt the need to find Liberty quickly. He got the same treatment on the way out.

# Chapter Ninety-Eight
## Yardies

"Jimmy, I have come in peace to make a good deal for both of us." Tazewell was wiping his glasses. His eyes when he lies go to the left. This is normally the case with people, a known trait for right-handed people. Jimmy knew this but he had to play along.

"It looks like it."

Jimmy was bailed up in his own office at the club. Tazewell sat opposite to him and there were four 'Yardies' standing in the office. They looking at and were touching everything, which annoyed Jimmy. There were more down in the club helping themselves to drinks and a few more outside.

Yardies came from Jamaica or were descended from there. The word 'yardie' came from when they worked for rich people in their yards in Trenchtown. They were now ruthless gangsters that had just started invading London in the poor black areas.

Dressed in designer suits, big gold watches and bling jewellery they liked to show off their gangster status. Easy to be insulted and very violent with the torture of killing anyone who disrespects them.

"These are the guys who got our drugs?"

"Russian drugs, Jimmy. Forgive and forget eh?"

"Why should I trust you?"

"I needed a better share and had to come up with other ways to make money. You and Nick are getting richer and not generous people with sharing."

"So?"

"So, we develop a partnership and we help these gentlemen expand and everyone wins."

"These guys act rashly and use extreme violence when they do. The police will always catch up with them and then us."

"Yo bro, ya know," the leader was objecting. Jimmy didn't have a clue what he was saying.

"Tazewell, Nick has been shot and is probably dying. I need to go up north right away to be at his side. Let me think about the deal. We have been devastated and need to start again with a new strategy. Let's meet in a few days' time and draw up a document."

Tazewell didn't notice that Jimmy's eye went left.

"I have brought one with me." He handed Jimmy an envelope. Jimmy took it and hoping that they would wait not to attack him now. He nodded to the

Yardies and gave them some respect. "Gentlemen, thanks for coming we will meet again and see what we can do." This seemed to satisfy them and Tazewell didn't interfere, he had the time and most of the Harkers trusted gang had been killed or were in prison. They were in a weak position.

# Chapter Ninety-Nine
## NFA (No Further Action)

DCS Allcock had just got back from a private meeting with the commissioner and the DAC. He was furious and frustrated. He needed time to weigh options and how he could position it with the team. Eager was the person he needed most to control as he was now a wild card in the normal police operations. He had taken many risks and delivered the Harkers, which now was almost a moot point. He would not be happy at all.

Eager saw Logan dangling from the winch rope on the helicopter. He jumped down near his car and ran over and jumped in. He was black from head to foot and smelt of peat. He said nothing but was breathing hard.

"Good morning, I trust you had a good evening," Eager was playing with him glad to see him alive.

McAllistar just looked at him through black peepholes.

"You're okay, that's all that matters."

"Thanks to the SAS, yes. It was a damn stupid idea."

"The Americans?"

"One dead, one wounded and they got away in their chopper. They are in pursuit now, using all the electronics they can. Although one had used this body which they threw out of the chopper to cover himself. They had to check the body for life signs before moving on. He is dead, they have his ID Roger White, they left him for the police."

"Wow, the MI5 guy! Are they all out there, the wounded and dead ones?"

"No, they have a policy, no one is left behind. They dragged them to the chopper, then too far for the sniper."

"Chief Inspector Fenwick?" "That's me."

"Army HQ here. Some of our guys whilst on chopper exercise spotted a dead body at the high peak. The coordinates are…"

His moustache and eyes were twitching. *Unbelievable!*

The publican used his outside hose pipe to water McAllistar down and get as much peat off as possible. Even so, it took stripping in the car park before he would let him inside. Big towels were provided so he could strip first.

The police had worked all night and you could see the body markings for the dead and wounded on the car park gravel. It had become a tourist attraction as the locals had been there all morning, looking and waiting for the pub to open to get the inside story. The publican was sure that they would be packed that day and maybe for a long time after. What, other pubs in the centre of town, there were four, had such an interesting yarn. He would be telling it as it happened for years to come, even though he was in the cellar when the action took place, a mere forgettable detail.

McAllistar wanted to stay in his cottage and Karlien chose to be with him. They didn't think the Americans would be back after today. Nick was in hospital in a dire condition and most of his gang out the picture. So, he went to the farm and got organised and visited Aunt Bessie. Logan dropped Eager and Liberty off at Derby train station and kept the Rover. Eager took the two guns and knife with him. DS Williams will be happy at their return and the fact they had never been fired.

Gavin found Liberty at Barney's, slightly sloshed. He had tried all the other watering holes the press visited in the area, knocked until his knuckles hurt on her flat door and then tried Barney's. It was more of an American style than the run of the mill pubs. She was sitting in a booth with a bottle of wine. Her second at least, he figured.

"Hi! Can I join you?" She looked at him coldly and for a moment he thought that she was going to scream or cry.

"Why not, Sir Gavin, would you like a glass of this particularly expensive Pinot Noir and, Chardonnay mix." She poured him a big glass and waited. He gulped a mouthful.

"This is good."

"Yes, the most expensive in the United Kingdom I am told. Nyetimber Tillington 79%, Pinot Noir and Chardonnay 22%, seventy-five quid as you Brits say a bottle."

"And this is my third. Don't worry, Sir Richard is paying for it. The waiter saw me with him the night we came here and he has an account. I am his bastard US daughter. Ha."

"Let me take you home."

"No, tell me what really happened?"

"It seems the government, that bully McClements, put the hard word on the board. More advertising or none from the government and his party or they had something on some of them, maybe the tapes? The tape, I am at a loss, although maybe Sir Richard gave it to them knowing I wouldn't. He put a fix on the children with high-level social workers and psychologists to ensure the evidence was seen as flawed. Then he had your work visa rescinded. You go away and it is all over."

"What about the other tapes the police have?"

"Not sure it has all been pushed under the carpet. John will know."

"I am going to fuck this government up and especially that little fucker McClements."

"How?"

"You will see, you don't think I have been sitting here drinking and not thinking." Pointing her finger to her head.

"So, you see it is all going to be handled by specialist working for the PM to ensure that the national interest is kept front and centre and the general public doesn't lose confidence in our institutions."

"So, it's a big cover-up?" Eager was the first to speak.

"No, I am assured it will be handled well and these people get what they deserve," Charlie looked to his left as he said this.

One of the team muttered, "More children." which Charlie ignored.

"Sir, the Harkers?" Denise Williams asked.

"We prosecute Nick Harker for the shooting in Bakewell, attempted murder on two counts. We leave alone the incident at the abbey as he could bring up more than we can handle."

"Meaning he knows and can identify the members of 'The hellfire' club which could be embarrassing to the government."

"What if he turns state witness for us?" she persisted.

"Which would embarrass the government." A chorus from the team.

Charlie made it clear that they need to move on. Lots more cleaning up and investigating for everyone to do. Eager stayed behind.

"Do not say it, John, no need."

"I wasn't going to say anything. Well, not true. How does the commissioner feel about this?"

"He fought it and is sick to the back teeth."

"Is he getting his lordship?"

"Not fair, John, he has earned that status through many years of excellent police work. His life's work."

"So, he is getting it."

"We are all being paid off if you want to think of it that way. You will be promoted for your excellent work to DCI and then in twelve months detective super and I will retire a commander with a much better pension."

"The press will have a field day."

"That has apparently been looked after. The *'Daily Cryer'* is publishing a retraction on Stephens and your young lady is being sent home."

"Retraction? Home?"

"Work visa being rescinded." Eager was visibly shocked. He needed to find her.

"It's all one big fix. What about McAllistar?"

"Gets to live in peace and have his record expunged and will be offered compensation for false imprisonment."

"If the Harkers leave him alone."

"If, yes."

"Charlie, what if there were copies of the tapes, what would you do?"

"Do you know that for sure?"

"Just speculating."

"Not sure what I would do. Take my promotion and then pension and then sell them to that Murdoch guy and live happily ever after and not feel that I failed a lot of kids."

"I would miss ya."

"Do they exist? No, don't tell me. Do me a favour though. I have left my notes for the handwritten report to the PM in my top left-hand side drawer can you get them and destroy them. Thanks."

# Chapter One Hundred
## Pieces of the Puzzle

"Ask him, officer, if he will see me? Tell him McAllistar is here."

"A friend?"

"I was."

"Not allowed, sir."

McAllistar and Karlien had just visited Aunt Bessie when it occurred to him that he could try and visit Nick Harker just to talk, he was not sure why but his gut said they had unfinished business. Just then Jimmy came out on his own. A few cold glances. He had two heavies waiting in the corridor he had never seen before.

"How is he?"

"What do you care?" and Jimmy walked away, had second thoughts, stopped and came back.

"Let me tell you this, it was not us and we have suffered the most because of you two. Tazewell Javelin orchestrated the American beating with her and he planted the drugs on you and tipped off Samuels, sold the rest to these Yardie gangs. He has been double-dealing with the Russians and Americans. He is now trying to take over our business. So, he is the guy you should be pursuing to get your revenge." He then walked away.

A nurse walked out the intensive care room and was asked how he was. As good as could be expected was the unhelpful answer.

*Not a good day,* Gina thought. The call from Sam was bad news, very bad news. One dead and one on the verge. Sam with a twisted ankle run-in with the SAS on the moors where McAllistar chose to meet them. They are dumb fucks; it was always a trap. Now she arranged for a black flight out of there back to the States and a medical team from a local US army base to shore up the injured. He would have to travel with the dead guy in the Learjet; no time for coffins or niceties. When things go wrong, they often get worse.

"Get your ass back here by tomorrow morning. You are suspended until a full investigation has taken place," the director of the CIA ordered as though he was a sergeant major talking to a new recruit.

"Sir, what is this all about?"

"You know, Gina, do not play games with me. Get back here and call off this rogue team that MI5 seem to think you are directing. Shoot outs in the United Kingdom, questions are being asked at the highest level."

"Rogue team, I am not sure what you mean really? Okay, I will be there as quick as I can."

*With the tape in my hand and see what you say then when I tell you who is involved.*

"I need those tapes now," Liberty shouted.

"No, too dangerous, they will take them off you and maybe kill you."

"Do you know what they have done to me, do you know?" She was drunk and in her flat.

"Do you," punching him in the chest with each word, "know what they have done to me?"

"Get some sleep and we will work a plan in the morning."

"Fuck you, smalls." Then she collapsed and he carried her to the bedroom. Put water by her bed and a basin on the floor just in case. He retired to the lounge room and made himself comfortable on the settee.

The abbey shootings and fire was put down to gang warfare and was still under investigation. It was described as a drug den and no mention of the real goings-on.

The two incidents with the Russian agents were covered up and apart from a 'tit for tat' expulsion of embassy staff, nothing got in the press. Scotty had his story down pat and his wife supported him. They came and said they were going to kill them all, Romeo attacked the guy and put him off balance and he fired in the air. His wife threw him the loaded shotgun and he fired at them before the woman, who was pulling a revolver and the man was getting up to fire. Scotty said that they were after revenge for the B&B killings where he had just been a friend and had no idea what it was all about, consistent with his previous statement. High powers had given the local police direction and no further action would take place.

The Peacock's shootings were put down to attempted murder on an undercover policeman who knew too much. Nick Harker was mentioned as the ring leader and being in the hospital in a serious condition. The SAS had helped out whilst on exercise in the area upon the request of the local chief inspector, Fenwick. The pub was now always packed and the publican was more than happy now. He made several interviews on what happened, even though he was in the cellar at the time. A good yarn always goes down well.

The shoot out on the moors was never reported. Some young people the 'bogtrotters' reported to the local police about the shooting, helicopters and a man, who seemed to be running for his life. The Blue Thunder helicopter was a giveaway for the SAS and seen by people around the area. The military response was that exercises were being carried out on the moors with dummy bullets, so no one was at risk.

Tazewell Javelin was interviewed and, the slippery lawyer he is, didn't get nailed for anything. Yes, the abbey was in his name, however, which he had bought for the Harkers at their direction. No idea what it was used for, he was just a humble legal advisor now out of work. It was not him attacking the abbey, it could be any guy with a balaclava. "A real-life slippery eel," one detective commented.

He was, though, working on his plan to take over and be the big guy in town.

# Chapter One Hundred and One
## Karlien

They were sitting by the cottage fire when he burst in. Sam aimed at McAllistar and fired twice. Karlien had got between them and took the bullets. She died instantly. They went through her into McAllistar, who collapsed with her on top of him. Sam checked that she was dead and McAllistar seemed also to be gone. He had achieved his goal. He didn't have time to confirm McAllistar as there was a knock at the door.

"Everyone okay?" the nosy postie was delivering and noticed the door wide open. He had not heard the shots as Sam was using a suppressor. Sam barged past him, knocking him over. He got up and looked in.

"Really people...oh."

They were laying there in a heap. No phone, on his bike down the hill faster than he had ever gone. Mail flying out of his bag which irked him being a devoted postie.

Chief Inspector Fenwick was not impressed, all his years and more has happened in two weeks than his total career. He was efficient and once McAllistar was on his way to hospital and Karlien was being attended to by the morgue people, he secured the scene and telephoned Eager. McAllistar was very tall and Karlien small, so the bullets in her chest slightly deflected and hit him in his thighs. No major organs were hit. "He's going to survive but not going to play football again."

*Prick,* Eager thought.

# Chapter One Hundred and Two
## Leaving on a Jet Plane

"Oh, not you again! You promised never to come back." The big tattoo guy at the video shop shouted.

"Here's a hundred quid. I just want to do twelve copies."

"Oh, be my guest," he said while grabbing the cash.

Eager had recovered the tapes that morning and was making sure these didn't disappear. He would send with Charlie's notes indicating the names and professions of the people on them he would courier to an address she had given him in the United States. The address could not be connected to her, not a relative, known friend or associate. It was an old school boyfriend so far in the past, no connection could be traced. She would call him on a payphone when she arrived in the States to hold the parcel for her.

He had driven her to the airport in silence. Not one of them had much to say. There was sadness between them. An exciting adventure turned sour. A love liaison lost due to distance and age. He saw her through the formalities using his police badge and stayed with her as they thoroughly searched her as they had done with her luggage. He noticed a lot of people looking at her. She had indeed had become famous.

They sat down in the British Airways' first-class lounge and ordered drinks. Hers white wine and he had a lager.

"Cheers, bon voyage."

Tears formed in her eyes but got no further.

"Always wanted to be an investigative journalist. My teacher told me I was such a busy body I should be one."

"You are and the best there is. No one would do what you did for you big story."

"DCI and then superintendent, how does that feel?"

"Feels sick. It is a payoff to shut up. I am not sure whether I should take my pension and move on. Scared of becoming a rent-a-cop though."

"Can I ask you a personal question?"

"Go."

"Would you have married me if I stayed?"

He thought about a little stunned. He needed another drink before answering.

"Twenty years ago, I would have for certain. Today it simply will not work because of age, lifestyle. You know that Dr Hook song when they sing about age difference? Well, I have been around for so many more miles than you. There's a social stigma to big age differences in relationships and one day you will wake up with an old man in your bed. I will be an old crock of a guy and you would feel obliged to take care of me for a long time. You will ache for a better life. I mean if you were staying, seriously would you have married me?"

Liberty had tears in her eyes listening.

She started laughing and crying he was not sure which, "Oh, of course not, smalls." He laughed along with her and they clinked their glasses together.

The flight boarding was called.

"Gotta go then. Promise me two things. One, you will visit me in the big apple and two, you will definitely send those tapes?"

"I promise both, cross my heart."

They kissed and hug several times. They both had glossy eyeballs.

"What are you going to do now?" she asked.

"Take a couple of weeks off and then nail all the bad guys I can. After retiring, to the country in a few years, maybe even go up near Logan and farm."

She laughed out loud. "I meant right now."

"Go home and feel sad for a while and then go to the pub."

"What are you going to do when you get back?"

"Last call for BA071 to New York."

"I am going to contact the Aussies, National Enquirer and German Media and make a lot of money out of those tapes, which mean I am going to fuck up this cover-up and bring down the whole lot of them!"

To be continued...